Spawn's She-Wolf

Iron Punishers MC #5

Ciara St James

Copyright

ISBN: 978-1-955751-62-9
Printed in the United States of America
Editing by Mary Kern @ Ms. K Edits
Book cover by Tracie Douglas @ Dark Waters Covers

Blurb:

Spawn's decision years ago to leave his past behind led to him unexpectedly meeting a biker who changed his life. He has repaid his MC family time and time again using his computer skills. When he helps one of his club brothers with a problem, it backfires, putting him in the right place at the right time to meet the spirited little nurse who goes toe-to-toe with him. He's intrigued. She's not backing down.

Kimera has no idea how her life will change after meeting a patient and the huge biker who comes to see her. She instantly becomes the other woman's refuge, but while trying to help resolve Troian's past, she puts herself in danger. Spawn and the Iron Punishers come to the rescue, but she's not able to let go of what happens.

When Spawn finds out Kimera left town without a word, he does his thing to find her, only to discover something that leaves him angry and unwilling to go after her. It takes his club calling him on his behavior and a friend digging into things to show him the truth. When he finds her and gets a dark secret out of her, it's worse than he imagines.

Now Kimera has Spawn not only wanting to claim her forever, but he vows to make her real-life demon disappear by releasing his inner demon and showing her why he's called Spawn. With a little help from a new MC, he makes it happen, and she ends up becoming Spawn's She-Wolf. A Spawn and a She-Wolf just might make the perfect couple made in hell.

Warning

This book is intended for adult readers. It contains foul language and adult situations and discusses events that may trigger some readers. Sexual situations are graphic. If these themes aren't what you like to read or you find them upsetting, this book isn't for you. There is no cheating or cliffhangers, and it has a HEA.

Iron Punishers Members/ Old Ladies:

Holden Grier (Reaper) President w/Cheyenne
Creed Donovan (Maniac) VP w/ Lark
Jamison Tyrell (Mayhem) Enforcer w/ TBD
Killian Hardison (Ratchet) Road Captain w/ TBD
Damian Tatum (Crusher) SAA w/ TBD
Austin Kavanagh (Ink) w/ Alisse
Derrick Tatum (Lash) w/ Troian
Vance Halliwell (Tinker) Treasurer w/ TBD
Aidan Priestley (Spawn) Secretary w/ Kimera
Carter McKnight (Sandman) w/TBD
Braxton Russo (Shadow) w/TBD
Dante Braun (Remus) w/ TBD
Dillion Braun (Romulus) w/ TBD
Colt Langley (Gravel) w/TBD
Rhaines Dallesandro- Prospect

Reading Order

For Dublin Falls Archangel's Warriors MC (DFAW), Hunters Creek Archangel's Warriors MC (HCAW), Iron Punishers MC (IPMC), Dark Patriots (DP), & Pagan Souls of Cherokee MC (PSCMC)

Reaper's Banshee IPMC 1
Bear's Beloved HCAW 5
Outlaw's Jewel HVAW 6
Undertaker's Resurrection DP 1
Agony's Medicine Woman PSCMC 1
Ink's Whirlwind IP 2
Payne's Goddess HCAW 7
Maverick's Kitten HCAW 8
Tiger & Thorn's Tempest DFAW 18
Dare's Doll PSC 2
Maniac's Imp IP 3
Tank's Treasure HCAW 9
Blade's Boo DFAW 19
Law's Valkyrie DFAW 20
Gabriel's Retaliation DP 2
Knight's Bright Eyes PSC 3
Joker's Queen HCAW 10
Bandit & Coyote's Passion DFAW 21
Sniper's Dynamo & Gunner's Diamond DFAW 22
Slash's Dove HCAW 11
Lash's Hurricane IP 4
Spawn's She-Wolf IP 5

For Ares Infidels MC

Sin's Enticement AIMC 1
Executioner's Enthrallment AIMC 2
Pitbull's Enslavement AIMC 3
Omen's Entrapment AIMC 4
Cuffs' Enchainment AIMC 5
Rampage's Enchantment AIMC 6
Wrecker's Ensnarement AIMC 7
Trident's Enjoyment AIMC 8
Fang's Enlightenment AIMC 9

Talon's Enamorment AIMC 10
Ares Infidels in NY AIMC 11
Phantom's Emblazonment AIMC 12
Saint's Enrapturement AIMC 13
Phalanx & Bullet's Entwinement AIMC 14
Torpedo's Entrancement AIMC 15

For O'Sheerans Mafia

Darragh's Dilemma
Cian's Complication
Aidan's Ardor

Please follow Ciara on Facebook. For information on new releases & to catch up with Ciara, go to www.ciara-st-james.com or www.facebook.com/ ciara.stjames.1 or www.facebook.com/groups/ tenilloguardians or https://www.facebook.com/ groups/1112302942958940 or https:// www.facebook.com/groups/923322252903958

Kimera: Chapter 1

The OR had been busy as usual today, which was the way I liked it. I always preferred being occupied to twiddling my thumbs, especially at work. At home, I could always find something to do, even if it was just spending time with Toro. Thinking of my dog made me smile. He was such a sweetheart and made me laugh. I needed that.

I really liked my job as a nurse because I loved helping people. It was hard work, and sometimes the heartbreak was too much. You had to have ways to decompress. While at work, you had to appear calm, confident, and in command at all times. You broke down in private, even if it was in a linen closet or a bathroom for five minutes. Losing a patient made me want to cry every time. Watching their family be told the terrible news made my chest hurt.

All those thoughts were wiped from my head though as I headed to bed five to check on the young woman in recovery. She was my age, according to her chart, and I'd overheard yelling not long ago when a man was made to leave her bedside. It was unusual for them to let anyone back to sit in the recovery area. I wondered why they had let him and what caused her to insist on him being made to leave. The other staff were gossiping about it, but I was working and didn't have time to find out why. Truthfully, it wasn't any of my business. I was here to take care of her, not stick my nose in her personal business. The others should do the same.

As I eased back the curtain around her hospital bed, I saw her curled up in the fetal position. I swear I heard her sniffling. Lord, I hated to interrupt what sounded like a crying session, but I had to. Softly, I called out, "Excuse me, Miss. I need to take a look at your bandage. I'm sorry."

She slowly uncurled herself and wiped her cheeks with her hands. I saw the wetness and how red her face was. Yep, she'd been crying. I couldn't keep the sympathetic expression off my face. It made her snort, then she responded, "That's fine..." She paused.

I saw her staring at my name badge. I was too far away for her to read it. I smiled to put her at ease and said, "I'm Kimera. Everyone calls me Kim, though."

"It's nice to meet you. I think I'll call you Kimera. That's a pretty name," she said. I didn't mind. I happened to like my name, but others found it hard to say for some reason, hence the shortening to Kim.

"Thank you. I love your name too. I've never heard it before. Do you mind if I ask where you're from?" I asked as I came to her bedside to lower the sheet and lift her gown.

I was glad to see her bandage was clean. I left it in place. The surgeon would raise hell if a mere nurse were to mess with his surgical dressing. Most of them were like that. They might perform the surgery and be great at what they did, but most thought they were gods, and the rest of us were annoyances here to boss around. Those in the know knew that the nurses were the true healers, but we rarely got any credit. However, I hadn't become one to gain recognition or accolades.

"My family is originally from Russia, and it means trinity. How about your name?" she asked.

"I have no clue. I've tried to find out its meaning, but it doesn't seem to have one," I explained with a shrug.

"Did you ask your parents?" Troian asked. I expected the question.

"I don't have any. I grew up in foster care after I was ten. My granny who raised me didn't know where they got it. She wouldn't tell me anything about my birth parents, so I couldn't ask. Granny said I was better off not knowing." That was my short, concise answer. It was the truth, as unsatisfying as it was. I'd tried multiple times to get the child services staff to share my file. They told me there was nothing in it that revealed anything about my parents. I wasn't sure I believed them, but what reason would they have to lie?

"Well, they gave you a very pretty and cool name. How does it look?" Her change of subject was welcome. I guess she noticed how uncomfortable talking about my parents made me feel.

I quickly answered her, "I can't see the incisions, but the dressing is dry, and there's no bleeding through, which is good. You'll need to be careful. No bending or lifting. They did a robotic laparoscopic surgery, so you have three incisions. They've been stitched with dissolvable sutures and then glued together. For the next six to eight weeks, you'll have restrictions that we'll go over in a bit. Can I get you anything for pain? You're due."

She took a few moments to think, then she nodded and said, "Yes, thank you. I'd like that."

I promised her I'd be back in a minute as soon as I got the medicine, and I explained how I'd put it in her IV so it would have an immediate effect. I didn't think she knew how much pain she was in while we talked, and she cried. Her grimacing and restless movement told me that she was, and it wasn't good to let it get too far out of control. She gave me a faint smile as I left.

In the med room, I quickly drew up the medicine and signed for it, as well as noted it on her electronic medical record. As promised, I was back in a jiffy. I cleaned the port on the IV line with alcohol and then injected the medicine. "There you go. That should help. You don't want to let your pain get ahead of you. Don't try to be stoic about it. You had surgery. It hurts," I kindly hinted, hoping she'd take my advice. I'd seen patients think they had to be tough, and it ended up making their situation so much worse. I believe it slowed their healing time.

Suddenly, her eyes widened, and she asked, "What is that?" as the medicine hit her.

I grinned as I explained. Most people had no idea about the different kinds of meds. Most wouldn't even ask the names of the medications they got, which wasn't smart in my book. You should always know what you're putting into your body, why you need it, and what it will do.

"It's oxycodone mixed with Toradol. The oxycodone is an opioid, and the Toradol is an NSAID, a nonsteroidal anti-inflammatory drug. It helps the pain med work better and reduces inflammation, which is common after surgery. They'll switch you over to oral meds soon, but until we get your pain controlled, this is what they want you to have."

"Thank you so much, Kimera—" She stopped as the curtain parted, and a huge scowling man walked into her cubicle. He was so tall I had to look way up at him. She shrank back, and my hackles went up. No way in hell was anyone going to hurt one of my patients. I watched as he registered her response, and I swear it looked like his face had fallen. His first words confirmed it.

"Don't do that, Troian. I'd never hurt you. I just need to talk to you," he said gruffly.

I didn't know where my extra courage came from, but I moved to place myself between him and her, and I got close to him. I knew I was in his personal space, but I wanted him to focus on me, not my helpless patient. She wasn't even an hour post-op and drugged to boot. She wasn't in any condition to defend herself. I tipped my head back all the way so I could see his face. His left brow inched up.

Swallowing my niggling fear, I told him sternly, "You need to back up and leave. She's in pain and recovering from surgery. She doesn't need to be any more upset than she already is. What's wrong with you guys? If you won't leave, I'll make you."

Instead of getting angry like I expected, he got a somewhat amused expression. His lips twitched. He thought I was playing with him, didn't he? His reply confirmed he did.

"Whoa, calm down there, Hotcake. No need to go all chihuahua on me. I'm not here to hurt, Troian. I just need to talk to her for a few minutes. There's been a huge misunderstanding."

His amusement and calling me hotcake and a chihuahua pissed me off. I'd show him a chihuahua. How about if I bit him? "Call me hotcake or chihuahua again, and you'll see what I do. Leave," I snapped back automatically, without thinking.

"Babe." He sighed.

I narrowed my eyes at him. *Babe.* I hated random men who didn't know me from Eve calling me names like that. I clenched my fists so I wouldn't punch him. Doing that might lose me my job. He was triggering a very aggressive response in me. Worse than any I could recall, and I'd dealt with some real assholes. "One," I uttered in warning.

"One what?" he asked with a sexy grin.

"Two," I said. *What is up with you finding his smile sexy?* I chided myself. *Focus.*

"Kimera, it's alright. I'll talk to him for a minute, then he'll leave. Won't you, Spawn?" Troian said out of the blue.

"Kimera? I like it," he told me as he winked at me.

"Like I care. Spawn, guess that's apt. Spawn of the Devil, no doubt. Say what you have to say, then get lost. She's gonna be asleep soon. I just gave her pain medicine," I said with a huff.

I crossed my arms so I wouldn't give in to my urge to take a swing at him. There was no way I'd leave her alone with him. He was massive and could crush her with one hand. His reply made me blink.

"One day soon, I'll tell you how I got that name, but right now, I can't flirt. I need to talk to my brother's old lady," he said as he casually walked past me and went to her bedside. A growl slipped out of me. God, I hope Troian hadn't heard that. I couldn't care less if he did, not that I intimidated him. I turned so I could watch him. I saw her grin, but I couldn't see his face.

"What do you want to say, Spawn? I can't think of anything we need to talk about. I'm tired. I want to sleep," she said to him wearily as her eyelids drooped.

"I want you to know that I was the one who did the investigation and found out one of your cousins is in prison for running a prostitution ring. I'm sorry you heard what you did. It was just a precaution to check into you to be sure you weren't involved. We'd have done it with anyone who was involved with our club. Lash didn't believe you were. He's hurting, sweetheart. You gutted him. Don't be mad at him. If you have to be mad at someone, let it be me."

Prison, prostitution ring, club? What the hell? That's when it registered that he was wearing a leather vest. The kind worn by bikers. It read *Iron Punishers MC* on the back. In the middle was a skull with wings and what looked like flames. The background was white, and the skull and the rest were black. Stark, but still scary. The name Spawn was making more sense. They kept going back and forth.

From what she said, it appeared he and his club and a guy named Lash thought she was involved in a whoring business, as she called it. Her mention of having amnesia struck me. Did the doctors know that? Poor woman. I wanted to hug her. She seemed so alone to me, and I knew what that was like.

She said more, and he immediately apologized and used the excuse they had to be sure because of a past attempt to infiltrate his club. What the hell did these bikers do to have people wanting to do that? Likely, it was illegal, so why wouldn't they welcome prostitutes? It would make them money if she hooked up with one of the guys like it sounded like she had. He tried to say none of them believed she was, and it was all paranoia. His remark about being an old lady didn't make sense to me. She wasn't old.

"Maybe in your world, but in mine, I can do anything I want. It's over. Once I'm cleared to leave the hospital, I'm gone. I don't want to be with people who lie to me and think terrible things about me. I don't want to see or talk to any of you," she said, teary-eyed.

Her tears made me want to kick his ass out, but

until he tried to hurt her or she asked me to do it, I'd watch. Maybe letting her have her say would be good for her.

"Babe, where will you go? It's not safe. You have to know he won't let you go. He can't. Losing you will kill him." I heard what sounded like pleading and worry in his tone. Wow, he could act. He made it sound like he cared.

She snorted. "He'll soon be back to screwing anything with a pussy. I was just a temporary diversion. He'll forget my name in a month. Now, I'm done. I need to sleep. Go." She closed her eyes.

"Fuck," he muttered. That was my cue.

Before he could go at her again, I intervened. "You heard her. It's time for you to go. Don't send any of your other friends back here. If you do, I'll have security throw you all out. She's made herself clear, I think. Don't you? Leave," I hissed.

"I'd like to see you try that, Hotcake. Don't get your tail in a twist. I'm going, but I make no promises that Lash won't be back here again. That's his woman, and even if she's pissed at him, they love each other. She has to let him make this right."

"I don't think that's happening. Now, you need to go. I have other patients to check on, and I'm not leaving you alone with her."

He studied me for a long moment, which was unsettling. Then he gave me a chin lift and turned to walk off. I started to relax as he did until he looked back and said, "I'll be seeing you, Kimera."

My heart almost jumped out of my chest. What did that mean? Was he threatening me? Unease filled me. I didn't want any trouble, but I couldn't walk away and leave my patient either. I'd have to be careful.

As I got back to work, I had to fight to push Spawn to the back of my mind. It wasn't long before Troian was moved to the ICU for observation. She'd thanked me before going. As I watched her be wheeled away, I felt sad. She seemed like someone I could be friends with.

Friends, yeah, like I had any of those. The other nurses I worked with were only work acquaintances, and we didn't spend time together outside of work. They had different interests than I did. Some had families and spent their free time with them. I wouldn't want to interfere with that. The rest, the single ones, only seemed to want to go out and get drunk and find men. That didn't interest me. As pathetic as it sounded, my one true friend was my dog, Toro. At least I wasn't a cat lady.

I finished off my shift without any more drama. On the drive home, I thought about Spawn. I couldn't stop myself. If I was being honest, the man did something to me. Yes, he was big and scary, but he was more than that. *Hell, just say it, Kimera.* The man was sex on two legs. He was hot as hell. A woman would have to be dead not to notice.

He was a giant. I bet he was six and a half feet tall. He was broad-shouldered, and his arms in his t-shirt were bulging with muscles. The tattoos that graced them only made them look bigger. His chest was wide and muscular. Again, the shirt didn't do anything to hide it or what I bet were rock-hard abs underneath. His body tapered down to lean hips and long legs. His skin was very tan. After his height and build, his face and hair caught my attention.

His features were bold and put together in a way that made him a very handsome man. There was nothing pretty about him. He was all male. His face was clean-shaven, with the ever so faintest hint of facial hair above his lip and along his jaw. His eyes were the darkest brown I'd ever seen, with long, thick lashes. His hair was a medium brown with lighter golden strands. It was thick and hung almost to the top of his shoulders. It fell over his forehead a little way on the left side, giving him a rakish look. Put it all together, and he was hot and made me squirm. I didn't notice guys, even the really good-looking ones, other than to acknowledge they were attractive. Why him? This thought occupied my brain not only for the rest of my drive but also into the evening.

Spawn:

The tiny woman I met standing guard over Lash's woman in the hospital wouldn't leave my mind. I should be trying to figure out a way to get Troian to forgive my brother, and I was, but I kept coming up empty. Instead, I continued to go back to the nurse. When she'd bowed up on me at Troi's bedside, it amused me for sure, but it also impressed the fuck outta me. There were very few men who would do that, let alone a woman and a petite, delicate one to boot.

I was a lover of women. I liked them in all sizes, shapes, and looks, although due to my size, I often ended up sticking to those on the taller and thicker side. The nurse was neither of those, but what I wouldn't give to have her naked and in my bed. I bet she'd be a wild one. Despite how feisty she was, she inspired this protectiveness in me too.

I'd been struck by her and had to fight not to gape at her like an idiot when I first saw her. It was more than just the fact she placed her small body between Troian and me. It was her utter beauty and her fierce protectiveness. She would be one to defend her man and family to the death.

She was younger than me. Probably, if I were to guess, her mid-twenties, which was Troian's age. That made me a good decade older. At six foot six, I was more than a foot taller than her. It didn't matter. Instantly, I knew I wanted her. Her pale, creamy-looking skin and her fit, petite, though curvy body made me want to touch her all over. She had the most beautiful blue-gray eyes, which were perfect with her delicate features of a small nose, high cheekbones, and full lips. That mouth of hers fueled some fantasies about what she could do with it.

I knew I was a dog, but I couldn't help it. She hit me hard, and it hadn't lessened in the last few days since meeting her. In fact, she occupied more and more of my mind even when I was supposed to be working. No woman had ever done that. I was known to be able to shut everything out and focus.

Add to all that her hair. She'd had it up in a bun, but I knew it would be long, most likely past her shoulder blades. It was a light brown color with lighter streaks in it. They weren't from a bottle either, I'd wager. They were natural. Her quick mouth and the fact she was a nurse told me she was smart. A stupid woman would bore me to death in seconds. They might be alright for a quick tumble and then send on their way, but I wanted more than that.

Like most, if not all, of my club brothers, I was getting older and wanted to settle down. Well, maybe not the guys still in their twenties—Sandman, Shadow, Remus, Romulus, and our newest member, Gravel. Hell, even our only prospect, Rhaines, might not. The rest of us were in our thirties or a bit older. We wanted to have a stable life with a wife and kids. Or at least I did. I found I was jealous, in a way, of Reaper, Ink, Maniac, and, hopefully, if we could get Troian to forgive him, Lash.

Shit, if she didn't take him back, I didn't know what would become of him. He loved her like crazy. You could see it. Losing her forever would kill him, literally. I wanted to love and want someone that much. That made me think of Kimera. God, even her name was pretty and so unusual. An unusual name for what I thought was an intriguing woman.

The one thing that ruined my daydreams about her was the thought she might not be free. Sure, she didn't have a ring on at the hospital, but not everyone wore one. Yes, I'd checked her left hand. However, in her case, I figured she was the kind of woman who would unless it was a work thing since she was taking care of people all day. I could see it then.

I wanted to know if she was married or in a serious relationship. If she was married, was she happy? Did he treat her like a queen? If the answer to any of those were no, then I'd have a hard time thinking it would be wrong to take her away from her man. To me, there was no moral dilemma. If he didn't take care of her properly, then I would. If she had a boyfriend, then that was even better. If there were kids, I wouldn't care. They were part of her, so they'd become mine.

God, what the hell was I thinking? This was crazy shit, especially after a single meeting that didn't last more than fifteen minutes if that. I needed to have my head examined. *No, you don't. You need to find out if our woman has a man. If so, run him off, whether he's a boyfriend or a fiancé. If he's her husband, then watch and wait to see if he's worthy,* my inner demon said.

That bastard wouldn't stop. He was the part of me that pushed me to do things I maybe shouldn't. I came by my name, Spawn, partially because of him. As I aged, I'd gotten better at ignoring him, but Kimera was arousing him to come out.

Ten years ago, when I came to the Punishers as a prospect, I'd been looking to leave the shit I'd gotten involved in behind. The thought of being in an MC sounded exciting and fun but also something I would love as I saw more of them. I loved riding and had a bike. I was fascinated by their lifestyle, even if I didn't know everything they did. I liked how they talked about how they were brothers. I came to them after I met Mayhem. We'd both been at a local bar having a few drinks. That had been an eventful night for both of us.

There had been a group of five men who were acting like total assholes. They were too loud, kept touching the waitresses inappropriately, and picked on other customers. I was at the bar, and my demon was pushing me to go do something to stop them. Yes, the bar had a bouncer, but he wasn't much of one. He sat on his ass at the door and looked at people's IDs. Earlier, there had been a shouting match between two men, and he hadn't done more than watch with interest. Luckily, they settled down and left.

Those five didn't. Instead, the main instigator eventually went too far. He grabbed one of the waitresses and dragged her onto his lap. He had his hand on her ass and was trying to get her to kiss him. She was protesting and struggling to get away from him. Others around the bar were watching the display but not doing anything to stop it. His friends were laughing, and even over the noise, you could hear their lewd comments. I threw off the reins

23

holding me back, and I was up and crossing the room in an instant. Just as I reached them, I noticed someone else had decided to stop them. I hoped. He was a biker, and based on his grim expression, he wasn't finding it any funnier than I was.

The biker gave me a chin lift and narrowed his hard-ass look at them. The idiots never looked up. They were too busy cheering on their buddy. I stepped up to stand right next to the grabby fucker. That was what got his attention. He glanced up at me and sneered. "What? Can I help you?" he asked.

"Yeah, you can let her go and take your friends and leave. No one wants to hear or see your shit. People are here to have a good time, not share air with fuckers like you. Didn't anyone ever teach you manners?" I snapped.

"Fuck you. Who're you to tell me anything, dude? Now, why don't you take your ass back to wherever you came from and let me talk to this bitch? Do it before you get hurt," he said with what I guess he thought was an intimidating glare. He didn't know what intimidating was, but he was about to meet it. I smiled at him, and I saw that it took him aback. I leaned closer to him.

"Listen, we can do this nice and easy, or we can get ugly. Personally, I'd love ugly, but it wouldn't end well for you and your buddies. Trips to the hospital could be involved. In fact, I guaran-fucking-tee it. Let her go, now," I growled.

"You asked for it," he said as he pushed the waitress off his lap, letting her fall on her ass on the hard, dirty floor. I heard the scrape of chair legs on the wood. I was ready. I

wanted to help her up, but I couldn't take my eyes off these assholes.

"Move, sweetheart. I don't want you to get hurt," I warned her. She scrambled up and away from us like a frightened rabbit. The one I was facing off with was rising up out of his chair like his companions. Suddenly, he launched himself at me, which he totally broadcasted. I nailed him with a right hook to his jaw. I heard a loud thump, and someone else cried out in pain. A darting glance to the left revealed the biker holding one of the other guy's heads to the table. I think he slammed it off of it. That must've been the thump I heard.

I couldn't help but smile seeing it. The guy I punched was shaking it off. I knew I'd rung his bell good. A third one came at me from the side at the same time as guy number one threw his punch. I ducked the punch, then pivoted to place an uppercut on the third guy. He went flying back and landed flat on his back on the floor. He was out cold. I danced away from the first one, who was trying for a second punch.

As I did, I saw the biker had knocked out the guy with his head on the table, and he was beating the ass off the fifth one. If he knocked him out, that just left my first idiot. I needed to get to work. Swinging back to fully face asshole number one when he came roaring at me, I gave him a right-left combo to the gut, and when he bent over holding his stomach, I placed a knee to his face while using my hands to drive his head down to meet my knee. That ended it. I heard the crunch when his nose broke, then he was falling like a felled tree, and he was out.

Swiftly checking that guy number three was still out

for the count, I swung around to see if I needed to help my new friend. I didn't. It seemed he was standing there waiting for me. He grinned. "Let's put out the trash, then have a drink. I hoped it would last longer. Barely worth it, except they won't be harassing the staff or bothering the rest of us. Nice job. My name is Mayhem. What's yours?" he asked as he lifted his first guy over his shoulder.

Deciding to do the same, I lifted my first one, too. Together, we ignored the stares and whispers and carried them outside past the gaping bouncer and threw them not too gently in the gravel.

"I'm Aidan. Thanks for the assist. I could've taken them, but they might've gotten in a few hits before I did."

He laughed. After we carried the other three outside, we sat down and ordered new drinks, and spent the next couple of hours talking. By the time the bar closed, I had an invitation to come check out his club. The rest was history.

Recalling that and how my life changed because of a chance encounter, I knew meeting Kimera was another life-changing moment. I'd wait and see what I found out. As much as I was dying to dig into her, I wouldn't. This time, I planned to learn about someone the way others did. It should be interesting.

Spawn: Chapter 2

The past three days since Troian booted Lash out of the hospital and had them place a security guard outside her room had been hell on him. For me, it had been a different kind of pain. I was seriously jonesing for another look at and to spar with Hotcake. I hadn't broken my promise to myself about investigating her, even if it was damn near impossible to resist. The one thing I did do was get into the hospital's employee listing and find out her last name. It was Jordan.

The urge to go further into their HR files was so strong I found myself starting to type and had to get up and walk away from my computer. No, I wasn't going to do that. I needed to learn about her for myself. However, that resolve was tested in church, and now, as I sit at my desk, working in the DMV system. All because the little minx helped Troian escape the hospital. I was typing away as Lash and a few others stood there watching me.

"Can you get a clearer picture of her license plate?" Lash asked.

I wanted to roll my eyes and ask him, *Are you for real? Don't you know me?* But I didn't. He was stressed enough. He didn't need me to be a smartass. So, instead, I said, "Yeah, give me a minute."

As I worked my keyboard, I couldn't help but

mutter under my breath some of the tamer things I'd like to do to Kimera when I found her ass. I knew they might hear me, but I didn't care.

"Spank her ass. Over my knee."

Several minutes later, I grinned as I told Lash I found her. "I have her address. How much you wanna bet she took Troian to her house? She lives outside of town."

When he stood up and thanked me, asking me to send him her address, I shot his idea down. I stood up, too. "Oh, no, I'm going. Me and little Hotcake have some talking to do," I said.

I saw them exchange amused glances, but the only one to say anything was Crusher. He questioned the hotcake remark. All I said back was, "Yep," and I kept heading out to my bike. The ride wouldn't be terribly long, but I found myself anxious to be there. Sure, I wanted to get Troian back for my brother, but it was more because I wanted to see Kimera.

Not long afterward, we pulled up in front of the small house where the nurse lived. I took it in. The first thing that struck me was how isolated it was. Instantly, I didn't like it. Anyone could come here and do God knows what to her. No one would hear her screams. The house was a small, white-siding cottage. There wasn't a garage, and I could see her car parked alongside the house. Surrounding it were a lot of trees, especially behind it. There wasn't a clear line of sight. Anyone could sneak up on this place.

As we approached the front door, Lash said softly

to Crusher, "I need you to go around to the back in case there's a back way out. Hide there until I get inside."

"Sure thing," was his reply before he took off. We'd told Colt to stay in the SUV. He was here to transport her if need be, not to stand guard. At least not unless we found we needed him to.

I approved of Lash sending Crusher to the back. Knowing how upset Troian was with Lash the other day, I wouldn't put it past her to run, even if she had to crawl. The woman was stubborn. I stood behind him as he knocked on the door. After the third unanswered knock, he called out, "We know someone is in there. Your car is here. Troian, baby, I just need to talk to you. There are things I need to explain and things you need to know. It's not safe for you."

Silence greeted him. I raised my brows. It seemed like we might need to do some breaking and entering. It wouldn't be the first time. He waited another minute or so, and then I pulled out a lock-picking kit. Yeah, most of us had one of those. You'd be amazed at the skills one picked up. Before I could get the door unlocked, we heard swearing and yelling from the back. It was Crusher. Lash took off running.

I kept jimmying the lock. I could hear them talking since they were so loud. "What the fuck is going on? Why did she scream, and why are you holding her?" Lash growled at Crusher.

The rest became muffled as the door opened, and I went inside. I wanted to catch Kimera. I wondered why she wasn't out there in the middle of it. I was confident she wasn't since I didn't hear her. A quick walk-through showed me she wasn't there. Was she outside after all? I walked out the back door to find out. A quick scan showed she wasn't there either. I frowned. I marched over to the three of them. Troian was being held in Crusher's arms.

"Where is she?" I asked.

"Who?" Troian played dumb.

"You know who. Your new friend who helped you leave the hospital against medical advice. The one who could lose her job for that shit," I snapped. I was upset Kimera wasn't here, and I knew I was taking it out on Troian, but I couldn't seem to help it. Disappointment was crashing through me.

"Hey, don't you dare threaten to get her fired! She didn't do anything wrong. I was the one who decided to leave. She was just nice enough to give me a place to get back on my feet. If you cause trouble for her, I swear to God, I'll—" she stopped telling me off abruptly.

It looked like she was trying to think of more to say. She was so irate-looking that I had to fight back a full-blown laugh. My lips twitched, though, as I responded to her. "And just what'll you do about it if I do?" I asked with an amused tone.

"She might not be up to doing anything, but I sure can," came the reply from behind Crusher. My whole body tightened with awareness. I knew that sultry voice. When Crusher swung around to face her, I saw Kimera. I avidly ate her up with my eyes. A once-over was all I got before I realized she wasn't alone. Standing next to her, alert with his ears up and watching us as if he was ready to eat us, was a large dog.

I recognized the breed. Although most people would assume it was a German Shepherd, it was actually a Belgian Malinois. It was tall and probably weighed at least eighty pounds, which would mean it was most likely a male. He was beautiful with a fawn-colored coat. I loved dogs. Kimera was glaring at us and had a hand on the dog's head.

"Hold on, let's not do anything crazy. I'd hate to hurt your dog, but if you give him the command to come after us, I won't have a choice. We're not here to hurt anyone. I just need to talk to Troian," Lash told her. Kimera didn't act as if she was worried.

"Why don't you have your friend there set Troian down and let her come to me? If she decides to talk, then we can all be civilized and move inside. However, if she doesn't want to, then you'll need to go. If you hurt my dog, I'll put holes in you." That's when I discovered why she hadn't been too worried. She pulled a gun out from under her shirt.

"What the hell are you doing with that?" I snapped at her. All I could think was she was handling a deadly weapon and, like many people, had no idea how to use it properly. Those people were the ones who ended up shooting themselves or others by accident.

"What kinda dumbass would I be to be a woman who lives alone and goes walking in the woods with her dog and doesn't have a gun? I don't know what bimbo idiots you're used to, but I'm not one of them," she responded with a roll of her eyes. I could hear the unspoken *duh* at the end.

"You can't get us all before we disarm you," Crusher said. I wanted to smack him. *Way to instigate her, dumbass*, I wanted to snap.

"No, but I can get at least one, if not two of you. Wanna find out which ones it'll be?"

Her confidence, along with her gorgeousness, made me tune out what Lash, Troian, and Crusher were saying. I only had eyes and ears for the woman before me. As I watched her defend one of ours and stand there with her dog, a new name came to mind. She objected to Hotcake. I wondered what she'd think of She-Wolf. Not that I planned to find out right this second, but I'd hold that back and surprise her with it later.

I momentarily zoned back into the conversation to back up what Lash had said to Troian. I reiterated what I told her in the hospital. I was the one to investigate her, and she should be mad at me. She quickly assured me she was mad at all of us and then ordered Crusher to put her down. He was still holding her. After Lash nodded to him, he did so. She didn't waste time limping over to Kimera. I shifted slightly. This brought up her dog's ears more.

"Babe, let me check your foot. What did you do?" Lash asked. I could tell he was worried.

"Don't call me babe, and I can have Kimera look at it. How did you know I was here?"

"I'll answer that if we can go sit down and talk

like civilized people. It's too exposed out here," he said.

"What do you expect? Someone to shoot me with a sniper rifle from a tree?" Troian asked.

"Don't fucking joke about that! You have no goddamn idea what you're dealing with. It's worse than we imagined."

I was surprised when Kimera bent forward to whisper in her ear and Troian considered whatever she said for a minute, and then whispered into Kimera's ear before turning to us.

"We'll talk, but when I say it's time for you to leave, you do it. Don't take this to mean anything has changed between us. And Spawn..." Troian paused until I glanced from Kimera to her. "Don't you dare do anything to get Kimera in trouble at work. She doesn't deserve her life destroyed. One of us is enough."

"Troian, sweetheart, I know you aren't able to believe it yet, but we're not the enemy. We want to make it up to you for what we did and how it hurt you. As for your friend here, I'll behave. Well, I will as far as doing that, anyway. Her job is safe." I couldn't help but smirk. I knew it would aggravate my she-wolf. I was right. She glared at me and gave me the bird. Troian snickered, and Crusher, Lash, and I all laughed. I winked and blew her a kiss in reply. Kimera pointed to the back door.

After Troian took a couple of steps, Lash was at her side, demanding, "Let me carry you, please."

"No, I can do it. Go."

I knew he wasn't happy about her refusal, but he

didn't fight her. He stayed next to her while Crusher and I went ahead of them into the house. Kimera and her dog brought up the rear. It was a risk to turn our backs on her with that dog and gun, but something told me she wouldn't hurt us unless we gave her no choice.

Troian took a seat once she got inside. The rest of us didn't get a chance to say anything before Kimera walked off to get stuff to take care of Troian's foot. She left her dog with us. The dog stayed close to Lash's woman and eyed us the whole time.

It was Crusher who voiced what we were all thinking. "That damn dog looks like he'd love nothing more than to eat one of us. Who do you think he wants the most?"

I should've known Kimera would pick that exact moment to come back, and she'd voice her opinion. "My pick is Spawn," Kimera said with a smirk aimed at me.

It didn't bother me a bit. I loved her snarky remarks and sassy mouth. There were so many delicious things I could think of that would calm them but never tame them. "Hotcake, you can threaten me all you want, but it won't do you any good. I'm called Spawn because I'm related to the Devil. You know, Spawn of Satan. I can control your hellhound over there," I informed her with a smile.

"Keep telling yourself that. Toro will take a chunk out of you if I tell him to, so behave and don't piss me off more than you already do. That means stop calling me Hotcake."

Ah, Hotcake really must get to her. There was

no way I'd stop, but I'd add more pet names and endearments to it. My smile got bigger as she fussed over Troian. Well, we now knew the dog's name and that it was a boy. When she was done and had cleaned her hands, she brought us all a bottle of water and sat down. After she did, Troian told Lash, "Tell me what you think I need to know."

"You know that we dug into your background and family. We were trying to rule out that they were involved in hurting you."

Troian interrupted him. "Yeah, and you needed to prove that I was involved in my cousin's dirty criminal activities. Oh, and that my amnesia was faked."

"Jesus, we're never gonna get past this if you can't stop bringing that up! I know we fucked up. That I did. Christ, every time I open my eyes and don't see you in our bed or house, I know it. I'm fucking sorry, but that's not what we need to worry about. It's what else we found out since your accident," Lash said.

"And what would that be?" Kimera asked.

"That her family, the Gusevs, aren't the people she thought they were. It wasn't only your cousin Andrik who was involved in the prostitution ring. We're positive it was all five of your male cousins," he told them.

"And what are you basing that on?" Troian asked.

"What my family told me," Crusher said out of nowhere, his expression grim.

"Your family? What do they have to do with

this?" Troian asked.

"You know my mother is Russian. Well, most of her family is still back in Russia. I do have contact with them, although not a lot. My father wasn't involved in their business, so when my mom married him, they lived here and outside the family circle."

"What was your family's business?" Kimera asked.

"My family is Bratva," he blurted out.

I half listened to them talk. My attention was taken with Kimera, who was pretending to ignore me, but I saw the pulse beating in her neck. She was more than aware of me. After telling them Crusher's mother's family was Bratva, Lash picked Troian up and sat her on his lap. She tried to fight him, earning him a growl from Toro. He ignored the dog and told her to settle.

It wasn't until I added to the conversation that there was a more violent response from Troian. "We're waiting for actual confirmation, but I think the reason you were beaten and left for dead is Andrik was convicted based mostly on evidence, not witness testimony, although there were a couple of people who did testify. That usually means an informant on the inside. We think you were that informant, and at first, no one knew it. Somehow, they found out and tried to kill you for putting him away and ruining a very lucrative business for them," I said.

Suddenly, Troian flung herself forward in Lash's arms and vomited. He swore, and Kimera got up and went to the kitchen. She came back with a bucket and mop. It had been sitting in the corner of the kitchen. I hazard a guess that earlier, she had been cleaning. She ordered Troian to sit while she cleaned it up.

"What caused that?" I asked.

"I saw images. I remember a flash of a man's face, then pain in my head. It was nighttime. Then voices and being beaten and kicked. I didn't see them, but it was men's voices, and I begged them to stop."

I took out my phone and brought up the five photos of her male cousins. I handed it to Troi and asked her if any of the men on it was the one she saw in her head. It didn't take her long to identify Zandro. Lash explained who he was and why it was too dangerous for her to be outside the compound because they'd be searching for her.

"Why? They dumped me. They think I'm dead," was her quick response.

This led to him explaining how one of the authors she edited for had reported her missing, and the police went to question her so-called family. As she cried, he reassured her we wouldn't let them hurt her, and we'd take her back with us where she'd be safe with fences, guards, and cameras. That's when Kimera surprised the hell out of me.

"Troian, I want to tell these guys to go screw themselves, but they're right. People like that are too dangerous to take the chance on them not finding you. Even if you go somewhere else, there's no guarantee they won't find you. I can try to protect you, and Toro will help, but I'm not here all the time. I have to work.

I have a suggestion if you're willing to do it. Oh, and if these guys can stay off my nerves." She said the last part as she gave me a challenging chin lift.

I snorted. "Let's hear your bright plan, Hotcake," I teased. God, sparring with her was like foreplay.

She bared her teeth at me for calling her Hotcake again, but she didn't say anything about it. She surprised us. "I'd like to come with Troian. I can help her and make sure she recovers like she should. Toro will come too. He's a trained guard dog. He'll be added protection for her. He'll tear anyone apart who tries to harm her or anyone else I indicate isn't a friend. He can be there even when I'm at work. Plus, I have a gun, and I know how to use it. If they somehow find a way into your place, I have no trouble putting them down like the vermin they are." Disgust was evident in her voice.

When none of us said anything, Kimera suggested we talk about it while she helped Troian to bed. We could see she was tired and in pain. I wanted to laugh when Kimera said when she got back, we could tell her all the reasons that would be a no, and she'd make us see how full of shit we were. As soon as the door to the bedroom was closed, Lash turned to Crusher and me and asked, "What do you think?"

"I think that woman needs a spanking," I grumbled, although I wasn't truly upset.

"And let me guess. You're not talking about Troian, and you're just the man to give it to her," Crusher teased me.

"Damn right, I am. She's got more balls than

sense, but in this case, I think she's right. If she comes, it'll get Troian back home, and the dog will be extra protection. We can keep an eye on her to be sure they don't find out she helped Troian," I told them.

As much as the idea of Kimera acting as protection went against my grain, if it got Troian back and my Hotcake there, too, I'd take it. We could keep them both safe. We debated it a little more and then came to an agreement, which was a good thing since Kimera returned seconds later. Lash tried to go into the bedroom, but she held him off.

"She's almost asleep. Let her get some rest. She's overdone it. We can talk out here. Sit," she ordered.

They'd barely started to talk when my hackles went up at her mention of not trusting us. She didn't blame Troian for it after what we had done, so I defended the club.

"Now, that's not exactly fair. Yes, we checked into her, but it was the right thing to do to ensure everyone's safety."

"How about I go digging into your life and do it because I think you're lying and can't be trusted? And then I'll blithely tell everyone I know that you're okay to be with? That wouldn't bother you or hurt you? Think before you answer," she warned me.

She had a point, but only a small one. I shrugged. "I can see how that might upset me, but Lash and she are in a relationship. You and I aren't." She didn't hear my very softly uttered, "Not yet."

She kept going to explain how she'd gotten Troian to agree to go temporarily, but only if she and Toro went. I had no issue with that at all.

Lash said they could stay in his house as long as Toro didn't try to eat him every time he saw him. I wanted to object to her staying with him and Troian. I had a house. She should stay with me, but I wisely kept it to myself. There would be time to make that happen after we got her there. Just like I knew my brother would find a way to convince his woman to stay.

There was a burning question that I had to ask her. "Why're you involved in this?"

"What do you mean, why am I involved?"

"You don't know her. You met her once for a couple of hours, at the most, in the recovery room. She's not your friend or a family member."

"Does someone have to be a friend or family in order to do something you know is right? Or for me to care that they're safe and not being hurt by someone? Or maybe I should sit back and assume she has a bunch of family who give a damn about her and will step in," she snarled back.

"Who hurt you?" Crusher asked. A brief flash of surprise on her face was all we got before she blanked her face. She pretended not to know what he was talking about.

That set off warning bells in my head. My pledge to not dig into her life got harder to keep. Crusher kept pushing it. "Either someone hurt you, or you've seen shit. I'm willing to bet at least one man was the cause. Why else get involved this much and have a dog like that?"

"I have a dog because I love animals," she defended.

"You can love animals but not have a trained guard dog. Those don't come cheap," I added.

She stared hard at me. "Go stick your nose in my shit and see what happens, Spawn. I have a guard dog because I'm a woman who works odd hours and lives alone out here. I'd be stupid not to protect myself in more ways than just my gun. I can't hide behind a fence with weapons and people at the ready. Some of us have to live out in the real, scary, and dangerous world."

Lash shut any more talk of her motives down. She seemed alright with it and offered to get packed. She relaxed until Crusher mentioned Colt. She got uncomfortable again. "There's more of you here?"

"Just one of our prospects. He brought the SUV. We didn't know what condition Troian would be in and figured she wouldn't be up to a ride on the back of my bike," Lash explained.

"Send him back. We'll use my car. I can't be without it anyway. I have to work."

"It won't hurt to have him stick around in case you end up needing to take more stuff with you. We're not sure how long this will last, so bring plenty," I told her.

"Make him come inside and wait," she demanded.

"He's fine in the car. He'll entertain himself," I assured her. There was no reason to bring him inside.

She stood up. "Either he comes inside where Toro and I can keep an eye on him, or you all go."

"Goddamn, why the hell are you so damn paranoid, woman? He's not gonna go busting in here at gunpoint and decide to kidnap and rape you," I snapped. I hated mysteries. I knew immediately that my choice of words was wrong. She turned pale and swayed on her feet. I shot to my feet and put my arms around her. Her damn dog growled at me, but I ignored him. No way would I let go of her. Not when she reacted like this.

"Call off your dog, babe. I'm not hurting you, and I don't plan to. You couldn't be safer than with me. I just want to know what made you react like that. We're not men who hurt women and kids. Yeah, we fucked up with my brother Lash's woman and hurt her emotionally, but that wasn't intentional. Tell me why you went pale and swayed. Did someone do that to you?" I asked.

She didn't answer me right away, but she signaled to Toro to relax. When she did answer me, I heard the lie. "I'm fine. My blood sugar must be low. That's all. If you'll let go of me, I'll grab a snack. Would you guys like something? Oh, and how about your prospect? Is he coming in, or are you all leaving?" I stared at her as she stared back at me. It was a battle of wills. What broke it was when Lash called Crusher "cuz."

She turned her head to glance at Lash. "Cuz? You're blood-related, or is that another biker term I don't know?"

"We're second cousins on our dads' side," Lash explained. "Hey, let me ask you something. Did you happen to get Toro from Flynn Farms down in Tennessee? Seamus and Laura?"

She pushed on my chest, and I reluctantly let go but didn't move too far away. She looked surprised. "Yes, I did. How do you know Laura and Seamus?"

Finding out we knew the Flynns and were good friends with their daughter and her man seemed to reassure her.

"How long have you had him?" I asked. Maybe if I knew that, it would help me figure out why she was so defensive and had reacted the way she did to my earlier remark.

"Three years. I got him not long after I moved here," she told us as she headed into the kitchen. We followed. She got stuff out for sandwiches and then told us to help ourselves. Her tension reappeared. I saw it because she kept eyeing the front door. I pulled out her chair at the table, which earned me a weird look. Trying to make her relax, I spoke up.

"Relax, he's gone. Didn't you hear the SUV leave? I promise there's no one from our club lurking around outside," I assured her gruffly.

"Nothing says he couldn't have been told to go down the road then sneak back on foot," she responded.

Crusher took his phone out of his pocket, pushed a few buttons, and then presented it to her. "Here, you can see that I didn't tell him that. He's really gone, darlin'."

She read it and then nodded. I opened my mouth to question why she thought he would do that, but Lash cut me off with a question about her being a nurse. This led to a casual conversation over our lunch, and then we cleaned up the mess while she began packing. I used the time to think about what could be behind her behavior. The thoughts that came to mind weren't good ones. I swear to God, if someone hurt her, I'd skin them alive before I killed them. As soon as she left the room, I whirled around to glare at Lash and Crusher. "There's something not right going on here."

"You mean more than just with Troian?" Lash asked coyly.

I rolled my eyes. "Duh, yeah, that's what I mean, asshole. You know it is. The way she reacted to my snide comment about kidnapping and rape and the fact she carries a damn gun and has a dog that'll eat your ass. Someone either scared her or actually hurt her. Shit, I need to figure this out," I muttered. I'd kill for one of my computers right now. Wait, I promised I wouldn't do that. Shit!

"Spawn, chill. You can't go diving into her past. You heard her. Why not see if we can gain her trust and then ask her? I agree it might be something ugly or maybe she's just cautious like she said. Either way, if you're interested in her, she's not gonna like it if you go digging into her past," Lash warned me as if I needed it.

I was not sure yet how comfortable I was with

anyone else, knowing how far under my skin Kimera already was, so I tried to dismiss Lash's remark about my interest in her. "Who said I was interested in her?"

This earned me a snort from Crusher. "Brother, you almost pissed on her, for God's sake. She's got your attention. Don't lie. Now, if it's because you want to get your cock wet, forget it. That woman isn't one to go around sleeping with men to scratch an itch."

"I'm not just looking to—" I halted. Damn, sneaky bastard. They laughed at me, which made me give them the finger. "Yuck it up, bastards. I'm not saying anything will come of it, but she's got my attention. There, now let's get this mess cleaned up and this show on the road." Thankfully, they let it go for now.

We had the kitchen cleaned in no time. Once it was, I escaped. "I'll be back. I want to make sure there's nothing outside that needs to be secured." I went out the door before they could say anything.

As I walked around the outside of her house, I not only identified areas where her security measures could be improved, but I thought of various reasons why she was so distrustful. None were good reasons. I tried every window and found them locked. Her front and back doors had deadbolts on them, although why they weren't engaged when I got inside, I didn't know. Even her car, when I tried all the doors, was locked. True, she didn't have a garage to put it in, but most people didn't think to lock their vehicles on their own property. In addition to that, a trained guard dog and the way she handled the gun, which was competent, made my alarms grow louder.

After I made it back inside, she came out a few minutes later with a packed bag. I chided her for carrying shit when she had the three of us to do it.

"Hotcake, don't be lugging shit around. You pack, then we'll carry that shit and load it into your car."

"I told you, don't call me Hotcake, and I can do this. I'm not a weakling," she protested.

"It has nothing to do with your strength. It's manners. Women don't open doors, carry stuff, or pull out their own chairs around us. Give me your car keys so I can unlock it and put this in there." I held out my hand.

When I confessed that I had tried the doors, she asked, "When did you do that?"

"While you were packing. I checked to see if there was anything outside that needed to be secured or needed attention."

"And you thought my car did?"

"No, I was testing out a theory, and you proved it with the locked car."

"And what pray tell would that be?"

"That you're overly cautious, and one day you'll tell me why."

"Don't bet on it," she muttered as she smacked her keys in my hand, turned her back on me, and walked back into her room.

I grinned at my brothers. "She's wearing down," I told them.

They cracked up laughing. She kept packing, and we kept hauling the stuff to the car. We were at it for close to an hour on and off before Troian rejoined us. She was moving slowly and looking sleepy. She asked what she could do after verifying we were still going. When Lash tried to tell her to rest, she told him off. Whatever he whispered in her ear got a reaction out of her and Toro.

Toro squeezed between them and gave Lash a look that shouted, *move or else.* My brother did it, but not without telling the dog off. "Listen, you little cockblocker, step off," he told the dog. Crusher and I laughed.

Kimera just looked curious before suggesting she help Troian get freshened up while we entertained ourselves. Crusher teased Lash about being twisted up by Troian. I knew how he felt. Kimera did the same damn thing to me, but I found I wouldn't trade it for anything. I felt more alive than I could recall being in years, maybe ever.

This led to Lash cursing Crusher with the same thing when he found a woman. It became apparent quickly that Crusher was delusional. He thought his future woman would fall at his feet, begging him to take her, and they'd live in bliss for the rest of their lives. This made us laugh. I had to say something to that.

"God, I can't wait to see how wrong you are. When she puts you in your place or on your ass, we want to be there and record that, so you can watch it again and again and know how full of shit you were for saying this. Why would you get someone like that when none of us have or will? That's not our kind of woman. We need 'em with fire."

"You wait. I'll get an angel who'll never go against my advice when it comes to her safety, health, or happiness," he replied. Lash and I were still laughing when the women rejoined us. They gave us curious looks but didn't ask.

After getting them in the car, we got on our bikes. I took up the rear position. It would allow me to protect them from behind while the others did it from the front, and I'd be able to prevent them from taking off just in case Kimera got that bright idea. There was no way I was letting her get away from me.

Kimera: Chapter 3

The past several days had been confusing, to say the least. While a small part of it was the Punishers as a whole, it was mainly one member, Spawn, who caused the bulk of it. He kept throwing me off-kilter, and I didn't know what to do about it. I tried to avoid him and thinking about how he made me feel.

The club had not only been very happy to see Troian back, but they'd welcomed me, a total stranger, too. Not only did that surprise me, but so did how they treat their women and kids. Most of the members were single, but they were still helpful and affectionate toward the women and kids.

I got a good dose of it when they had Arya's first birthday party. She was Alisse and Ink's daughter. The clubhouse's common area had been cleaned and decorated in purple-and-teal balloons and streamers, and all the table covers, paper plates, and other decor matched. She'd gotten a ton of gifts since every member bought her more than one thing. Her cake had been a masterpiece. Other than her and Lily, Cheyenne and Reaper's daughter, there was one other child, Flynn.

I was surprised to find out he was the adopted son of Maniac and his wife, Lark. They treated him as if he was their natural-born son. It brought up memories I didn't want to think about. They were too painful, even if I was happy they treated him the way they did.

I'd laughed so hard watching Arya bury her face and hands in her piece of cake and get it everywhere. Her daddy instigated her to do it, too. The adults hung out, talked, and had a few drinks, but it was mainly about the kids. They played with them and had a ball. What would it be like to grow up being loved and wanted like that?

The compound was awe-inspiring. Not only the size of it but what they had. There were several houses, along with a big clubhouse and play and picnic areas. I was told back through the woods there were a couple of storage buildings, too. Toro was in heaven. He had acres and acres to run to his heart's content. Sure, my place had a large yard, and my neighbor allowed us to walk on his property, but I didn't let Toro run wild. I was afraid he'd get hurt, or someone might take him or shoot him, thinking he was a stray, even though he had a collar and was microchipped. It would kill me if I lost him.

The guys went to the clubhouse more than once for mystery meetings. Troian had explained they called those church and they discussed things. I asked Lash what they talked about and got a vague answer that it was club business. I asked her what club business was, but she could only say she didn't know. Their unwillingness to answer made me huff in aggravation and to be wary. What did they have to hide?

I kept to my work schedule at the hospital. It wasn't like I could take off from work just because there might be a slim possibility I could be hurt by Troi's twisted family. If the threat of them kept me hidden, I'd never leave the property. She kept an eye on Toro while I was at work. He loved having someone to fuss over him. Usually, he stayed at home in the house while I was working.

The one thing that irked me was the club insisted I had to have an escort to work and back. I argued it wasn't needed, but they refused to listen or pull it, so I bided my time. Hopefully, they'd see soon that such a thing was overkill. Truly, it was Troi's pleas and worry for me which made me stop fighting it.

Today, I was off work, and we were in Lash's backyard playing ball with Toro. He had us laughing. He needed his exercise and things to keep his mind active, or he'd get into mischief, and that could end up costing Lash his furniture. I didn't think he'd appreciate it. She was swearing Toro had a doggie smile, which I had to agree, he sort of did.

He was giving it to us again. Our giggles were cut short by the arrival of Lash and Spawn. My whole body tightened seeing Spawn. The man might make me want to fight with him, but he also caused me to have a physical sexual reaction to him, which I was more wary of than anything. The looks on their faces made me grip the arms of my chair tightly. Toro ran over to stand between them and the two of us. Troian asked them what was wrong.

"Babe, we just found out something. I need you to stay calm. There's nothing to worry about. We've got you," Lash said firmly. I knew he was trying to reassure her. She insisted he tell her.

I steeled myself to hear it. I knew it couldn't be good, although having been beaten and left for dead was pretty damn hard to top in my book. I was wrong.

He grimaced before telling her they had more information on her other male cousins. Somehow, they'd confirmed that the four remaining ones who weren't in prison were part of the business, too, with the one who was in prison, Andrik. We knew that was a possibility, and the club wanted to know for sure if they had anything to do with her being beaten. It was the latter they confirmed to us. A text was sent, and it consisted of her family talking about checking if the body had been found. They were headed to Bristol soon to find out.

She bent forward in her chair and gasped as she held her stomach. I shifted to go to her, but Lash beat me to it. He dropped to his knees in front of her and wrapped her in his arms. I could see the love he had for her on his face. In that instant, I knew he'd do anything for Troian, and he'd never hurt her as he had with his momentary need to confirm she wasn't involved in that awful business.

He pleaded with her. "Baby, please, don't be scared. We're not gonna let them get near you. Now that we know it was them for sure, we can take care of this once and for all." As he finished, his tone changed. It hardened. She pulled away to look at his face. He wasn't smiling at her. Shit, this wasn't good. She knew it, too. She immediately told him not to do anything that would get him or the others hurt or killed. She said her family wasn't worth dying over or going to prison for. I wanted to holler and tell them the same.

Glancing at Spawn, I saw he was just as determined and unhappy as Lash. My heart fluttered. Lash put on a smile and assured her she had nothing to worry about. He seemed convinced they wouldn't go to prison and would have the tools they needed to make it back alive. It was his next comments which made me take even more notice.

"This isn't our first rodeo with people like this. Surely, the old ladies told you their stories."

I hadn't heard the other women's stories, but Troi appeared to have. She admonished him even if they had done it before. There was no guarantee. He listed a few things that could happen to them in everyday life. She lay her head on his chest and closed her eyes. He held her and rubbed her back. Spawn came over to stand next to me. I didn't look up. I couldn't. If I did, I'd start telling him not to do anything to end up hurt, in prison, or killed. Eventually, she lifted her head and shifted her gaze to us, then back to her man.

"I'm not saying that I can stay. I haven't decided that yet, so if that's a condition of taking care of them, you now know it and can forget going after them."

I expected him to argue that she needed to make her decision right then. I knew he loved her, but what if she left him? It was most likely he and his club would wash their hands of her, and she'd be on her own. Well, not alone because I'd stick by her. In the short time I'd known her, we'd gotten close. I had what I considered a best friend for the first time. I wasn't gonna let her go it alone.

His declarations left me beyond stunned. A man was pledging that not only would he protect her even if she left but that she would always be his in his heart. It was heartwarming. She'd always have someone or something watching out for her. That last part made me think he meant there was something Spawn could do. I was learning the man was a whiz with computers.

She pushed Lash on that by asking what would happen if she found someone else. He didn't look happy at the thought, but he was adamant he'd make sure she was safe, and that meant from whomever she was with. And he wouldn't stop trying to win her back until she married.

"Lash, you can't do that! What about your happiness? Having a wife and kids? You said you want that," she cried.

"I want that with you. If I can't have you as my wife and old lady, and those kids aren't ours, then I don't want them," he said.

Troian sat there speechless at his revelation. She glanced at me. I gave her a speaking look, but she appeared too dazed to understand it.

I cleared my throat. "I think you've given Troian enough to think about. Tell me if I'm wrong, but you're okay with them doing what needs to be done to protect you. Right?" I asked her. Troian nodded yes.

"Okay, then, why don't you guys go do whatever it is you do, and Troian and I will fix something to eat? Are you hungry?" I asked as I rose to my feet.

Lash offered to bring in dinner rather than having us cook. I couldn't help but tease them about forgetting about the ribs and pork we'd been cooking all day, along with baked beans and coleslaw.

Spawn was the one to answer first. "Hell no, you're not wrong! Tell me what you need me to do."

"Stay out of the kitchen. I don't need you in my hair. Go plot with the guys or entertain Toro."

"I'd entertain your dog if he didn't look at me all the time like he was plotting ways to kill me and hide my body," he told me as he and Toro exchanged looks of challenge.

I held back my giggle, but I did say, "Well then, I suggest you get to know him better, and maybe he'll stop plotting. Give us an hour, maybe an hour and a half, and it'll be ready. Shoo, we'll be fine." Surprisingly, my wave made them leave. Boy, they must either love barbeque or were starved, maybe both.

I hooked my arm through hers and walked her inside as I teased her to stop mooning. I assured her she wasn't weak for likely forgiving his stupidity and how he made me melt when he told her how he'd watch over her and protect her even if she was with another man. Toro came inside with us and did his customary walk-through while we went to the kitchen.

The next hour was spent talking, cooking, and laughing. I had her help with my barbeque recipe. She questioned why we weren't using the store-bought one in the fridge. I had to teach her that Yankees like her didn't know what a religion barbeque could be in parts of the South. I teased her about how deprived she had been all her life, and I'd get a marriage proposal out of her after she tasted it. She thought it was hilarious.

The men rejoined us at the end of the hour and set the table for us. That was something else I wasn't used to—men helping with household chores. Lash had cooked the other night. I'd seen him doing laundry, too. My experience was men thought of those as women's work and would rather die than clean a dish or wash a load of laundry.

We got the food on the table, and we were all seated. Spawn pulled out my chair like Lash did Troian's. I thanked him, and he winked at me. "You're welcome," he said.

We filled our plates and took our first bite. I loved ribs and pulled pork. Along with those two, brisket was up there too. I hadn't found any in the freezer and didn't want to ask Lash to go get some when Troi and I decided to do this yesterday. I smothered my laugh as Troian got up and came to my chair. She carefully kneeled and then took one of my hands in hers. The guys gave us puzzled looks.

"Kimmy, I love you. Will you marry me?"

"What the fuck?" Spawn choked out. He furrowed his brow and glanced at Lash.

"Hell, if I know. Maybe she took too many pain pills," Lash answered.

He sounded so serious that combined with Spawn's reaction, it had us exploding into laughter. We looked at them. She assured Lash she wasn't high, then explained. When she said she could convince me to change teams to be with her, I laughed even harder.

I had to fight to choke my mirth back enough to say something. "Well, I guess I'll have to take it back. Let's run away with each other," I offered her.

Lash had something to say about it as he helped her to her feet. Spawn didn't disappoint me when he had his own remark to make, but what he said did stun me so much so that I didn't warn him not to call me Hotcake.

"Hotcake, you don't have to switch teams. If you want a proposal and an undying love declaration for your cooking, I'm your man. When do you want to get married? I'd like at least three kids, so I hope you're on board with that."

I scrambled to think and come up with a suitable comeback. I couldn't let him know he was getting to me. "Well, Studcake, that's nice, but I believe Troian's offer is better. If you're good, I might let you come to the wedding. Do you want to be the ring bearer?"

"Babe, you know you can't resist me. Keep trying. I know you'll see the light soon," he told me as he smirked.

My snarky reply came out without me even thinking about it. "Oh, great, so I'll be dying soon then because that's the only light I'll be seeing."

His retort that he would rock my world made my heart beat faster. I'd never tell him, but it made my nipples harden. I had to stop this line of talk before I spontaneously combusted or begged him to take me on the table. I told him to eat and not let it get cold. He surprised me when he did it without a quick comeback. The noises the guys made and how they cleaned their plates made Troian and I grin.

I stood up. "Now, who's ready for dessert?" I asked. The guys groaned.

"God, woman, you can't expect me to eat dessert too," Spawn growled.

"You don't have to. You can watch me and Troian eat it. It's just homemade banana cream pie. No biggie," I said as I shrugged.

He bounded to his feet, almost falling as he ran to get clean plates and a knife. Lash whispered something in Troian's ear. Spawn came back, and I cut the pie and scooped out slices for all of us. They inhaled it and didn't leave a lick of it on their plates. Spawn's moans were making me squirm. Lash called him on them before I did because I was about to excuse myself and go to my room to masturbate.

"Man, you gotta stop moaning like that. It's indecent. You sound like you're having sex."

"Don't judge me. You have no idea what I'd do for pie like this. Hotcake, who do you want me to kill? Or wipe their existence off the internet? I can make them disappear if you promise to make this once a week for the rest of our lives."

I fought to hold on to my smile so they wouldn't know how his offer hit me. I could think of someone he could kill. However, I couldn't tell him that. He kept talking and teasing about the wedding being next month and asked if three kids were acceptable to me. He was willing to adopt, he said.

I wasn't able to resist, telling him I thought six was better and a month was enough time, but making him this pie weekly would have him getting fat, although I didn't see that happening. The man was ripped and worked out. You could tell it. That wasn't just good genes, though they helped. He said he would exercise more to counteract it, then asked where I learned to cook like that. My memories made me smile.

"My granny taught me. She loved to cook, and I spent a lot of time with her in the kitchen when I was a young kid. She made sure I knew how to cook and bake."

"I take it she's gone? You used the past tense," Spawn said.

"Yeah, I lost her when I was ten, but I have my memories and a book filled with her recipes. She'd love to know people were eating them and enjoying it."

He reached over and took my hand and then squeezed it. "She's dancing then because this is wonderful. Bet she's watching you from heaven with a smile," he said. I patted his hand.

Troian broke the spell by asking if it was alright that she'd written down Granny's barbeque sauce recipe. I assured her there was nothing my granny loved more than people enjoying what she made and asking for her recipes.

While the guys cleaned up after dinner, she and I went to sit in the living room to pet a content Toro. He'd inhaled his small portion of pork. I saved him some without the sauce. I didn't feed him a lot of human food, but some things like the delicious pork, I did.

Spawn:

The more time I spent with Kimera, the more time I wanted. She might make me want to growl and order her about, but if she'd been a woman who never said a word back or didn't have a mind of her own, I wouldn't want her. Meek and mild wasn't what I fancied.

After washing up after dinner and Lash's examination of Troian's incisions, I thought we'd just kick back, maybe watch some television, or maybe I'd get lucky and convince Kimera to take a walk with me. Something I hadn't tried to do yet. Only that wasn't what happened. Instead, a challenge was issued by her, and it called our manhood into question. What kind of men would it make us if we didn't step up to take the challenge? Piss poor ones, that was what.

Now, having her refer to herself and Troian as superwomen didn't offend or challenge us. We had no problem agreeing with her statement. It was being called mere mortal men and told God chose women to have the babies since we were too weak to do it. That we objected to. I had no choice but to defend our manly honor.

"Now, don't disparage the strength of us men, especially your future husbands. I'll have you know, I'm tough, and I could have the babies if I was able to."

I knew it was too much to hope she'd take it back, but she laughed and added more. She seemed to think that if I puked once or had an ache, it would kill me, or I'd lie around the whole pregnancy and for years afterward lamenting about it and would never have another kid. While I agreed there were some men like that, they weren't bikers. We were a hearty breed apart.

Lash tried to get his woman to tell mine that he could do it, but she teased him that she didn't want to hurt his delicate man feelings. Those were fighting words and what formed our bet. Since we couldn't actually have a baby to prove it, we'd have to inflict pain another way. For us, that was a fighting match.

I had no problem participating in one or more. I knew our other brothers would want in on it, too, for no other reason than it had been a while, and they loved any reason to fight. However, no good fight was complete without a reward for winning. Lash brought it up, and I agreed.

"Oh really, and what pray tell is a suitable reward in your book?" Troian asked.

Since it was his woman asking, he answered. "You let me do anything I want in the bedroom for one night. I promise I won't hurt you. All you have to do is relax and go with it. I'll make you scream harder and longer than you ever have."

Instantly, I knew I wanted the same from Kimera. When she rolled her eyes at me when Troian didn't object to Lash's statement and asked me what mine was,

I told her, "Well, Hotcake, I think Lash has the perfect idea. So the same. I hope you don't have to use your voice for a while afterward, say a few days, because you won't have one when I get done with you," I said with a big smile.

I was pleased to see I stunned her, but she recovered quickly and couldn't leave it alone. She accused me of talking big, and it would be more than just her and Troi who would judge us. She wanted the other old ladies and Annie to help them do it. I wanted to snort at her assertion they would be unbiased judges. I told them that wasn't unbiased, but when Troian asked if we wanted to call off the bet, there was no way in hell I'd do it. Lash was of the same mind.

That's when the idea of adding money to the bet was voiced and agreed upon. I told them to give us a few days to get the fight night set up with the other guys and taunted them that they couldn't back out if they were scared.

It was with reluctance that I said I had to leave not long afterward. I wanted to stay and keep sparring with her, but I had some work I had to get done tonight. Kimera couldn't let that last opportunity for the night to razz me go. She grinned at me as she piped up with, "Goodnight, Studcake. I know why you're really leaving. You have to start intensely working out for the fight, but it's no use. You'll still lose, so save the sweat."

"You won't know what hit you, babe. Dream of me winning tonight," I told her as I made my way to the door, flexing as I went.

I decided to go to my house rather than the room I had at the clubhouse. I still stayed at the clubhouse, but not often. Usually, that only occurred if I was working on something and fell asleep. I'd lived most of the first several years happily in the clubhouse. We all had, well, except for Reaper. He'd had a house since his younger sister, Harper, had lived with him. As time passed, a few more of the guys built houses and placed them inside the compound fence, like our friends, the Warriors, did. Even if we were single, we liked the idea of having the security of the fence, our brothers, and more. That was even more important now we'd begun to have families.

While I worked, I tried to see my house objectively. Was it a house Kimera could see herself living in and being happy? I thought it was a great one, but if she didn't, then I'd be willing to have another one built. This one could be bought by one of my brothers. I'd always secretly wanted a family, even if I believed it wasn't a guarantee I'd have one. With this goal in mind, I didn't build a small one or two-bedroom house. Mine had four big bedrooms. Although if she wanted those six kids she spoke of, we'd have to either add on or they'd have to share.

Growing up, it had been me until I was ten years old, and my baby sister, Alecia, was born. We never shared a room, and I took on the role of being her protector from the moment she came home. We were still close, even though she lived in Montana, where our parents still lived. I hated that I only saw them a few times a year, along with her four-year-old son, Tommie.

She'd married her high school sweetheart. I didn't

know him well since I was all the way in Virginia and part of the Punishers, but the times I'd met him, I'd never taken to him. There was something unsettled or flighty about him. I tried to talk her out of marrying him right out of high school, but she was determined. They got married a month after graduation, and two years later, she gave birth to Tommie.

It wasn't long after she had their son—Tommie was six months old—that her husband, Bryan, came home one day and told her that he didn't love her anymore and he wanted a divorce. She'd been devastated, and no matter how many times she had asked him why, he wouldn't explain himself. Rather than beg him to stay with them, she walked out and granted him a divorce.

Bryan didn't waste time moving away to Utah. I think he thought it would keep him from having his ass beaten by our dad. Hell, if it wasn't due to Alecia's pleas to let him be, for Tommie's sake, I would've flown there to find him and laid his ass out. The bastard had next to nothing to do with his son, and Tommie didn't understand why.

Hell, he wouldn't even pay child support, though the court ordered him to do it. Each time she took him back to court to force him to do it, he'd mysteriously lose his job or have to quit due to his physical ailments, which he claimed prevented him from being able to work consistently. In truth, he was a goddamn lying piece of shit. He worked under the table and hid his money under his new wife's name.

Luckily, he hadn't had more children. So, doing

what I did best, I made sure the bastard didn't live the good life while not paying for his son. It seemed every time he stashed money away, made extra, or whatever, he'd end up being hacked or otherwise losing his cash. The bank couldn't seem to figure out how or who was doing it. When he thought he'd smartened up and kept his money in the house, it was stolen. When he buried it, lo-and-behold, it disappeared too. I'd keep finding ways to make him miserable until my nephew turned eighteen, then I might let him off the hook. It wasn't because he dared to divorce my sister that I did it. It was his refusal to help care for his son.

I'd been trying to convince her and Tommie to move to Virginia, but they wouldn't do it as long as Dad and Mom were in Montana. I couldn't blame her. My parents helped out a lot with my nephew. He adored their small property. It was the horses he loved. He was big enough now, though, that I was hoping to get her to bring him here to visit me rather than me going to see them. Mom and Dad had come a few times over the years, but never her or Tommie. Finding an old lady might be the way to get her to do it.

It was with these happy thoughts in mind that I finished up what I was working on and crawled into bed hours later. If all went well, we'd soon have Lash's woman free of her disgusting excuse of a family, and I'd be free to spend the bulk of my time pursuing the woman of my dreams. I was determined to make Kimera mine.

Spawn: Chapter 4

Looking back over the past few days, I thought I was upset enough, waiting for the Gusevs to get off their asses and make their way to Bristol. Sure, we could've gone after them in Richmond. since we knew without a doubt they were involved in the illegal shit with Andrik, and they were the ones who hurt Troian and left her for dead. I didn't know how Lash was keeping himself together. If I were in his shoes, I'd want to kill them. However, going to them rather than letting them come to us posed bigger risks.

In Richmond, we didn't know the area like the back of our hands. We'd have no places to easily take them and carry out their punishment like we did here. Not only did we have places, we knew people and had our allies close at hand. We didn't stick out here like we would there. People noticed things that were out of the ordinary, especially bikers.

No, the smart thing was to wait for them to come to where we had all the advantages. We'd be able to make them disappear and do it with the least amount of risk to us. As much as we told the women there was nothing to worry about, there was. As careful as we were and the planning we did, there was no guarantee that something wouldn't go wrong. Some of us could be hurt or killed, or we could be caught. However, it was a risk we'd all gladly take. This was about keeping not only our brother's woman but also other people safe.

It was this goal that was on my mind when I got an alert from the dump site. Watching the video and seeing it was them, sent a thrill through me. We could now end this. I sent out the notification to all my brothers.

Me: They're here. Just triggered the cameras at the site. They're losing it. Get back as soon as you can. I'll have them tracked with the other cameras in town. We'll figure out where they're staying and do our thing. See you in a bit.

The replies came back one after the other, with my brothers promising to be here as soon as possible. I knew it might take some longer than others to wrap up whatever they were doing at work, but Lash would be one of the first to come back. His reply backed up my assumption.

While I waited for them to get here, I worked the other camera feeds I was able to access around town to use to track them when they left the dump site. Their conversation pissed me off. These bastards deserved everything they had coming.

It wasn't long before I heard a knock on my open door. I glanced up to find Reaper standing there with an expectant look on his face. When he saw he had my attention, he walked in. As president, he really didn't need to knock before entering, but he did. He leaned over and put his hands on my desk as he studied me intently. "Tell me you know where they're at," he ordered.

"They're still searching the site, but as soon as they leave, I should be able to track them on the other cameras. Don't worry, if I have anything to do with it, those dirty, no-good cocksuckers will be dead by morning at the latest."

He laughed. "Getting more bloodthirsty in your old age, Spawn?"

I rolled my eyes. "Pres, you know me better than that. I've always been bloodthirsty. I have the name Spawn for more than one reason," I reminded him.

"That's for sure. Poor bastards don't know what they have unleashed against them, do they? I only hope with this information, we can keep Lash calm until we're ready to roll."

"He'll struggle, but he'll hang tight. This is too important for him not to. He'll do anything to protect Troian."

"Yeah, he loves that woman. Think she's gonna stay? I know she's still upset with all of us."

"He does, and I'm hopeful. She was talking more the other night and joking around. She said she wasn't promising to stay, but the way she acts with him, you know she loves him too," I assured him. Reaper worried about us like we were not only his brothers but sometimes as if we were his kids, even if he wasn't much older than some of us.

"How's it going with her new friend? I ain't talked to her much, but she seems to be a feisty one, and she appears genuine in her friendship with Troian."

"She is her friend. It might not have been long since they met, but those two are tight. She's an interesting woman."

He grinned at me and raised a brow. "Interesting? Is that all? Hell, I thought you were over there all the time because she caught your attention, but if not, you should tell your brothers. More than a few checked her out at Arya's party. I bet they'd like to get to know her." He smirked.

Heat filled me as a bolt of white-hot anger flared through me at the thought of anyone wanting Kimera, let alone it being one of my brothers. I snapped before I thought about it. "If one of them goes near her, I'll beat his ass into the ground. She's not available!"

Reaper burst out laughing and lightly pounded his hand on the desk. "Hot damn, I knew it! The little nurse has you by the balls, doesn't she?"

I scowled at him and tried to cover my slip. "She doesn't have me by anything. She just doesn't need men panting after her. She's not here for hookups."

"Who said anything about a hookup? She could be an old lady for one of them. Tinker has been looking for years for a woman. Hell, so have Mayhem and Crusher, although they might deny it. I think she'll be a good fit with the club and the other women. I overheard Alisse picking her brain about being a nurse. You don't need to worry about her being treated like a hang around or bunny. She'll be snapped up as an old lady," he said confidently.

I knew I had to cut this line of thinking off even if he might be saying it to instigate me, so I gave up the pretense. He could warn away any of the others thinking they had a shot with Kimera. I stood and leaned over the table toward him. He watched me with a slight smirk.

"Pres, I say this with total respect and love, but if any of them dare to make a move on Kimera, they'll get to meet my inner Spawn. Kimera isn't gonna be the old lady of one of my brothers."

He leaned even closer. "Then whose old lady will she be?" he asked softly.

"Mine, you baiting, provoking, infuriating fucker. Kimera is destined to be my woman."

A satisfied look came over his face. "Good. That's what I wanted to hear. I think she's perfect for you. How does the pursuit go? Do we need to order a property cut yet?"

"She's stubborn and thinks she's here until we get Troian's problem settled. Then she'll go home. I'm working on her. It takes time and finesse with her. I'm not ready for the cut yet, but when I am, you'll know it. Do you think I should announce to the guys she's hands off?"

"I don't think you need to. They can all see the way you watch her when you've both been in the clubhouse at the same time. And they know you practically live at Lash's house rather than yours. They know," he said.

"You're not planning to hold another get-together soon, are you? If so, give me a heads-up so I can get her cut made. No way I'll let her walk around without one if those horny shits, the Warriors, Pagans, Horsemen, or Marauders, come around. She'll wear it if I have to tie it to her," I growled, thinking of them.

He chuckled. "Nah, I don't have one planned yet, but you never know. I'll give you at least two weeks' heads-up if something changes. Now, from the sound of the noise coming down this hall, I think most, if not all, of the brothers are here. Let's go tell them what you found and get this moving."

"One sec, I just need to let Smoke know I'm stepping away," I told him. I used my phone to send my computer sensei a text. Once it was sent, I nodded and followed Reaper to the common room.

The noise was much greater there. Reaper got everyone's attention when he let out a loud, ear-piercing whistle and then lifted his finger to circle it in the air. We all knew what that meant and headed into church. I was in the lead with him. Hurrying to my seat, I opened my laptop to pull up the video for them to watch and listen to.

"You know why we're here. Spawn has the Gusevs in Bristol. Show them the video," Reaper ordered— short, sweet, and to the point. It wasn't long before I had it projected on the wall, and they watched. I had to switch cameras when the Gusevs walked out of sight. This showed them getting into a Tahoe and driving off. When that happened, I shut it off.

"Please tell me you were able to pick them up in town?" Lash pleaded with me.

"I have, and that's being monitored by Smoke right now while I do this," I said smugly. He, Everly, and the other hackers were all working on it.

"How did you get so much video? I thought those only took short snapshots with the audio," Mayhem asked.

I explained how I tinkered around with the store-bought ones to make them better before telling them the Gusevs were aimlessly riding around town. I assured them, "As soon as they stop for the night, we can put our final plan in motion."

"What if they don't stay in town?" Sandman asked.

"I don't see that happening. They're too anxious to finish this and make sure their operation isn't about to be blown to hell and back," Maniac said before I could. Reaper agreed with him and ordered us to relax until I had the location, then we'd move out tonight. They all got up and filed out. I stayed behind to get my laptop stowed and to check something before heading over to Lash's. I knew he'd go straight home to tell Troian the news. I wanted to be there for the discussion.

Minutes later, when I walked up to his house, I only slowed down long enough to knock on the front door before entering. We didn't stand on ceremony around here. Unless you locked your door, you had to expect someone to walk in. The couples had learned to do that, although we did try to wait to be invited inside those houses. Close calls in catching them having sex had made us learn that lesson. The women seemed to get embarrassed, and our brothers were mean when someone saw their women naked. I understood their reactions now. No way did I want anyone to see Kimera naked.

As I rounded the corner into his living room, I sought out Kimera. She was seated with them, and she wasn't smiling. When I glanced at him and Troian, he gave me an amused look. I sat on the couch next to Kimera. "Did you tell them already?" I asked.

"I was just explaining it, yes. They know they're here and riding around town and that we'll go tonight once we know where they're staying."

"Well, at least you're home tonight, and we don't have to worry about you going to work," I said to Kimera. That would make protection easier.

"Actually, I'm not off. I have to be on-call, and if they call, I have to go in," she informed me.

That was the last thing I wanted to hear. I frowned. "You can't. We'll need all the guys here or with us. You'll have to tell them you can't do it."

She glared at me as if I'd suggested something terrible, like kicking puppies. "No, I won't. First of all, I was the one to say yes when someone called off. Second, this is my work. I have obligations. Third, you don't tell me what to do. Fourth, I don't need anyone to escort me. I've been telling you that. No one knows I even know Troi. There's no reason to target me."

"And what if we're wrong and someone saw you pick her up outside the hospital? And that someone just happens to get asked by one of her cousins, and they share it? It can happen, and it's not worth the risk," I argued back.

"Spawn, you're talking crazy. The odds of that are a million to one, if that. No one saw me, and even if they did, why would they tell perfect strangers that information if asked? No, I'll be fine. You guys just take care of those bastards and protect the women and kids here. I'll be good. I have my gun if I need it."

"You don't think they'll have guns too? Goddamn it, woman, listen to reason. I know you're tough. No one doubts it, but you can't take risks like this."

"I'm not at risk! How will they know?"

We glared at each other. Troian interrupted our staring contest. "Won't it be dangerous and more likely someone might see you guys with them if you have to go into a hotel or some place to get them?"

"It is, but we'll be careful," Lash was quick to assure her.

"Why risk it? Instead, why not get their attention while they're out riding around town and lead them to somewhere private?" she added.

"Babe, that's a good idea, but how would we do that?" he asked.

"You take me to town, and you let them spot me. As soon as they do, we leave town, and they follow us. We lead them to your brothers so you can ambush them," she said calmly.

That set off Lash, and he told her it wasn't happening and why it wouldn't work. He was loud doing it, not that I blamed him. She bucked up to him. "Lash, don't you take that tone with me. I'm not your child, nor will I be yelled at."

He tried to backpedal and then used her recent surgery as an excuse.

"In that case, let me do it. I'll call off and tell them I have a family emergency out of town. I won't go to work if you let me pretend to be her," Kimera said out of nowhere. A moment of stunned silence was quickly replaced by me shooting it down. I tried logic.

"And how the hell do you think you can pull that off, woman? You're shorter than her, and you have a totally different hair color," I pointed out.

"If I'm in the car, they won't notice a few inches less, and as for my hair, it's about the same length. I've got a box of hair color. At night, it'll fool them at a distance. I can have it done in an hour. I'll style it like hers and be ready to go."

"That's the dumbest idea I ever heard. No, you can't do it. And Troian isn't either," I snarled. Over my dead body, she'd do it. Setting herself up as a target was insane.

"Oh really? What's wrong with it? They won't get their hands on her, and she won't be out there potentially risking her health so soon after surgery. I can use a gun, and if they get stupid, I can help. You won't need to surround the car with a bunch of men. Surely, you have guys stealthy enough to hide in plain sight." Kimera scoffed.

"We do have guys stealthy enough, but that's not the point. The point is, we don't let our women put themselves in harm's way. We protect them and eliminate threats to them," I explained as calmly as I could when all I wanted to do was snatch her up and lock her away.

"Well, I'm not one of your women, so I don't count," she replied.

I knew commanding her wasn't working so I went for humor, not my usual method. "Did you forget we were talking about how many kids we want? I'd say that makes you one of our women," I reminded her.

She rolled her eyes. "I believe that was to be determined with a fighting match that you men have no hope of winning, so that's not going to happen. Even if you did win, I don't see you settling down, Studcake."

"Why the hell not?" I asked, knowing I sounded offended, which I was.

"You're a player and used to having women fall at your feet and giving it up at a snap of your fingers. You go for quantity. I need quality and monogamy. We're not compatible. Although, if all I wanted was sex—one and done—then I'd give you a whirl."

I found myself sputtering. It was painful. As I searched for my voice, Lash jumped back in. He told them no one was going out and they needed to stay here. He also told Kimera that if she did get called into work, Colt would be the one she had to take with her as an escort slash guard. They didn't give up. I left, although I hated to, so I could continue to track the men. Once I knew where they were spending the night, I let Reaper know, and he called everyone back for church.

Kimera:

Driving away from the Punishers' compound, I tried not to let guilt consume me. My biggest argument with myself was, *what did I have to be guilty about? I wasn't doing anything wrong. I was protecting and ending a nightmare for my new friend.* After that came the thought that *I hoped they would understand and that Spawn would forgive me.*

I huffed out a breath. Why should I be concerned if he did or not? He wasn't anyone more important than the other Punishers and less important than Troian. Who cared if he forgave me?

Even as I thought it, I knew I was full of shit. It did matter. I found it mattered more than almost anything other than protecting Troi. Spawn made me feel so many things, and most of them were conflicting. He could annoy, frustrate, infuriate, and confuse me, along with making me anxious. On the flip side were excitement, exhilaration, attraction, protection, and safety, to name a few.

As much as he might make me want to fight, he made me feel passion, and that was disturbing. I might notice men due to their looks or personality, but I couldn't recall one making me want to experience his kisses or have sex with him desperately. Spawn did, and it scared me.

I knew my decision to go against what he and Lash forbade would earn me his displeasure, but I had to do it. I was better equipped than Troian to deal with her fucking cousins. Recalling what they did to her filled me with rage. Monsters like them and others deserved nothing but pain and to pay for their sins. You might not be able to get rid of your own monsters, but if you had the chance to get rid of someone else's, then you should. Troian had immediately gone from a stranger to a patient and then to a friend, which I never had before.

I wasn't blessed with a family or a ton of friends like some people were. I was too guarded, I guess, for that. There were things I wasn't comfortable sharing, and if you wouldn't share, people tended to move on. Troian, though, I didn't see her being like that. She was one person I might be able to talk about my past with one day. It was these things that had me leaving her with Lash after Spawn left the house. The two of them continued to argue while I supposedly rested. In reality, I prepared. I wasn't sure I'd get a chance to do anything, but if so, I would.

As luck would have it, I got a call while the men were in church. I didn't recognize the number, but it gave me my opening. I told the old ladies I had to take the call, that it was work. It wasn't. It was some telemarketer trying to sell me different car insurance, but they didn't know that. When I returned, I lied and said I had to go to work. That was when the guilt started.

Not to raise suspicion, I had them get Colt. He'd go with me to the hospital and then return when I called to let them know I was ready to come back. I would only wait until he left the hospital and then get in my car and ride around town. It was a risk, seeing as the Punishers might be out and see me, but there wasn't anything they could do, short of kidnapping me, to stop me.

I dragged off the hat I'd put over my hair once I colored it. It was close to the color of Troian's. It was purely a fluke that I even had it. I bought it before I met her and was toying with the idea of changing my color. What made me pack it when we moved to the compound, I don't know, but it could've been divine guidance. Colt was riding behind me. Hopefully, he couldn't see my hair. I shook it out. I'd put my hat back on before we got to the hospital, but for now, my head needed some air. I was sweating.

As I drove, I tried to think of where I'd show myself first. The logical thing was to go through the main part of town. After that, I'd work my way through the secondary streets and alleys. I wasn't sure if residential areas were worth it. Would they go there to find her?

Glancing ahead, I saw our town was quickly coming up. I needed to concentrate. If I did catch a tail once I got rid of Colt, I'd head to the compound and call the guys to give them a heads-up. If they'd planned this with me, we could've led the Gusevs elsewhere, but since that wasn't the case, this would have to do.

Suddenly, a loud engine sound caught my ear. I

swiveled my head from side to side, trying to see where it was coming from. The road had been mostly deserted. This vehicle, whatever it was, was loud. By the time I spotted it, there was nothing I could do. I screamed uselessly, "Look out," to Colt.

I watched in horror in my rearview mirror as a big dark blue SUV came up behind his bike, and he went flying off the side of the road. I kept screaming as the car kept coming, not bothering to even slow down. I hit the gas, but it had a bigger engine than my little car did.

The driver pulled up alongside my side of the car. A window came down, and a hand with a gun in it pointed toward the ground. There was a loud pop. I heard another pop right after it, and then I began to fight the car. Shit, they'd shot out my tires! I had to fight to keep my car from going off the road and hitting the trees. My heart pounded as I fought the steering wheel. By the time I got my car under control, they had blocked me, and I had to come to a stop. I scrambled to get to my gun and phone. Both were in my purse, which had been on the passenger seat but were now on the floor on that side.

I wasn't fast enough. Before I could use my phone that I had just snagged, my door was yanked open, and hard hands reached in and jerked me out. I barely had time to stuff my phone in my hoodie pocket. It was off because I worried if the club figured out what I did, they'd track me. I heard cruel, sinister laughter. Hard hands bit painfully into my arm. I punched and tried to kick as I was jerked out of the car. I added screams to it. Maybe I'd get lucky, and someone would come along, and I'd be saved. *Please, God, let Spawn and the others come*, I prayed.

I knew what Troian's evil cousins looked like from the photos we'd been shown by Lash and Spawn. I knew it had to be them when they shot out the tires, but seeing their faces made it worse. Jarek was the one manhandling me. His grin was menacing. It quickly morphed into confusion. He turned his head to tell the others joining us, "It's not Troian. I don't know who this bitch is."

Hope filled me. Maybe I could play this off, and they'd leave me alone and get the hell out of here before they were seen. Worry for Colt filled me. I needed to make sure he was okay and call for help. At a minimum, he would need to go to the hospital.

"Let go of me! Who are you? Why would you do this? I'm on my way home to my husband," I spewed. As I said it, I was scanning for a chance to get away. I'd hate to leave Colt, but I wouldn't be able to help him if I was dead. Jarek shook me and jerked my shoulder higher. I hissed at the pain.

"Shut up, bitch! Zandro, it's not her. What do we do?" he continued.

The other three came to a halt and stared at me. I felt like a bug. Their expressions weren't reassuring. Eyes ran up and down my body. I had to fight not to shiver.

"Well, well, what do we have here? A tasty little morsel, it seems. The hair is the same, but not the rest," Kaz said with a leer. My skin crawled, and my stomach heaved.

"*Proklyat'ye!* Goddamn it! You idiot, this isn't Troian. You said it was her," Zandro shouted.

"I thought it was. She has the same hair, and we've had no luck in town," Jarek protested as he shook me.

"Hey, I don't know who you are, but you need to let me go. My husband could come by here any moment," I said.

"*Tikhiy,*" Zandro snarled at me and Jarek. I didn't know for sure what they were saying, but the tone and looks were enough to get the gist of it. He wanted us to shut up.

"Zandro, what're we to do?" Laszlo asked as he fidgeted and kept glancing up and down the road.

Zandro examined me coldly. After several tense moments, he smiled. It wasn't a pleasant one. "Why, we take her with us, of course. Even if she isn't our cousin, she can still be useful. Put her in the car. Hurry," he ordered.

I screamed and renewed my fighting, but it was too late. A punch to the face made everything hazy, and my knees almost buckled. Despite that, I kept kicking, squirming, screaming, and throwing my head back. Laszlo joined Kaz, and they manhandled me toward their SUV. I turned my head, got Laszlo's upper arm between my teeth, and bit him. He howled and then slapped me. My ears rang. Zandro had the back door open. I kicked at him. He laughed. As I was thrown inside, I knew I wasn't likely to get out of this alive. My only recourse was to fight until the end.

Spawn: Chapter 5

Finishing up church, I was pleased with what we'd done. Our time preparing for our assault to take the Gusevs had been well spent. I'd knock out the security and surveillance at the place they were staying. It was on the edge of town and although not remote, it wasn't one of the more popular motels where most people liked to stay. It was clear by staying there, they hoped not to be noticed. It was one of those places where the doors to each room were on the outside of the building. At least no one would get off the elevator or walk down the hallway and see us dragging their no-good asses out of there. Not to say that we couldn't be seen, but we planned to go in during the dead of night after most people would be asleep.

However, my good mood was spoiled when I found out Kimera was gone. It wasn't what I wanted to find when I got to the common room, but at least she took Colt with her. I had to pick which battles to fight and win with her. This was what I was thinking, as I told Annie. At least she'd listened and taken him. I was cut off from saying more by a loud crashing sound.

We all whipped around to find the front door to the common room had been flung open, and in came Rhaines. He wasn't alone. Under one shoulder, with an arm held across his shoulders, was Colt. He was covered in blood. He was being half-carried by the other prospect. Alarm shot through me. Exclamations of surprise, shock, and outrage rang out. The women cried out but were cognizant enough to jump up and grab the kids. They didn't need to see this. Alisse, Lark, and Chey took the kids outside. Annie remained behind, and Lash got to his feet to run over to help Colt into a chair. All of us were shouting questions at the bloody prospect all at once. It was Reaper's sharp whistle that made us get quiet. I was trying not to think the worst.

"What the hell happened? Did you wreck your bike? Where's Kimera? You were supposed to be escorting her to work," Reaper asked our hurt prospect.

Fortunately, Colt was still conscious, although grimacing in pain. He answered hoarsely and with a slight stammer, "I-I'm sorry, pres. I tried."

It vaguely registered with me when Lash told Crusher to go get his bag out of the treatment room.

"Tried what?" I asked in fear.

"Tried to keep them from..." he paused. His panting became harder as Lash ripped the hole in the leg of his bloody jeans, making it bigger so he could see his wound. It appeared to be the spot with the most blood. Colt hissed. There was a deep wound there. I wanted to scream at him to finish, but the poor guy couldn't breathe. Once he could, he continued, "I tried to stop them from taking her. I didn't know she did it."

My worst nightmare was confirmed. Rage and terror fought to take control of me as I shouted at him. "Take her! Who? Did what?" Unconsciously, I'd moved closer and was standing over him with my fists clenched. I wanted to throttle him. How could he let this happen?

"Spawn, dial it down. Give him a chance to breathe," Maniac ordered me. I wanted to tell him to go fuck himself. My woman had been taken. I wanted answers. His wife and child were safe here.

What stopped me was Troian softly moaning, "My cousins took her, didn't they?" Fear and despair were in her voice.

Colt's next words made me lose more self-control. He confirmed it was the Gusevs, and they'd made him wreck. He'd been thrown from his bike and knocked out. When he came to, they were forcing her into their SUV. She'd been alive, at least. She fought them. It was his further revelation she'd dyed her hair the color of Troian's against our wishes that made my control slip.

"Why didn't you fucking call? How did you get here? Where did this happen?" I shouted. *Jesus Christ, why didn't he call so we could be working on this rather than wait until he got back?*

"Just before you get into town. I was behind her. I couldn't call because when I went down, I busted my phone. It was faster to ride back than dick around finding a phone to use. Thankfully, the bike could still run. They headed west. I'm sorry," he groaned. It was too much for him, I guess because he slumped over. The rising of his chest told me he merely passed out. Lash was busy working on him. Troian was crying as Annie comforted her. That's when I lost it.

I began to destroy the common room. Chairs were picked up and smashed into pieces on the floor. Next, I pounded a table with a broken chair leg and my fists until it split in two. My brothers tried to get me to stop, but I slipped out of their hands and jumped the bar. I swept bottles off the shelves behind it. It took Mayhem, Ratchet, and Shadow to get tight holds on me for me to stop, although I still struggled. What made me stop altogether was Reaper coming up, grabbing the back of my neck, and placing his forehead on mine. Seeing the determination and promise in his eyes let me clamp down on my out-of-control emotions.

"Take a deep breath. We need you. Kimera needs you. You have to get control and then get on your computer. You can find her. You already knew where we could find them. Let's see if they went there or not. If they didn't, your cameras should tell us something. What about her phone? Maybe she has it with her. Go," he ordered me.

I didn't waste time. The guys had let go after Reaper came up to me. I raced out of there to my room. My hands shook so badly I could barely type. As I brought up my camera feeds, I called Smoke. He answered on the second ring.

"Hey, man, I've been watching, and they haven't shown up yet at the motel. Are you all set?" he asked.

"Smoke," I croaked out.

I heard his swift intake of air, and then he asked, "What happened? What do you need? We can have guys there within two hours. Sooner if I call Jinx."

This was what it was like to have friends who had your back no matter what. However, waiting two hours wouldn't get it, not even an hour. "It's Kimera. They took her. The fucking Gusevs ran Colt off the road and took her. He's hurt to hell, and I need to know where they are."

"Motherfucker! Are you kidding me? Shit, okay, I'll get to work on searching for sightings of their SUV. You watch to see if they come back to their motel. I'll get the other guys searching outside of town. How long ago did they get her?"

I could hear frantic typing on his end. I checked the time. "I don't know, maybe thirty minutes. She was gone fifteen minutes or so before Colt was brought in. He rode his damaged bike back. It happened outside of town right before you hit the town limits. Fuck, I don't know!" I half-shouted.

"That's fine. It gives me a window I can work with. Do you want me to have Terror and Jinx send guys?"

"No, not unless we can't find her. Give me a few. Can you get them on standby? Goddamnit, I don't know. Smoke, what if—" I was cut off by him.

"There's no what-if. We'll find her, get her back, then make those motherfuckers pay. Get to work. I'll let you know as soon as we find anything," he assured me. His no-nonsense attitude settled me.

"I will. Thank you."

He replied, "Never have to say thanks. It's what

family does. Later," before hanging up.

While I spoke to him, I hadn't been idle. I checked if I could locate her phone. A quick search netted nothing. It was off. After that, I brought up and checked the feed from the motel. Not seeing the dark blue Tahoe anywhere, I opened a different screen and rolled it back. I watched intently. By the time I got to now, there was no sighting of the SUV. Fuck, I knew it was unlikely they'd go there, but I'd hoped they would. I left that running and brought up more cameras., I didn't know how long passed before a message popped up on my screen. It was from Beast with the Marauders. I read it with a sick stomach.

Beast: I found them. Check out this address. Good luck, and we're ready to roll.

I brought up the address in the link he sent. I realized he'd found her by tracking her phone. Jesus Christ, when did that come back on? I hadn't checked it that long ago. Noting the address, I got my program tracking it on my phone then I answered him back.

Me: Thank you a million. I'm headed there now. We'll let you know if we need ya.

Beast: Make them bleed.

Me: We will.

Filled with hope, I raced out of my room and back to the common room, where I knew the others were waiting. I knew I must look insane, but I didn't care. Hopeful expressions greeted me.

"We've found them. They didn't go to the hotel

they checked into, but I didn't think they would. Something was interfering with her phone's signal, and then we got lucky. Load up, we're going." I didn't say more. I headed for the outside door to get my bike. The others all followed me. I hoped they could keep up.

As we raced through the cold night, I couldn't help but speed. It was a miracle I kept it from being totally reckless. It was my concern for my brothers with me that kept it that way. I didn't want any of them getting hurt because of me. I knew they'd do everything they could to keep up. Maniac was beside me. I wouldn't let him get hurt. Lark and Flynn needed him. The others fell in behind us.

Our destination was outside of town. No surprise there. I had no clue if this was a place they'd had all along or if they'd lucked out and found it. Seeing that we were close, I slowed up and gave everyone a hand signal to pull off the road, which they did. It was a deserted stretch of road that saw very little in the way of traffic at night. This rural area was mostly open fields.

As we got off the bikes, I heard Lash snort. We all looked at him to see why, but all he did was shake his head. We got into a huddle. I took out my iPad. I saw the amused looks on their faces in the light Maniac had provided with his phone. We had flashlights, but no need to light the night up that much. I tapped on it until I got what I needed to come up. I showed it to them.

"This is where we are. This red dot is where her signal and one other are coming from. They must've had their phones off for fear of being tracked, so that's why I couldn't find them initially, but then Laszlo turned his back on. As far as I can tell, there are no houses out here. So they must have her in an old outbuilding, a barn, or something. It could be a cabin. We won't assume there's no more than the four of them, even if it's unlikely. We go in quiet, and we bring those fuckers out. I don't care how beat up they are, as long as they're still breathing and we get to spend time with them. Any questions?" I asked.

Maniac took over and issued commands. I was fine with that. It was his place anyway as VP. I gathered my stuff while they got theirs. We'd packed for just about any situation. Guns were a must, and we had a variety, with more than one per person. I placed my earpiece first so we could communicate. To get through the dark woods, we'd have to travel, so we put on our night vision. It was weird to use, but we'd done it enough and had practiced using it many times, so it wasn't hard for us to adjust. Our brothers who'd served had worked with us on many of our combat skills.

I shivered as the cold rain, which started as we rode, registered. It wasn't a downpour but rather a drizzle, but it was still cold. As soon as I saw they were set, I took off. I'd guide them using my tracker. My iPad was stowed on my bike and I was back to using my phone. The trek was too slow for me, but I knew we were doing it as fast as we could due to the terrain and the night. I didn't know how long it took us to get to the spot, but it felt like an eternity.

I was taken aback to see we were at what appeared to be an old church. By the look of it, it hadn't seen parishioners in decades. The road to it was overgrown, and it would be hardly visible from the road we'd come from. It was falling apart, but a dim light was visible through one of the windows.

Glancing at Maniac, since he was leading the charge, so to speak, he gave us a hand signal to split up. We quickly did and soon were on all four sides of the church. There were no guards that we could see. The fools had left their perimeter vulnerable. Good for us. I was at the front door with Maniac.

What grabbed my attention was the arguing and thumping sounds. I wondered what they were fighting about. I didn't have but a moment to think before Kimera's scream tore through the night. Maniac gave the go order just as I shoved him aside, and I charged for the door. I heard him swear, but he let me go. Kicking it in with him on my six, I frantically scanned the one-room church. The sight before me made me sick and insanely furious at the same time.

In front of me was a sight I never wanted to see. It was one of my worst nightmares and one thing I'd been praying wouldn't happen. Kaz, Laszlo, and Jarek were standing together, arguing, and pushing each other. Their pants were undone. Next, my eyes landed on Zandro, who quickly turned around. His pants were down, and his cock was in his hand. Hanging over the pew in front of him was my Kimera. She was naked from the waist down, and her other clothes were torn. She was struggling, even with her hands tied behind her back, and I heard her sobs.

Hate and fury unlike any I'd ever felt rushed through me as I gave a roar. I didn't know how I made it to Zandro that fast, but the next thing I knew, I was on him. The others weren't my concern. He was. The feel of his flesh under my fists was so satisfying but not enough. I struck him again and again. I wanted to pulverize him. Beat his head in and see his brains on the floor. I wanted to make him suffer as I bathed in his blood.

All I saw was red. It wasn't until I was pulled off him and took a swing at the person who did it and realized it was Lash that my utter rage started to recede. Lash yelled at me as he pulled me off the cocksucker. "Spawn, stop! You can kill him later. Go take care of Kimera. She needs you."

It was his mention of Kimera and that she needed me that broke the spell. I dropped Zandro on the floor and slowly approached her. She was shaking and crying while still over the back of the pew. She had her head down. My chest hurt so badly I thought I might be dying. My stomach wanted to rebel. God, did we get here in time, or were we too late? Had the bastard raped her? What about the others? Jesus, how would she recover from this? I reached up and turned off my earpiece before I spoke to her.

"Kimera, babe, it's Spawn. You're safe, honey. They can't touch you again. I'm gonna untie your hands and help you, okay? I'm not gonna hurt you."

She kept crying but didn't say anything. Moving slowly, I cut the rope around her hands first. Then, I gently touched her shoulders to raise her up. She flinched and was shaking so hard, I swear I could hear her teeth rattle. As I stood her up, I glanced down at the floor. I wanted to cover her nakedness. Immediately, I saw I wouldn't be able to use her pants or underwear to do it. They were cut or torn into shreds. Rage simmered harder in my gut again, but I fought it back.

"Stand still. I've got this," I told her. I tore off my cut and hung it over the pew so I could get to my shirt. Once it was off and my cut was back on, I eased her around to face me. She kept her gaze on the floor.

"Raise your arms, baby."

She did. I slid my shirt over her head and put her arms through the arm holes. Once it was in place, I pushed them down. My shirt on her was more like a short dress. It hit her mid-thigh. It would cover the vital parts. I knew she wouldn't want anyone seeing her like this, and I didn't want anyone to see her either. Vaguely, I knew my brothers were behind us, and they'd subdued the other three and had them secured, but they weren't my concern. Kimera needed me.

"Honey, let's get you out of here. Give me a couple of minutes to get us a ride." After telling her that, I turned my earpiece back on and ordered, "Rhaines, come get us. Bring the SUV."

He immediately answered back, "I'll be right there."

I stood there dying to hold her, but she wasn't ready for anyone to touch her. Her flinching as I put on the shirt told me that. She had her arms wrapped around herself, and her head was still hanging. Utter anguish and fury lived and breathed inside of me. Those motherfuckers would pay for daring to take and touch my woman. I began to think of the various ways I could make them bleed and hurt. I was an imaginative man.

The moans of the four Gusev men made me want to scream. Before they could say anything, which I figured would come next, my brothers guessed the same, so they cut strips off their clothes and used them to gag them. It wasn't long before Rhaines told us he was here and about to come through the door. Smart guy. I saw the anger take over his face when he saw Kimera and the men with their cocks still hanging out. I wanted to cheer when he walked by them because he kicked them in the crotch and muttered, "Filthy fucking animals."

That there would get him my vote when it came time to decide whether he patched in or not. Maniac snarled orders to him. I was glad since I was too scattered to do it now. "Take Spawn, Kimera, and Remus back to where we parked. Remus, you bring the van for these four fucks. The rest of us will walk back or catch a ride with you. Let's get them out of here and back to where we can have long and very painful discussions."

Rhaines ran out. Remus went ahead with him and the others got the four men up and further secured. It was long before I heard the hum of engines outside. I turned back to Kimera. I went to pick her up. I hated it, but there was no way I thought she could walk. We had no idea what injuries she might have, and walking could aggravate them. I gritted my teeth as I swung her up in my arms. "It's alright, babe. I'm just carrying you to the car now. Rhaines is here to take us back to the compound."

She didn't say anything, but she did give me a tiny

nod to show she heard me. Her head was still hanging. This whole time, she hadn't made eye contact with me once. Walking outside, before I got in the car that Rhaines had the back door open to, I saw Ratchet.

"Ratchet, I need you to ride my bike back home. I'm staying with Kimera." He nodded. The others went to the van and shoved our prisoners inside it roughly. Putting them to the back of my mind for the time being, I held her on the quiet ride home.

Later, as we got out of the car at the compound, I tried to carry her inside, but she moved away and shook her head. She was stooped over when we entered the clubhouse. I heard gasps, and then Troian burst into tears when she saw Kimera. Lash told me, "Take her to my exam room. I'll be there in a minute to examine her." He rushed over to Troi.

I followed closely beside Kimera but made sure not to touch her. She knew where the treatment room was. I opened the door for her, and she went in and took a seat on a chair. We sat there in silence as we waited. I wanted to say something, but I didn't know what to say. I wasn't sure how long we were like that before there was a soft knock at the door.

"Come in," I called out.

The door opened to reveal Lash, as I expected. Alisse was with him. She gave me a sympathetic look and then teared up when she saw Kimera. I watched her fight the tears back. Lash went to my woman. He didn't touch her, though. "Kimera, I'm here, and so is Alisse. Sweetheart, we need to check you over. Do you want me to get Troian, too?"

She emphatically shook her head no on the last part. He grimaced but didn't say more. He faced me. "Spawn, I need you to wait in the hallway until we're done."

"No, I'm staying with her. I can turn my back when you need me to."

He came to stand next to me. He whispered in my ear, "I need to ask her what they did to her. Was she raped? If you're here, she may not say. Please, I'll let you see her again as soon as possible. I know this is killing you. I get it, but this is for her." He squeezed my left shoulder hard.

Knowing he was right didn't make it any easier to do it. Reluctantly, I gave him a chin lift. Before I walked out, I had to say something to her. "Kimera, I'll be in the hall. If you want me to come back, just tell them, and they'll come get me."

A very faint "Okay" came out of her.

Her first word since we found her. I closed the door and sank to my ass to sit, leaning against the opposite wall. I stared at the door as if I could see through it. There were murmurs on and off, but nothing I could understand. The wait was torture, and I timed it. It was twenty-two minutes later before the door opened, and he came out. He had a grim look on his face. My nausea increased. I stood up.

"What is it? Does she need to go to the hospital?"

"No, she doesn't need to go to the hospital. She's

bruised and sore, but nothing is broken as far as I can tell. She doesn't want to go there either."

"Then why the grim face? They raped her, didn't they?" I blurted out. At least I kept my voice low so she wouldn't hear me.

He shook his head. "I don't know, brother. She refused to tell us and wouldn't let us do an exam. I tried to convince her, and so did Alisse, to let us look, but she got agitated, so we stopped. Spawn, she's traumatized, and I want you to go easy with her. Don't push her to tell you what happened. If you do, it could make her worse. As impossible as it might be, we have to let her tell us when she's ready."

"Jesus Christ, Lash, I don't know if I can. If she was raped, she needs to be tested for sexually transmitted disease. And what if she's pregnant?"

"I know she needs those tests, but we can't force her. As for pregnancy, if that happens, then we help her deal with it. She can get an abortion, put it up for adoption, or keep it."

"Keep it?" I asked in shock.

"Yeah, keep it. We've known more than one woman who did that. Why? Can't you raise it and treat it as yours?" he asked sternly. "Or is that no longer an option since she's been raped? You don't want her anymore."

I reacted by shoving him against the wall and grabbing his neck. He didn't fight me. "Don't you ever fucking say that again. Of course, I want her. It doesn't matter to me what they did to her. She's the same woman. I only asked because I don't think she'd want to do that. I know Brielle and a few others have, but not everyone can. No matter her decision, if that happens, I'll be with her every step of the way. If she wants to keep it, that child will have a father and never know I'm not his or her biological dad," I hissed.

He smiled at me. I eased my grip. "That's all I needed to hear. You're right. It may take some time and convincing, but you can do it. Now, mind letting go of my throat. If you bruise me, Troian might kick your ass," he teased. That got a laugh out of me despite how bad the situation was. I let go and moved away.

"Okay, I know you want to see her. She's trying to rest. Alisse will stay with her. Go tell her you'll be back. I think it's time to work off some aggression, don't you?" he said as his smile changed to an evil smirk. I was all for that.

"Give me a minute to tell her."

I knocked and then opened the door when I heard Alisse say, "Come in." Kimera was lying on one of the beds, curled up. I went over to her.

"Kimera, honey, I've got to do something with Lash and the guys. I'll be back as soon as I can. Alisse is with you, but if you want me, just have her text me or Ink. I'll come back. I wish I didn't have to go, but I do."

For the first time, she met my gaze. I saw misery and shame there but also rage. "Make them hurt," she whispered.

"I will, babe. You have my fucking word on that. Now, rest while I'm gone," I told her. She nodded, then closed her eyes. I knew I shouldn't do it, but I couldn't help it. I leaned over and placed a kiss on her forehead. She flinched. I reluctantly moved back and then rejoined Lash. It was time for payback.

Spawn: Chapter 6

I didn't remember the ride to the bunker underneath the storage building where we had our interrogation room. Thankfully, someone drove me there. When I got out, I didn't wait for anyone. I headed right for it. Inside, I entered my thumbprint to open the secret door to the bunker below and then again to get into the extra special room.

I noted that Maniac and Rhaines had been busy in the short time we'd been at the clubhouse. They secured our captives to chairs in the center of the room. They remained gagged, but they had bruises and a few cuts. I heard Troian gasp. I wasn't sure I agreed with her being here. This wasn't something we'd usually let any of the women see. However, that was Lash's call as her old man.

I was impressed when she moved closer to them. She put a hand on my arm. I looked at her. She waved for me to come closer, so I had to bend down. She whispered in my ear, "I know you want to kill them and make them suffer for Kimera. I'm all for that. Please let me get my piece out of the way, and then you can go psycho nutbar all over their disgusting fucking asses. Okay?"

I almost chuckled at her psycho nutbar comment, but instead, I whispered back, "You got it. Just don't make me wait too long. My nutbar meter is rising."

She smiled, then glanced at my brothers and asked them to take off the gags so she could hear what her cousins had to say. Lash tried to object, but she cut him off and assured him she knew it would be disgusting and ugly. No one moved until Lash gave a chin lift, and then Crusher and Maniac removed their gags. The captives didn't waste time starting their bullshit. Laszlo went first. It was the standard threat that we were dead, and we had no idea who they were. He called Troian a whore, which it was a miracle Lash didn't punch him for it, but he held back.

Troi didn't appear phased by it as she responded to his threats. "Save your breath, Las, you're gonna need it. I can't wait to watch you beg, cry, puke, and suffer. It's the least you deserve for what you've done."

He didn't answer her. It was Kaz next who spoke up. He went for the low blow of telling her how taking in her ass was the worst day for his family, and she should be grateful they did and that they made a mistake not selling her. Immediately on the tail end of that rant, Jarek chimed in to ask why we were helping her. He thought we should talk and do business together. He was obviously one of the ones who thought all men in MCs were immoral bastards.

Finally, Zandro spoke. "I should've drowned you after I beat you, bitch. It felt so good pounding on you and hearing you scream and beg for mercy. It made me hard. I should've fucked you first, though. I've wanted to do that for years."

That was the remark that set off Lash. He hurled himself at Zandro and started to pound on him. The rest of us stood back and watched the show. I'm not sure how long we would've stood there if it wasn't for Troian. She bent over and was crying as she panted and had her mouth open, but nothing came out. Her face was a mask of horror and pain. Reaper, Crusher, and I grabbed Lash, and all of us were hollering for him to stop. It took Reaper to tell him she needed him to make him quit beating Zandro. Lash ran to her as he ordered us to gag them. He wrapped her up in his arms. The rest of us stood there waiting as he talked to her although we did gag the bastards. A few minutes passed, and still, there was no word out of her.

He picked her up. "I'll be back. Save me some," he told us.

This made her struggle, and she moaned. He reassured her he was taking her to the house. When she looked up, she hissed, "Put me down. I'm not done."

What the hell? When he didn't do it right away, she tried to get down herself. He lowered her to her feet, and slowly, she straightened up. He whispered something to her. She shook her head and whispered back, which had them whispering back and forth more. I was about to ask what they were saying when she moved away from Lash and toward her cousins. She addressed Laszlo's accusations first and then went down the line through the rest until she got to Zandro.

They were trying to speak around their gags, but it wasn't working. They were jerking on their restraints like they thought they could get loose. It would take bigger and stronger men than them to break those. I was starting to get antsier. I wanted to start on them.

She revealed to Zandro that she had amnesia, and what we knew was mostly due to me. She pointed to me as she told him. I was staring at them hard, hoping they saw my hatred and what was in store for them. Then, she surprised all of us when she revealed his words had triggered her memories to return. She told him she remembered everything.

Her description of her beating and what they did made me angrier. The fucker got hard from doing that to her? When she hit him with the accusation she thought he was into boys and that she had a real man, I thought his head would explode. As he howled and jerked harder, we laughed and made jokes about them, especially about Zandro.

After a while, we calmed down, and she went on to admit to him she was the one to turn in Andrik and how she regretted she hadn't known they were involved so they could be enjoying prison, too. It was her next remarks that stunned me, although I wasn't sure why. "I hope he's being ass raped every day. It's only a small bit of justice for those poor women and girls you animals forced to be prostitutes all these years. It'll be a pleasure to see his end, too. Now, I think I'll watch for a while, then I'll get back to you."

That was my signal. I found my fists were clenched tight. I no longer held in the rage I felt. I took off my cut and gave it to Ink. I didn't want their blood on it. Next to come off was my shirt. No need to ruin all my clothes. Ink picked it up off the floor, where I dropped it. I was never prouder of my body than I was at that moment when they took in the size of me. Fear entered their eyes. I knew I was intimidating, and I loved it.

"You motherfuckers have no clue the hell you released, but you will. I promise you that. We'll take more than a pound of flesh, but you..." I stopped in front of Zandro. "You, I'll really enjoy punishing. The woman you had naked just a while ago is mine. I'll make sure you live long enough to regret ever touching her or any other woman or girl. Hell, like Troi said, you've probably been doing it to boys too."

Once I said that, I turned to Troian. I told her she should leave if she didn't want to see their pathetic cocks. She waved for me to keep going, so I did. My brothers came forward with their knives and cut off our prisoners' clothes while Reaper went to the thermostat. I knew what he was doing.

Reaper ordered my brothers to get them up and to let them stretch so we had room to work. I did Zandro myself. We got them standing and chained their arms above their heads onto the hooks hanging above. Zandro tried to fight me, but he was no match. When they were all hung up and spaced apart far enough, I heard Troian burst out laughing. Lash asked her what was so funny.

Her answer made my brothers all laugh their asses off and me smirk. "Oh my God, it's true. They do have tiny ones. No wonder they're so hateful to women. Not one could really satisfy a woman, and I bet they've been laughed at a lot. Too bad you can't show them what a real one looks like."

Remus, the nut, offered to show our captives what a real cock looked like. I thought Lash would stop him, but when Troi closed her eyes and smarted off about not wanting to know what ours looked like, he didn't. This earned her another laugh. Remus carried through with his threat. He unashamedly took down his jeans and underwear, gripped himself, and held it up to them. "That's what a real one looks like, boys," he said with a grin.

Not to be outdone, his twin, Romulus, joined him and did the same. "In case you need to see two." He snickered. The rest of us kept ours in our pants. Lash whispered something to a red-faced Troi. She answered him and then giggled as he nipped her ear.

When Remus and Romulus got their pants back up, I got back to it. "Take off their gags. I want to hear their screams. It's time to get this show on the road. Troi, you can look, sweetheart."

I should've known Zandro would speak first once the gags were off again. I let him. Nothing he could say would change what was about to happen. "You can't kill us. If you do, our family will slaughter every single one of you, including your families. You're fucking with the Bratva," he announced proudly.

Crusher got great enjoyment out of telling him that his branch of the Gusev family wasn't Bratva. Of course, Zandro told him he didn't know shit. His expression when Crusher spoke Russian to him was hilarious, and it made all four of them pale. Troian was nice enough to translate for us. He'd hit them with Kirill's surname. This caused Laszlo to ask Crusher who he was.

"I'm Damien Tatum. You might know of my cousin and godfather, Kirill Razin. He sure knows you and your so-called Bratva family in Russia. As we speak, he and the others are set to wipe them out, just like we plan to wipe you and your filth out here," he told them with a grin. They were shaking before he was done. I'd like to believe it was due to their fear, not the temperature.

"Y-you can't," Kaz stuttered, then shut up.

"What? Nothing to say?" Crusher taunted Zandro. He didn't say a word.

At Crusher's nod to me, I got closer to Zandro again. I didn't waste my breath with more talk. It was time to inflict pain. I punched with as much force as I could. I'd been known to pound on the big punching bags so hard seams gave. I hoped the same happened to this fucker. I landed the first blow to his ribs. The crack as his ribs broke was audible even despite his cry. I did the same to the other side. I liked symmetry.

My brothers got in on the action and paired up with one of the other three bastards. They'd have to take turns, but we'd all get our licks in today. The next several minutes were a symphony of cries of pain and the thud of fists on flesh. More cracks were heard, too. It was music to my ears. I enjoyed every sound immensely as I methodically beat Zandro. All I could see was the image of him with his cock out, and Kimera bent over in front of him.

I was broken out of my trance when Troian handed out brass knuckles to us. I gave her a wink as she did. God, she was quickly becoming my favorite old lady. Not to say I didn't love the others, but she was my woman's friend and Lash's woman. It gave her double points, and then to have her do this just added to her score with me.

After she gave them to us, she walked around her cousins. She was studying them as she tapped a finger on her chin like she was in deep thought. She finally spoke. "I think you should give them a few more punches, then change things up. What do you think? If I remember correctly, not only did I have bruises all over me, but I had cuts too."

Lash was quick to agree and asked her how to say Hurricane in Russian, which she told him. Calling her *Uragan,* he asked her where to cut Laszlo, who was the one he'd been pounding on. Her answer was perfect in my mind. She wanted Lash to duplicate where her cuts were when we found her. Lash would know since he had been her doctor. He practically purred as he took out his blade. The first cut was on the ribs. The rest of us took out our knives and copied him. Cut after cut was made. We'd wait between one cut and the next until he showed us where to place them. By the time we were through, blood was dripping onto the floor despite not cutting too deep. We didn't want to risk them dying yet.

The little minx then voiced her wonder if they could hurt more. Damn, Lash better hope she didn't get pissed enough at him to torture his ass. She swiftly followed up her question with an unexpected punch to Zandro. She did it on top of one of his larger, deeper cuts, making him shout in pain. That's when we all realized she had a pair of brass knuckles on, too. She hit him a few more times before saying to him, "You're so right, Zandro, it does feel good. I bet kicking would, too."

Like lightning, she kicked him between the legs. That even made me wince. She was a hurricane, alright. His shout was much higher this time. I enjoyed her going down the line, kicking the rest of those animals in the same spot. Kaz was the only one to puke when she did it, though. When she was done, she thanked us and then gave us permission to continue playing with our toys. I had to chuckle.

Lash warned her, "Babe, there's more that we plan to do. A lot more. It's gonna get bloodier and more gruesome. I'm not sure you want to stay for that."

She promised she could handle it, then asked if he was worried about her not being able to handle it or if it was her seeing what he was capable of. He was honest and told her both. She assured him the latter wouldn't happen, and if she thought she was getting to the point where she couldn't continue to watch, she'd leave.

That seemed to release Lash's inner beast. He stripped off his upper clothing after kissing her. Before he could start back on his man, Reaper suggested we take a break and let the others work off some aggression. I didn't want to, but I did. I knew no one would need a break, but everyone deserved a piece of them. Rhaines handed us bottles of water. I'd worked up a thirst and a sweat, so I gulped it down.

Not only did they beat them more, but other painful techniques were used. Salt was rubbed into the open wounds, in addition to more cuts being made with objects not as sharp as our knives. I smiled as their nails were ripped out with pliers.

It was too long for me before the original four of us were given the go-ahead to get back to work. I looked at Lash. I knew what he would be dying to do. "Lash, brother, do you want to show them how you got your name?"

After sparing a glance at Troian, he went to his special cabinet on the wall and opened it. Troian got her first look at how her man got his road name. It was filled with a variety of whips. He was a master with them. I'd never seen anything like it. Troian told him which two she wanted him to use, and he brought out his bullwhip first. The brothers and I moved back, and she joined us.

Zandro and the others tried to see what he was doing, but they couldn't. He held the whip behind his back until he faced them and snapped it. The loud snap made them jump and try to turn away. He explained his name and how he got it. Their eyes bugged, and then I smelled piss. Checking their crotches, I saw Laszlo had pissed himself.

"No! Please, we surrender. We won't bother you again," Kaz yelled.

"God no," Laszlo sobbed.

"Please," Jarek pleaded.

Even Zandro begged. "We'll do anything you

want. Just stop."

"You seem to be under the impression there's anything in the world you can do or promise us that'll stop this and make us let you live. You're really stupid, aren't you? There's nothing you can say, do, promise, swear, or anything else that's gonna save your miserable lives. You're dead men," I snarled. Stupid bastards thought there was something in the world they could do to save themselves. Never.

Watching Lash work his magic was almost mesmerizing. Each cry of pain and new wound made me smile, but none as much as when he sliced open the head of their worthless cocks at Reaper's suggestion. All of us brothers moaned, cupped ourselves, and winced. After that, he switched to Troi's other pick, the cat-o'-nine-tails. Their backs got the full measure of it. Reaper called a halt to it so the bleeding could be stopped. His request for volunteers to do it was eagerly accepted by Ratchet, Ink, Tinker, and Sandman.

Our metal tools had been heating up in the burn barrel. They each took one and placed the glowing ends against the larger wounds to cauterize them. The smell of burning flesh quickly filled the space. Troian gagged. The rest of us had grown used to the smell and no longer gagged. Lash tried to get her to wait outside, but she declined. Then, she called him over to talk to him in private. We whistled when they started to kiss.

When they broke apart, Reaper asked, "How else do you want them to suffer?"

I loved Shadow's suggestion. "They used their

hands to touch women and girls, and God knows who else when they shouldn't have. I say we break them."

We all took turns breaking every one of their ten fingers. However, when we were done, it became obvious they were weak and were on the edge of dying, even though we'd cauterized their wounds. It appeared they weren't nearly as tough as they thought. Maniac offered the choice to let them rest and get more medical attention or just finish them. Our brothers left the decision to me and Lash. He gave his choice to his woman since she was the one harmed by them. She said she was good, and so did he. They all looked at me.

I stood there thinking. There was a part of me that was hungry to inflict more pain and spill more blood. They hadn't suffered enough, in my opinion. But the other part of me wanted this over with so I could get back to Kimera. Being away from her was making me grow more worried. I needed to know what was happening with her. I wanted to be the one to watch over my woman and comfort her. Making my decision, I told them, "There's one more thing I want to do, and then we can be done with this. If I didn't want to get back to Kimera and take care of her, I'd say let's keep going. However, they've breathed enough air."

"They're all yours," Lash told me.

I went over to grab a pair of nylon gloves. For this next part, I needed them. After I had them on, I picked up the knife again that I had laid on the table. I turned it over so the serrated edge was facing downward. I walked up to Kaz first. As I sneered at him, I grabbed his worthless cock and sawed through it. His screams were music to my ears. The other three screamed in horror as they discovered their fates. I dropped his severed cock on the floor and moved onto Laszlo.

His horrified look made me smile at him as I cut his cock off. As I worked my way down the line of them and through Jarek, none of them were able to say a word. I was happy with that. I didn't want to hear any more of their shit. Well, it lasted until I got to Zandro. I saved him for last. The image of Kimera still wouldn't fade from my memory. It would take a long time for those images to fade, and they would never be forgotten. "This is for touching my woman and all the others before her," I snarled at him.

"I didn't! I never raped her. I swear," Zandro yelled.

"Even if you didn't, you were going to. Tell the Devil I said hello and to make it extra hot for you in hell," I hissed. I stared into his eyes as I took my time slowly sawing his cock off. His agonizing screams filled me with happiness. It wasn't until I finally dropped his cock on the floor that it registered that anyone else was still with us. Lash picked up Troian and walked out.

A slap on my shoulder made me jerk. I found Reaper standing there with my cut and shirt. "Spawn, why don't you head back and let us take care of disposing of these vermin? You should be with Kimera. Tell her they're no longer a threat to her. Let us know what she needs," he said softly.

"Thanks, Pres. I think I'll do that."

The others all gave me nods or chin lifts as I

walked out. Kaz had already bled to death. The rest weren't long for this world. Outside, I kept walking. I didn't stop until I reached my house. There was no way I'd risk Kimera, the other women, or the kids seeing me like this. I took off my boots and jeans outside. I'd spray them down later. I had another pair of boots I could wear. I'd carried my shirt and cut inside with me.

I went straight to my bathroom and stripped off my underwear while the water heated up. I stared in the mirror. I looked like something out of a horror movie. Blood was splattered on my chest, arms, and even my face. Thank God Kimera didn't see this. She'd run away in terror, no doubt. As soon as the water was hot enough, I got in.

I let it beat down on my tense muscles and watched the blood swirl down the drain as it was rinsed off me. I didn't stay like that long before washing my hair and then my body. I did it twice to be sure I got all the blood off. When I was done, it didn't take me long to dry off and get dressed and presentable. Checking my nails to be sure they were clean, I put on my clean boots and cut before heading to the clubhouse.

I came in the back way since I didn't feel like talking to the women. It wasn't personal. I just needed to get to Kimera as fast as possible. I'd been away from her long enough. I knocked on the treatment room door. There was no answer. I waited a few seconds, then knocked again. Finally, it was opened by Alisse. She walked out and shut the door behind her. She was frowning.

"Is she alright?" I asked urgently.

"She's okay. She's sleeping right now."

"That's fine. I'll just sit with her so you can go," I told her as I went to pass her to open the door. Her hand on my chest stopped me.

"Spawn, that's not a good idea. Before she fell asleep, she told me she didn't want any visitors. She specified you were included in that."

"What? That can't be. Surely, she wants to see me and Troian at least. I can understand the others," I argued.

"She doesn't want her either. Listen, she's shaken by what happened. I tried to get her to talk about it, and she shut down. I think she just needs time to get her thoughts straight. I know you won't stay away long, but maybe you should for now. It'll show her that you respect her wishes. She needs to feel like she's in control after what happened to her. Don't take that away, or you could push her further away from you and deeper into her trauma."

As much as I wanted to ignore what Alisse was saying, I knew it was sound advice. The last thing I wanted to do was hurt Kimera mentally more than she already was. It was with great reluctance that I backed off.

"Okay, I'll go, but I want regular updates. Tell her I was here and she has nothing to worry about. Those animals will never hurt her or anyone else ever again."

"I will. Go get some sleep if you can. Lash will spell me soon. I'll make sure he knows to update you as well. I'm glad to hear they're gone."

I gave her hand a squeeze and then slowly made my way to my room here. Even if she wouldn't see me, I planned to stick close in case she changed her mind or if something happened. I didn't want her to wait when she decided to see me. I didn't know how long I could hold back, but I'd try for her.

Kimera: Chapter 7

They were so concerned and hovered. I knew they were doing it because they cared. Or at least that was why Troian and Lash were. I wasn't sure why Spawn was. Shouldn't he be spending time at the clubhouse? It was where the men gathered to have a good time and find companionship. I knew what the bunnies and hang arounds were for, even if I hadn't met them yet. Since I'd been here, I'd stayed well away from the clubhouse when the women came to party, but I'd heard about them.

Thoughts of Spawn with them made me sick, but I didn't have a hold over him. He was free to do whatever and whoever he wanted. Yes, he'd been with the group that rescued me, and afterward, he hung around until they went to take care of business, but I knew that was him being a good brother to Lash. The slight possibility of any interest he might've had in me prior to that night was a thing of the past. I would've thought my refusal to speak to him would be enough to show him I didn't expect his attention. I didn't need pity or whatever you called it from him.

I'd begun to enjoy our sparring contests up until I was foolish and got myself taken. He made my heart beat faster and my temper rise. I felt alive when he'd debate with me or look at me. Now, all I felt was dead.

I wanted to be left alone. I needed to figure out my life and how to proceed. Everyone had paid me a visit at least once, and the old ladies more than once. Troian was with me every day. Although I stayed here at the compound for the first couple of days, I couldn't confide in anyone, not even Troian. Especially her.

I knew her well enough to know she blamed herself for what happened to me. I could see it on her face every time she looked at me. That wasn't a burden I wanted her to carry. I told her several times none of it was her fault. She said she knew that, but her actions said she didn't believe it. She wanted me to talk about that night and what occurred. Lash and Alisse had tried more than a few times to examine me and begged me to let them get me treatment. I told all of them no. I just wanted to forget and get on with my life.

Lash and Troian practically forced me to come back to live at their house. I was tired and let it slide, but I wouldn't impose on their hospitality for much longer. I needed to be in my house, where I was alone with my thoughts and dreams. Every night, I know I woke them with my screams. The nightmares wouldn't stop. As hard as I tried to either not have them or to not scream, I did it every time. Afterward, I usually couldn't go back to sleep, or it would take a long time before I could. I was surviving on catnaps.

I'd stayed in their house, not venturing out, but today, I wasn't given a choice. I was told I was going to the clubhouse. Troian said Lash would carry me there himself if I didn't go on my own two legs. His nod showed me they were dead serious, so I reluctantly agreed to go with them. I had no idea why they insisted

I be there.

I was surprised when I was led not inside the clubhouse but to the area between the barbeque area and the playground. I noticed they'd set up seating and even heaters in that spot, and someone had sprayed a large square on the grass with white paint. *What were they doing?* I scanned around me, trying to figure it out and to see where everyone was.

Troian and I joined Annie, the kids, and the old ladies. She and I sat close but not right next to any of them. They greeted us with smiles and said how great it was to see me. I gave them faint smiles. Hopefully, they wouldn't want to talk to me. I wasn't up to it. Lash disappeared as soon as we got there, and I didn't see a single one of the guys. Were they in church? What were the ladies waiting for?

Suddenly, the door to the clubhouse opened. I saw Rhaines holding it as the men marched out. The other women, along with Troi, called out taunts and booed the men. The guys were all stripped down, only wearing loose sweatpants. Their upper bodies were bare, and I had to admit that they made an impressive sight. All were fit and muscular and had numerous tattoos. My eyes couldn't seem to stop staring at one man in particular. Spawn was a perfect specimen.

When I tore my gaze away from him, I saw they had colored tape wrapped around their hands. It dawned on me that they were having their fight night. The one Troian and I had egged Lash and Spawn into doing and placing bets on the outcome. God, it seemed like ages since we talked about it and teased Spawn and Lash about making those bets. It will be a week tomorrow since we issued our challenge. They lined up around what I now guessed was the dirt ring in front of us. Reaper faced us.

He was very businesslike as he addressed our small group. "We're here tonight to settle a bet that was recently made. Two of you ladies challenged the manhood of the Iron Punishers in regard to our ability to handle pain. The exact charge was we wouldn't be able to stand the rigors of childbirth if we were able to have children. Troian and Kimera were adamant it wasn't possible, and I believe they said we'd curl up and whine or something to that effect."

The old ladies, along with Annie and Troian, snickered. I let a small smile slip. It seemed our challenge had been taken to heart by the whole club. This just might be interesting. Once the other women quieted some, Reaper continued. "Of course, there's no way we can give birth to prove it, so an all-out no-holds-barred fight was suggested. We men will engage in it and not hold back. The ladies will then judge when we're done if men could stand to have babies."

"And what else do you get out of it if you win, other than your male pride?" Annie yelled.

"Well, for those of us just supporting our two brothers, it'll be pride and satisfaction as well as a damn good workout. As for Spawn and Lash, well, that's between them and those two." He pointed to Troi and me.

"We'd like to know what it is unless it's a secret,"

Annie insisted.

Lash gave her an answer. "Part of it was we all put money down on the outcome. If the men win, we pick a worthy organization to receive the pot as a donation. The losers double the pot amount to make it a better donation. The other part of it is personal and between us and the ladies."

"Oh, I gotta hear that part. Ladies, we'll talk later," Annie teased us. I felt my cheeks heat up, and Troian blushed, too. There was no way I was telling them what the second part of the bet was. It was a moot point now, anyway. There would be no pleasure or children between me and Spawn. Troian and Lash would be the ones to do that. All the old ladies grinned and told us they had to hear it, too.

I was thankful when Reaper took back the conversation. "Enough talk. It's time to get this started. This is based on total honesty, so no cheating, just to be unified against the men. The rules are we won't permanently maim each other, use weapons other than our hands and feet, and a match will go until it's called due to being pinned and unable to break loose, one man is unconscious, too hurt to continue, or one of the fighters taps out. We won't kill each other either. Those are the rules. The refs for this will be Colt, me, and Mayhem. We'll take turns. Do you ladies agree to be unbiased?"

"Agreed," rang out from all of them. I kept my mouth shut.

I didn't know what to expect, but as the first fight

got underway, I learned. They were fighting all out, and I flinched more than once at the blows that landed and how hard they fought each other. The first fight was between Remus and Shadow. They didn't start hitting each other right away. They bounced around and let loose with some halfhearted jabs. That lasted a minute or two, and then they started to really fight. Neither man took it easy on the other just because they were friends and club brothers. They had us ladies gasping. It was Shadow who won it by knocking out Remus. He was helped to the sideline to recover while the next match was chosen and started.

Pair after pair were called into the ring, and the fights were brutal. Ink and Tinker fought, and Tinker won after putting Ink in a submission hold he couldn't get out of. Next was Rhaines and Romulus. The prospect held his own for a long time, but ultimately, Romulus won when he made Rhaines tap out. Reaper fought Mayhem, and it was the best fight to that point. The swearing and yelling were much more frequent and louder for their match. They were bloody and bruised. Finally, Colt, the ref for their match, called it a tie since neither man could get the upper hand or would submit.

Crusher and Maniac went up against each other after those two. Lark flinched the entire match and chewed on her thumb while their son Flynn watched it avidly. I didn't think he ever blinked. I was finding myself more and more in awe of their skill and dedication to proving us wrong. Eventually, the match was called due to the amount of blood. Mayhem was worried one or both had been seriously hurt.

Ratchet and Sandman were next. They tried to

get me to draw the names for their match, but I told them to let one of the other ladies do it. Their round was filled with jabs and kicks. It was a fluke, I think, when Ratchet got Sandman in a hold, and he couldn't break it, so Sandman had to submit. They didn't leave the ring mad. They were laughing, joking, and slapping each other on the backs as they left.

I didn't know if it was intentional or just luck, but the last fight was between Lash and Spawn. Troian and I exchanged worried glances. I saw Lash wink at her. Spawn actually came over to me. "Kimera, you don't have to worry. We know what we're doing. We'll both be fine."

He didn't give me a chance to respond before he walked off and got into the ring with Lash. He shook Lash's hand. They wished each other good luck and hoped they would win their bets. They said more, but it was said so low we couldn't hear it, but they appeared very serious as they spoke. There was a flash of fury on Spawn's face for a couple of moments. Then, it was replaced with a grin. The bell rang, and the fight was on.

They exchanged blow after blow and kick after kick. Neither seemed to slow down or lose the power behind their punches and kicks. They went on and on. My anxiety increased as each minute passed. Would they keep doing this until someone got hurt? Why didn't Reaper or one of the other refs stop it? My fear peaked when Lash hit Spawn in the temple, and he fell to his knees. A scream escaped me. Tears filled my eyes, and I stood up. I had to get out of here. I couldn't watch any more. I took off running for the house. I heard my name shouted, but I didn't stop. How I wish Toro was with me. I'd left him at their house so he could chill.

I was past Maniac and Lark's house, coming up on Lash and Troian's when my arm was snagged, and I was whipped around. I wasn't jerked hard or anything, but it scared me. I let out a scream. It took a couple of heartbeats for me to recognize Spawn had a hold of me. He was frowning in concern.

"Kimera, what's wrong? Why did you scream then take off? Surely you didn't think we were gonna hurt each other."

I didn't know what to tell him, so I tried to deflect him. "I don't know why I did that. I'm fine. I just want to go to the house and lie down. I'm suddenly really tired. Please, go back to your brothers. I bet everyone will be in the common room celebrating. You don't want to miss it or the entertainment later."

He frowned. "What entertainment? Sure, some will have a few drinks, maybe shoot pool, or play darts. Others will just relax and talk. I wouldn't call that entertainment."

His coyness pissed me off. Why did men have to lie and sneak around? Why did they have to only care about themselves? "You know what I mean! Those women who come in after the wives leave. The ones there to fuck you and your brothers. The bunnies and hang arounds. I meant them. They'll all be gone if you don't get back," I said snidely.

He reared back in surprise. He didn't say anything for a couple of beats, then he denied it. "Babe, I'm not interested in going back to the clubhouse and hooking up with anyone. Yes, later, there are women like that coming, I have no doubt, but they're for my brothers, not me."

"Why not you? Don't you like women?"

He narrowed his eyes on me. "You know I like women. I made a bet with you, didn't I? Why would I touch one of them when you and I are planning our marriage and kids?"

I yanked my arm loose. His words made my stomach knot and my eyes water. "That's never happening between us. It's cruel to tease me about something like that."

"What!?"

I didn't stay to debate it with him. I darted off, and somehow, I made it to Troi and Lash's house and inside. Toro came running to me. He followed me as I ran up the stairs as fast as I could to reach my bedroom. I locked the door behind us and then threw myself on the bed. Tears poured out as I sobbed. Too bad crying didn't ease my pain. I didn't think anything would. I wished I could find oblivion for a little while. Toro climbed up and curled himself up against me. I threw an arm over him and bawled. He was the one to wipe my tears away with his tongue.

※※※

The days since the fight night had been nerve-racking for me. Troian kept asking me why I left and what Spawn said to me. Spawn wouldn't stop coming by the house and spending hours here when Lash was around. Why couldn't they respect that all I wanted was to be left alone? Their poking and prodding into my pain and life wasn't needed. It was more than illustrated tonight when Spawn and I got into a yelling match. He'd joined us for dinner. I tried to eat in my room, but Troian begged me to join them, so I did.

We were almost finished eating when I casually mentioned my plans. "Troi, Lash, I want to thank you for having me here. I know that three is a crowd, especially when you're just establishing your lives together. You'll be happy to know that I'm planning to go home in the next day or two. It's time I got back into the swing of things. My work can't wait forever, either. Thank you both very much."

The clatter of metal against something hard made me turn my head. Spawn's spoon was half lying off his plate. He was staring at me with a stunned look on his face. Troian was giving me a pleading look while Lash watched with worry on his face.

"Kimera, you're not imposing on us. We love having you here, and we don't want you to leave," Troi said.

"Troi, you're sweet, and I love you for being such a good friend to me by allowing me into your house, but it's time for me to go home. It's been sitting empty. Lord knows what's happened to it. I thought tomorrow would be a good day for me and Toro to go back."

"Like hell, you will. You don't need to be out there all alone with just your dog. If you don't want to stay with Troian and Lash, there are plenty of other places you can stay. Besides, you're still recovering. You need to be where you have people who care for you and will be available if you need anything. Your house is fine. I've been checking it

for you," Spawn said gruffly.

"It wouldn't just be me and Toro. Did you forget I have guns? I know how to use them, I assure you."

"Why don't we calm down and talk about this?" Lash asked calmly.

"There's nothing to talk about. She's not going, and if she tries it, I'll lock her ass up here," Spawn snapped.

"Fuck you, Spawn! You can't tell me what to do!" I yelled. How dare he talk like that. Who did he think he was?

"Fuck if I can't. I'm not letting you get hurt to satisfy some asinine idea that you have to do everything alone."

"Screw you and your asinine comment. No man tells me what to do!"

"This man does, so get used to it. You're not going, and that's final," he snarled.

I shoved back my chair and screamed at him. Toro was alert and growling. He didn't know what the hell was happening. "Fuck you! No man will ever control me again. So watch me."

Tears made an appearance, much to my embarrassment. I ran from the room with him yelling for me to come back. He ended up following me and sitting outside my room, trying to get me to talk to him, but I wouldn't. I wrapped pillows around my ears so they would muffle his words. He sat out there for a good hour before it got quiet. Toro relaxed once he was gone. Until then, he stood between me and the locked door and paced.

That was yesterday. Today, Troian and I spent the

day entertaining Toro. We didn't talk about my plans to leave. I was still determined to do it, but not today. I figured if I tried it, Spawn would have someone at the gate to stop me. I had to do this smartly. Also, I couldn't leave Troi when she was worried about Lash. He left in the middle of the night, according to her. I found this out when I got up this morning. She had no idea what he was doing other than it was club business. I couldn't help but wonder if the reason I hadn't seen Spawn today was because he was out with Lash and other members completing this club business.

I was in my room reading while Troian was watching a television show. She asked me to join her, but I needed a bit of alone time. A knock at my bedroom door got me to put down the book. I'd been struggling to get into the story anyway. "Come in," I called out when I heard her say my name. I sat up on the bed.

"Hey, Lash is back. He says the guys need us to come to the clubhouse. They have something to fill us in on. He said it wasn't anything bad."

"Really? I wonder what it is. Give me a minute to brush my hair, and I'll go."

She ended up waiting for me, and we walked into the living room together. Toro was on my heels. I was full of apprehension despite Lash's assurance to her. He smiled at me, and the three of us, along with Toro, walked over to the clubhouse. There were a ton of bikes out front. Inside, the club members were everywhere.

They nodded at us, but no one said anything. Lash kept walking, so Troian and I followed him. The guys fell in behind us. We were taken into a room with a huge table and lots of chairs around it. From my tour when I first came here, I knew this was where they had church. Why were we there? Women weren't allowed in here, just patched members. I stumbled as I saw Reaper and Spawn were already at the table.

As we approached Spawn, he jumped up and pulled out a chair next to him. After catching my attention, he pointed to it. I thought of arguing but then decided that wasn't the way to go, so I sat down. Troian sat further along beside her man. After the others took their seats, Reaper hit the table with a hammer-like thing and spoke.

"Ladies, welcome. Thanks for joining us. You have to be wondering why you're here. First, let me tell you, it's nothing bad. In fact, it's damn good. We wanted to tell you together. You need to know, as the newest members to our family, we don't make promises we don't keep, nor do we leave things not tied up," Reaper told us, then paused.

Troian thanked him and then told him she knew that about them. He said actions spoke louder than words, and as their family, she should've been safe. He even apologized to me for getting hurt while trying to protect Troian, my friend. He thought it was their fault I was hurt. They should've assigned more than Colt to me.

I couldn't let his recriminations go unchallenged. "No, it wasn't your fault. I was the one who colored my hair and rode around like that. I got Colt hurt. He could've been killed. I'm the one who should be apologizing. You've been nice enough to let me stay here despite that, but I want you to know I plan to get out of your hair."

This earned me a rumbling growl from Spawn and a glare. I glared right back at him. Reaper continued talking about Crusher's family in Russia and how they were taking care of the Gusev family there. That left just Andrik, the one Troian put in prison here. He finished up that interesting speech with, "I'll let Lash and Spawn tell you the rest."

Lash was given a chin lift by Spawn, so he began to talk. "Last night, Spawn and I made sure Andrik will never see daylight again. He met with an unfortunate accident which landed him in the infirmary of the prison."

"What kind of accident? And how will that keep him in prison? He only got a ten-year sentence," Troi said.

"He did, but then he took a hard tumble down the stairs," Lash said with a grin.

This got my attention. I had to ask. "How did he fall down those stairs?"

"It seems someone started a rumor that he was not only in there for pandering but he likes the kiddies. Rumor was he not only pimped out women but kids too, and he sampled them," Spawn said, sounding short. Then Lash explained Andrik's prison record was altered, and an inmate saw the notation and told others.

As amazing as it sounded. I asked the obvious

questions, or at least they seemed obvious to me. "How does this keep him there, though? Won't they just put him in protective custody? That's what they do to those filthy bastards."

It was Spawn who answered me. "Usually, yes, but it seems his luck got worse once he got to the infirmary. See, there's an inmate who's in for life. He was a doctor, so the warden let him work there. Free labor, you see. It appears that recently, one of his nephews was molested. He's only ten years old. Suffice it to say his uncle is furious that he's not able to do anything about it. I guess when a cho mo appeared in front of him, he couldn't resist," Spawn added.

Troian asked what a cho mo was. I had no idea, either. When he told us it was prison slang for a child molester, I wanted to say duh to myself. I wasn't sure where knowing prison slang would come in handy in the future, but I filed it away. Troian asked how they knew all this. I found out truly how cunning and talented Spawn was. Of course, I'd never tell him this or that I admired his skills. I also learned to fear them a bit when Lash said they had people on the inside to help with problems like this.

I had no remorse for the man, even if Troi voiced a bit of guilt over a lie getting Andrik killed. Spawn quickly told her there was no lie. He'd found evidence of Andrik's guilt. He not only molested kids, but he sold them in his sick sex ring. Hearing all of this, while relieving me on one hand, brought up terrible memories. A sob slipped out, and then another. I rocked in my seat.

I was stunned when Spawn reached over and lifted me up like I didn't weigh a thing and sat me on his lap. He rocked me, and I was too drained to fight him. I let comfort seep into me as he whispered in my ear.

"Baby, don't cry. All those animals are gone. They can't hurt you again. You just need to focus on healing."

I sobbed harder. How could I remind him that they weren't the only monsters in the world? There were so many and most we didn't know about until it was too late. They ruined lives, and most got away with it. I don't know how long we sat like that before I realized the others had left the room. I sat up and wiped my wet face.

"I'm okay. You can let me up now. I think we should go see what the others are doing." I tried to get up, but he held me to him.

He searched my gaze. "Are you sure you're ready for that? We can talk. I'm a good listener, you know."

"I'm sure you are, but I don't want to talk."

Sighing, he let go so I could stand. "Well, if you change your mind, I'm here. You'll talk to me one of these days."

I hurried out of the room when he said that. What he just said was what I was afraid of. I couldn't tell him or anyone else here about it, but especially him. I had to get out of here soon.

Spawn: Chapter 8

I was gonna paddle that woman's ass when I saw her. She waited until I was gone for the day doing a job for the club I couldn't do remotely, well not totally anyway and she ran back to her house. I yelled at my brother Lash for letting her go, but he tried to tell me he couldn't force her to stay. Like hell, he couldn't!

It was super late when I got in last night, so I went straight home, took a shower, and tumbled into bed. It wasn't until I got up this morning and came over to Lash's to see her that I found out she was gone. My reaction hadn't been a pretty one.

Standing in Troian and Lash's living room, I stared at them like they'd grown two heads. What Troian had just told me didn't compute. Well, it did, and that was the problem.

"What the fuck do you mean, she's gone!? When? How!" I half yelled.

"Don't fucking yell at Troian. It's not her fault. Kimera has been telling us for weeks she wanted to go home. We couldn't keep her here if she wanted to go. You know that," Lash barked back.

"With all you big men around, not one of you could keep her inside the goddamn compound?" I snapped back.

"Only if we wanted to be accused of holding her hostage and being like some other people we know. I tried to talk her into staying, too. She was adamant, so we escorted her and Toro home. We checked it was safe and left her with all our numbers and her guns loaded," was his reply.

"Why didn't you text or call me and let me know?"

"Because Reaper told us not to. He didn't want you distracted and then end up hurt or dead. I know this isn't what you wanted. It wasn't what we wanted either, but we had to do it. You can still work on her to get her to see reason and return. Just don't yell at her like you are us," he told me with a stern look.

I yanked on my hair. "Goddamn it, I'm sorry, Troian. It's not your fault. I'm just frustrated that I can't seem to break through to her. Has she said anything else to you about what happened that night?"

She gave me a sad shake of her head. "I've tried, and she shuts me down every time, Spawn. She says she's fine even though we can all see she's not. The other ladies have tried more than once, too. We tried not to push too hard because we didn't want her to leave, but it happened anyway. I begged her not to go yesterday. She said it was time to stop hiding and to get back to her life. I think her work has been hounding her to come back. They don't know what happened to her. She lied and said she was in an accident."

I hadn't known what excuse she used at work. On the one hand, I understood their need for staff, but on the other hand, I was angry at them for pushing her. Her physical bruises might've healed, but her psychological ones hadn't.

"I'll be back. Later," I told them, making up my mind.

Lash followed me outside. Before I got on my ride, he stopped me. "Go easy on her, brother. Don't blast her for it, or it might make her worse," he warned me.

"I'm gonna try. Shit, how would you feel if it was Troian?"

"Like going over there and dragging her kicking and screaming outta that house and back here, but it would be the wrong thing to do. We learned that when I had to fetch Troian, remember? No matter what, it has to be her choice. Yeah, I made some threats to get Troian here, but in the end, I let her make the decision. That goes against our alpha male tendencies, but we have to sometimes."

I chuckled because he was right about those tendencies. "I hear ya. I'll do my best. Wish me luck."

"Good luck," he said with a grin.

On the ride out to her place, I tried to calm myself and think of things I could say to her that would change her mind. I wasn't sure anything I came up with was gonna do it, but I'd try. Usually, I was a guy who could maintain his temper. It only came out to play when I was pushed too far. Then, it was worthy of the devil, hence my road name. What happened to Kimera pushed me there with no ramp-up needed.

When I pulled up in front of the house, her place looked deserted, and I didn't like it. Turning off my bike, I swung off and removed my helmet as I scanned the area. Nothing looked out of place. I'd been coming out here a lot to make sure no one messed with it, and I knew I'd notice if something were out of the ordinary. I didn't see her car, but she might've parked it in the back to make us think she wasn't home.

Walking to the door, I briskly knocked and waited. I heard Toro bark and then get quiet. I noticed that at the compound. He'd only bark long enough to alert her and then stop. He was a very well-trained dog. I did feel better with him guarding her, but it still wasn't enough. I needed her behind a fence with cameras, weapons, and lots of bodies to keep her safe.

When the door didn't open, I knocked again. I wasn't leaving until she talked to me. I could wait as long as I had to. I'd slept in worse places than on her porch. If she really weren't home, I'd wait. Finally, after a couple of minutes, the door eased open, and she peeked out at me. She didn't open it all the way, though. She was glaring at me. *So this was how it was to go? Okay.*

"What're you doing here?" she asked aggressively.

"I came to see how you're doing since you snuck off while I was gone. Can I come in?" I asked with a smile, even though there was a bite to my tone.

"I didn't sneak off. I came home. I can't help it if you were off gallivanting somewhere. I didn't need your permission to leave."

"Permission, no, but common courtesy would dictate you should wait until everyone is present to say goodbye. I would've thought you knew that."

I saw her hand tighten on the door. Shit, I wasn't increasing my odds of getting inside to talk to her by being confrontational with her. "Hey, sorry, I was just disappointed, and I would feel better about you being home if I checked that you were secure."

"Lash and some of the guys already did that yesterday."

"Yeah, but they aren't security system savvy like me, no offense to them. Last time I was here, I saw you had what appeared to be a security system. I'd like to check to be sure it's working properly or if you need something better or not."

She gnawed on her bottom lip for several moments before nodding and opening the door wider. "Okay, if that'll get you off my property, then do it. It's always been more than adequate before this."

As she stepped back, I saw Toro was hiding behind her. His ears were up, and he was alert. She gave him a command, "*Bleib*." He relaxed a bit. I knew enough German from my school days to know she'd told him to stay. I'd heard her use several commands while at the compound. The Flynns trained some of their dogs using Irish Gaelic but others in German, which was more common.

As I came inside, he nudged my hand with his snout. I rubbed his head. "Hi boy, how're you? Keeping your momma safe, I see." He gave me a doggie grin and head-butted my hand for more rubbing.

She laughed. "I swear, Toro, you'd sell me out for head and belly rubs and treats, wouldn't you?"

I followed her into the kitchen. He let me

continue to pet him but stayed between us. She pointed to the stools at the counter. "Can I get you something to drink? I have water, soda, lemonade, and tea. Sorry, no beer."

I sat down. "I don't drink beer as much as you might think. I'd love lemonade, please. And for the record, Toro would never sell you out for those things. He loves you and would gladly rip out anyone's throat if they were a threat. He's still guarding you right now even if he appears relaxed, and that's with him knowing I'd never hurt you. If he thought I would, he'd be eyeing me like a treat."

She laughed and nodded as she got two glasses out of the cabinet. "Yeah, you're right. He's a smart boy, aren't you? Yes, you are." She praised him as she poured lemonade over the ice she filled the glasses with. He perked up.

As soon as she sat my drink down in front of me, she got into a jar and got out a treat. He sat on his butt without being told and waited for her to give it to him. His tail was wagging a mile a minute. With it in his mouth, he lay down and started to gnaw on it. She stayed standing on the other side of the counter. That bothered me. Didn't she trust me?

"Why don't you have a seat and relax while we talk? I promise I won't bite unless you ask me to," I told her with a grin.

She hesitated for a couple of seconds, then came around the counter. I jumped up to pull out the stool closest to me. She eyed it warily, but she did sit. I pushed the stool closer to the counter and then sat. I heard her inhale deeply. I waited.

"Hopefully, the woman you went to see isn't upset you had to leave so quickly. Shouldn't you spend more than a day or so? Or is that all the longer Reaper will allow you away from the compound and whatever it is he has you do?" Came out of her mouth. It surprised the hell outta me.

I addressed the last thing she said first. I had to in order not to lose my cool over her thinking I'd been with some woman. Was she blind? If so, it was time to let her know she was the only woman I wanted, and I'd wait until she was ready for us to go to the ultimate conclusion. I thought I made myself clear about other women when she mentioned bunnies and hang arounds, but I guess not. Maybe if she knew how serious I was, she'd stop fighting me. Up until now, I hadn't outright said I wasn't just teasing her.

"Reaper didn't limit my time away. He wouldn't unless there was a very good reason. I'm lucky that most of my work for the club is doable anywhere as long as I have a computer and internet. In this case, there was some boots-on-the-ground work to do, and I was the best qualified to do it. I deal in anything computer-related. I set up cameras and security systems for the club's businesses and the compound. I do research into people who're bothering the club or we have questions about. I sometimes help the other clubs do investigations, although Smoke and his old lady, Everly, in Dublin Falls do it more."

I paused to give her a chance to say something

before I went on. She glanced down at the counter and then back up to me. "Do you mind if I ask how you learned to do all that? No offense, but you don't strike me as the computer type."

I laughed. "Do you mean I don't look smart enough to do it, or because I'm a biker, I wouldn't be capable or interested in it?"

Her face flushed. "Well, you have to admit, a computer-savvy man isn't what most people think of when you say biker, and there's a certain image that goes with your kind of person, too. It sounds terrible saying it out loud, but shouldn't you be a skinny, glasses-wearing nerd?"

This really made me laugh. I had to sober up a bit to answer her. "Darlin', I was exactly that growing up. I was super tall and skinny, and I wore glasses. You would've never recognized me if you saw me then and now."

"So what happened? And why a motorcycle club? Did you grow up around your club?"

I heard what sounded like genuine interest in her voice. I went with it. I'd still tell her the rest, but later. "I started to work out to put on some weight and muscle to take care of the skinny part. I was twenty before I beefed up a decent amount. The super tall you can see I had no choice in. I've been six foot six since I was twenty-one. I hit six feet when I was around thirteen. As for glasses, I do wear them sometimes when I'm tired of contacts, or I'm at home and have the contacts out and wanna read."

"Really? I just can't picture you as any of those things."

"I'm glad. I was a total nerd. As for why an MC, no, I didn't grow up around any clubs. I was born and raised in Montana. I grew up with real horses, not steel ones. I can tell you when I discovered motorcycles as I got older, my mom almost had a heart attack. She begged me to stick to the animal kind, but after taking a ride on a friend's bike, I was hooked."

"Motorcycles and computers, not the likeliest combo. When did you get into computers?"

"I've loved computers since I was a kid. I think I was ten years old when I started using one at school. To me, they made sense. When I graduated high school, it was the only thing I could see myself doing, so it's what I got my degree in, in college."

"You went to college? Shit, there I go again. Sorry. I truly don't mean it like it sounds," she quickly clarified.

"Yeah, I did. I have a bachelor's degree in computer science. I could've gone on to get my master's, but honestly, by then, I was doing shit beyond that level on my own. A lot of stuff I do now was self-learned or from having those in the field showing me. I'm not the best there is, but people like Smoke and Everly, who are, share their knowledge. I'm fortunate to call them friends."

"Can I ask how you ended up in a club if you didn't grow up around one and how that ended up being here rather than in Montana? If I'm being too nosy, tell me."

"You're not being nosy. I don't mind. I came to be part of the club by accident. I left Montana ten years ago to get away from, of all things, a woman. She was someone I thought I was head over heels in love with, and when she chose another guy over me, I was heartbroken, or I thought I was. I couldn't stand to see her with him, so I packed some of my shit and got out of town on my bike. I didn't know where I wanted to go, so I sorta wandered, and soon, I was no longer in Montana. From there, I went from state to state, seeing the country. I'd never been anywhere before."

I paused to take a drink. It was weird to be talking about another woman with her, but she asked, and I wanted her to know about me. She'd soon find out I knew what I had with that woman wasn't love because she never hit me a tenth as hard as Kimera did.

"What did your family think?"

"They hated it. They were worried about me and would ask me to come home every time we talked. Anyway, I eventually landed in Virginia. I'd started to see bikers all over the country, and some were in clubs. I didn't know much about them, but they seemed exciting to me. I was in a bar one night, and I saw five guys being idiots. They kept harassing the waitresses, being loud and obnoxious, and picking on other customers.

"I was at the bar, and I watched as long as I could, then one of them grabbed one of the waitresses and pulled her down on his lap. The bouncer was worthless, and I knew he wouldn't do anything. I'd had enough and went to intervene. People saw the guy do it, but none of them did anything. When I got to their table, I noticed another guy walking up, a biker. He didn't look happy either. The guy with the waitress on his lap noticed me and popped off his mouth. I told him to let her go and take his friends and leave. I said no one wanted to hear or see their bullshit and asked whether no one taught them manners."

"Let me guess. The answer was no, and he took a swing," she said with a smile.

"Yeah, you could say that. The next thing I knew, I was brawling with them along with the biker. We put them down and then out of the bar. That biker turned out to be Mayhem. Afterward, we talked and had a few drinks, and he invited me to come to the compound. I never left and ended up a prospect. Best decision of my life. I came to hide and lick my wounds only to find the wounds weren't really that deep. She hurt my pride more than anything."

"Coming to the rescue seems to be your thing. You're a knight in shining armor."

"Babe, I wouldn't ever claim to be a knight. Yeah, I hate to see people get hurt, especially women and kids. That's kinda par for the course in our club and those we call friends. My dad raised me better than those idiots. I have a temper, and I work to contain it, but seeing shit like that, what happened to Troian and you, it brings my inner demon out to play, and I play hard and for keeps."

Immediately, I knew I'd made a mistake in mentioning what happened to her. Her ease evaporated, and she became stiff and closed off. It was like a wall went up around her. Shit! "Kimera, don't do that."

"Do what?"

"Close yourself off. I know that night was hell for you. No woman should ever go through it. I wish you'd talk to someone about it. It would help. Any of us is willing to listen. You have nothing to be ashamed or embarrassed about. It's not your fault." I took her hand as I began to talk. By the time I was done talking, she jerked it away and stood up.

"Spawn, I appreciate you wanting to help, but I don't need it. Talking doesn't solve anything. I just want to get on with my life. Thank you for stopping in to check on me, but as you can see, I'm fine. I hate to cut you short, but I have a lot of stuff to get done before I go back to work." She edged away from me.

I stood, too. "Kimera, tell me, do you think checking on your security system is the only reason I'm here?"

"You said it yourself. You're protective of women. Yes, I can see you totally doing that, but it's not needed."

"It's true, I am, and I'll check it out, but it's not the main reason I came."

"Did Troian send you?"

"She didn't. I came because of you. Surely, you know what I feel? All our talk about the bet should've told you."

"You're a flirt. I didn't take it seriously. I promise,"

she said hastily. She was moving toward the front door. I had to stop her.

I got between her and it and slowly raised my hand to touch her cheek. She saw my hand coming, and she still flinched. God, how I hated that. I rubbed my thumb soothingly over her cheek. "Baby, I'd never hurt you. I hope you know I won't. As for me flirting, yes, I was, and I am, but it's not just something I do with all women. I'm gonna just lay this out for you, so there's no doubt about what I intend."

I saw her swallow hard. There was panic on her face, but in her eyes, I saw something more. I was pretty sure it was desire. My heart skipped a beat. Taking a deep breath, I told her.

"I know you have healing to do, and I'll help you in any way I can. I'll be here no matter what because when you're ready, I want us to be together. I'm more than interested in you, Kimera. You mean more to me than any other woman ever has. I wasn't away seeing another woman. None of them attract me. I wasn't kidding about the whole number of kids thing. I want them and you. I want you as my old lady when you're ready," I whispered.

For a moment, I saw stunned surprise and maybe hope on her face, but then it was gone, and she started to shake her head and move away from me. "No, no, that's not possible, Spawn. I can't be what you want even if you did mean it. Besides, give it a week or two. You'll forget all about me. I'm not anything special for you to settle for."

"I'm not settling for you! And it's more than possible with us both wanting it."

She darted around me, got to the door, and had it open before I could stop her. "Well, I don't want it. Now, it's time you leave. I don't want you here. Tell Troian I'm fine and I'll talk to her soon. Please, don't come here again."

She was close to breaking down, I could tell. As much as I wanted to stay and argue, I knew it was the wrong move. If I did, I ran the risk of alienating her permanently. So, as much as it hurt, I walked out the door. I turned before she could shut the door. "I'll give you some time to think, but we'll talk about this again. Take care and call us if you need anything. See ya later, Hotcake," I said before striding off to get on my bike. I had a campaign to plan. Operation Win She-Wolf was underway.

Kimera:

I sank to the floor with my back against the door and let the tears fall. Why did he have to go and say all that? He just had to go and present me with my dream when I knew it wasn't ever going to happen, not now. There was a tiny part of me that had wondered if he might be interested in more than just someone to tease and argue with from the start. That thought had filled me with excitement. I'd been tempted to see if it could become more if he was serious, but not now. It would've been hard to do it with my past but add this latest horror to it, and I wouldn't do that to him.

There was obviously something wrong with me. I attracted monsters, and even if I knew he was the exception, I wouldn't let the ones who'd touched my life ruin his. If he knew everything, he'd run a mile anyway. It was better to let him think I didn't want him than to tell him the truth. Which was horrible on more than one front. It meant my friendship with Troian would have to be abandoned. There would be no way I could be her friend and not see him or at least hear about him. When he found another woman, I knew Troian would mention her, and it would hurt too much. *God, why did my life have to be so unfair?* Sobs shook my whole body. Toro whined and nuzzled my cheek. I rubbed his ears. "It's just you and me, Toro," I whispered brokenly.

Images of that night weeks ago and of the past assailed me. I screamed, "Why?" Hate and despair filled me. Slowly, I got to my feet. It was time to dull the pain. It had been a long time since I had the urge to do this but today was my breaking point. My newest monsters might be gone, but the past wasn't.

Spawn: Chapter 9

My anger over finding out Kimera had left town was throbbing inside of me. How dare she do this? Why would she up and leave without a word to anyone, especially Troian? It had been only minutes ago I found out she was gone.

Walking into the clubhouse to see Troian and get a report on whether she'd talked to Kimera or not today since no one was at Lash's house, I noticed it was eerily quiet. Glancing at my watch, I realized it was early. Most people would still be at work. It wasn't the weekend. I saw Rhaines behind the bar stocking it. He gave me a chin lift along with an odd look. Scanning the room, I saw Lash, Troian, and Reaper sitting at one of the tables. They were staring at me. Both men frowned, and Troi appeared upset. Immediately, I knew something was wrong. I hurried over to them.

"What happened? Tell me," I ordered.

"Have a seat," Reaper said, pointing to an empty chair across from him.

I shook my head no. "I don't want to sit, just tell me. You talked to her, didn't you?" I directed the last bit to Troian. She exchanged a worried look with Lash as she nibbled on her bottom lip.

"Spawn, sit, and then we'll tell you," Reaper said firmly. I knew from his tone that he wasn't about to bend on this, so I jerked the chair out and dropped into it. I leaned forward over the table. "Go," I ordered.

She hesitated for a moment, then softly, she began to talk. "I went to the house to see Kimera today. She wasn't answering my calls, and I was concerned something might've happened or she was deeper into her depression and was cutting me off completely. She's never not answered when I called her before. Although she won't talk about what happened, she'll at least talk to me about other stuff."

I wanted to tell her to hurry the fuck up and get to the point, but I knew Lash would hit me, and Reaper might do the same. Besides, I didn't want to be ugly to Troian. She didn't deserve it, so I held onto my temper and silently prayed she'd hurry up.

"When I got there, her car wasn't where she usually parks it. I knocked on the door anyway, but there was no answer, and I didn't hear Toro barking. I thought she might be in town running errands, so I stayed for a while. An hour later, I gave up and decided to go to town and see if I could spot her. I didn't, which led me to call the hospital to check if she was working. It's her day off, but she gets called in all the time, you know."

"Babe, Spawn's about to explode. Just tell him," Lash urged her gently.

"She wasn't at work. They said she had a family emergency, and they didn't know when she was coming back," she said in a rush.

"Okay, so where does her family live? It could be she's caught up with whatever took her out of town," I said, trying not to think the worst.

She shook her head. "She doesn't have a family. She was raised in foster care after her granny died. Remember, she told us about her. The reason she raised her was there was no one else, I think. She told me that when I asked what her name meant and if she'd asked her family, she said she didn't know. If there was anyone, she wouldn't be close to them. No one took her in when she lost her parents. She's gone, and I have no clue where she went. What if she never comes back?"

A shaft of pain went through me. She was gone. Where? Why? What if she was gone for good? All those questions went through my mind until I shut them down. I could find her. I reached across the table and grabbed her hand. I gave it a gentle squeeze. "Don't worry, I'll find her. You stay here. How long ago did you find out she was gone?"

"About an hour ago," she told me. I didn't yell and ask why no one had called me to tell me; instead, I stood up.

Before I could walk out, Reaper sternly demanded, "You find out where she is, and we'll help you go get her. It was time we made her see we're here for her, and no matter what, we always will be. Go find your woman, then we'll go after her."

"Thanks, pres. I'll let you know as soon as I find something. I need to do some searching for her to find out if she has anyone to go to."

He nodded. Lash gave me a sympathetic look. The closer I got to home, the more my facade of calm slipped until I walked into the house, slamming the door behind me. I stomped into my office. I needed peace and quiet to track her down. And when I did, I was going after her and spanking her ass before bringing her back. Sitting down and bringing my computer to life, I did what I swore I wouldn't. I began to dig into her life. First, I tried the easy thing, and I sent her a text message.

Me: Hey, Hotcake, it's Spawn. Where are you? You've got us worried to death. Troian is freaking out. Text or call me.

I waited five whole minutes, and when I still had no reply, I tried to track her phone. My program came up with zilch. She must have it turned off, or it was dead. Next, I got online and started to investigate her. I started with her name and driver's license, which I knew. From there, I got into the employee files at the hospital, only this time I went into the personnel files. I found she had no emergency contact or anyone listed as her next of kin. I did find a former employer, but it was someone not in Bristol.

Working from there, I slowly pieced enough together to get me to the state she was born in. Most people didn't know their social security number indicated where they were issued the number. The first three numbers were the area, and based on hers, which was four-three-four, that was Louisiana. Working through prior addresses and the child services there, I was able to piece together more about her. I found out she'd been raised by her maternal grandmother until she died when she was ten years old. That was the one she told us about who taught her to cook.

When her granny died, Kimera went into the foster care system. She was never adopted, although she did live in a few foster homes. The first was from the time she was orphaned to eleven. It had been only temporary. The home she was in from eleven until thirteen ended when the mom unexpectedly died. The social worker's notes indicated if she hadn't died, the family planned to keep Kimera. The last one was from fourteen to sixteen. The file only said it ended when the family said they could no longer keep her. She spent the last two years living in a group home.

As soon as she turned eighteen, Kimera left town and moved to the other side of the state. She worked and put herself through school. It was after she graduated that she moved to Virginia. Once I had this information, which didn't tell me much, I left it be and went to search her social media to see if there might be clues there on where she might be.

I was disappointed to see she had very little she ever posted about. Nothing which would lead me to where she was or someone who might know. It was basically an empty profile. She didn't post pictures and stuff like a lot of people did. Dropping this search, I brought up her credit cards and bank account. I had an alert set to tell me if she used her phone or turned it on. It would automatically trace the cell tower closest to it.

It was when I was researching the latter two things that I found a charge on a credit card she never used. It was in Lake Charles, Louisiana, which was where she was originally from. It was at a hotel there. Excitement filled me as I worked to see if I could find and gain access to cameras at or around the hotel. I decided to do that to confirm she was there rather than just ride off to find her. However, it would be too much of a coincidence for a charge to register there and her not being there.

My luck held, and in short order, I had found and gotten into the hotel's CCTV. It was really disheartening to see how easy it was to break into security and closed-circuit systems. You'd think they'd make them much more hacker-proof, but it was lucky for me they weren't. I checked the time of the charge and saw it had been posted early this morning. We didn't know exactly when she left, and it would've taken over twelve hours to drive there, assuming she'd taken two days to do it, so I searched for her vehicle and went back into the recordings.

It wasn't a quick process. I was about to say forget it when I noted her car on the tape. It was time-stamped at eight o'clock Central last night. I saw her go check in and then come out to her car to grab her suitcase and go inside again. I left it running as I searched for flights and was about to shut it down and go get my stuff together to go after her when my heart dropped, and acid filled my belly. There was a shot not long after she checked in. It showed her leaving the hotel, except she wasn't alone. Walking out with her was a man.

They had their arms wrapped around each other and were smiling. I watched as he opened the passenger door to another car and helped her inside. When he got in on the driver's side, she leaned over to him. It was obvious from the way he was facing her and how he bent his head that they were kissing. Absolute fury careened through me. I let out a roar. It took everything in me not to sweep everything off my desk, including my computer.

She'd left to go be with another man! A man who no one here knew anything about. Why? If she had a man, why keep him a secret? Furiously typing because I had to know who he was, I tapped into the Louisiana DMV and ran his license plate. It wasn't long before I knew his name, date of birth, and address. From there, I traced him further and what I found made me more furious. He was married and the father of two kids. The reason for her secrecy and running off without a word was that she was having an affair with a married man. A man who must travel for his work. This was the only answer for how they saw each other when they lived so far apart. She was his out-of-state mistress. No wonder she didn't talk about him or want anything to do with me. Disgust filled me, along with extreme anger.

❦❦❦

I was over this celebration. All I wanted to do was get drunk and forget. Forget I ever met a woman named Kimera. I knew no one would miss me if I slunk off to my house. In fact, they'd be glad to see me go. Even though I knew it wasn't any of their fault, I was taking my "pissed off at her" attitude out on them. I had to stop that. They didn't deserve it.

Tonight was supposed to be all about celebrating Colt getting his patch. I was glad for him. I really was.

I just couldn't seem to express it. All I could do for the past week was think about how she'd been hiding shit and was involved in adultery. I would've never thought she'd be involved with a married man, let alone one with kids.

I'd kept myself from searching further into him and her, but it had been hard. I wanted to know what he had that she found so damn attractive. I would've given her anything she wanted and treated her like a queen. He couldn't do that. He had to hide her existence. Unless he divorced his wife, he couldn't marry her. Would they be happy to keep their relationship a secret and at most have a second family together? The thought ate at me.

A hand coming down hard on my right shoulder got my attention. I looked up through blurry eyes to find Reaper, Lash, Mayhem, Maniac, and Crusher standing there, frowning at me. Shit, I guess they were here to get to the bottom of my attitude and tell me to get over it. Believe me, if I could, I would.

"Get up and come with us," Reaper growled.

"I know what you're gonna say, Pres. I swear, I'll stop being a bastard to everyone," I promised, hoping I could do it. The last thing I wanted was to ostracize my brothers.

"Damn right you will, and we know how you can do it. Let's go," Maniac added.

Knowing it was useless to argue with three of the officers and Lash, I sighed and wearily got to my feet. I hung on to my beer, though. I had a feeling I'd need it and a lot more after this talk was over. As

I followed them away from the party and to Reaper's office, I wondered if I was about to get an ass beating to adjust my attitude. Maybe it would do some good. Fuck if anything else seemed to help.

Lash closed the door, and I was pushed down into one of the chairs. The others stood around the room, with Reaper taking his seat behind his desk. He crossed his arms over his chest. "Talk. Tell us what the hell happened with you and Kimera."

"Nothing happened. She left. You know that," was my immediate snappy reply.

"Brother, it was more than her just leaving. When our women left, we went after them. We thought you were doing the same, and then bam, you backed off and became a total fucking bear. What's stopping you from going after her and making her see her place is here with you? Hell, you went with me when I fetched Troian back when she was pissed with me," Lash reminded me.

"You and Troi and the other old ladies were different. Kimera isn't interested in me or in being here."

"How do you know that? Did you ask her? She's hurting after what happened to her," Maniac added.

I snorted. "Yeah, believe me, she's not hurting. She's just fine."

"What the fuck is that supposed to mean?" Crusher snapped.

"It means she's where and with whom she wants. Let's drop it. I'll stop being a bear." I went to stand up, but Mayhem pushed me back down.

"You sit your ass right there. See, we wondered what the hell was going on with you, so I asked a favor. You're gonna listen and keep your mouth shut," Reaper barked. As I stared at him, he picked up the phone and dialed. I wondered who the hell he was calling and what this was about. It wasn't long before a voice answered. I recognized it immediately. It was Smoke.

"I take it you got his ass with you," Smoke said as a way of greeting.

"Yep, he's across the desk, glaring at us right now. You said you found something and wanted to talk to us. Tell us," Reaper ordered.

Uneasiness began to worm its way inside me. What had Reaper done, and what did Smoke have to tell us?

"Got it. So I did what you asked since it seems Spawn wasn't doing it or sharing what he knew. I can tell you that he found her. I came across his digital footprints." My heart jumped. Shit, he'd gone searching for Kimera. How the hell did he know what I did? I swear I covered my tracks, but then again, he was the best.

"There's no need for that," I told him gruffly.

"Shut it. Keep going, Smoke," Reaper said.

"Well, I found her in Lake Charles, Louisiana, where she grew up. It seems she went there. She has been staying at a hotel in town. I don't know if she shared much with you, but she was orphaned at ten and was raised until she was eighteen in foster care."

I worked to tune him out. I didn't need to hear what he found. I had no doubt he was about to tell my brothers about her secret man and how I'd made a fool of myself over the bitch. Disgust not only with her but also with myself increased. A loud slapping sound jarred me back to attention. It was Lash.

"Are you listening to Smoke?"

"I already know what he found. Let me save him some time. She's there with a man. She has a boyfriend, a married one with two kids. Apparently, she couldn't wait for him to travel this way for his work, so she went to him," I snarled. Stunned disbelief appeared on all of their faces.

"That can't be," Crusher said gruffly.

"It is," I said.

At the same time, Smoke said, "It's not."

"What the fuck do you mean it's not? I saw them on the security camera at her hotel the night she got there. They were kissing in his car after he picked her up. He's married."

"I don't know what you think you saw, but she's not his mistress or girlfriend or whatever you want to call it. Did you bother to dig deeper once you saw whatever it was and found out his name and that he was married?" Smoke asked.

"There was no need," I told him.

"Yes, there was. You need to get your ass to Lake

Charles if you can't get her to come back, and you need to talk to that woman. There's shit happening you have no clue about, and if what I suspect is true, it's ugly. Worse than what happened with the Gusevs. Fuck, she should've asked for help," he muttered.

"What do you mean? What have you found out?" I snarled as I sat forward in my chair. I wanted to come through the phone and shake it out of him.

"Enough to know she's not involved with that man the way you think, and there are too many unanswered questions. She's been spending time with him, his kids, and his wife. If you don't wanna help her, then I'll talk to Terror, and we will," Smoke snapped. He was truly pissed at me. I sat there feeling poleaxed. What had I missed? Right on the heels of that thought came dread.

"We'll take care of it, although we appreciate you doing this, Smoke. Depending on what we find out, I'll let Terror, or you know if I think we need reinforcements. Would you send me what you have? By the looks of Spawn, he might be broken," Reaper said.

"Sure, I'll send it over. And Spawn, if she's the one, you'd better beg to get her back, and when you do, tell her what you thought. You don't want this coming out down the road, and believe me, it will. Later," Smoke said before hanging up.

I put my head in my hands. Jesus Christ, what did I do? It was eerily quiet for a minute or so, and then I raised my head to meet their gazes. I saw pity, sympathy, and disappointment. I met Reaper's eyes. "I need to see what he sent. And I need to go to Lake Charles."

"Before you go running off, we need to talk. You said you saw them kissing in his car. Are you sure? Hell, the sparks the two of you gave off were enough for us to know there was interest on both sides, even if she was subdued after the attack. Why didn't you tell anyone what you found out?" Pres asked.

"Because it gutted me, and I felt like a fool for thinking she was the one! It was like..." I paused, not wanting to say it.

"It was like history repeating itself," Mayhem said quietly. All of them had been part of the club when I joined, but Mayhem was the one to whom I told my story the night we met. I hadn't talked about my old girlfriend to anyone else, that I recalled.

"Yeah, it reminded me of the girlfriend who picked another man over me all those years ago. It's why I left Montana and was wandering the country when I met Mayhem. I guess seeing Kimera with him made me feel like it was happening again, only I feel more for her than I ever did the first one by far. There's no comparison."

"Can you show us what you saw?" Maniac asked.

I didn't want to see it again, but if they wanted to verify it, I'd show them. "I can. It's on my computer in my office. We'll have to go there." I didn't say aloud that as painful as it was, I'd saved it. I think I did it so that if I ever got weak and wanted to go after her, I'd have it to remind me not to. Seeing their nods, I got up, and we all went to my office. It didn't take me long to bring it up. I made myself watch it.

When she and the man drove off after kissing each other, it was Lash who broke the silence. "I can see how maybe it could've been seen as a kiss, but it's not for sure. Add to it what Smoke said, and I think you owe it to both of you to call her. Ask what she's doing there and when she's coming back. If she doesn't tell you, then you can decide if you want to go after her or not."

"I agree. There are other explanations for what that was. It's getting late. Do you want to call her tonight or tomorrow? Has Troian talked to her?" Reaper asked Lash.

"She has a couple of times. Kimera wouldn't say where she was or why she left other than she needed time to get herself together. It's causing stress for Troian, which I hate," he said.

"What do you want to do?" Maniac asked me.

"I'll call her tonight and see if I can get her to talk to me. If not, then I'm headed to Louisiana. I was a goddamn idiot, and I refuse to continue to be one. I may be gone for a while, convincing her to give me another chance if I'm wrong about him and her," I warned them.

"You do what you have to do. We'll survive. Let us know what you need. Now, I think we should get the hell out. No one needs to listen to this call," Reaper added with a smirk.

The others mumbled their agreement, and before they filed out, they patted my arm. As the door shut behind them, I took a few moments to collect myself before dialing her number. It was ten at night our time, which meant it was nine in Louisiana. It wasn't too late. *Let this be a huge misunderstanding. God, don't let me fuck this up*, I pleaded. Hope was beginning to rear its head.

My hand actually shook a tiny bit as I pushed the call button. I was about to hang up after letting it ring several times when she answered. I heard the hesitancy in her voice as soon as she said hello. "Hello? Spawn? Is that you? Is everything alright?"

"Hello Kimera, yes, it's me. Everything is good. I was calling to see how you're doing. You've been gone for a couple of weeks. Everyone is wondering when you'll be coming home. You missed Colt's patch-in party tonight."

"Oh, I'm glad he made it. Tell him I said congratulations. I bet he's happy," she said softly, but I could hear she was glad he'd gotten it.

"He is. He's called Gravel now. The guys have been teasing him, saying it's because he wrecked, but really it's his voice."

I heard a soft chuckle. "That's so mean of you guys, but funny. How've you been? Busy?"

"I've been okay, not too busy. I'd be better if you came back. I miss you. You didn't say how much longer you'll be gone. Troian is missing the hell out of you, too. We all are. Where are you?"

She didn't answer immediately, so I waited as patiently as I could. Finally, she did. "I needed time away to get myself straightened out. I'm not sure how much longer I'll be. I miss everyone, too. I'm visiting an old friend."

"If you miss everyone, then that means you miss sparring with me, I see. I admit, no one here likes to go at it with me like you do. You can't expect me to go from that to cold turkey, Hotcake. I'm in withdrawal," I teased her. I didn't want to cause her to worry or stress.

She laughed this time. "Okay, Studcake, I'll let you know when I know I'm coming back. Try to resist going into a funk because you miss me. I hate to do this, but I'm at my friend's house, and I can't talk."

"That's alright. I'll let you go. Just promise if I call or text, you'll answer me. I'm worried about you."

"You don't need to worry about me, but thank you. Yes, I'll answer your texts, and if I can, I'll answer your calls. That's not as easy to do as texts are. Take care, Spawn."

"I will darlin', and you take care, too. Talk soon," I softly said before she hung up.

As soon as the line went dead, I got to work on purchasing an airline ticket. There was something going on. I could hear it in her voice. She'd be talking to and seeing me way sooner than she imagined.

Kimera: Chapter 10

A day later, I was still thinking about Spawn's call last night. Seeing his name appear on my phone had shaken me. I almost didn't answer but found I couldn't resist. I hadn't heard a peep out of him since he'd texted me after I left Bristol. At the time, I didn't trust myself to answer him, so I didn't. When he never texted again or called, I figured he'd forgotten all about me. After all, why would he keep trying to talk to me? The first time was merely because of Troian, no doubt.

Hearing his voice made my whole body tingle and made me miss him more than I already was. Which sounded crazy when I thought about it. We'd only known each other for less than two months. Most of that time, we'd spent arguing with each other. I should be happy to be away from him, but I wasn't. Even when he called me Hotcake, I smiled. The name was growing on me, although I wouldn't tell him it was.

When I rejoined Claudia and Sonny after ending the call, they'd asked me who was on the phone. I'd told them about the Punishers and their families. I hadn't said much about Spawn. I tried to downplay it.

"Oh, it was just someone back in Bristol wanting to check on me," I said as I sat down on the couch. It was quiet since the kids were in bed.

"Who? Troian?" Claudia asked.

"No, not her. Is that one of the kids I hear?" I asked, trying to divert her.

"Kimera, you don't have to tell us if you'd rather not. I was just curious. Sorry," she said with a hesitant smile. I felt bad for making her uneasy.

"No, it's alright. Sorry, I didn't mean to act weird. It was actually one of the men. His name is Spawn. He wanted to know how I was doing and if I knew when I'd be back. They had a party tonight for one of their prospects, Colt. He's now a patched member and going by the name Gravel."

"Really, that sounds like fun. I can't believe you know a motorcycle club. It seems wild and so different from the way you said they are and what I've seen and heard," she said.

"They are. I admit I was surprised when I first got to know them. They're a great bunch, and the guys are totally protective of their women and kids."

"Why would Spawn call you and not Troian? Is he someone special?" Sonny asked.

I was taking a drink from my glass when he asked. I choked. As I sputtered and turned pink, he laughed, then said, "I guess that answers my question. So, tell us about him. What's he like? What does he think of you being here? Why didn't he come with you?"

I had to wait until I could speak to answer him. Claudia might back off, but I'd found Sonny wouldn't. I liked him better for it, at least when it came to Claudia *and their kids.* "He's their computer expert, a hacker, I guess you'd call him. He's nothing like I thought a hacker would be. He's good friends with Lash, Troi's man. As for what he thinks of why I'm here, they don't know why I came. All I told them was I needed time away." *I didn't tell them more because I didn't want to give away the fact I'd been attacked in Bristol. They didn't need to know that.*

"Why? God, are the two of you involved, and I caused trouble between you? I should've thought more before calling you," *Claudia fretted.*

"No, we're not together. Please, I'm happy you reached out to me after all this time. I've always wondered what happened to you. I didn't know what to tell them."

That statement led to us talking more about why I was there and what we'd been able to do so far, which wasn't much. I was frustrated and on the brink of asking for help, but if I did, then I'd have to explain why to the club. I wasn't sure I could handle them knowing.

My phone buzzed, making me jump. I glanced at it. It was a message from Claudia asking if I was still coming over for dinner. I hurried to tell her yes. As soon as I did, I got up from my hotel bed and went to the bathroom to freshen up. There was no use daydreaming. Tonight, we were planning our strategies more.

Ten minutes later, I was ready to go. She wouldn't care if I came early. It was better than moping around here. Grabbing my purse and a jacket, I checked to make sure I had everything I needed. Seeing the phone I'd left on the bed, I grabbed it. Putting it in my pocket, I hurried to the door. I opened the door and then froze. Standing there with his arm raised was Spawn. He had a somber expression on his face. My purse fell out of my nerveless hand to the ground.

"Kimera, hello, sweetheart," his deep voice made me shiver.

I didn't know what to say. All I could do was stare at him like an idiot. My legs went weak, so I had to grab the door frame to keep from falling. Seeing me do that, he frowned, and then I was swept back into the room as he closed the door. His arm wrapped around me and supported me to the bed. I thumped down.

"Babe, are you alright?"

"I-I'm...W-what're you doing here? How did you find me?" I croaked stupidly. Duh, he was a hacker.

He sat next to me. His arm around my shoulders soothingly rubbed lightly up and down my arm, adding to my goosebumps. "Let me get you a drink. Then I'll answer your questions. Stay," he said before he got up and picked up the empty glass on my nightstand. He went to the bathroom. While he was gone, I struggled to get my brain to work.

He was back before I accomplished that. After sinking down in front of me, he held it up to my mouth. I tried to take it away from him, but he held onto it. I let him tip it up so I could take a sip. I pressed his hand away once I had enough to wet my dry mouth. "Thank you," I said.

"You're welcome. Now, you wanted to know what

I'm doing here and how I found you. Let me answer the last question first. You know what I do for a living, baby. I'm a hacker, among other things. You've been gone for two weeks and wouldn't tell Troian or me where you went. You told me last night you had no idea when you were coming home. I had to come and make sure you were alright. I'm here to help you with whatever brought you back here. I didn't get the impression you had friends here."

"How did you know I was here in this hotel?"

"I can access camera systems, the DMV, credit card accounts, bank accounts, phones, and more. It wasn't that hard," he explained.

Terror filled me. "What else did you find when you went searching for me?"

"I didn't dig into more. I wanted to give you a chance to tell me what's going on. Who are you visiting? Why?"

"Please, don't ask me that, Spawn. I need you to turn around and go home. I'm begging you," I whimpered.

He frowned and shook his head no. "Baby, I can't do that. It's obvious from the way you're reacting that it's something serious, and you're scared. Let me help you. Surely you know me, and the club will help you?" He was holding my hands as he said it.

I hung my head and stared at our intertwined hands. God, the feel of his hands on mine felt so good. Just a tiny touch and I felt safe. "Spawn, I know you all would. It's not that. It's the fact you shouldn't have to deal with it."

"Do you remember what I told you when you went back to your house? How I wanted you to be mine?" he asked. I nodded yes. I had thought about it so many times.

"That right there makes this mine to help you deal with, no matter what it is. Even if you weren't, as a friend to Troian and the club, I'd still do it. First, let me get us something to eat then we can talk. You're pale as a ghost. I don't want you fainting."

I gasped. "Oh God, I have to call Claudia. They're expecting me for dinner soon."

"Whose Claudia? Is she the woman you've been visiting while you're here? The one with a husband and two kids?"

"I thought you said you didn't dig further!"

"I know about them, but only their names, nothing else. Were you going over just for dinner, or is there more to it?"

"Spawn, don't—" I went to plead, but he cut me off.

"I'm not leaving until you tell me everything. And I have some things to confess to you as well. Something I'm not proud of, but you need to know. Now, we can do it just the two of us or with them since I think they're involved. Your call, but before you decide, I do have something else to ask you first."

I could see that he wasn't about to let me get away with not telling him. I'd been debating anyway if it was time to tell the club to see if they might be able to help. My shame wasn't worth letting this continue. Plus, I was tired. "Fine, we'll talk. Ask what you want, and then I'll let them know that I'm not coming tonight."

"Good. What I want is for you to call me Aidan, at least when it's just us. Will you do that, please?"

"Aidan? That's your name? I thought you only went by your road name."

"Yes, it's Aidan Priestley, actually, and we typically don't allow people to use our actual name unless it's someone special, as in our old lady or sometimes our blood family. Nothing would make me happier than to have you use it, Kimera."

My heart skipped. I was stunned but also excited. Surely, he wouldn't want me to do that unless he was serious about us despite the way I'd pushed him away and what happened with the Gusevs. But would he knowing the whole truth make him change his mind? "If you want me to call you Aidan after we talk, then I will, but you might change your mind once you hear what I have to say."

"There's nothing you can tell me that will do that. Unless you're already married or have a boyfriend."

"No, I don't have either of those."

"I'm relieved to hear it. Would you like me to get us something to eat before we do this? I can bring it in, or we can go out if you prefer."

"No, no food yet. I wouldn't be able to eat it, and if I did, I'd probably throw up. Let me do this before I chicken out."

He eased around on the bed, putting his back to the headboard. He patted the bed beside him. I slowly moved up there. He took my hand again and gently squeezed it. Taking a moment to compose myself, I began to tell him about my past.

"My parents couldn't raise me. When I was three, they gave me over to my mom's mother to raise. She's the one I told you taught me how to cook. I had her until I was ten. When she died, there was no family to take me in, or at least none I knew of, so I was sent to be a foster kid. I was matched to a family for about a year, but it was only temporary while the foster system tried to find me a permanent place. When I was eleven, I went to another family. They were great. I really liked them, and they treated me well. I think I would've stayed with them until I was eighteen, except the mom got sick and died when I was thirteen.

"I wasn't placed with a family again until I was fourteen. They'd had foster kids before me. They treated me well overall. I had no complaints. I was with them for almost a year when they took in another girl. She was three years younger than me, and her name was Claudia."

"Claudia, the same woman you've been visiting?"

"Yes, the same one. It was great having a younger sister. I always wanted one growing up. We were close, and we were the only foster children in the house at the time. The family had a natural son, Paden, who was older than us, but he didn't live with them. He lived a couple of hours away and was in college. I never even saw him the first year I was there. It was several months after Claudia came when he came home claiming he needed a break from college." I paused because talking about this was hard. I'd only wanted to forget it, but recent events made it impossible.

"Kimera, what did he do?" Spawn growled.

I fought back the tears that wanted to fall from my eyes. I wasn't able to meet his gaze. His hand gently gripped my chin and raised it up, not giving me a choice. "Tell me. Let it go," he said softly.

"He seemed not to pay much attention to us unless he was picking on us. He would play practical jokes on us all the time, but they were never funny. They were humiliating or cruel. We kept wishing he'd go back to school, but he didn't. His parents thought he was an angel, and telling on him got us in trouble, not him. Then, two months after he moved back in, his parents were out of town for the night for a class reunion. They left him in charge. Claudia and I were in bed. We were lucky enough to have our own bedrooms, which wasn't usually the case."

His hand tightened on my face a bit. God, this was so hard to do. I wanted to run out of the hotel and hide, but I'd come this far. I had to finish it.

"I woke up because I heard a weird noise. At first, I had no idea what it was. It was dark in my room, and the clock showed it was after one in the morning. I was about to go back to sleep, thinking I had imagined it when he appeared next to the bed. I let out a little scream and asked him what was wrong. I thought something happened with his parents being gone like an accident."

My stomach was cramped, and I wrapped my arms around it. "Finish it," he urged me. There was a fire which had started to burn in his stare.

"He stared at me funny, and it made me begin to worry. I was about to tell him to leave when he lunged at me, pinned me down, and put his hand over my mouth. He told me he had been watching me, and I'd teased him enough. It was time to give him what he wanted. I tried to fight him, but he was much bigger than me. We struggled and fought, but I couldn't get him off me. We fought for a long time, and then he-he raped me," I whispered.

Spawn let out a loud roar and jumped to his feet. The rage on his face was scary. I moved further across the bed. When he saw me do it, he tried to school his features to be calmer. He paced back and forth as I huddled there for several minutes before he said anything.

"What did his parents say when you told them?"

"I didn't tell them," I mumbled.

"You didn't tell them! Why not? It wasn't your fault, you know that, don't you? He was an adult, and you were a child. How old were you?"

"I was fifteen, close to sixteen. I couldn't tell

them. He threatened me if I did. He said if I told and if I didn't let him have me whenever he wanted, he'd get it from Claudia. She was thirteen but developing fast, Aidan! I couldn't let him do that to her, so I submitted." The tears escaped. Now he knew my biggest shame. I felt so dirty telling him.

He was over to me and back on the bed, holding me in a flash. "Shh, baby, don't cry. It's alright. Is there more? With that happening, why come back here even to see Claudia? You can't have good memories of this place."

"There's more. He kept it up for the next four months. Thank God he used a condom every time, or knowing my luck, I would've gotten pregnant."

"Why did it stop?"

"I finally got the courage to tell his parents."

"How did they take it?"

"They thought I was lying, and they sent me back to the orphanage. I was terrified he'd target Claudia next, but I heard he left and went back to college a few days after they sent me back to the group home. After I turned eighteen, I got far away from here, went to school, and ended up in Bristol. Claudia was moved to another foster home, too, eventually, and I lost track of her. That is until she contacted me two weeks ago and said she wanted to see me. She said we needed to talk. That's why I packed up Toro and we came here."

"Speaking of Toro, where is he? Why isn't he with you?"

"This hotel has a policy against animals, even if they're a service animal. I tried to tell them he was my protection, but they didn't care. I tried to find one that would allow him, but they all said they were full. I don't think it's legal for them to do that, but I didn't have a choice. He's been staying at Claudia and Sonny's house. The kids love him, and he's getting all kinds of attention, so he's in heaven."

"I need to know what Claudia wanted to talk to you about. Then you're gonna tell me that fuckers full name and anything else you know about him. Is he still here in Lake Charles?" he snarled.

"We think he is. Claudia called me because she saw him in town. He approached her on the street and was inappropriate. She was running errands and he scared her. When she told Sonny, he tried to find him, but he couldn't. She wanted to tell me about it and what he said in order to warn me. He mentioned my name to her, and that clued her into what he did to me. God, it was all for nothing! I let him continue to hurt me to protect her, never knowing he was doing it to her too and using the threat that if she told and didn't submit, he'd come after me," I sobbed.

Thinking about it and how I'd felt and then to have Spawn know it made me sick to my stomach. It rebelled. I shot off the bed and ran into the bathroom. I lost what little I had in my belly. As I heaved, my hair was pulled back. I moaned. He was standing there helping me. I didn't want him to see this. It was gross.

"Please, go, you don't need to see this," I moaned.

"Like hell, I'll leave you alone. How is your belly feeling? Better?" he asked. I'd stopped throwing up after the third heave. I nodded my head yes. It wasn't rolling nearly as much.

"Good, stay there," he said as he stepped away. I watched as he got a cup off the sink and filled it with water and some of the mouthwash I had on the counter. Then he wet a washcloth before bringing both to me. The washcloth was placed in my hand, and the glass was put into my other hand. "Swish and spit."

I did as he instructed. I was too tired and drained to argue. When I was done, he gently wiped my face and then helped me to my feet. He held onto me as he guided me out of the bathroom and over to the bed. "Lay down, babe."

I crawled onto the bed, and he sat beside me. He rubbed my back. I was facing away from him. "Babe, why didn't you tell us this, especially after what happened with the Gusevs? It had to have brought back all the shit that fucker did to you. We could've found him and taken care of him already. You don't need to be doing this alone," he chastised me a little.

"I couldn't ask you to do that! You just took out five men. You and the club didn't need to add more bodies to your resume. The more you do, the more likely it is you'll get caught. Yes, the Gusevs brought things back I thought I'd conquered, but you need to know something."

"What's that?" He sounded tense.

"They didn't rape me that night. It was close, so close, but you bursting in when you did saved me. Zandro was about to do it when you guys came storming in. I couldn't say anything because I was afraid I'd blurt out what happened when I was a kid. I don't want to make this your business. It's Claudia and I's fight. It's time he was made to pay for what he did. God knows how many others he's done this to. I should've gone to the police, but when his parents didn't believe me, I figured no one else would either."

"When are you going to realize that anything that happens to you is my business? The club isn't letting this go, and I sure as hell won't. You'll be safe. I promise you that. Tell me his name. Let me protect you. It's my job and my honor to do it, my little She-Wolf."

"She-Wolf? What's up with calling me that?" I asked. I'd never heard him use it before. It was always Hotcake or Babe. Coming from him, I now found I didn't mind being called babe or baby.

He grinned. "You are so feisty and ready to defend others even if it places you in danger. You're like a she-wolf protecting her cubs. Would you prefer Hotcake?"

I pushed him, and he barely rocked. "Keep calling me Hotcake, and I may have to beat you. As for she-wolf, I think I like it. It sounds strong. God knows I need to be that. It might help."

"Kimera, you're already strong. Look at all you went through, and you're still standing. That bastard can't run and hide from me. He'll get what he has coming to him, and it'll be because of you. I think we should let you rest and then I'd like to meet Claudia and her husband. I need all the details I can get to track him. Also, I have to make sure you're safe. If he's around, I don't want him seeing you and trying anything. Will you take me to meet them?"

I didn't want to involve him or the club, but it did make me feel better knowing they would help and have our backs. After a minute or so of silence, I answered him. "Yes, I can do that. I need to check with them to make sure they're alright with it, but I don't see them minding. Anything to make Paden pay."

The way he twisted his mouth told me that he had some very painful ideas on how to make him pay. I knew I wouldn't mind them at all. Some might even coincide with mine.

"I'll call them right now," I told him as I took my phone out of my pocket. I found Claudia's name and hit the call button.

It took three rings before she answered. "Hey, are you on your way yet? We're running a bit behind."

"I haven't left the hotel yet, but I have someone here who wants to come meet you and Sonny. He can help us. Would that be alright?"

Her cheeriness switched to caution. I could hear it in her voice. "It depends on exactly who wants to meet us. I thought we were the only ones who knew about you-know-who." I heard Sonny murmuring in the background, asking her what was up. She told him she'd tell him in a minute.

"Remember I told you about Spawn with the Iron Punishers? He's here, and he knows what happened. He wants to help and to do that he needs all the information we can give him."

"What!? He's here? Oh my God, a real biker is offering to help. Yes, bring him to dinner. Hurry and get here," she said excitedly.

I laughed. "Control yourself, Claud. He'll be afraid to come with you acting all hyper," I teased.

"Hey, I'm an old married lady. I have to get my thrills somehow. No, Sonny, I'm not trying to replace you, but I've never talked to a real biker before. I've seen them. I wanna meet him and ask him some questions," she told him in a whisper that wasn't really a whisper. I glanced at Spawn to find he had an amused look on his face. He winked at me.

"Tell her I'll answer her questions and ask her what's for dinner. Do we need to bring anything? I'm starved."

I had it on speaker, so she heard him. A squeal came through the phone. "Oh, goody. No need to bring anything but yourselves. Toro is waiting impatiently for his momma. See you in a bit, and Spawn?"

"Yeah."

"Be prepared for a lot of questions."

This earned her a laugh. I told her we'd see her soon, then hung up. I sat up. "Give me a couple of minutes to make myself presentable, and then we can go," I told him as I scooted off the mattress.

"I'll be right here waiting, although you're more than presentable, babe."

I didn't know what to say, so I didn't say anything. I went to the bathroom to compose myself. I hoped I wasn't making a mistake involving him. If something happened to him or the club, I'd never forgive myself, but I'd run out of ideas to find the bastard.

Spawn: Chapter 11

Knowing Claudia wanted to meet a real biker as she called me, I rode the bike I'd rented rather than riding with Kimera in her car. I wanted to be close to her, but I hated being in a cage, too. I made sure to stick close. It only took maybe twenty minutes to make it to the small community where her friends, I guess you'd call them, lived. The street was quiet as we pulled into the driveway of a small red brick house. It was two stories. The lawn was neat and there were plants in flower beds, although this time of year, they were rather dead-looking. It screamed young family home to me for some reason. I pulled in beside her.

As I got off the bike and removed my helmet, I heard a woman chattering as she came around the corner from the front door. There was a man right behind her. Toro bounded past them and up to Kimera, who dropped to her knees to pet him and get his kisses. When he saw me, his tail, I swear, wagged faster, and he gave her one final doggie kiss and then came to greet me. I scratched his head between his ears. He closed his eyes, and I swear he groaned.

"Hey boy, I've missed you. Have you been taking care of your mama? I bet you've been loving people making over you, haven't you?" I gave him a final scratch, then a pat on his side. Straightening, I walked over to Kimera and put an arm around her. I could tell she was nervous. I squeezed her closer to me. I wanted, no, actually needed, her touching me. I was happy when she put one of her arms around me in return. I smiled at the man and woman standing before us. I held out my hand to him first. The husband was sizing me up like I was him.

"Hi, I'm Spawn. Nice to meet you. Thanks for agreeing to let me come over and help."

"Hello, I'm Sonny, and this is my crazy wife, Claudia. If she gets too personal, just tell her no. She's been bouncing like a ball since she talked to Kimera. Come on in," he invited. Before he could turn to lead the way, his wife broke away from him and came to stand in front of me. She looked up with awe on her face.

"God, you're so tall. He's a giant, Kimmy. You can climb him like a tree. And look at those muscles. Can I see your leather vest and your bike? Do you ride one all winter? Isn't that cold? How long have you been in a biker gang?"

"Honey, let the man get in the house and something to drink before you go crazy asking your million questions," Sonny said with a tolerant smirk on his face.

"Oh, sorry. Yes, let's go inside. It's nice to meet you, Spawn. I need to check on the kids anyway. They're napping. Come," she ordered before heading back the way she came. Kimera smiled indulgently after her.

I bent down to whisper in Kimera's ear as we followed them. "Bet you're smiling because you're imagining climbing me like a tree. Go ahead, admit it. I don't mind. You can do it anytime, She-Wolf." I winked when I was done teasing her, although it wasn't really teasing.

A vision of her arms and legs wrapped around me as I held her against a wall and pounded into her or me holding her while standing in the middle of the room with her riding up and down on my cock came to mind. I began to harden and had to think of something else. I knew after what she confessed about her past and the incident with the Gusevs that she wouldn't be open to a man doing something like that to her any time soon, but God, when she was, I planned to pleasure her until she begged me to stop and I couldn't keep going.

Walking into the house, I took in the decor. It was nicely done and felt homey. There was as much pride in their home on the inside as on the outside from what I could see. The small entry opened directly into the living room. Off to the right was the kitchen. We followed them there. I could smell wonderful things cooking. Sonny indicated the stools at the bar, so I hauled one out for Kimera. As soon as she was seated, I took a seat next to her. The first few minutes were spent giving our drink orders and getting them. Sonny did it while his wife went to check on their kids. Once we had our drinks, she was back.

"The kids are still asleep. I'll let them be until it's almost time to eat. If I don't, they'll be cranky and want to eat as soon as they wake up. So, Spawn, I've got to ask how you got your name and what your real one is. And what about the questions I asked outside? Oh, and why're you here when yesterday you were in Virginia and never said you were coming?" She fired them off one right after the other.

Sonny sighed and gave me a sympathetic look. I grinned. "Well, let's see. This isn't a vest. It's called a cut. On the back is my club's emblem and name, and you can see here that my road name is on it, which is what Spawn is. I pretty much wear it all the time unless I'm somewhere it'll offend another club. It just so happens that our VP knows someone in the Dom club in your area, which is the dominant club, and they gave approval for me to be here and to wear my colors while I am. I'm called Spawn because when provoked, I can become like the devil. As for my real name, sorry, but only special people in my life, like Kimera, know and use it. I do ride most of the winter unless it's very snowy or icy. It's cold as hell, but you get used to it. I'm in a club, not a gang, and it's been ten years since I joined the Punishers as a prospect. I became a member nine years ago."

"And how did you end up here? I thought Kimera said she didn't tell anyone in Bristol where she was or what she was doing. Did she tell you?" She asked much more seriously.

"Claudia, maybe we should save this until after dinner. Let Spawn get to know us, and we get to know him. I need to put the steaks on the grill anyway if we want to eat soon. Spawn, you wanna come hang with me? We'll do the manly grill work and leave the women to talk about how great we are."

"Sure, sounds good."

As he took the plate with the steaks out of the fridge, I felt Claudia studying me. I didn't mind. Before going outside, I went up to Kimera and kissed her mouth lightly. She gave me a surprised look. I wanted to get her used to my touch a little at a time, and this seemed like one way to do it. "If you need me, just holler, baby. Okay?" I told her.

She smiled. "I'll be fine. I promise not to tell Claudia any of your secrets. Go cook my steak. I like mine medium. I'm starving."

"Bossy thing," I teased as I left. Her laughter followed me. Once we got outside and Sonny put the steaks on the grill, the real interrogation started. He faced me and crossed his arms as he frowned.

"Tell me, what the hell brings you here? I know for a fact Kimera was adamant that your club not be asked to help us. I want to know what she told you and what you plan to do about it, if anything. We're not fooling around with our intentions."

"First, tell me what she told you about my club and me, and then I'll answer your questions to a point," I countered.

If he thought he could intimidate me, he was wrong. Sure, he was a big guy. I would say six foot two and two hundred pounds. He was fit, too, but he would be no match for me. I calmly waited and let him see I wasn't scared of him and could out wait him. As we stared at each other, I saw his unease and worry. He was truly concerned about his wife, at least, if not Kimera, too. I respected him for protecting his wife. It was my job to protect Kimera.

"She just said that she has a friend who's dating a man in a motorcycle club. The club is very protective of them both. His club helped her friend out of a tough situation. Listen, I don't want us to get involved in anything to do with your businesses. I just want help with this for my wife."

"What do you think we do for businesses? Drugs? Guns? Extortion? Kidnapping and murder for hire?" I rattled off.

He grew tenser as I named them. I hated that those things were automatically the ideas people had about us just because we were in an MC. It was true. We might've dabbled in less than legal and nice things in the past, but never kidnapping, murder, or extortion. Sure, guns and selling weed had been part of it, among other things, but that was long behind the club.

"I don't want to know," he said abruptly.

"I can assure you, we're not involved in any of those things. We do have several businesses, but they're all legal. Hell, I oversee a storage unit facility. I can promise you, those units aren't full of dead bodies, illegal guns, or drugs," I said, chuckling. Part of the reason I laughed was that I thought of the places we actually did have the bodies, but he didn't need to know that.

"Really? A storage facility? Wow, okay, I feel stupid for making assumptions. Okay, tell me how you plan to help and what brought you here?"

"I'm here because I was worried about Kimera and why she abruptly left town and wouldn't say why, where she was, or anything. The whole club is concerned. After two weeks, enough was enough, and I tracked her down. I have skills with computers and finding people, among other things. If I can't do it, I have friends who can. She told me what happened years ago and that the man responsible was sighted by your wife in town. I plan to find him and make sure he never hurts anyone again."

"And by not hurting anyone, what do you mean? Put him in jail? Beat his ass and threaten him? Kill him?"

"What do you want to do to him for raping your wife repeatedly as a child?" I countered gruffly. I wouldn't outright admit anything to him. I had to protect myself and the club.

He clenched his fists and stared off into space for several heartbeats before he looked at me and answered. "Jail is too good for the fucker. I want him to hurt and never be able to do it again or for her to run the risk of laying eyes on the fucker."

I read between the lines. He wanted him dead. I gave him a single nod. "Then we agree, and I don't see us having any issues."

"Good, so tell me how you ended up running a storage unit," he asked with a grin. Chuckling, I told him why. It left me with a lot of time to devote to other things for the club. It didn't take long for the steaks to cook, and then we were back with the ladies. They had the rest of the food on the table. It was somewhat chaotic because while we were outside, the kids got up.

Their three-year-old son, Brent, was running around in excitement and playing with his cars and Toro. Their one-year-old daughter, Brie, was toddling unsteadily around, grabbing everything she could get her hands on, which at times was Toro. It was a full-time job watching and making sure they didn't get into anything they shouldn't.

Just like she was at the compound, Kimera was hands-on with them. She smiled a lot. I could see her being the same and more with our kids. God, I had to get her to see we were perfect for each other. I wanted this— quiet nights at home with our kids, maybe some friends over for dinner, and then time alone together at night.

Dinner ended up being really good, and I enjoyed it. As we ate, we kept the conversation to general topics. They told me what they did for work. I told them about what I did in general for the club, nothing too heavy. After we were done, it was time for the kids to play a bit, then get a bath and go to bed. It was a while before the house settled down. With the kids in bed, Toro was laid out on the floor in front of their fireplace. It was cool, so they'd turned it on. He was dozing.

"Sorry for that. They would've interrupted us the whole time if we'd tried to talk while they were awake," Claudia apologized.

"You don't have to feel bad for me. I understand. We don't have that many kids in our club family yet, but the ones we do are the same. We have a one-year-old, another who is close to a year and a half, and then a five-

and-half-year-old. They run us ragged. I could sleep for a whole day after watching one of them," I admitted.

I saw stunned expressions on all three faces. It was Kimera who broke it. "You babysit them? On your own? I knew you guys paid attention to them at gatherings and such, but not that you did more."

"Yep, so you see, I'm quite the catch, babe. I know how to change diapers and feed and bathe babies and kids. I'm ready for ours. Remember, you promised to marry me if I won the bet," I said with a wink.

She blushed. Claudia jumped on my remark. "What's this? You didn't say anything about you getting married and having kids, Kimera. Where's your ring? You're keeping secrets."

Kimera hastily answered her. "We're not getting married. Spawn is teasing me about a bet Troian and I made with him and his club brother, Lash. They ended up winning it, and part of it consisted of him teasing me about us having kids. He didn't say anything about marriage though."

"Tell us the bet," Claudia urged.

Seeing Kimera squirm, I decided to tell them for her, so I quickly recounted the basics of the bet and how we won. When I was done, Claudia was sitting there with her mouth hanging open, and Sonny was grinning.

"Oh my God, you watched a bunch of bikers fight? Tell me, were they all the size of him and covered in tattoos? If so, I need to see a rematch," she said.

"Hey, none of that shit. You ogling men on the covers of those books you read is one thing, but I draw the line at live ones," Sonny objected half-teasingly. It was obvious from the way they acted, they were in love with each other.

"Honey, you know I only love you," she cooed before kissing him.

As they did, I addressed what Kimera said before. "Baby, I asked you to be my old lady. Did you forget? In my world, that's more serious than an actual wedding, but that part was implied. I want you to have my last name, too. Once we get this shit with this bastard Paden settled, we'll plan it."

"Spawn, stop kidding around like that, or Sonny and Claudia will think you're serious. If you don't, I'll say yes, and then what'll you do?" she asked with a smirk.

I leaned closer to her. "I'll run home and get your ring and be back here as fast as I can to place it on your finger and get you to set our wedding date. I don't want a long engagement. The old ladies will help you plan it. Hell, the ladies at the two Warriors' compounds are experts at it. They'll be more than happy to help, too. We need to do our part to help the Punishers catch up on kids. I think Dublin Falls alone has fifty kids now."

"Fifty? Are you kidding me?" she gasped.

"Nope, and they have, I think, at least twenty over in Hunters Creek. You said six kids, right? We may have to up that number," I teased further.

I loved the flush it brought to her skin, but it also made what appeared to be desire peek through on her face. If she was totally uninterested in me, she wouldn't react like that. It gave me hope. I leaned in the rest of the way and kissed her softly on the lips. I wanted to devour them, but this wasn't the time or place for it.

"More than six? Oh no, I'm not doing that," she weakly protested when I drew away from her.

"You don't have to have all of them. I'm willing to adopt or foster, remember? However, we should talk about it later. We have some less pleasant stuff to talk about first."

A dark cloud came over her expression. I hated to do it, but I needed that information so I could get started on finding the bastard and ridding her of him. Claudia's smile fell away. Sonny curled up his top lip and took his wife's hand. I took Kimera's hand.

"I'm sorry, babe. I know this is hard for you ladies, but we need to know about him so I can find him. Also, I have to get the club mobilized."

"Mobilized? Why?" Claudia asked in confusion.

"Because we'll have to make sure he doesn't get away and keep doing this to other women, girls. I don't believe he's stopped doing it all these years, do you?"

"I hoped I was the only one. It was that thought that kept me from losing my mind all these years, but when I found out he did the same thing to Claudia, I knew I just fooled myself. I have no doubt he's done it to more girls. Whether he does it to grown women, who knows," Kimera said quietly.

We were sitting on the couch together. I tugged her closer to me when I saw her shiver. I knew it wasn't because she was cold. "Babe, I hate to say it, but it would be extremely unlikely you're the only two. Men like him are predators, and they keep doing shit like he did until someone puts a stop to them. I have a question. Do you have any idea how many young girls his family fostered before you two? What about afterward?" I was trying to gauge how many he hurt just in his parents' home. The chances of even more outside of it were high as well.

"I have no idea of either," Claudia said.

"I was told by the parents when I came they started taking in foster kids when he was fourteen. He was six years older than me, which would make him thirty-one now. They had pictures they showed me one time when I asked about their past kids. There were five girls and two boys. I have no idea how many they might've raised after I left. Claudia said his parents moved a few years ago. She has no idea where," Kimera added.

"Okay, I can find out the names from the foster system's records. What I need is anything you remember about him. Obviously, his name, although that too I can get from the system. Who were his friends growing up? Were there places he liked to hang out or things he did for fun? Hobbies? I understand you ran into him, Claudia, and that's how you knew he was in town and why you contacted Kimera. I need to know what he said to you and how you found Kimera. She said she lost track of you. The smallest detail can help more than you imagine," I explained.

"I can do that. Well, let me start with how I found her. Since her name isn't exactly common, I went online and did one of those things where you pay for someone to get you an address and phone number. I didn't know which state she was in, but I knew it would be highly unlikely that there'd be another Kimera Jordan, or if there was, not many. I was right, and it only came back with one."

As she talked, I took out my phone and opened the notes section so I could jot down anything I needed to remember. I had a good memory but you could never be too careful. "That's the easiest way to do it if you're willing to pay and the name isn't common. What about your run-in with him? Where was it, and what did he say?"

"I was in town running errands. I literally bumped into him on the street outside the post office. At first, I thought I was seeing things when I looked up and saw his face. It wasn't until he opened his mouth that I knew it was him. I'd never forget his voice," Claudia said with a shiver.

"Is there something unique about it?" I asked.

"It's deep, but it was always the way he said his words, and he'd make these funny humming sounds. When he first came home to live with his parents, we thought he was just a bit weird, but after you got to know him, it's like he has this uncontrollable noise he makes. It's a half moan and half hum."

"Does he do it all the time?"

"No, when he was talking with his friends or parents, he wouldn't, but if he was talking to us or we were in the room, it would happen on and off. It's not very loud, so I think most people don't realize he does it," Kimera added.

"Got it. Keep going. What did he say to you?" I prompted Claudia.

"He got this big smile on his face, which made me sick, and called me by name. Said it was so good to see me and that he'd thought about me a lot over the years. He saw my wedding rings and asked me who the man was and if he appreciated the skills I had when we met. I told him to go to hell and tried to walk off, but he grabbed my arm. He leaned close to me and told me he couldn't wait to see Kimera and we should have a reunion to relive old times. He made me so sick to my stomach. I don't know how I kept from puking on him."

She paused and took a shaky breath and a gulp of her drink. Sonny was rubbing her back with one hand while holding the other hand in his opposite hand. She had a sick expression on her face just from retelling her story. I hated to make her do it, but I needed all the information I could get.

"Take your time," I told her. She gave me a faint smile and nod before launching back into it.

"I jerked my arm loose and began to walk off. As I did, I told him to never speak to me again and to stay away from me. I also told him that he didn't need to worry about seeing Kimera because she didn't live here anymore. He laughed and called out that he'd have to find her so we could have that reunion. He'd show us the time of our lives, and he knew we missed him. His last parting remark was he'd be seeing me really soon. I got around the corner and took off, practically running."

"She called me on her way home, crying hysterically. I had to have her pull over the car and not drive. I went to pick her up. My parents watch the kids while we work. They were with them, thank God. She'd used her lunch break to run to the post office. I had her call her office to tell them she wouldn't be back and that she had gotten sick. I let my boss know I had a family emergency and stayed with her. When she calmed down a bit, she told me what happened," Sonny added.

"Did you already know her history with him, or was that the first you'd heard about it?"

"I knew about it. When we first met, she had some reservations about men. When I didn't give up trying to convince her to date me, she explained what happened. That cocksucker has caused her years of pain and fear. Even though it happened a decade ago, she would still occasionally have a nightmare about it, or a smell or sight would trigger her to recall it. Since she saw him, she's rarely slept a whole night. I despised the bastard when she originally told me, but now, I hate his guts even more and want him gone. This is my chance. Before, we didn't know where he was or have a way to find him, although I guess we could have done what we did to find Kimera, but that could've been a fluke in her case. That's why I want us to find him as fast as possible before he leaves town. I don't know if he lives here or was visiting."

"It doesn't matter if he doesn't live here. I can find him. No matter where he does live, we can get him. Do any of his friends still live here? If so, what are their names?"

"He didn't hang out with many people that we knew of other than two guys who he said he'd been friends with since they were young kids. One was Asa Ledger and the other Linden Faris. They were the only ones I ever really heard him mention by name, and they'd come around to the house sometimes to pick him up. I don't know if they still live here," Kimera offered.

"Asa did the last I knew, but Linden moved not long after Paden went back to school," Claudia supplied.

"Did either of them ever try anything with you ladies or say anything to make you think they knew what he was doing to you?" I asked next.

"They'd make teasing comments about how pretty I was becoming but never touched me. What about you, Kimera?"

She didn't say anything at first. She was staring off into space. My gut clenched. Jesus, please don't tell me either of them had done something to her, too. If so, how would I ever make her trust me? "Baby, look at me. What did they say or do?"

"Sorry, I didn't mean to space out on you. They never raped me like he did, but when you asked, it made me remember that Asa one time touched my breasts and another time my ass. I thought they were purely by accident, but thinking back and then remembering him snickering to Paden about how he didn't know how he could stand to leave the house, maybe he did. I don't know, honestly. I found every way I could to escape whenever he was in the house. I wish I could tell you for sure if either did."

"You have nothing to apologize for. Okay, what's Paden's last name? The parents no longer live here, as far as you know, but are there any other family members in town?"

"None I ever met. As for his last name, it's Gallagher. His parents are Beck and Dorothy," Kimera said.

From there, I had them tell me anything they could recall about his hobbies, sports, or places in town he liked to go. Since he'd been an adult, they didn't know much about what he did when he was away from the house. Mainly, he seemed to talk about partying a lot and bragged about the girls who chased him. I could tell my questions were wearing on them, so I didn't ask more after they finished telling me that much. It was Sonny who started to ask me questions.

"You said you can find him and would make sure he can't do this to anyone again. How? It'll be their word against his. The cops might not be able to prove it. Won't they question why it's taken this long for them to come forward? And we don't know if there's a statute of limitations on it. We thought about asking a lawyer but haven't. If there's a limitation or they can't prove it, then he still gets to walk free and keep doing it."

"Let me answer your questions. Before we left

the hotel to come here, I asked a friend to do some digging on this for us because I thought it might come up. Here's what he said. In this state, it's considered a felony if someone seventeen or older has carnal knowledge of someone thirteen to seventeen years old when the defendant is more than four years older than the child, which would be the case with Kimera and Claudia. If he was closer to their ages, it would be a misdemeanor. Since they weren't younger than thirteen, it's considered second-degree or forcible rape. He prevented them from resisting by using both force and threats of physical violence. If convicted, he could be sentenced anywhere from five to forty years imprisonment with hard labor. The more counts would most likely add to the years given. They're nowhere close to the statute of limitations. Of course, the biggest risk is proving he did it."

"So they could go through all this, and he still gets away with it," Sonny snarled.

"Yes, it's a possibility. There's no physical evidence to support their claims, so it would all fall to circumstantial. I won't lie and say it would be easy or a guarantee of conviction. You asked how I could make sure he never does it again and that he pays for what he did. All you need to know is I can. He'll never darken their lives. That's all I'm gonna say on that. I believe he's done this with more than them, but I might be wrong. It doesn't matter. I'll find him regardless of whether he lives here or in Timbuktu. He can run and hide, but eventually, he'll be found." As I explained the last part, I made sure to stare hard at each of them. I knew Kimera understood what I meant. She knew what we did to

Troian's attackers. There was no way in hell I'd do less for her.

"You'll kill him," Claudia said softly. I didn't respond. "Okay, I get it. What do you want us to do next? How can we help you?" she asked.

"You tell me anything you might remember that could help us find him. Leave the rest up to me and my club. If we need more boots on the ground or help, we have friends who can do it. If you run into him again, don't confront him or indicate in any way he's on anyone's radar."

"We can do that," Sonny said.

"Good. That's all I can think of at the moment. We'll be around, so I know we'll be seeing you," I told them.

"Yes, we will. Now, it's getting late and you both have to work in the morning. We're gonna let you get to bed. Thank you for dinner," Kimera told them.

We spent the next few minutes saying goodbye and thank you for having us, and then we left. On the ride back to the hotel, I thought through what I wanted to talk to her about as well as the research I'd start tonight. I wouldn't be able to rest much without being with her, and that wasn't something I saw her doing. Before I went to her room earlier, I'd gotten a room next to hers even though I wanted to be in her room and hold her. I knew it was too soon to do that.

Kimera: Chapter 12

I tossed and turned all night. My dreams were filled with memories and nightmares about Paden. I was up and down several times. When I was awake, I couldn't stop thinking about Spawn. I was still stunned he'd come all the way here to find me. I'd been mortified that he had to find out about my past the way he did, if at all. However, as last evening progressed and we talked more with Claudia and Sonny, my mortification lessened.

More than anything, as I thought about Paden, the angrier I got. I didn't want him to continue to affect my relationships or my happiness. I'd never been able to fully trust a man since him. This led me to only have a couple of actual boyfriends. I'd never been comfortable enough with them to tell them what happened to me when I was a teen, nor to fully open up and commit to them. Sexually, it was hard to relax, and I know it was a big part of what led to us never lasting. However, I didn't want that to happen with Spawn. I'd tried since meeting him that day at the hospital to deny he did anything other than make me mad, but I'd been lying to myself or trying to. Being away for these past couple of weeks had been hard, and it had as much to do with leaving Troian as it did with leaving him. I missed seeing and being with him.

Every single day, he'd come to see me, or I'd see him at the clubhouse. Even after my kidnapping, I tried to push him away, but I wanted him near, too. I think the shock of what almost happened to me on top of what did happen when I was a kid and how similar they would've been, in a way had pushed me to try to protect myself.

Now, with him confessing how he felt about me and asking that I call him Aidan, it opened my eyes to what I'd deep down subconsciously wanted, which was for Spawn to be as attracted to me and to want me as much as I did him. You'd think realizing this would make the next part easy, but it didn't. I had to figure out how to tell him all that and then carry it through. I was nervous as hell about having a physical relationship with him.

What if I froze or freaked out during sex? What if I couldn't satisfy him? Or if he wanted things I couldn't give him, and if I said no, would he say so long? Getting out of my own head enough to relax and enjoy sex in the past had been an issue. I went around and around in circles in my brain, which explained why I was dragging this morning and was willing to kill to get good coffee.

Last night when he walked me to my room, he'd pointed next door and said that was his room. I was surprised but pleased. We planned to go get breakfast at nine, and he said he'd come get me. I was dressed and pacing as I watched the minutes tick closer to the designated time. Even though I was expecting him, I still jumped when there was a hard knock at the door.

Smoothing my sweaty hands down my jeans, I hurried to answer the door. His sexy, smiling face greeted me and made me long to kiss him. I smiled back. "Good m—" I was cut off by him stepping into me and taking my mouth as he backed me into my room, letting the door slam shut behind him. One of his hands buried in my hair and held my head while the other tugged me against him.

His mouth ravished mine, and I got lost. Up until now, his few kisses had been mere pecks. This was a full-on devouring, and my whole body went up in flames as he did it. I clutched him close and stood on my tiptoes so he wouldn't have to stoop so low. As I kissed him back eagerly, he let out a low growl, then I was lifted up by him, and he walked me backward until he reached my bed. He lay me down and hovered over top of me, kissing me. I tugged on his hair and teased his tongue back. I don't know how long we kissed before he reluctantly parted our mouths. I whimpered and tried to chase his mouth with mine, but he moved out of reach.

His expression was slumberous and full of heat. "Shit, we've gotta stop, Hotcake, or I'm gonna explode and end up doing something I know you're not ready for. Jesus, that's the best fucking kiss of my life. I didn't mean to let it get that crazy, but I'm not mad it did. Come on, we need to get the hell outta here before I attack you again," he muttered hoarsely.

"Well, I didn't mind it, in case you didn't notice," I said with a grin.

He groaned. "God, don't tell me that. You're supposed to be helping me resist, not encouraging me! Nope, I'm not letting you lead me astray, woman. Up, we're going to get breakfast."

I pouted as he got up and then helped me to my feet. He headed for the door at a trot. I barely had enough time to grab my purse before he had me out the door, and we were on our way to the elevator.

I tried not to giggle as I overheard him muttering. "Eggs, bacon, no kisses. Coffee, hash browns, no, you can't kiss her again. Pancakes, waffles, God, her lips are sweet like strawberries."

I burst out laughing. I couldn't help it. "Aidan, are you trying to talk yourself out of kissing me or what?"

We stepped onto the elevator alone. He grimaced. "I'm trying to convince myself that food is more important than your kisses, but my brain and body are fighting me."

I tried not to look at his zipper, but I couldn't stop myself. The bulge I saw there made me gulp. God, he looked huge. I felt the heat in my cheeks. I quickly glanced up and caught him smirking at me. "Stop," I ordered.

He grinned. "Stop what? I'm not doing anything. I'm just standing here minding my business."

"Yeah, like you didn't start all this by attacking me at the door. What'll you do if there's a little old lady in the lobby? You'll give her a heart attack sporting that."

"Baby, it might just make her day, or if she's with her man, make his week," he joked.

"You're terrible," I told him as the door opened and we got out.

Immediately, I spotted three older ladies in the lobby. I laughed, and they glanced over at me. I saw their eyes widen as they got a look at him. I couldn't blame them. He was something else to look at. He came up beside me and wrapped an arm around my shoulders. As we passed them, he gave them a big smile and said in that deep voice of his, "Ladies, looking good."

I heard them sigh as we walked by. I glanced back to find them watching his ass. I held in my glee until we were outside, and then I let it out. "O-oh, my God, you just made their month, and they were checking out your ass. I can't take you anywhere, can I?"

"Babe, don't get jealous. You're the only one I see or want. Who cares if they use me as spank bank material later? You can have the real thing, not just an image."

"You're just so modest, aren't you?" I pretended to sniff. He walked me over to my car and his bike. I took my keys out of my jeans pocket, but he snatched them away before I could unlock my car and backed me up against it.

"I like to tease, but I can promise you one thing for sure. You're the only one I'll let touch me, and it's you I dream about. Shit, sorry, I don't mean to come on so hard. I'll tone it down. I promise." He began to ease back, but I grabbed his hips to stop him.

His erection hadn't gone away, and the feel of it digging into me was turning me on. With anyone else, I'd be running a mile, but not him. "I really enjoyed our kiss and the fun stuff, too. I can't promise nothing will freak me out or make me hesitate, but I don't want you to walk around scared to say or do anything, either. Just be yourself, and we'll figure it out as we go."

Excitement filled his face. "Does this mean what I hope it does? Are you willing to see where this goes between us? You know what I want. I wasn't blowing smoke last night when I said those things about kids and marriage."

I gulped. I was hoping he meant it but to hear him say it aloud was scary but also exhilarating. "I'm starting to see that. And yes, it means we'll see how it goes. Now, take me to get breakfast and coffee before I savage someone. Lesson one, I'm not a morning person unless I have my caffeine," I admitted.

"Just give me a minute," he said right before he kissed me again.

I melted even faster than last time. By the time he lifted his head, I was panting and ready to drag him back upstairs for an intense kissing session, but my stomach growled, making its need for food obvious. He winked as he moved me aside, got the car unlocked, and opened my door. It was then I realized we were on the passenger side. "I'm driving. You're not dressed to ride, and I can't be away from you this morning, not even for a few minutes," he said.

I let him help me into the car. He even went as far as to latch my seatbelt, but I think he did it so he could rub his hand over my body even though it wasn't anywhere offensive, just my stomach and thighs. I fought to calm down as he rounded the hood and went to get in. I laughed when he grunted and had to unlatch the seat and push it back as far as it would go. His legs were so long they wouldn't even fit between the seat and the dash when he tried to sit. He did it standing outside the car.

"Goddamn, that's one way to take someone out at the knees. I'll have to remember to check before trying to get in an automobile after you've driven it. Where to? I assume since you've been here and grew up here, you know the best places to go for breakfast?"

"I do. Head west on the main road in front of the hotel, and I'll direct you from there. It's only a couple of miles away. It's called Paulette's, and they do breakfast the best anywhere around here, in my opinion. Their coffee is great, too."

"Can't wait," he said as he put it into drive, and we took off.

In a matter of a few minutes, we were parking. The parking lot was still more than half full. Everywhere you looked around town, you could see the holiday lights and decorations up. That's when the date registered with me. I'd been in such a fog of trying to recover from my kidnapping and then trying to find Paden I hadn't paid much attention. I knew it was Christmas because Claudia and Sonny had put up a tree and some decorations for the kids, but it hadn't clicked that it was this close. People and businesses seemed to put up their stuff earlier and earlier every year.

"Aidan, I just remembered! It's Christmas in a week. You can't stay here for that. The whole club will be having their huge celebration. I heard the old ladies planning it. Why don't you head back? You can do your research online from anywhere. After Christmas, once we find him, you can come back. No way will I have you miss it with your club."

He studied me in silence for several moments before he answered me. "Babe, I'm not going back unless you are too. If we stay here, we can celebrate together and be there next year. I won't die if I miss one Christmas with the club."

He got out and came around to open my door as I sat there, thinking over what he had just said. When I got out, I answered him, "I don't want you to do that. You should be around your family."

"So should you, and as of now, they're your family too. So, if you miss it, I do, too. End of discussion."

He held my hand as we walked into the restaurant. The chatter of voices was loud. Staff was bustling around like busy bees. We stood and waited to be seated. "I haven't had a family since I lost my granny. It hasn't been a big thing in my life, having no one to share it with. I won't notice if I miss it, not like you will. And what about actual family? Do you have any? I've never thought to ask. If you do, won't they expect to see you too?"

He didn't answer right away since a hostess came up to seat us. She looked harassed as she grabbed two menus and showed us to a table. After a quick, "Someone will be over to take your drink orders soon," she hurried off again.

He didn't open his menu. Instead, he was watching me. "Not having had a real Christmas since you were ten is even more reason to celebrate it this year and every year. As for your question about whether I have an actual family, I do. I have both my parents, a younger sister, and a nephew. Unfortunately, we don't get to spend Christmas together unless I go to them. They all live in Butte, Montana."

"That's where you grew up? Was it on a ranch with horses and cows?" I asked a little excitedly. I'd always loved the thought of living on a ranch for some reason. It had left me with the desire to learn to ride, but I'd never learned. As much as I thought horses were beautiful creatures, they were scary. I tried to picture him dressed as a cowboy. I couldn't. He looked like an ideal biker in his cut and with his tattoos.

"It's a small one, not a great big one like you see on TV or read about in books, but yes, we had horses and a few cattle. I was born and raised there. I was put on my first horse when I was two, I think."

Again, conversation halted while a waitress came to take our drink orders and ask us what we wanted to eat. I knew what I wanted, but he hadn't gotten a chance to look over the menu, so all we gave her was our drink orders. She was a young girl, maybe eighteen at the most. She gave Spawn an awed look tinged with wariness.

After she walked off, I teased him. "I think you might've stunned our waitress. She's never seen anyone like you, it seems. I wasn't sure if she was going to run or ask you to take her for a ride...on your motorcycle."

He rolled his eyes. "I didn't notice. A lot of people are scared of bikers, and others think we're something special. We're just people who live a different life than them. That's what attracts people like her."

"No, it's not. You can't be oblivious to the fact you're very easy to look at, Spawn. A man like you will always attract attention, and women will want to be with you, even some men." Thinking about it, I felt sick. He'd always have women throwing themselves at him. How in the world could I ever keep his interest? My appetite fled.

He grabbed my hand across the table. "Whatever you're thinking, don't. You went from happy and smiling to frowning and looking upset. What brought that on?"

I glanced down at the table and traced the wood grain with my fingernail. I didn't want to tell him. He waited. Sighing because I knew he wouldn't let it go, I answered him. "It was me recognizing that a man like you will have women wanting you and offering themselves to you all the time. I don't believe I can compete with that. There'll be a lot of them, I imagine, who'll have much more to offer you than me. Maybe we should reconsider pursuing a relationship."

I sucked in a startled breath as he let go of my hand and stood up. He had a grim expression on his face. *Here it was. He was leaving*, I thought. Only that wasn't what he did. Rather, he came to my side of the table and yanked out a chair to sit right beside me. He hooked his arm around me and tugged me flush against his side. He regarded me with an intense scowl.

"That's the one and only time I want to hear that crap outta you. I'm not some fickle young horny idiot running around trying to score as much pussy as he can get. Have I slept with women? Yes. Did it mean anything to me? Not in a long time. But that's not us, Kimera. What I feel already for you is so damn fierce there's no way I'll want another woman, no matter what she offers me. I know what and who I want. It's you," he growled before kissing me.

I don't know what would've happened if our waitress bringing our drinks hadn't interrupted us. Probably me making a fool of myself and getting us arrested as I stripped in the middle of the restaurant. I blushed, which made him grin. He didn't apologize to her for the display, nor did he move back to the other side of the table.

He asked her to give him a minute to look at the menu. I was surprised when she stood there waiting for him. I filled the silence with my order, although it was hard for me to talk. It wasn't long until he gave her his, and she went on her way. As soon as she was gone, he faced me again. "Did that clear up your doubts, or do I need to take it further?"

"You can't do that, or we'll be arrested," I hissed.

"It would be worth it. Is that what you want?" He inched closer.

I hurriedly put my hand over his mouth. He chuckled. "Behave, you're giving me and every other woman in here a heart attack. I'll accept your declaration, but I have another question. But first, tell me about your family."

I sat back as he told me about growing up in Montana and his family. I felt sorry for his poor sister and her son. To think the boy's dad wanted nothing to do with him. What was wrong with people? Why have kids if you don't want them? My parents had been the same.

"Your nephew is lucky he has your parents, you, and your sister. It sounds like his dad is like my parents. Some people don't deserve to have kids. He's better off without him."

"You said your parents gave you to your granny. Why? Do you mind me asking?"

"No, it's alright. They just weren't cut out to be parents, according to Granny. They barely paid attention to me. She was always taking me for days on end so I wouldn't be neglected. They were more into lazing about, smoking weed, and partying with their friends who were like them. She kept begging them to stop, but they didn't. Finally, one day, they came to her with me and said they were done. They said I was too much work and they gave me to her. I'm not sure legally if they severed their parental rights themselves or if she made them, but I never saw them again. I don't remember what they look like."

"It's the best thing they could've done, babe. God knows what would've happened to you if you had stayed with them. At least you had your granny for those next seven years. I wish you still had her. My parents were the complete opposite. They've always been loving, and I've never doubted they wanted me or my sister. I'm more than happy to share them with you. They'll love you."

"Whoa, hold on, I'm not ready to meet your folks yet, but thank you. Can I ask if you're so close, why do you live in Virginia, and they live in Montana? I understand why you left originally, but that was years ago."

He gave me an uncomfortable grimace. Uh oh, what was up with that? I waited for him to answer. After almost a minute of silence, he answered me. "Originally, it was all because of that woman I told you about before. Now, don't get upset and start thinking the shit you were a few minutes ago. Let me explain. I said I hadn't had a woman mean anything to me in a long time." He paused.

"Back home, the woman I told you about was when I was in my early twenties. She and I had dated for two years. I was all into her, and I thought she had the same feelings about me. Only in the end she broke up with me, claiming she was in love with another man. I tried to change her mind, but then I found out she'd been seeing him behind my back for months. I knew it was no use. It was the prospect of seeing them together all over town that made me leave Montana, as I said. I had a bike even then, so I got on it and just started to wander the country. I don't know what I was looking for other than to escape. It was the night I was in a bar near Bristol and ended up meeting Mayhem that changed it all for me. I'd seen lots of bikers and found their life appealing. He invited me to come to the clubhouse, which I did. I've been there ever since."

"No one could blame you for staying away from seeing your first love happy and having a life," I said.

"No, that hasn't been a factor in years. Yes, at first, I stayed away because of what I thought was a broken heart. Only as the years have passed and I've watched my friends and brothers find their true loves have I come to realize it was never love between us. I was in love with the thought of it. I lusted after her, and it wounded my pride to have her choose another man over me. I stay in Virginia because I like it, and I have the kind of life I love there. Hell, I've tried for years to get my family to move closer to me. Dad and Mom are getting older, and they can't keep doing the stuff on the ranch forever. My sister tries to help as much as she can, but she works and has Tommie. Maybe one day they'll move. I think six grandbabies would be the thing to do the trick," he added with a wink.

That made me laugh. "Keep it up, mister, and you'll have me running for the hills. I was only teasing you about six. You're assuming I'll be a good mom. What if I suck at it? Other than Granny, I had some bad examples."

"Baby, I have no doubt you'll make a great mom. You're a compassionate woman who helps others. Look at what you did for Troian more than once and how you're trying to help Claudia. No, you'll do more than fine at it. Hey, here comes our food. We can continue this discussion after I get you fed. I've been taking my life into my hands, distracting you long enough."

We ate a leisurely breakfast, and I got my caffeine fix, which he drank as much as me, so I thought he might be as much of a caffeine hound as I was in the mornings. He wouldn't let me pay and left a sizable tip for the waitress. By the time we left, it was almost eleven. Knowing Sonny and Claudia would be at work, we headed back to the hotel. I thought we could spend time doing some research. I was anxious to find Paden.

Spawn: Chapter 13

The past three days have been busy. I'd found out a lot about Paden Gallagher, and the more I found, the more questions I had. I knew we were all anxious to have him removed from the picture, but I couldn't hurry it along and leave too many unanswered questions or loose ends. Those considerations and the fact Christmas was in a few days led to us putting on hold making any moves. Just until we knew more and Christmas was past.

Sonny and Claudia deserved to celebrate the holiday with their kids. They invited us to do it with them, but in the end, Kimera insisted we had to go back to Bristol to spend it with the club. She used the excuse of how much the kids there would miss me, as well as my brothers, and the need to get more things from her house. I don't know if it was really those reasons or if she needed a break from her old hometown. I could tell being there took a toll on her. She was tense and couldn't relax.

Rather than driving, we got a flight back. We planned to return the day after Christmas. Flying with a dog was new to me. I found Toro wasn't just a guard dog but also an emotional support and service animal. Apparently, Kimera had anxiety and depression from what happened to her all those years ago, which

I would've been surprised if she didn't. She'd ensured Toro was certified as a service dog and, to prevent any pushback, had a letter from her therapist stating he could be used for emotional support, too. The airlines had to allow him in the cabin with us. We knew he wouldn't cause a disturbance or problems. He was too well-trained for that.

The flight back had been an experience. Toro was calm and collected, but the other people on the plane weren't. Most wanted to admire and pet him, although we cautioned them not to do it since he was working. There was only one who caused a stink and had me ready to beat his ass and throw him out of a door mid-flight. The man was sitting across the aisle from us in the bulkhead row, which they gave us to make enough room for Toro at our feet.

Since the moment we got onboard, Toro has been resting there with his eyes closed or just watching people. He didn't bark, approach people, or growl—nothing. He was content with our attention and people-watching. The man started as soon as he saw him.

"What's that thing doing on this flight?" he asked with a sneer at the flight attendant.

"Sir, the dog is allowed on this flight. If you'd rather sit somewhere else, I can move you."

"Why should I move? Make them move that animal!" he demanded.

"I can't. They need the extra leg space, so he's out of the aisle. Either you can move, or you have to stay. He won't bother you." I could tell she was fighting her impatience

with him.

He snorted and muttered under his breath, but he stayed where he was. As we took off, he kept glaring over at Toro. Trying to be helpful, Kimera leaned across me and told him, "Sir, I promise Toro is well-behaved and won't disturb you."

He sneered at her but didn't bother to say anything. I wanted to punch him in the mouth at that point. It was later when the urge to throw him out of the plane came over me. If it weren't for Kimera, I probably would've done it. Fuckers like him pissed me off to no end.

They were coming around to serve drinks and snacks in the cabin. Toro raised his head with interest as we got ours, but he didn't beg for anything. Kimera did give him some water and a treat bone. He was contentedly chewing on it when the man got vocal again.

"I can't eat with him watching me. Look at him chewing on that bone. He'll attack someone in a minute for their food, and then what'll we do? He's a killer. You can see it. Why do they allow people to have them on planes? What's your disability? You look perfectly fine to me," he snapped at Kimera.

She was polite as she answered him while putting him in his place. "Sir, not all issues are physically apparent, and I'm not required to tell you what mine is, nor will I. I assure you he's not about to eat you or your food. People with disabilities have as much right to fly as you do."

"I demand to know! I want to see your paperwork to have him on this plane! You're probably just lying so you can bring your mangy pet with you," he snarled. That's when I had enough. I stood up. He gulped when he saw I had to stoop over because I couldn't stand up straight. I didn't have my cut on, but my tattoos were visible. I don't know if he hadn't noticed them before, but he did then.

"I've listened enough to your shit. The only one disturbing this flight is you. The dog hasn't come near you. He hasn't barked. He's fine. My woman doesn't have to tell you or show you anything. I suggest you shut up and give it a rest. You're disturbing the other passengers."

As I got done telling him this, those around us began to clap. His face turned beet red, and he blustered at me. "You can't talk to me like that! I'll have them throw you, your dog, and that woman off the plane. Stewardess, stewardess," he yelled. Christ, who still called them stewardesses?

The one from boarding came up the aisle. She was fighting not to glare at him. "Yes, sir," she said politely. The woman deserved a medal or, at the very least, a Xanax. I could never do her job.

"I want the pilot to land this plane and kick these people and their dog off. I won't be talked to by this man. He threatened me. His dog is a menace. I demand we land."

"Sir, they haven't done anything to you. I'm sorry, but I won't tell the pilot any such thing. The dog is a perfect angel. You're the one causing the problems. If you continue, I'll have to ask the pilot to land and eject you from the flight," she told him with a pleased look on her face. This caused the other passengers to cheer and clap louder.

I'd retaken my seat when she came up the aisle, but I was out of it again quickly when he lunged at her. "You *fucking bitch!" he yelled as he raised his hand and pushed it at her. His hand landed in the palm of my hand. I squeezed it, making him howl in pain.*

"That's it. You don't yell or hit women in front of me. Miss, if you'd like to go speak to whomever, I'll make sure he stays here."

"There's no need for that. I can take it from here," said a man behind me. As I turned, he continued. "I'm the air marshal. I was in the back of the plane and didn't know there was an issue. I'll take it from here. Sir, you need to come with me. We're moving, and if you continue to cause trouble, when we land, you'll be handed over to the local authorities," he told the man.

I let go of his fist but stayed alert. I didn't think he'd do anything with the marshal there. In fact, he was so pale I thought he might faint. He was escorted back to the rear of the plane, and the rest of the flight passed peacefully.

Even thinking about it as we rode back to the compound made me grin. The man wouldn't make eye contact as he left the flight. The marshal took him off the plane first. He was nowhere in sight when we got off. Good riddance. I'd seen him drinking several alcoholic drinks on the flight, but it hadn't helped his attitude.

Rhaines picked us up at the airport. It made no sense to pay for a ride. He filled us in on what had been happening while we were gone. The closer we got, the quieter Kimera got. She was fidgeting when we came through the gate. I had him take us straight to my house. As soon as we got out of the car, Toro gave us a pleading glance. We laughed, and she told him to go.

He took off running. He'd explore for a long time. He was so happy to be able to run. I had no doubt he'd find someone to play with, too.

I wanted to be alone with her before I asked what was bothering her and to give her a tour of my house. She had never come here before she left, although I had planned to bring her. I was nervous about what she would think of it. It reflected where I came from. I loved living in Virginia, but I missed all the cabins back home, so that's what I'd built.

I opened the door and motioned for her to enter. She was examining the outside and the porch. It was one that wrapped ninety percent of the way around the first floor. In the back, where it didn't, that section had a breezeway that connected the house to the three-car garage and storage room. Inside, I'd kept the natural wood logs exposed in the walls, floor, and ceiling. The first floor had a great room with a stone fireplace, dining room, and kitchen with a walk-in pantry and a big island. There was a laundry room, a half bath, and what was called a hunting closet right before going out the back door to the breezeway. A guest bedroom and bathroom were downstairs, too. One of the things I loved was in the master suite. Besides the bedroom and bathroom with its walk-in closets, there was a small safe room.

Upstairs, part of it was open to below, and the rest contained a storage room, two more bedrooms, a full bathroom, and a room I could use as either another bedroom or something else. In the original plans, it was called a bunk room. Since it was just me in the house, I hadn't furnished all of it. The living room, kitchen, master bedroom, and guest bedroom all had furniture. Since I had seating for six at the island, I hadn't bothered to put in a dining table. The only ones likely to visit would be my family from Montana, and if that happened, I would've done the others. I was glad I hadn't because it meant Kimera could help me do it and change anything she didn't like. If she hated the idea of living in a cabin, it would hurt, but I'd be willing to change and build another house.

I left our bags in the entryway as I showed her around. The expression on her face made me relax. She appeared to really like what she was seeing. We ended up back in the kitchen when we were done with the tour. I had to ask. "So, what do you think?"

"What do I think? I think your house is freaking amazing, Aidan! I love it. It's so cool that you built a cabin. All this wood is beautiful. Although it's a lot of house for just one person. How do you keep it clean? And that safe room in the master is brilliant," she exclaimed.

"Really? You like it? Damn, that's a load off my mind."

"Why?"

"If you hated it, I'd have to build another house, and I love the cabin feel."

"B-but why would you do that? It's your house," she stammered, appearing stunned.

"We're working on a life together, aren't we? You said we'd do this," I reminded her.

"Sure, I remember, but that doesn't mean I'd assume anything. And your house is gorgeous, and you should never give it up for anyone. What kind of bitch would that make me if I came in here and said I hated it, and you had to build me a whole new house if we worked out?"

"We'll work out, and I don't see it as you being a bitch. If you hated it, I'd want you to say so. Sure, I love it, but I can live without it. Something tells me I can't live without you."

This put a smile on her face and earned me a kiss. I eagerly devoured her mouth. Kissing her made me so damn hard. We'd been making progress in the intimacy department. Nothing that led to taking off our clothes or having full-blown sex, but the kissing sessions and the petting drove me wild. She'd confessed she was worried she wasn't experienced like I was used to. That didn't mean shit to me, and I told her that and showed her often how much I wanted her and loved what we did together. I didn't want to know about the men she'd been with before me, but I knew I had to listen when she spoke of generalities since it would help me not do something to upset her.

I hoisted her up and sat her on the island. This put her at the perfect height to kiss her. As our tongues twisted together, I ran my hands up the back of her shirt to rest on her warm, soft skin. She had such silky skin. She moaned and shivered before tugging my shirt free of my pants and easing her hands up to my chest. She told me she liked the rough texture of the hair on my chest on her palms and to run them over my muscles.

I longed to put my hands on her breasts, but I didn't want to push her too fast. We had time. No one had literally died of sexual frustration that I knew of. She pressed closer and then broke our kiss. I growled in protest.

"I want you to do something," she whispered against my lips.

"Whatever you want, I'll give it to you, beautiful," I told her as I nibbled on her lips.

"I want to feel your hands on my breasts. Underneath my bra. Will you do that?" she asked.

Would I do it? Was she kidding? "Baby, if you're sure you want that, it will be my damn pleasure to do it. You have to know I've been dying to touch you there, but I didn't want to push it or make you uncomfortable. I'm going at your pace."

"You haven't been pushing me, and I want it so much. Please, touch me," she moaned.

That broke me. She never had to beg me for anything. I slid my hands to the front after putting a bit of distance between our bodies, then inched them up to her bra-covered breasts. I watched her face to make sure I didn't see any panic or unease. If I did, I'd stop. There was none. As I touched them, I noticed her bra snapped in the front. I unsnapped it and let her firmness fill my hands. Jesus, they were perfect. I knew it from feeling them alone. I gently kneaded both and ran my thumbs over her nipples. They were already more than half hard at my first pass.

She whimpered into my mouth and clutched my pecs, making me groan as her nails bit into me. I greedily kissed her as I played with her breasts. In between kisses, I could hear us both panting. I decided to see what she might like by moving from stroking and kneading her to actually twisting her nipples. I didn't do it too hard, but enough to give a tiny bit of sting. She went rigid, but the loud moan she let out told me it was because she liked it.

Reluctantly, I let go of her mouth to speak. "Does my She-Wolf like a bit of bite, a taste of pain with her pleasure?" I asked half in jest.

"I like what you're doing. As to whether I'd like more, I don't know. I've never had anyone ask or try it. Do you like it too?" she asked as her nails bit in more.

"Fuck, yeah, I like it. And I do enjoy pushing boundaries, but only as long as we're both enjoying it. Once it begins to be just pain or unwanted, I don't. Never go along with it if you don't like what I'm doing, babe. That'll piss me off."

"I won't. I just don't know what I like. You'll have to test the waters, and I'll tell you yeah or nay. Being spontaneous and exploring are things I have to work on, but I want to. God, I want to. I need to make you feel as good as you make me, so I want you to promise to always tell me your needs."

"I promise, and you do the same. If you're unsure of something, tell me, and we can slow down, stop, and try again later or decide it's off the table. I do have something to tell you."

"What?"

"Just feeling your breasts tells me they're perfect. It's probably a good thing I can't see or taste them, or I might just embarrass myself," I told her. It was only half teasing. My jeans were tight over my erection.

"Oh yeah, well, let me help you," she said.

Abruptly, she pulled further away from me. Before I could ask what she was doing, she had her top pulled off and shimmied her bra down her arms to rest on the island. My mouth went dry as I saw her. Each nipple was dark pink and so tight they were begging for my mouth. I lowered my head as she bowed her back. A hand landed on the back of my neck as I sucked one nipple into my mouth and teased the other with my hand.

She tugged on my hair and moaned while pressing me harder against her breast. I tongued her nipple, then used my teeth to nibble. "Oh God, Aidan, that feels so good. Don't stop," she whimpered. I growled and shook my head slightly as I tugged harder with my teeth and pinched the other one between my thumb and finger harder. She let out a slight scream and shook. Jesus, did she just come?

I could feel precum leaking from the head of my engorged cock. The urge to tear open my jeans and give myself a hand job or, better yet, have her mouth on me was almost unbearable. It was only my fear of scaring her that held me back. I pressed my groin into the vee between her legs. She responded by rubbing against my cock through our clothes. She gasped and humped me. I had to make her stop.

I released her nipple and pleaded with her. "Baby, please stop, or I'm gonna blow in my jeans. Shit, I'm sorry, I shouldn't have pressed into you like that, but you just feel so good," I groaned.

"I'm glad I make you feel like this, Aidan. I don't want you to walk on eggshells around me. As for apologizing for pressing into me, don't. It felt amazing. However, I don't want you to mess up your pants."

I went to pull my groin away, but her hands came down and grabbed my hips, stopping me. I gave her a puzzled look. She shook her head. "I don't want you to do that. Why don't you take them off so you're more comfortable? You can leave your underwear on."

"God, you're making this hard, no pun intended. I want to do that more than you know, but isn't this too fast? I don't expect more than you've already given me, even if I want more. I meant that."

"I know you do, and I can't tell you how much it means to me. I can't explain it better than this. Yes, I'm scared but not scared of you. You make me feel so out of control, and I want you. I'm terrified of not being enough, of not being able to satisfy your needs and wants."

I rested my forehead on hers. She closed her eyes. "Baby, I know it can be scary, but I've got you. If you're sure, then I have a suggestion. Let's go to the bedroom where we can be comfortable. We can take our time and do whatever you're comfortable with. You tell me. Or if you want to stop, then we stop."

I silently prayed she'd say yes and not call a halt after having a moment to think. My erection had edged away from coming, but it was still hard. I was fighting not to look at her breasts again. If I did, I'd lose it and carry her to my bed. She wrapped her arms around my neck as she opened her eyes, and I caught a smile.

"What're you waiting for? Show me how big and strong you are, and carry me to your bed. I've always wanted a guy to do that. It's what men always do in the romance books."

Not wanting to be outdone by fictional men, I growled softly as I tugged her hips closer. She wrapped her legs around my waist. I easily hoisted her in the air. She didn't weigh enough to break a sweat. I turned us around and strolled through the short hall that passed the back door and led to the master bedroom. Kicking the door shut, I let go with one hand to lock it. I didn't want anyone accidentally disturbing us. We were known to walk into each other's homes, although not the married guys' houses. No one knew she and I were together yet, so it was a possibility.

Lowering her to the bed, I admired her as I removed my boots and socks. I paused. "Last chance to keep these on," I told her as I pointed at my jeans.

"Take them off, Aidan. Stop making me suffer," she said. She was raised up on her elbows, watching me. Her gorgeous breasts were tempting me.

Unbuttoning the button, I unzipped them carefully and then pushed them down. She sucked in a breath as she saw my underwear. Unlike a lot of guys,

I didn't wear boxers. I preferred the tighter briefs. My erection was clearly outlined through the taut fabric. I groaned when I saw her lick her lips as she stared at me.

She sat up higher and beckoned me with her hand. I stepped to the bed and crawled on it to hover over her. "How's this?" I asked gutturally.

She answered by grasping me behind the neck and pulling me down to meet her seeking mouth. As soon as our lips met, the flames started to burn like a bonfire again. As I hungrily used my teeth on her rapidly swelling lips, I interspersed those nips by twinning my tongue around hers. Our breaths were loud as we panted. Every whimper or moan out of her made me want to beat my chest and roar.

Suddenly, I had to get my mouth back on her breasts. I was kneading and stroking them, but I wanted more. Releasing her mouth, which made her whimper in protest, I kissed and nipped my way down her neck, which made her arch her back, causing her to thrust into my hands harder. Slowly making my way down, when I reached them, I stopped to admire them again. I'd never get tired of looking at them.

Her mounds were full and, even in my large hands, gave me a more than nice handful. Her pink nipples were pebbled into hard beads. I sucked the right one into my mouth. I sucked hard and increased it before flattening my tongue against it, then biting down enough to be able to tug it when I moved my head back. She moaned louder and thrust her pussy into my torso. Her hand came up to tease my nipple and tug. I twisted her other nipple.

The sounds she was making and how she squirmed on the bed made me leak in my underwear. I ground my cock into the mattress. Fuck, what I wouldn't do to have her hand, mouth, or pussy surrounding it right now. My balls were tightening. I reached down between us to tug them down to stave off my coming like I had threatened earlier. Her hands in my hair, pulling my head up, made me frown.

"What's wrong, Hotcake?"

"Nothing, Studcake. I just thought you might want me to help you with your problem. It seems you need some relief, and I think I can help you get it."

My heart stopped beating, I think, at her words. Did I understand her right? Was she offering to get me off with her hand or, better yet, her mouth? Fuck, surely I was dreaming. I studied her face. She didn't look afraid or like she was kidding. I swallowed hard before I croaked out a reply.

"Baby, you don't have to do that."

"I know I don't. I want to. Please, I need to see you and touch you. Take off your underwear and lie on your back, Aidan. Unless you don't want me to," a trace of uncertainty crept into her voice. Fuck that.

I quickly stood up and lowered my underwear, allowing them to drop to the floor. I stepped out of them and then lay down next to her. She sat up, and I saw her eyes widen and her mouth fall open. I wanted to grin. Yeah, I was blessed in that department. My cock matched my size. I wasn't the thickest guy in the world, but I was long and more than satisfied the ladies. Some even said it was too much. God, I hoped she wouldn't think that. I fisted myself and stroked it a couple of times. I groaned at how good it felt, but I let go. I didn't want to blow yet.

She swallowed, then tentatively reached out. She stopped short of touching me. "You can touch me, baby. Hell, you can do anything you want. Although if you walk off now, I might cry. Talk to me."

"You're beautiful, Aidan. God, I never thought a man's cock was beautiful, but yours is. It's so big. Will it fit? And I didn't expect those," she said as she pointed to my piercings. Yeah, I could tell those were a surprise, and she was fascinated.

I'd gotten Sunshine at Ink's shop to do them one night about five years ago. It was on a dare, and they'd hurt like a motherfucker, but when they healed, I loved how they felt to both parties. I snorted at her "will it fit" comment. "Kimera, it'll fit. As for those, this one up here is called a king's crown piercing," I said as I pointed out the curved barbell one, which was through the ridge at the base of the head on the topside.

Then I pointed to the one at the base of my cock, right above my sac. "This is called a lorum."

She lightly ran her fingers over the top one and then down my shaft to the bottom one. My cock jumped, and more precum leaked out. The head was covered in it. "So they hurt?" she asked.

"Not now, but they did when I got them."

"Why did you get them? Do they really enhance your pleasure that much?"

"It was on a dare from some of the guys. Yes, they do enhance pleasure, but not just for me. They do it for my partner, too. Don't be afraid to touch them, darlin'. As long as you don't yank the hell out of them, you can do just about anything, although you have to be careful if you ever want to give head. I don't want you to chip your teeth."

I moaned as she wrapped her hand around me. She slowly stroked the whole length. I hissed, then put my hand over hers. I tightened her grip. "You can hold me tighter. Yeah, fuck like that. Jesus, I'm gonna apologize now, but I'm not gonna last long, baby. Your hand feels way fucking better than mine."

She hummed, and when I let go, she kept up the perfect tightness and worked my cock. Shit, a hand job had never felt this good. My balls drew up again. Before I could tug them down, she did it. The look of awe and desire on her face was too much for me. I had to close my eyes. I didn't want to be selfish, but she had me so in need I couldn't do anything but lie there and fight not to come. In my head, I pictured her mouth on me. *Fuck, don't do that*, I told myself. I jumped when the image got so real I swore she was doing it. When the sensation got tighter, I opened my eyes and got the surprise of my life.

Kimera: Chapter 14

I was stunned and mesmerized by Spawn's cock. I never imagined we'd get this far this fast, but I couldn't resist him. Then, to see what he was packing and those piercings, my desire ramped up even further. It didn't take much for the hand job not to be enough. I wanted to know what he felt like in my mouth and how he tasted. The thought of his piercings in there was a turn-on, too.

What was even more of a surprise was giving head wasn't one of my favorite things. I did it in the past with my couple of boyfriends, but it was for their benefit, never mine. I sure never told them their cocks were beautiful. His was, and the size was intimidating, but I wanted to see how much of him I could swallow.

Seeing the strain on his face as he fought not to come, I wanted to push him past it. I needed him to come, and I wanted it to be hard. Leaning forward, I sucked the cum-covered head into my mouth. Jesus, I couldn't believe it, but he tasted good. That was another thing. My past experiences had always been that cum tasted nasty. I sucked harder and took a bit more of his cock inside. I could feel the piercing rubbing on my tongue. He jumped. Glancing up, I saw him staring at me in shock.

Keeping my fist pumping his base, I held his gaze as I lowered my head. Heat filled his gaze. He ran a finger down my cheek. "Fuck, I didn't expect this. God, yes, just like that," he moaned. I fluttered my tongue on his shaft before licking my tongue up to tease his king's crown. I was determined to put everything I could into this blow job. I wanted to blow his mind.

My panties were drenched. Giving head had never turned me on like this, either. My whole body was humming. I knew he was too long for me to take all of him, but I would do my best. As I worked more of him inside my mouth, his hand came up to rest in my hair. He didn't press me down and try to force me to take more. One guy had done it more than once, and that had ended me doing this for him.

However, in Spawn's case, I wanted him to do it to me. That was weird, but the thought was exciting with him. Hoping I wasn't making a mistake, I placed my hand over his and pressed lightly, lowering myself a tad more. He hissed, then muttered hoarsely, "Are you sure, Kimera? I don't want to hurt or scare you."

I hummed and nodded as best as I could. The hum made his hips flex, driving him deeper. That's what broke him, I think, because the next thing I knew, he was pressing me down. He didn't do it aggressively or force me to take all of him at once. It was slow. By doing it that way, I was able to adjust. He stretched my mouth wide.

I bobbed up and down, getting more turned on by the second as I played with his balls. His groans and grunts were music to my ears. When he hit the back of my throat, I gagged, and he backed off. I found I didn't want that. I wanted him to go further. I literally wanted to choke on his cock. Inhaling deeply, I pressed myself down and past the back of my throat. He shouted, "Goddamn," when I did.

I hummed, and he cried out. "Stop, God, stop before I blow. I'm close, babe. So damn close. You gotta stop," he panted.

I could feel how tight his balls were, and his cock was jumping in my mouth. Looking up at him, I let him see my intent, and then I pushed deep again and hummed hard and long. The look of utter bliss on his face as he grunted and then began to shoot his load was empowering. I loved the fact I'd made him feel that good.

I struggled a bit, swallowing all of it, but I did it. When he stopped coming and softened a little, I slowly lifted up, bathing his length with my tongue. When he popped out of my mouth, I placed a gentle kiss on the head and then sat up. I yelped in surprise when he grabbed me, yanked me down to his mouth, and kissed me. I knew he had to be able to still taste himself on me, but he didn't seem to care. He growled as he kissed me literally into a stupor.

By the time he let go, I was dazed. He eased me onto my back and straddled me. His expression was even hotter than before he came. He was breathing hard. "That was the best fucking head of my goddamn life, woman. I didn't expect it or for you to swallow, but shit. If you ever want to do that again, my answer is fuck yeah."

I smirked. "I think you can be guaranteed I'll do that again. Aidan. I've never liked it much, but I love taking you like that."

"Then I'm one lucky bastard. Now, I think I need to give you some relief. What do you say? Can I take the rest of your clothes off and taste you? Please?" he pleaded.

I was helpless to say no. As nervous as I was to have him see the rest of me, I needed him more. Nodding yes, I watched him give me a satisfied smirk, and then he was up. He dragged off my shoes and socks, then undid my pants and tugged them down and off. He stood there admiring me in my bikini panties for a couple of moments, then he hooked his fingers in the waist and slowly inched them down. I think he was giving me time to say no, but I wouldn't.

As soon as they were off, he spread my legs. I wanted to cover myself, but I didn't. I hoped he liked what he found. Even if I weren't involved with anyone, I'd always hated having hair down there. It drove me crazy, so I'd gone a few years back and had it waxed off for the first time. It was painful at first but worth the result, so I kept it up. I was completely bare.

He stared hard, and I shivered when he licked his lips. He met my anxious gaze. "That is the most gorgeous pussy ever, baby. I love you bare. There's nothing between my mouth and you. I want you to feel everything I do. Let me know if you don't like something, otherwise prepare to come and come hard.

Oh, and once isn't enough," he warned me.

I thought I should warn him. "Aidan, it's hard for me to orgasm, so don't be disappointed or think it's you if I don't or if I come only once. I was surprised I did it earlier, to be honest. That's never happened before."

"Challenge accepted, She-Wolf. I'm gonna make you howl for me," he promised right before he lay on his stomach between my legs and spread me open wider. His hand parted my folds, and I swear I heard him inhale like he was smelling me. Shit, I had a shower this morning, but what if I smelled bad? My face went beet red, and I tried to close my legs but couldn't.

He growled. "Don't. Fuck, you not only look gorgeous, but you also smell so good. I've gotta know what you taste like, baby." As he finished telling me that, I jumped as his tongue swept from my entrance to my clit. He moaned and kept lapping at my folds, and then he sucked my clit hard, thrashing it with his tongue and biting down on it gently.

I shuddered at the sensations zinging through my body. I'd never felt anything like this. If he kept this up, I'd be coming in no time at all. My hips lifted off the mattress. He growled and nuzzled harder between my legs. His slight five o'clock shadow rubbed deliciously against my nerve endings. I almost cried when he lifted his head to speak.

"I want you to come hard and give me all the delicious honey you can. Shit, you were made for me," he muttered before going back down on me.

I got lost in his lips, tongue, teeth, and fingers

teasing me. He thrust a finger inside, and it sent me careening into a forceful orgasm. As I cried out and shook, he didn't stop. He kept going. From there, he proved me wrong. I could orgasm more than once, and they were the most intense ones of my life. I got lost in a haze, and I think it was after the third one that he let me rest. He laid his head on my stomach and smiled up at me.

"So, what was this about you can't come, and if you do, it's only once?"

I smacked his shoulder. "No need to fish for compliments, honey. You know you're a sex god. I stand corrected. Lord, I could take a nap now," I said, yawning.

"Well, why don't we go take a quick shower, then we'll both take one? I'll let Rhaines know to keep an eye on Toro until we get up."

"I'd love a shower, but I don't think I can walk."

He got up, and I saw he was hard again. He lifted me up. I squealed, and he laughed as he took me to the bathroom. I wondered if he'd let me suck him off again in the shower. I'd never tried it there. Hmm, it might be fun.

When we eventually crawled into bed, I was done for. He hadn't let me suck him off, but we both gave each other hand jobs, and they were amazing. I think my head barely touched the pillow before I was out. He had his arms around me, and my head rested on his shoulder.

৶৶৶

A loud knocking sound made me surface. I did so reluctantly. I was warm and comfortable. I didn't want to wake up. I heard a muffled swear, which made me open my eyes. My warmth moved away, and I realized Spawn was getting up. I watched as he dragged his jeans on. He saw me watching him.

"Go back to sleep, babe. I'll see who it is, then come back. Whoever it is, they'd better have a good reason for disturbing us," he grumbled.

"Maybe it's Rhaines, and he needs us to take Toro. I should get up. He's probably hungry," I said as I threw back the covers. He stalked over and put them back over me.

"Stay. If he needs food, I can get him taken care of." He gave me a brief, hard kiss and then left. I strained to hear if I could hear who it was and what they needed.

There was a murmur of voices, but I couldn't make out what they said. When he didn't come back and the talking continued, I got up. Now, my curiosity was piqued. I tossed on my pants, and then I remembered my top and bra were in the kitchen. God, I hoped whoever was in the house didn't see them. I went to his closet and got one of his T-shirts. I hoped he didn't mind. My feet were cold, so I put on my socks and shoes. Once I was decent, I padded out. I wondered if they weren't in the kitchen if I could get there and grab my stuff without being seen. I went as quietly as possible. I was almost to it when I froze. It was Lash by the sound of the voice. I heard my name. What he said turned me from smiling to hurt then furious.

"Well, I guess since she came back with you and you've been staying out in Lake Charles with her, she's forgiven you for thinking she was hooked up with a married man. What's he like, this husband of the other woman that bastard raped? I told you she wasn't a woman to have an affair with a married man. Aren't you glad you listened to Smoke and went after her?"

"Shh, keep your voice down. She's in the bedroom. If you must know, I haven't told her what I thought."

"What? Spawn, you said you would tell her. You can't keep this from her. She'll find out eventually," a second voice said gruffly. This one belonged to Reaper.

"I know, but things are still new, and I don't want anything to ruin it. I'll tell her, eventually. I know I fucked up when I tracked her down online right after she left and saw her in that car with Sonny. They didn't kiss like I thought. He's happily married. They're nice people, and he wants the same thing we do. To put an end to Paden Gallagher once and for all. You said you wanted to have church. Do you mean right now or tomorrow?"

My fury over him thinking such a thing about me overtook my senses. Instead of finding a way to get out of the house, I marched through the dining room and great room to reach where they stood in the foyer. The smile on Spawn's face slid off when he saw my expression. I heard Lash mutter, "Shit, not again."

I clenched my fists tightly. I wanted to punch Spawn in the face so badly I ached. He started toward me, but I stopped him by raising my fist. "I swear to all that is holy. If you touch me, I'll hit you, Spawn. Hell, I might, anyway. So, you thought I was a whore who would have an affair with a married man. That I ran off to be with my married lover in the same town where he lives with his family. Well, I'm glad to know what you think of me. Fuck you, Spawn. Fuck you and everything you ever said to me. Forget coming back to Lake Charles with me. I don't need or want your help. In fact, I'll sell my body on the street to find another way to track him," I hissed.

This pushed him into action. He came at me as Reaper and Lash slipped out the door. I slapped his hands as he got near me. "Don't touch me!" I yelled at him.

"You need to let me explain and calm down. I know hearing that hurt, and I'm sorry. I was fucked up when you left. I wasn't thinking clearly."

"No, I was the one not thinking clearly. I should've never listened to you. Tell me, was the lure of sex with someone who didn't fall at your feet and drop her pants right away so big that you had to play games and make promises you didn't mean? Hell, according to what I just heard, you thought I was no better than those women you guys fuck at the clubhouse. Maybe I should apply for their job. I wonder who'll be my first fuck," I snapped.

He let out a roar, and despite how I slapped, punched, and kicked, he hauled me up and over his shoulder. I struggled and screamed profanities as he carried me into his bedroom. When he dropped me on the bed, I kicked him, catching him in the thigh, then scrambled across the mattress to get to the other side. A hand grabbed my ankle and jerked me back to him. I tried to kick with the other leg, but he caught it, and then I was pressed into the mattress by his hard, heavy body. I tried to hit him when I couldn't kick, but he pinned my hands over my head with one of his. I glared up at him, seething.

"Get off me and let go. I'm leaving."

"No, you're not. You're staying with me where you belong. Nothing I told you was a lie, Kimera. I want all those things with you. I'm not just looking for a piece of ass. And it'll be over my dead body before you'll sell yourself on the street or fuck one of my brothers. You're mine," he growled as he scowled at me.

"No, I'm not. I take it back. Go back to your whores. I'm sure you'll forget me by tomorrow. I bet you're pissed you didn't get me to fuck you before I found out, aren't you? Sorry, but hand and blowjobs are all you'll get," I hissed. The anger was still there, but the hurt was edging it out. I didn't want that to happen until I was away from him so he wouldn't see me cry.

"I regret hurting you. I regret not telling you myself what an idiot I was. I cherish what you allowed me to do and what you did to me. Do I want to make love to you? Hell yeah, and I will one day. We're not over. I need you to let me explain."

"There's nothing to explain. It was pretty plain to me that you think I have no morals, and I'd have an affair with a married man and not care if his wife knew it or not. Maybe you think I still am. After all, a woman like me could stand in front of his wife and pretend to be her friend while I was screwing her husband. Oh, and make over his kids, too." The tears were coming. I could feel them.

"No, you couldn't, and I know that. I knew it then, but I was so twisted up over you leaving the compound, what happened to you here, and then you disappearing without telling anyone that I went a bit nuts, I think. I was desperate to find you and terrified. When I did, and I saw you get in that car with Sonny, I didn't know who he was, and it looked like you two might've kissed. It gutted me. I walked around here like a bear, snapping everyone's heads off for a week. No one could stand to be around me. I hated my own company."

"So you just suddenly thought, hey, maybe I'm wrong? What did they mean about Smoke? What does he have to do with this?"

He sighed deeply and then lay his head on the bed next to my head. "Reaper got tired of me acting out and called Smoke, asking him to do some digging. He knew it was because of you. When Smoke called, he informed Reaper that I'd found you. He explained to us how you were orphaned and that it was your hometown. When I found you there, I didn't go further, and I should've. Anyway, I told them what I thought I saw, and Smoke said I was full of it. He was the one to hint there was more going on, and he thought it was worse than what happened with the Gusevs if his guess was right. He offered his club to help you if we wouldn't."

"So it took a stranger to convince you I wasn't this terrible person. That's rich." I snorted.

"No, it took him to make me think and realize there was no way you'd do that. The dread it made me feel made me sick. That's when I researched what I could, and then I headed to Lake Charles to find you and get the rest of the story. You need to know I intended to tell you, but not yet. Not until..." he petered off.

"Not until what?" I challenged him. Tears streamed down my face, but I didn't let my voice tremble. With his face still buried in the bed, he didn't see them.

"Until you love me as much as I love you," he whispered brokenly. Despite how mad and hurt I was, hearing him confess such a thing made my heart lurch for joy. I fought to stop it. I wouldn't let myself believe it.

"You don't love me. If you did, you'd never have believed me capable of that."

He lifted his head, and that's when I saw tears on his cheeks. He looked devastated. He wiped at the ones on my face. "Baby, please, don't cry. I do love you so fucking much it hurts. This isn't the way I wanted to tell you, but it's no lie. Please, you have to forgive me. Tell me what I have to do to earn your forgiveness. Don't leave me. It'll kill me if you do."

I wanted to tell him to go to hell, and I never wanted to see him. However, my damn heart wouldn't let me. I'd fought not to fall for him for weeks. Despite trying not to, I had, and I think those feelings made what he did seem so much worse. I tried to see it from his perspective. Could I forgive him and move on?

Spawn:

I watched as emotions flitted across her face. I saw them all. There was anger, hurt, worry, sadness, and even a soft expression or two. It was those that gave me hope. I held my breath as long as I could, afraid to even breathe. I hadn't lied. I knew I loved her. I was a fool not to confess my stupidity the moment she opened her hotel door, but I couldn't do it. If my stupid mistake in ever thinking such an asinine thing caused me to lose her, I'd cut out my heart because it would be useless.

I don't know how long she remained silent as she contemplated what I told her. I could hear the thundering beat of my heart in my ears. I found myself praying. *God, don't let her leave me. I'll do anything if you just make her forgive me and stay. I'll love her like no other.*

I jerked when she spoke. It took me by surprise since I was lost in my prayers. "You hurt me, Spawn. I can't tell you how much. Thinking I could possibly do that shows you don't know me at all."

When she paused, I had to say something. It didn't sound good for me. "I know I hurt you, and you have no idea how much I wish I could go back and do it differently. Instead of letting my hurt pride dictate what I did, I'd go with my heart. I'd have flown out to see you then, and we'd possibly have this whole thing taken care of, but I can't change it. I don't know everything about you, but I know you'd never do that. It was temporary insanity."

She shook her head, which made me queasy. "No, it means we don't know each other. Looking back, I know it's my fault we don't. You've tried over and over to get to know me since the moment we met, and I kept pushing you away. I have this bad habit of not letting people get close to me. It's a protection mechanism. All I remember after Granny died was being disappointed again and again by the people who were supposed to care for me. It's a miracle I let Troian in as much as I did, although even with her, it wasn't all the way."

"I knew someone had hurt you. I even wondered if you'd been raped at one point before the whole mess with the Gusevs, but I prayed it wasn't true. I knew you were wary, and I had to take things slow. Earning your trust and love is all I want. How can I do that? Please, I'm begging you, don't say it's impossible."

"I can't just sweep it under the carpet," she said, which made bile inch up to the back of my throat. She continued. "But I can agree to us spending time together and getting to know each other. However, what we did earlier can't happen again. Sex will only cloud the situation. I won't sleep with you unless I know I can trust you not to hurt me. If you can't agree to do that, then we'll stop this now."

The thought of not being able to touch her, taste her, and ultimately make complete love to her made me cringe inside, but I'd do it if this were the only way to win her. "Okay, I agree. Only don't get mad if I slip up and give you a kiss now and then. Is hand holding or caring touches permitted? I don't think I can control those."

"If you want to hold my hand or place your hands on me in appropriate places, that's fine. As for kissing, I don't know. It clouds my mind. Let's just say you'll do your best not to."

Seeing this was the best I could hope for, I nodded. "Agreed. Now, what should we do? It's getting late. I think we should find Toro and get ourselves and him fed some dinner. Tomorrow, we'll meet with the rest of the club. I have a lot to do until Christmas. Our flight back is the day after. Hopefully, I'll find him by then, and we can figure out what's to be done with him."

"Sounds like a plan. Let's go find my dog, and if there's anything I can do to help, let me know. I don't like being idle or feeling useless."

I sat up when she did. "You're never useless to me. The online research I'm doing isn't something you can help me with, but I do have something you can do. I have several gifts I need wrapped for Christmas. It's mainly things for the kids and small things for the old ladies. Would you mind wrapping them for me? When I do it, it looks like a toddler did it."

She smiled. "I'd love to do them. I can't wait to see what you got. Which reminds me, it's only a couple of days until Christmas. I have to do some shopping. While you work, I'll go to town tomorrow and shop."

"Babe, you don't need to buy anyone anything.

The kids will get plenty of stuff, believe me."

"Regardless, I want to. Okay, let me wash my face and comb my hair, then we can go get Toro and find food. I'm starving," she said firmly. I didn't argue. As we got up, I thanked my lucky stars she was willing to try.

Kimera: Chapter 15

Spawn was hard at work on his sea of computer monitors. He'd been at it since early this morning when I woke up to find him working. I had no idea when he started. I'd gone to bed in the guest bedroom and tossed and turned for a long time before I finally fell into a fitful sleep. I knew he wasn't happy with my decision not to sleep with him, even though he asked and promised he wouldn't touch me. The reason I didn't was it would test my control too much.

Even as angry as I still was, the desire to be with him fully tugged at me constantly. I needed a distraction, and shopping would provide it. When I mentioned I was still going to do it, he wanted to come with me. I told him this would waste valuable searching time. I urged him to stay and work, and I'd return as soon as possible. In the end, he wouldn't agree unless I took someone with me. As it happened, Troian was happy to go along. I knew it would provide us with an opportunity to talk about what happened. I'd hurt her too by leaving like I did.

We'd talked a couple of times since Spawn showed up in Lake Charles, but I didn't go into a lot of detail. I hadn't told her about my history, and I wondered if she knew. I figured all the men did, and wouldn't they tell their old ladies? Would it change how they treated me? I hadn't seen the rest of the club yet, and I was nervous about it. The brief glimpses of Reaper and Lash last night hadn't revealed anything. They'd left too quickly. When Troian and I left, she met me at Spawn's house, so I didn't get a chance to see or talk to Lash. As we drove into town, the silence was awkward. Tension could be felt. This wouldn't do.

Instead of going to where the main shopping was, I detoured and took us to the park. I parked at the edge of it, where there were no picnic tables or kids' playsets. We shouldn't be disturbed there. Since it was winter, we stayed in the car with the heater on. She turned in her seat and studied me.

"I need to apologize for leaving like I did and making you worry. It was never my intention. I hoped I'd resolve the issue and be back soon. It didn't happen, as you know. I didn't tell you or anyone because I didn't want to involve you. All of you deserve a rest after what you went through with your family."

"That's where you're wrong. This is our business, Kimera. You're my friend, dare I say, my best friend. I've befriended the other old ladies, but it's you I think of as my bestie. I won't lie. It hurt when you left without a word, but it also scared me. I was confused, too. Spawn had been so attentive to you. I thought he was into you, and when you left, he was so upset. He went to find you doing his thing. Then suddenly, he refused to talk about you and wouldn't say what he learned. He walked around, biting off everyone's heads. Just as abruptly, a couple of weeks later, he up and goes to Louisiana. Now you're back for a bit, but I heard you'd be returning there after Christmas. What the hell is going on?"

I was surprised Lash hadn't told her. Maybe the whole club didn't know, or just the women didn't. I wondered why they kept it a secret. Knowing I had to tell her, I steeled myself to retell my story. It seemed that was all I had done lately. "What did Lash tell you?"

"Lash said there was something serious happening, and I would have to ask you what it was. He said it wasn't his place to tell me. I've been patient, Kim. Please tell me so I can help you. You helped me. I'm here for you no matter what."

This brought tears to my eyes, but I didn't let them get the better of me. Now wasn't the time for crying. As concisely and as quickly as possible, I told her about my foster care days and what happened with Paden. Suffice it to say she was shocked, angry, and sympathetic to me. She cried when she heard. I then explained how Claudia found me and what happened to her with Paden. I even told her what I overheard yesterday. When I was done, she had a determined expression on her face.

"I wish you'd told me. To think you carried this around all these years and then to have my cousins do that to you. It's a wonder you didn't lose your mind."

"Troi, your cousins scared me, and it did trigger bad memories, but they didn't rape me. The guys got there in time. It's been hard. Those months with Paden did shape me. It took years before I would even try to have a relationship with a man, and even then, sex was not great. I could never let go. The couple of guys I let get that far with me couldn't cope, and they walked. I don't blame them. Even now, the thought of opening up to Spawn scares the crap outta me. What if I can't do it? Or what if I can't give him what he needs and wants? If he walks away, it'll likely hurt me in a way I'll never recover from," I confessed.

"I can tell you one thing. He was an idiot to ever think you'd be a home-wrecker, but I know that man is crazy about you. Nothing you say or do will make him walk away. If you give him a chance, he'll help you open up and let go. Sex with him will be pretty spectacular, I think. Only don't tell Lash I said that." She giggled.

I couldn't help but giggle, too. "I know, I think so too. God, the man makes me melt, and I can't think straight. His kisses are lethal, and when he…" I stopped and blushed.

"Oh, ho, do tell. Have you two done the deed?" She wiggled her eyebrows at me.

I playfully shoved her. "Not what you're thinking. There was one make-out session that got pretty hot, but then I found out what he thought. We had an argument and then talked, and we've agreed to get to know each other without adding sex to the mix."

"God, you're stronger than me. I fell for Lash, and even when I was mad at him, I desperately wanted him. It didn't take much for me to give him my virginity. And let me tell you, whew, that man…" She fanned herself.

"Stop it. I don't want to have images of you two doing it in my head. And you were a virgin? Bet he loved that."

"Oh yes, he did, but enough about my man. We're talking about yours and that bastard who hurt you. You're part of this club, and the guys will do everything in their power to make him pay for you and Claudia and to keep all women and girls safe. He'll deserve whatever they decide is his fate."

She'd never told me exactly what they did to her cousins. I knew she'd been present for it, and when she returned from wherever they took them, she'd been quiet for a few days. I wondered if I asked now, would she tell me? It wasn't that I had doubts the guys could handle Paden. I wondered how they might do it.

"What exactly did they do to them? I hate to ask, but I need to know if they find and kill Paden, will he suffer? Is it wrong of me to want him to? I have this burning desire to inflict pain on him, but I'm a nurse. I should only want to help people. Am I a horrible person?"

She gasped, then leaned over the console to tug me closer. She hugged me. "No, you're not a horrible person. You're a very loving person, but we all have our limits. What he did to you and her is unforgivable, and I can guarantee you, he'll suffer. We don't talk about what the guys did to protect them. However, you need to know. If it were ever discovered, I'd go down with them. I had my hand in inflicting pain on my cousins, and it was cathartic for me. Do you think you'd like to do the same? You don't have to. In fact, Lash and the guys didn't want me to do it, but I had to."

I thought about what she said. On one hand, I

wanted to make him suffer personally. On the other hand, I felt bad that I did. In the end, I gave the only answer I could. "I don't know, maybe. I guess when the time comes, I'll decide. I swear I won't ever say a word to anyone about what any of you did. Your bastard cousins deserved it, and so will Paden. I'd like to think the law would put him away and throw away the key, but there's no proof other than our word. He might not get convicted, and even if he were, he'd likely get out in the future. It's rarely a 'life in prison without parole' sentence. Spawn explained what he might get."

"True. Okay, enough of this depressing talk. I forgive you as long as you never do something like that again. If you do, I'll kick your ass. Oh, and you have to promise to really give Spawn a chance. Has he told you he loves you yet?"

I blushed, but I nodded yes. She smiled. "Good. Believe it. Now, let's go shopping. I feel like spending some money. You said you wanted to get some things for the kids and a few others. Let's do the kids first. They'll be the most fun, I think."

She was right. We had so much fun and laughed ourselves silly, especially in the toy section. I was lucky I had decent savings even if I wasn't working at the moment. I'd never lived extravagantly. I not only bought things for the kids, but I got something for each of the old ladies. I made her go for a walk while I got hers. She picked up a few more things. As for the guys, I found some badass skull caps at the Harley dealership. They depicted different images with skulls, flames, and the company logo. They were a thick material that would keep their heads warm since they all seemed to ride in the winter. I had my fingers crossed that they would like them. Troian told me they would. The last one I shopped for was Spawn. I was hoping he'd like what I got.

By the time we were done, we were exhausted and starved. We decided to have a late lunch in town before heading back. As we sat in the restaurant, we laughed more. I noticed we were getting a lot of looks. At first, I didn't know why, but then I realized it was her property cut. Some were merely curious, but others were curling up their lips. It was those who pissed me off. After catching more than one doing it, I couldn't keep my mouth shut.

I turned around in my seat to face the table with the biggest number of culprits. It contained five women who'd been watching us and saying stuff just low enough we couldn't hear what they said, but it was clear they were talking about us. I stared at them. I saw a couple squirm and look away. The one I tagged as the leader gave me a defiant look. This would be fun.

I was no longer the shy young girl in foster care. After I turned eighteen, I did a lot to become strong and protect myself. The thing with the Gusevs hadn't shown my skills much, but I had them. And one of the things I didn't put up with was bitches. Enough of them had made me miserable growing up. I refused to let them do it to me as an adult or to keep my mouth shut.

"Do you have something you'd like to say loud enough for us to hear? I mean, if you're gonna run your mouth about us, at least have enough guts to say it to our faces. You've been staring and mouthing shit for the last twenty minutes. Speak up," I told them boldly. The other customers got deathly quiet.

The leader, a fake dye-job blond bitch sneered at me. "I don't talk to trash. Why don't you and your biker whore friend eat somewhere more your style? Can you even afford it here? I think it's disgusting she's wearing something that proclaims her as property. What century are we in?"

"Oh, we can more than afford it, and we're not trash or whores, although from the looks of you, you are with your fake dye job and even more fake tits," I told her with a smirk. She gasped when I said it, but I kept going. "As for her property cut, that's not ownership. That's a declaration from a man who's so in love with her he's marked her so anyone who fucks with her knows he'll protect her in any way he can. And so will every single one of his brothers. It's a goddamn compliment that she has one. I don't see a ring on your finger. What's the matter? Can't you find some man dumb enough to marry you? That's a claim of property, too, but I bet you'd kill to have one." I smirked more as I said it.

"How dare you speak to me like that! You're nothing but filth. I don't have to put up with this. Waitress! I want to see the manager. These people are bothering me," she called out loudly.

I glanced at Troian, hoping she wasn't too upset with me. What I found was a smiling woman who winked at me. "You're doing great. If you need a break, let me know, and I'll take over," she said quietly. I laughed.

"What did the bitch say?" Blond bitch squawked.

"I don't know, what did you say?" I countered her.

Her face was getting redder and redder. It was then that a man in a dress shirt, tie, and slacks came hurrying up. He was bald on top, and you could see he was already sweating. He didn't make eye contact with me or Troian. I knew how this would end, but I was gonna enjoy it as long as I could. He went to Blond Bimbo Boobs Barbie, or B⁴ as I now thought of her.

"Yes, how may I help you, ma'am? Sara said you wanted to speak to me. I'm Jeremy, the manager."

"Yes, these two women are disturbing our meal and being very confrontational. I'd like them removed, please. I would think an establishment with your reputation would be more selective about the type of people you let in here. If this is what I have to look forward to, I'll be sure to find a new favorite spot and tell my friends they should, too," she threatened.

His face went pale. He was sweating even more. He darted a glance at us, then back to her. I wasn't about to let her have all the say. "She and her friends started it by staring and talking about us for at least twenty minutes. I just told her to say it so we could hear her and shared a few truths when she said stupid stuff. She needed to be educated. As for her boycotting you, if she's that thin-skinned, you're better off not having her here. I know plenty of people who would love to eat here. Don't you, Troian?"

She smiled. "Oh yes, the club and the other

women would love it. And we can't forget all the people you work with, Kimera. I'm sure they'd love it too. Your business will increase, I bet."

His nervousness was apparent, and he was conflicted. He stared at Troian's cut. She'd moved, making the back more visible. I smirked at the outraged B^4.

She sneered. "And where do you work? The strip club? I hardly think he wants your kind or those disgusting bikers and their other whores in here," she snipped.

"If you call my friend, me, or the other old ladies whores one more time, I'll teach you some manners. As for where I work, I'm a nurse at the hospital. What do you do? Sit on your ass and wait for someone to take care of you? You're not smart enough to do much of anything else. If anyone is a stripper, it's you, although that's giving them a bad name by comparing them to you." I wanted one of her friends to say something, but they all seemed terrified. I guess they were cowards.

"If you touch me, I'll have you arrested and sue you," she said outraged, then she turned to Jeremy. "Throw them out or else."

"I-I, well, can't we just forget this? All of your meals are on the house."

"I don't want to forget it or a free meal. I want them gone. I can't eat with them here. The smell is awful."

I'd had enough. I stood up and walked closer to

their table. I saw her momentary look of fear, and then she masked it. "The only smell in here is you, your friends, and your nasty skank asses. As for arresting me, did I say I'd touch you? No, I didn't. I said I'd teach you manners. Don't worry, we're leaving. I'll make sure to let the club know how we were treated here. I think all of them and their various businesses and customers will find this enlightening. Don't worry. When I get done, you'll have this whole place to yourself whenever you want. Come on, Troian, it's time to go home and tell the guys about our day."

She stood up with a smile on her face. She made sure to turn so everyone in the place could see her cut. I took money out of my purse and laid it on the table. She did the same. Jeremy was standing there open-mouthed as we leisurely strolled out. He tried to apologize and followed us to the door, but we didn't stop. He was a spineless man, and I didn't have time for him. When we got to the parking lot and into the car, I told her to hold on. She gave me a puzzled look but didn't ask why. She saw me staring at the restaurant's door, so she did, too. It wasn't long before B^4 and her friends left. They all parted ways and got in their various cars. When she pulled out of the lot in her car, I followed her. I didn't think she knew we were doing it.

"What're you gonna do?" Troian asked, sounding a trifle worried.

"I'm gonna scare the shit out of her. I'd like to punch her in the face, but she'd whine and call the cops, and I can't be in jail right now. Besides, it could cause me to lose my nursing license. See that light, it's yellow. We're gonna pull up beside her and wave. I bet she'll shit herself."

I was feeling evil today. I think my "turn the other cheek" meter was broken. We pulled up next to her car. She wasn't paying attention so I laid on the horn hard and long. When she turned her head and saw us, it was amazing to watch the horror spread across her bitchy face. We smiled and waved at her until the light turned green then we kept pace with her until the next light. When it turned green, we took off and left her behind.

We laughed most of the way home. Were we terrible, yeah, but that woman and her friends were worse. I'd stood up to her, and maybe next time she'd think, or maybe her friends would before talking shit about people. Although, her kind was pretty stupid. If not, at least I got it off my chest. Probably not very mature in some people's minds, but I didn't care.

When we got back to the compound, I dropped Troian off at Lash's house and then headed to Spawn's. I'd barely parked before he was out the door. He opened my door and helped me out. "I missed you. I'm glad you're home. Let me get your bags."

"Okay, but I'm carrying this one," I told him as he opened the back door, and I grabbed the black shopping bag. He raised his brow but didn't ask. He was able to carry the rest on one arm. How did guys do that? If it were me, my arm would fall off. Inside the house, I insisted on taking them to my room and putting them away in the closet. After I finished, I joined him in the living room. He had a drink waiting for me. I sat next to him.

"How did your research go today?"

"I don't know yet. I think it might eventually give us a clue. I have to wait and see. How was your shopping?"

"It was a lot of fun. We found everything we wanted."

"Did you do anything else besides shop?"

"Like what?"

"Oh, you know, laugh, have fun, or maybe go eat and cause a scene in a restaurant?" He said the last bit with a raised brow.

I looked at him in astonishment. How did he know that? "H-how did you know that?"

He grinned. "Babe, there's not much we don't find out in this town, especially if it involves one of ours. One of the regular customers from Punisher's Mark, Ink's tattoo shop, was there. He called Ink and told him about it. He thought we should know. He said you handled it, but in case they got too ugly, he was standing by to get involved if you needed him."

"Really? I can't believe it. Lord, that woman and her friends were so rude. I stood it for as long as I could, then I had to say something. I'm sorry if it embarrassed you and the club, but I won't stand for it. They said hateful things to us, especially Troian. I put up with people like that growing up, and I don't anymore."

He wrapped his arms around me and gave me a brief kiss. I hated it when he pulled away. I wanted more, but I kept quiet. I didn't even call him on kissing me. "She-Wolf, you don't need to apologize. It was great. I don't want you to ever keep your mouth shut when someone acts like that. I would've preferred if you had backup, just in case. Ink said he'll show us the video."

"Video? The guy recorded it?" I squeaked.

He laughed again. "Yes, he did. Ink said to tell you, way to go. I think he was disappointed you left and didn't beat her ass."

"She would've had me arrested, and I could've lost my nursing license. Otherwise, I might've. I have to confess, though, we did follow her when she left and let her see us. We waved and smiled. I think she might've shit or pissed herself. She was a total bitch."

My confession only made him laugh harder. I snuggled into him and hoped he'd still be laughing when he saw the video. He was getting to know a whole different side of me, and I hoped it wouldn't scare him off. To be honest, I kind of wanted to see the video myself.

"Is there anything else you need to do while we're home?" he asked.

"Yeah, I should go see my boss at the hospital and let them know I need to extend my leave. Right now I've been using my vacation time, but that'll run out soon. Hopefully, they'll grant it and not just fire me. If they do, then when I get back, I'll have to get hot finding a new job which sucks, but whatever."

"If they do that, then you'll find something else,

I have no doubt. Nurses are in demand, according to what Alisse and Chey say. I don't know if you only want to work in a hospital, but if not, the doctor they work for might need a nurse. Alisse has a while to go before she's done with her nursing school. If not there, they might know of others looking."

"I'll ask if or when the time comes. I might not even get to speak to my boss while I'm home since I'd have to go tomorrow, and it's the day before Christmas. She could be on vacation herself for all I know."

"Doesn't she have an assistant or someone who covers when she's out?"

"She does, but I don't know if she can grant those kinds of things or not. Don't worry. I'll go see whoever tomorrow."

"I'll take you. Just tell me what time you want to go."

"I don't want to take you away from work. If I can borrow your car, I can go, or I'll see if Troian can take me."

He gave me a stern look. "Babe, I want to spend time with you. Yes, it's important to find Paden, but I don't have to be at my computer all the time to do it. I have help to search for the bastard. I want to take you."

"Okay, if you're sure, then yes, you can take me. Maybe we can go back to that restaurant and see who else I can piss off," I teased him. He laughed harder and then gave me a passionate kiss. I let him wipe all thoughts from my head.

Spawn: Chapter 16

We were back in Lake Charles. Our flight yesterday had been a bit crazy with after-Christmas travelers, but we made it. I was glad we'd left Toro in Bristol. The club offered to take care of him. It was hard to leave him, but I knew he'd be in good hands and have a ball.

The trip home had been quick, but we'd enjoyed Christmas with everyone. It was an added celebration for one couple. Lash chose Christmas Day to ask Troian to marry him, and he presented her with a ring. Of course, she said yes, and the women excitedly talked about planning a wedding.

Kimera had been so happy for her friend and promised she'd help her do anything she needed her to do to plan it. The rest of us knew it wouldn't be a long, drawn-out engagement. Once we hooked our women, we didn't like to wait. I wish I could've asked Kimera to marry me, but it was too early for her to handle it. We still had stuff to learn about each other, and I had to lock her down. I would've been satisfied if I could've given her the property cut I had on order, but I knew I needed to wait until after this shit with Paden was over, and she said yes to being mine without reservation. I hoped it wasn't long until it happened.

There had been some progress on the Paden front, too. A dive into his parents revealed that right before he spoke to Claudia on the street, his parents had withdrawn a large sum of money from their bank account. There was no subsequent deposit in any of his, but they could've easily given it to him in person. Our research showed they'd kept in contact over the years, and when they moved away from Lake Charles, they moved to a town near him in Athens, Texas, which was barely over four hours from Lake Charles. Having him on the same planet was too close, in my opinion.

He still wasn't using his bank accounts, and his phone wasn't showing as active. The only reason I could think for him to keep it turned off was he knew it could be used to track him or at least to show where he had been. His car hadn't been found on any camera feeds in town either, but again, we could only assume he was using his own vehicle. He hadn't rented one from any of the big rental companies because if he had, it would've shown up on our search. Even if he paid cash, they'd enter it into their systems and have to have his driver's license. Monitoring the major car rental companies wasn't hard. It was the tiny mom-and-pop ones we had to worry about. We had no way to know or watch all of those.

The average citizen wouldn't think to hide their paper trail or digital footprints; however, my dive into him told me he wasn't just anyone. He had a computer background, not at my level, but enough not to be totally stupid, unfortunately. It was him being so careful, which made me positive he was up to no good and intended harm for Claudia and Kimera.

His comments to Claudia were a threat, not just him spouting nonsense.

We were waiting to go over to Sonny and Claudia's this evening once they got home from visiting family and had the kids settled so we could talk. We offered to bring everyone dinner so no one had to cook. They said it wasn't necessary, but we insisted.

To pass the time, I did more searching, but not the whole day. I wanted to spend time with Kimera and she was bored, even though she tried to stay busy. One way she did that was to search for jobs back in Bristol. When she went to see her boss about extending her leave, she was told she could take another week, and if she weren't back after that, she'd have to let her go and get someone else. Since we couldn't guarantee we'd have this wrapped up by then, even though we wanted to, she was planning for the worst and doing a search now. Even if she couldn't interview, she'd know what the market had to offer.

Alisse promised to talk to her boss, Dr. Simpson, to see if she was hiring soon. They didn't have any openings, but she was in the process of taking on a partner, and when this happened, they would need more staff. I was hoping she'd get on there. Dr. Simpson was great to work for, and she understood the MC life. She never explained how, but we'd met her, and she treated us great. She obviously had been around bikers before. Her flexibility with Chey and Alisse was wonderful, too. They didn't take advantage, but sometimes things happened, and she had no problem covering them or having us around to keep them safe.

I didn't want to keep us holed up in our hotel the whole time, so we went out to lunch, and she took me around to show me the town. It was probably a good thing since, upon our return from Bristol, we'd moved into the same room. It had two queen beds, but we decided to do this so we could spend more time together. It tested my restraint, but I would resist the temptation. I was waiting for her to let me sleep with her, even if all we did was sleep. I meant what I said. I would go at her pace, but it didn't mean it was easy.

When I first suggested we go out in the town, she worried what would happen if Paden saw us, but then she realized how that would be to our advantage. I felt confident I could protect her from him, and if it let us find where he was hiding, all the better. In order to be ready if or when I should say we found him, a few of my brothers were coming in tomorrow.

Maniac's contact in the area Dom club, the Savage Highwaymen MC, had come through in a big way for us. It seemed they were a club despite what their name suggested, who was like us. They weren't a typical one-percenter into illegal shit and making war. A lot of them had been in the military and had a code very similar to ours. They'd fuck you up and kill you if you deserved it, but they had hard lines they didn't cross.

He'd explained why we were in their area. The enforcer for them happened to be a biker Maniac had met and befriended years ago named Abyss. They'd stayed in contact, but we hadn't ever needed to ask for their help or them us until now. With us being in Virginia and them in Louisiana, we didn't have our paths crossed. When Abyss told his president and the rest of his club about what we were doing, they offered any assistance we might need.

I doubted we'd need any of their men to help capture the fucker, but we would need a place to take him to when we did. It would be easier to torture and kill his ass here and get rid of the body rather than risk transporting him across multiple state lines to do it at home. Tomorrow, once my brothers got here, we were to go to their clubhouse to meet all of them.

When I told Kimera we'd be going and I wanted her to go, she'd been nervous. Ideally, I'd never take my woman to another club's clubhouse unless I knew them personally, but Maniac vouched for not only our safety, but hers, too. He said they had some old ladies, and Abyss told them to bring her so they could meet her. I knew she was nervous being around anyone who wasn't part of our club, but this would help her to see there were others like us. At least until we got a chance to have her meet our friends closer to home.

We spent a few hours around town. She showed me where she went to school and her favorite spots. After we had lunch and before going back to the hotel, she wanted to take me to see what had been the Gallagher's house. I told her it wasn't necessary. In the end, she agreed to do it another day. I wanted to avoid her having to look at it. I could go alone to see it. I had the address.

I didn't want it to trigger even more bad memories. I'd discovered last night she had nightmares. She'd awakened me with her whimpering and begging someone to stop. It had torn out my heart and made me even more determined, as if that was needed, to end the bastard. I'd ended up crawling into her bed and holding her. She never woke up, but she did settle down and sleep peacefully the rest of the night. I got back in my bed before she woke up this morning.

We were on our way to have dinner at Claudia and Sonny's house. We'd all decided last night that pizza, wings, and breadsticks would suffice. Brent was old enough to eat the pizza and breadsticks, and he loved them. Baby Brie would have to stick to her baby food and breadsticks. I grabbed a twelve-pack of beer. Sonny drank it, and we both could agree on a brand. For the ladies, they had a bottle of wine. I'd have a couple of beers with him, but not enough to make me unable to drive. I was hoping Kimera would relax if she had a couple of glasses of wine.

Sonny answered the door and waved us inside with a smile when we knocked. He laughed. We could hear Brie crying, and Brent was running around the living room, making airplane sounds as he waved a toy plane in the air.

"Welcome to the insanity. Run while you can because if I close the door, you're trapped," he teased.

"I'm used to this, and I think Kimera is more than capable of standing it. What has upset little Brie?" I asked.

He closed the door before he answered. "Better close it before the neighbors hear and call the cops. Well, let's see. My sweet daughter has taken exception to her bath tonight or getting dressed. She's decided we'll all have to listen to her displeasure until she is ready to stop."

"Honey, go take the stuff to the kitchen will you, and I'll go see if I can help Claudia," Kimera suggested. Sonny took the bag she was carrying. I had the bulk of the food and the beer.

"We got this, babe. Go rescue her," I told her before I gave her a quick kiss, and she hurried off. I followed Sonny to the kitchen. As we worked to get things organized, we talked.

"So, what did you guys do today?" he asked.

"I did more searching for you-know-who. Then Kimera took me around town and showed me some places, and we had lunch. It was pretty low-key. When did you all get back from visiting your family?"

"A couple of hours ago. God, I do like to see them, but it's exhausting. We've gotten them to come together for the most part, so we only have to go to one or two places on the holidays. Before we had Brent, it was running from house to house and even more tiring. Soon, we'll have to start having them come to us when they get a bit bigger, especially for Christmas. The kids don't truly understand Santa yet, but Brent's getting there. I can't wait until that day. Dragging all those gifts to the parents is a pain in the ass."

I chuckled. "I can imagine. I guess us all living on the compound makes it easy."

"Yeah, I think that would be so cool. Although,

don't any of you have family you spend holidays with?"

I was about to answer him, but the ladies joined us. Brie was still crying. Kimera had her. Claudia looked frazzled. I held out my hands. "Let me have a try," I offered.

"Are you sure you want to do that?" Claudia asked.

"Oh, let him. He's the baby whisperer back home. I swear he gets a hold of Lily or Arya or even Flynn, and they settle right down for him. It's rather disgusting, actually," Kimera told her as she gave me the baby.

I inhaled that fresh baby smell. Man, I knew I'd lose my man card if I admitted I loved the smell, but I did. I tucked her against my chest and cuddled her to me. Almost instantly, her little fist went into her mouth, and her eyelids began to get heavy.

"See, I told you. He pisses me off the way he can do that," Kimera said as she huffed. Sonny and Claudia were watching me with surprised expressions.

"Hey, you'll love it when we have our kids," I told her.

She blushed but didn't deny it. I glanced back at Sonny. "To answer your question, yeah, some of the brothers have family, and a few are close enough to go visit them, but most either don't have anyone or they're not close to them. I go see my family a few times a year in Montana. So far, I haven't gotten my sister and nephew to Virginia, but I'll keep trying. I wish they'd all move there. I told Kimera that once we have kids, I might convince them to move. Don't wait for me. Dig in. I'm content right where I am," I told them when I saw they appeared to be waiting for me to eat.

"Thanks. Just tell us when you wanna give her back," Sonny said. I stood gently patting and bouncing Brie while they got their plates and had a seat.

"So, you and Kimera plan to get married and have kids?" Claudia said with a smirk.

"Absolutely. I'm just waiting for her to say the word. She'll be my old lady and then my wife not long afterward."

"Old lady? Kim, smack him for calling you that," she said in outrage.

Kimera laughed. "It's not an insult the way he uses it. In the biker world, an old lady is the same as a wife. Guys don't claim an old lady unless they're serious. Most don't marry them because it's more serious to them than an actual marriage. They give their ladies a property cut."

"Property cut? So why is Spawn saying he'll marry you too?" she asked in interest.

I answered her so Kimera could take a bite. "I wear a leather cut, what you'd call a vest. It has my name, the name of my club and our logo on it. Our old ladies get the same thing. Only theirs are different. Kimera's will say on the back Property of Spawn with our logo. On the front will be her club name, which I'll give her. In our club, we not only make our women our old ladies but also our wives. We like to cover all the bases. It makes it harder for them to get away," I joked. I winked at Kimera as she gave me a stunned look.

"Oh, so the truth comes out. I have news for you, mister. I can run no matter what," she threatened.

"You can try, but I'll just chase you down and beg and plead until you come back. I've done it once already."

This made her blush again, and Claudia's mouth fell open. "You're admitting you begged her to have you and go back to Bristol with you when you came here?"

"Damn right, I did. I've been an idiot a few times, but she's forgiven me, and we're working out any issues. I'll always do that to keep her with me and happy."

Claudia got a satisfied smirk on her face. Kimera snorted. "As if I could hide from you. The man is lethal on a computer, and if he can't find me, he has friends who can. This Smoke I've heard about sounds interesting. I can't wait until I meet him."

"Who's Smoke?" Sonny asked.

"Smoke is part of the Archangel's Warriors MC in Dublin Falls, Tennessee. Our clubs are really close. He's their computer guy. Hell, he puts me to shame, and I can admit that. He and his wife, Everly, are two of the best hackers in the world. Our other friends' clubs don't have slouches in the hacker department either. The other chapter of the Warriors in Hunters Creek, Tennessee, has Outlaw. The Pagan Souls in Cherokee, North Carolina, has Wire, and their chapter in Lake Oconee, Georgia, has Shadow. The Horsemen of Wrath is our newest friendly club in St. Augustine, Florida, and they have Micro. The last one is Beast in the Ruthless Marauders. They're in Knoxville, Tennessee. We have friends with a security company with their own people, but I don't know their individual names. Believe me, when we need to, we can find anyone. That's why I have no doubt we'll find who we're looking for."

"Sh-crap, I had no idea," Sonny said. He stopped himself since Brent was there. I was trying really hard not to swear in front of him or the kids back home.

We chatted for a bit longer, and then Sonny took his daughter so I could eat. While he put her down to bed, I ate. Brent was excitedly talking to me about my bike. He'd learned I rode, and he was in awe. I let him see pictures on my phone of my bike and some of the others. When he saw the custom ones Ghost, Falcon, Blaze, and Tiger built in Dublin Falls, he was so excited I thought he was gonna pass out.

I glanced over at his mom. "I think you might have a future rider on your hands. Watch out."

"Oh God, that's scary. Have you ridden on his bike yet?" she asked Kimera.

She shook her head. "Not yet. He offered before, but I said no. Although when we go back, and the weather is warmer, I want to try it. He rides even in the winter, and that's too cold for me. He rented a bike when he was here before. All the Punishers are nuts to ride in winter," she shivered.

"Babe, that's because I have a tough hide, unlike you and your soft, beautiful skin. Don't worry; if you ride with me in winter, I'll make sure you're toasty warm—heated jacket and gloves and the works." I told her before kissing her. I made it brief.

"Ahh, that's so sweet," Claudia cooed.

Sonny chose that moment to return. He leaned down and kissed her, then stood up to give me the stink-eye. "Thanks for making her expect more out of me," he joked.

"Hey, we have to keep our women happy, man. Can't have them running off on us. They have options."

We talked more as we cleaned up and let Brent play a tad longer. He and I got down on the floor and drove his toy motorcycles around. He made me miss my nephew even more, just as Flynn did back home. We talked more about our lives, just getting to know each other. I liked them. It wasn't until Brent was down for the night that we got around to talking about Paden.

"Tell us. Any progress?" Sonny asked.

"I'm pretty sure his parents pulled out money to give him. I can't prove it, but I'm almost positive they did right before Claudia's run-in with him. He's staying off the grid. He's a computer guy, so unfortunately, he knows stuff. Tomorrow, a few of my brothers are coming to join us here. As soon as we find him, we'll be having a talk with him." I refused to say we were killing him, even if they knew that was what I meant.

"We're not gonna ask for details, Spawn, but you don't know the area. I can try to help you find a place," Sonny offered.

"Thanks, I appreciate it, but it's better if you don't know. Besides, we have another club who has offered to assist us. They're like mine, and they don't like raping pedophiles any more than we do," I growled. Every time I thought of what that man did to Kimera, Claudia, and who knows who else, I wanted to roar and have my hands beating his flesh. I planned to do a lot more than just beat him, but it was a start.

"How did you luck out there? Or do you have another, what do you call it, a chapter out here?" Claudia asked.

"No, not one of ours or the others I mentioned, but we know people and one of our guys knows a guy in a club near here, and there you have it. In fact, tomorrow, after my brothers get here, we'll be going to their clubhouse to meet them. We want to be prepared to make our move as soon as I track Gallagher's ass down."

"Spawn, I need to ask a favor," Sonny said hoarsely. I already knew what he was going to ask.

"Sonny, I know what you want. Since this involves more than just my club, I can't promise that. I'll ask and see if the other one will be alright for you to have some time with him, but they may not be comfortable taking that risk."

I could tell this didn't sit well with him, but I had to be upfront and not put anyone at risk. Finally, he sighed and nodded. "I get it, I do. Thanks for asking. I just want to help make him pay for what he did to Claudia. I can't help but think of others he might've done the same fucked up stuff to. If they aren't comfortable, make sure you give him pain for me."

"I do, too. I swear if they don't have an issue with it, you'll get your turn. If they do, I'll give him some hard, painful licks for you."

"He will, Sonny. I promise. Not long ago, something happened, and people who hurt a friend of mine tried to hurt me, too. They're not a problem anymore," Kimera assured him. I was impressed by how she didn't give much of anything away.

"Really? What did they try to do to you?" Claudia asked, aghast. I guess Kimera hadn't shared that with them before I came. I waited to see what she'd tell them. I wrapped my arm tighter around her shoulder. We were on the loveseat together.

"They thought I was her, and they took me. They were gonna rape me. Then God knows what else, maybe kill me or sell me. They were into forced prostitution. Anyway, Spawn and his club found me in the nick of time. It was so close. Both of our nightmares were taken care of."

I felt her tremble as she retold it. I kissed her temple. Claudia gasped. "Oh my God, no! Oh, Kimera, I'm so sorry. To have that happen at all is horrible, but after what we went through. How're you doing? When did this happen?"

"I'm still dealing, but it's better, I think. It was about a month or so before I came here to see you."

"And you came here? I wish you'd told me. If I'd

known, I wouldn't have bothered you. God, I feel sick," Claudia moaned as she held her stomach. Sonny had his arm around her now.

"Please don't. To be honest, it was kind of a relief to come here. Coming lets me put distance between me and those memories there. I'm happy you called me. To be able to face this and take Paden down is a dream come true. I dreamed of it for years but never thought it would happen. I don't want you to worry about it for a second."

Claudia nodded, but I saw the tears. We sat and talked for a while longer, and I gave them some information on the things I'd investigated. After we were done, we went back to talking about ordinary things until we called it a night. On the way back to the hotel, Kimera was quiet. I hoped our talk tonight hadn't been too much for her. I wondered if she'd have a nightmare. I wouldn't be surprised if she did. Maybe I could convince her to let me sleep with her to drive the demons away before they could bother her.

Kimera: Chapter 17

I thoroughly enjoyed our night with Claudia, Sonny, and their kids, even if we had to talk about Paden. He was the only downer of the night, really the whole day. As the day progressed, I'd been thinking more and more about something. By the time we made it back to the hotel, I'd come to a decision.

Any doubts or hesitation I might've had in regard to completely committing to Spawn were gone. What he'd done when the Gusevs kidnapped me, plus what he was doing now, erased any lingering upset over what he thought when I left Bristol without telling anyone.

When we got in our room, he was a gentleman and insisted I take my shower first. I got my clothing together out of the drawer and went into the bathroom. I'd washed my hair last night, so there was no need to do it again. I thoroughly scrubbed and exfoliated my body and freshly shaved my pits and legs. I'd made sure my wax job was done again while we were at home. Once I was done, I got out, dried off, and applied body lotion. It was a special kind I hoped he liked. A swipe under each arm of deodorant came next. Brushing my hair and teeth were the final steps before I slid on my clothes. I checked myself out in the mirror. I appeared flushed but presentable.

Deciding not to linger any longer, I opened the door and confidently walked out. I saw the way his gaze burned as he scanned me from head to toe and back. His tongue peeked out for a moment as he licked his lips. I smiled at him. "It's all yours."

"I won't be long," he said rather hoarsely, I thought. He had his clothes in his hand. I couldn't tell what it was.

He hurried past me and into the bathroom. The shower came on moments later. Knowing I didn't have much time, I turned off all the lights except the one between the two beds. Once I did it, I went to the bed he'd slept in last night. I pulled back the covers. I left mine as it was. Crawling on the bed and under the top sheet, I felt the butterflies in my stomach. God, it had been so long since I'd done this, and whenever I had done it in the past, it hadn't ever been what I called good.

When I was home, Troian and I had talked about sex. She was new to it, but at least it seemed her experiences with Lash were all very positive ones. She glowed when she talked about it. She didn't go into details, but she did say he rocked her world every time. I didn't know what that was like. When I was with the other women, they let tidbits drop, which told me they had no complaints in that department with their men either. Was it a biker thing? I hoped so. Otherwise, I was worried Spawn would be disappointed.

All my past sexual relationships had been disappointments. Overall, I thought I had tried to be an active participant despite what happened to me at fifteen. The guys always got off, but I rarely did, and when it did happen, it wasn't anything to talk to your girlfriends about, if I had any. Mostly, I couldn't wait for it to be over. The men got off, rolled over, and went to sleep. There was no cuddling or sweet talk or intimacy. They only gave me enough foreplay to get me wet, and then they got to the main event. Why they were upset when they suggested we do other things and I said no, I couldn't understand. Surely, they knew I didn't orgasm. I didn't fake it. I got wet, but that was it. In order to get any satisfaction of my own, I'd go to the bathroom after they fell asleep and masturbate in the bath or shower. I kept hidden under the sink a vibrator which was waterproof.

I prayed hard for it to be different with Spawn. The oral sex we'd shared had been amazing and nothing I'd experienced before. If he could do that with his mouth and hands, surely he'd do as much with his cock. I wasn't expecting it to be better. He was already way better than anyone I'd been with. Hell, oral sex hadn't been a frequent thing with them, at least not with me receiving it.

I was so lost in my thoughts and feeling nervous that I didn't at first hear a new noise. When it registered, I strained hard to figure out what it was. It was coming from the bathroom. Spawn was making low groaning noises. They sounded like the ones he made when I'd given him a blow job. Throwing back the covers, I tiptoed to the door and listened. Yep, it was louder and definitely sounded like he was pleasuring himself. My pussy began to get wet. Turning the knob, it opened.

I slowly pushed it open, far enough for me to squeeze inside. I swallowed nervously. My mouth was dry. I hoped he wouldn't get upset.

The shower had one of those opaque glass doors on it. I could see him through it, just not in detail. Taking a deep breath, I went to it, whipped off my nightgown, then slid the shower door open. He had his head thrown back. One hand was on the wall, and the other was wrapped around his cock. He was fisting and working it fast. His strokes went from the base to the tip, where he twisted his hand over the head, dragging precum down his length. Even in the water, I could tell he was leaking. That sight made me even wetter. Before I could lose my courage, I stepped in and closed the door. It was a large shower for a hotel.

I don't know if I made a sound, he felt my presence, or cool air got in, but whatever it was, his eyes snapped open, and he whipped around. I saw the surprise on his face then he lowered his gaze and took in my naked body. It was true he'd seen me before, but this was different. He already had an aroused expression on his face when I got in. It doubled within seconds of seeing me. I fought not to cover myself and let him look his fill. Lowering my gaze, I scanned his body.

Last time I'd been able to enjoy his cock and a bit more. I hadn't explored his whole body with my hands or mouth. My mouth went from dry to watering at the sight of the man in front of me.

"Kimera, what the hell are you doing? You shouldn't be in here, She-Wolf. I'm not in control right now. Go out, and I'll join you when I am," he asked hoarsely.

"What if I don't want you in control, Aidan? What if I want to stay and see what you're like when you let go completely?"

He groaned as if he was in pain. I couldn't help but stare. He had muscles for days that were covered in delicious tattoos, and then there was his cock. It was standing tall and begging to be touched and licked. His piercings called to me to play with them. My pussy was soaked, and my nipples were hard beads. I had to fight not to touch myself.

"Jesus Christ, you don't know what you're asking for, baby. If I let myself go, I'll scare you, and I don't want to do that. I can't just give you oral sex tonight. I'm sorry." he grimaced as he said it.

Deciding to show him rather than talk about it, I stepped closer. He tried to back away, but he was close to the wall and didn't get far. I reached out and placed my hand over his heart. It was pounding. I ran it down to his taut nipple and flicked it. He moaned. I then gave it a pinch like he'd done to mine during our one night together. This made him moan louder.

"You've gotta stop, babe. Please," he pleaded. His fists were clenched, and I swear he was shaking a little bit.

"I don't want oral sex. Well, I do, but it's not all I want. I'm ready, Aidan. I'm ready for you to take me. I want to know what it's like to have you inside of me. To feel your cock filling me and you making love to me. I don't mind if you lose control. I know you won't hurt me."

I knew that even if I was nervous and worried, I had to convince him that I wanted to try. That was the main thing, and I wanted to make it good for him.

"God, you have to be sure. Don't do this unless you're one hundred and ten percent sure. I don't want to scare you or anything else," he said.

I slid my hand down his chest past his washboard stomach to his cock. I fisted it and stroked up and down once as I said, "I'm beyond sure. Make love to me, fuck me, I don't care which, just do it. I'm hurting," I whimpered. That wasn't a lie. I ached deep inside my core.

He growled, and then I was flush against him as he yanked me to him. My hand was still around his cock, but it was trapped between us. He lowered his head and took my mouth in the most aggressive kiss I'd ever had in my life. He was growling like a beast as he kissed, nibbled, and licked my mouth. When I opened my mouth, his tongue darted inside to wrestle with mine. I moaned at the taste and feel of him.

I raised up on my tiptoes to make it easier for him to kiss me. The next thing I knew, he cupped both of my ass cheeks and lifted me up. I squealed and hurried to get my arms around his neck and my legs around his waist. I moaned louder because this brought my nipples in contact with the hair on his chest, which made them tingle, and my pussy was rubbing along his hard cock. He groaned and kept kissing me for at least a good minute or two before he broke it.

His face was flushed like I knew mine was. I could feel the heat. His gaze was smoldering with desire and so intense. "I fucking love you, and I'm gonna show you that tonight. I need to ask. Are you on birth control? I have condoms, but I'd prefer if I could take you bare. I'm clean, I swear."

"I'm clean too, and yes, I'm on birth control. I've never gone bare, but I'm willing to with you."

"Thank fuck. I've never done it either, but between us, I want nothing, not even a thin layer of latex. I need us both to feel everything. Let's get out of here and to bed so I can do this properly. We'll have shower sex some other time," he said with a wicked smirk. I panted a little as he lowered me down. He made sure to drag my nipples through his hair and my pussy along the entire length of him. I moaned, and he smiled.

I wrapped a hand around his cock. He shuddered. "Just remember, paybacks can be a bitch."

"Fuck, I hope so," he muttered as he shut off the shower then maneuvered me around. "Let me get out and get you a towel. Stay here. It's warmer." The next thing I knew, he was out and shut the door. It was only a minute or so before he opened it again and wrapped me in a towel. He lifted me out and briskly, although gently, dried me thoroughly. He caressed my skin, and I saw him checking out everywhere his hands touched me. He paid extra attention to my breasts, ass, and pussy. I moaned again. I couldn't seem to hold them in. He flashed me his sexy grin.

When he was done. He lifted me in his arms like I

was a bride and opened the door somehow. "Aidan, I can walk, baby." I reminded him.

"I know you can, but I want to carry you. To me, this is our wedding night." His declaration filled me with more warmth and happiness. I nodded and smiled at him to proceed. He swiftly carried me to the bed and laid me down gently. I didn't know why he was so concerned about losing control. He was very controlled.

Or he was until I was spread out then he showed me what he meant by being out of control. He growled again like a beast, and the next thing I knew, he was straddling me. He took my mouth again. His hands were buried in my hair, lightly tugging on it. It stung a bit, but I found it only made my desire heighten. I had no idea it would make me do that. We consumed each other. I gave as good as I got in that kiss, I thought.

As we kissed, our hands were busy, too. Each of us had them on the other's chest. I played with his nipples and ran my fingers through the hair on his chest and outlined his pecs while he kneaded my breasts and tugged on my nipples. I shuddered and had to rub my thighs together. I was trying to get some kind of relief from the burning down there.

This caused him to lift his head away from me. I tried to chase his mouth with mine, but he shook his head and grinned. "Nah, no more of that right now. I promise we'll come back to it, though. No one kisses like you, baby. Why don't we see if I can help you with what's bothering you." He slipped a hand between us and into my folds. I cried out and jerked. "Fuck, you're so damn wet. I've got just the thing for that."

"Wait," I said breathlessly.

He froze. "Are you alright?"

"I'm more than alright, but I didn't get to explore you last time like I wanted. Let me do that," I pleaded.

"I don't know that I have the control to let you do it, then have me pleasure you before I have to have you. You're so damn beautiful and luscious. You're driving me wild. Feel my cock. It wants inside of you now. I want to pound that sweet pussy until I make you scream and come, then fill you with my cum. I've gotta mark you as mine. It's primal, baby. Do you know what a primal hunter Dom is?"

I shook my head no.

"It's considered a kink by many." When he said that, my eyes widened. He hurried to continue. "It's nothing painful or dangerous. I'd never do anything you don't want or like or hurt you. I like to growl. I might snarl or grunt loudly. I like to use my nails and teeth. Pull your hair. Maybe one day if you're willing, I'll be rougher with you, but again, it all depends on what you want, need, and can handle. I'm not gonna do it tonight or even soon. I just wanted to explain before you hear me get going," he smiled and winked when he said it.

"Do you do more than those things? Are there other things a primal does or likes? What am I if you're considered a hunter?" I was scared to a degree, but my curiosity was bigger. To be honest, the thought of exploring kinks was kind of exciting to me. Rather than our intermission causing me to become less aroused, it was growing.

He ran his nails over my skin on my chest, over my nipples, then down to my stomach. He didn't break the skin, but it did sting a tiny bit. "You would be called primal prey, and yes, primal hunters like to do other things, like chase their prey. It can be inside or outside. They like to take them down and ravish them," he whispered. I moaned as his nails bit into my hip harder.

"D-d-do you like to chase women and capture them?" I stuttered.

"I've not been able to do it, really, although I won't lie, I've thought about it a lot. What would you say if I told you I thought about visiting a kink club in Nashville before you to explore that? One of the guys in Hunters Creek, Payne, belongs to it."

"Really? An honest-to-God kink club? What's it called? Would you want to take me there?"

"Yes, an honest-to-God club. It's called the House of Lustz. I wouldn't go now unless you went with me. There's no touching other people for me or you, baby. You're mine, and I'm yours. I don't mind being watched or even seeing others, but if anyone actually touched you, I'd fucking tear them apart," he ended that declaration with a low rumbling growl.

Instead of this scaring me into running out of the room screaming, I found I was intrigued and more than curious. I'd never watched anyone have sex other than in porn movies. I had to admit, it turned me on. I had no idea if I could let someone else watch us. He saw me thinking, so he added, "Kimera, don't worry about it. We don't need to go. I'll be more than happy with whatever you give me. No pressure. I planned to talk to you about this once we were closer to having actual sex, but you surprised me. I'm sorry I dropped it on you like this, but I wanted you to know. The sounds might scare you. Was the scratching I just did alright? I've bitten your mouth and nipples. What about that? If you like it, I'd like to do it harder to see if you like it even more.

"I like your nails, the way you pull on my hair, and how you've bitten my mouth and nipples. Do you like that done to you? As for the club in Nashville, can you go there and not do anything, you know, just observe? And if you do something, does it have to be in front of people?"

I saw surprise cross his face, then amazement. "Babe, are you saying you'd be willing to at least go check it out even if we do nothing more than watch and never return?"

I nodded. "Yes, I think I could do that. I'd never be able to have sex in front of other people, but watching them might be hot. Oh, and as for the sounds you make, please do. I've loved what I've heard so far. And if you want to chase me and catch me one of these days after we get back home, I think I'd like to see what that's like. No drawing blood, though," I warned him.

"Goddamn," he muttered.

"What?" I asked.

"You're perfect for me, Kimera. So goddamn, mind-blowing perfect. You have no idea what it does to me to hear you say all those things. Why don't we start out slow and we'll go from there? Nails, teeth, sounds, and maybe hair pulling tonight?" he asked. I saw hope on his face.

I raised my head and captured his mouth. I bit his bottom lip as I scratched down his chest to right above his cock. He hissed and growled. I let go. "I think that sounds good. I'm not sure how I'll react, but go for it. But first, I need to explore you," I reminded him.

He groaned like I asked him to run a marathon, but he did roll to the side and lay on his back. He flung out his arms and spread his legs. "Do what you will, but I make no promises on how long I can hold back. You may have to wait a while to be able to do a thorough exploration."

Before he could change his mind, I got up and straddled his middle. I rubbed myself on him. Yes, I knew I was tempting the beast, but I wanted to. After hearing about him being this primal hunter, I wanted to experience more of that. I still wanted to touch and taste him all over, but I wouldn't mind when he broke. Something told me Spawn would be able to talk me into almost anything sexually. My hang-ups and fears in the past might just stay in the past.

I leaned up and began at his mouth. I worked my way down. I looked at, touched, and tasted his mouth, neck, and then his impressive chest, which was huge and wide. I traced his tats with my tongue and nipped at his skin. I tugged the hair on his chest and sucked and nibbled on his nipples. When I got to his stomach, his muscles jumped, and his breathing sped up more. I smiled up at him. His hard cock was digging into my stomach now.

"Can I put my mouth on your cock, baby?" I asked him softly.

"Jesus, yes. If you don't, I'm gonna die. Although I'm not sure how long I can hold back from coming. Shit, you're a temptress," he muttered.

This gave me the confidence to do more. I raised up and laid down until I was face-to-face with his massive cock. I swear it looked even bigger than the last time I was about to give him a blow job. It was covered in his precum and my slickness. Not wasting time, I grasped the base firmly and swiped my tongue across the head. He moaned loudly, and his hips flexed up, which drove it into my mouth. I lifted up to say one more thing.

"Aidan, I want you to fuck my mouth like a primal. Make me take it and gag. Come down my throat as I suck your huge, beautiful cock," I begged.

I saw when he let one of his figurative chains loose. He let out a louder, snarling sound and grabbed me. He flipped me on my back and came over the top of me, straddling my chest. His cock bounced and tapped my mouth. He grasped it and hit my mouth again, only harder. "Open that sexy mouth and suck your man's cock. I want tongue and teeth and to go deep," he ordered.

I felt wetness flood my pussy. I opened my mouth and took it. He fed his cock to me, and I worked to take as much as I could while tonguing him and using my teeth as he ordered. The almost feral look on his face drove me on. Fuck this was hot. I moaned when he grabbed my hair and tugged. This time, it was harder than the last.

I sucked him deeper to show him I liked it. He began to take over and thrust in and out. Each time, he went deeper. The growls, grunts, and snarls coming out of him were crazy sexy. I felt like I could orgasm without him touching my pussy at this point, and that had never happened to me in my life except once with him.

"That's it. Take it. I'm gonna go deep, babe. Are you ready?" he asked.

I nodded as best as I could with a mouthful. He thrust his hips forward. When he hit the back of my throat, he held it there for a few seconds and then backed off. "God, you're doing so good, Kimera. It feels so fucking amazing. I'm gonna do it again. I want you to swallow and see if you can take me down your throat. Take a deep breath. On the count of three, okay. One, two, three," as soon as he said the last number, he thrust. It was a hard one, but not enough to hurt me. I fought to swallow despite gagging. I could feel him past the back of my throat. I was glad I took a breath because there was no way I could do it now. My eyes watered, but I kept swallowing, and then I hummed. He jerked and grunted, then slid back out.

"Hotcake, I've gotta do that again. I'm so close. Can you take it?"

I nodded. I could do it. He didn't count this time, but as he thrust forward, I inhaled and swallowed. He groaned loud and long. He tugged on my hair and began to thrust faster. I could barely keep up, but I loved his expression. He thrust a few more times, then suddenly a hand was on my throat, lightly squeezing as he buried his cock down my throat and hollered, "Fuck," as he came.

He jerked again and again. I had to fight to swallow it all and not panic when I couldn't breathe. As my air supply was cut off for longer, I began to panic. Even in the throes of his release, he instantly knew, and he eased back so I could breathe. He ran his fingers gently up and down my throat as he gazed at me lovingly.

"Kimera, baby, that was so goddamn incredible. I've never... shit," he whispered as he pulled out and lowered his head to kiss me. I eagerly twined my tongue around his. It still shocked me that he didn't care if he tasted his own cum. He kissed me breathless and stupid before he stopped.

He gave me a sexy smirk. "Now, it's my turn. Prepare for me to eat your pussy until I make you scream over and over.

"Oh God," I said. He chuckled as he kissed his way to my soaking wet pussy. I grabbed the headboard. I knew I was about to be taken on the ride of my life. I might not survive to get to the main event.

Spawn: Chapter 18

My head was practically spinning as I went down on my woman. She was beyond anything I could ever have hoped for. I hadn't expected her to be so open to what I wanted. I knew I had to warn her if nothing else. But to have her agree to try pretty much whatever I wanted, even to go as far as letting me chase her, had stunned me. Add to it agreeing to maybe go to the House of Lustz, which had knocked me for a loop.

I sniffed her. I forgot to tell her smelling was part of being a primal. Her scent flooded my nose. I inhaled deeply and let out a low rumble. I remembered her taste and smell from last time. My mouth was watering. I nuzzled her and slowly lapped at her folds. She was so wet. She moaned and jerked. Taking my time, I laved her from top to bottom and vice versa. I used my teeth more this time and bit harder. She didn't tell me to stop, and more cream spilled from her.

I ran a nail over her hard, protruding clit. She wailed, and her whole body spasmed. She was close to coming. I thrust my tongue into her pussy and fluttered it as I twisted her clit. She came screaming my name, "Aidan!" I kept pleasuring her as she jerked and orgasmed.

She was slow to come down because of it, which

was what I wanted. I had to give her at least two orgasms, if not more before I took her for the first time. My cock was already recovering and hardening. The bastard wanted her. I ruthlessly drove her back up. This time I used my fingers to fuck her as I nipped and bit on her clit and folds. It didn't take her very long to come again, and she was shaking so hard the bed squeaked.

I wanted to make her come a third time, but I couldn't use my mouth to do it. I had to be inside of her, or I was going to die. Raising up, I pulled her hips onto my folded thighs. She gasped, and her eyes widened as I pressed the head of my cock to her opening. "Ready?" I asked her.

She nodded, but I saw the apprehension there. "Baby, if you need me to stop, just tell me," I told her. I meant what I told her, but if she told me to stop, I might die. The need for her was insane.

"I don't need you to stop. Please, do it. I want you, Aidan. God," she cried, then she thrust down, driving the head inside her. We both moaned at the feeling. Christ, she was tight. It was hard to get inside her. She was snug and fit around me like another layer of skin.

"Motherfucker," I groaned.

"What's wrong?" she panted.

"I won't last, babe. You feel too incredible for me to last. Tell me if I get too rough. I'm sorry," I pleaded before I thrust all the way inside of her. She wailed louder, but she didn't appear to be in pain. Seeing this, I let my last bit of restraint half-slip. I snapped my hips back and thrust harder and deeper. When she didn't tell me to stop, in fact, she threw back her head and cried out. The rest of my restraint snapped, and I began to hammer in and out.

I gripped her hips and tried not to leave bruises as I powered into her. I did it over and over. Fuck! She was taking all of me, and I was climbing to the point of no return so fast. However, no matter how much I enjoyed it, I had to be sure she was alright. I gritted my teeth so I could speak. "Kimera, sweetheart, is this okay? Am I hurting you? Too rough?"

"No, No, don't stop. Oh my God!" she screamed then she came. She almost strangled my cock in half. It was half painful, but it threw me into a frenzy as the tingling in my balls came rising up. I got two more thrusts in then I was roaring, growling, and grunting, hell I might've snorted as I flooded her pussy with my seed, and she milked me dry. It was, without a doubt, the hardest I ever came in my life. I almost blacked out. It was so good, and she squirted when she came. I was helpless to do anything but keep thrusting until I eventually began to soften. I was breathing like I'd run a race. She was lying limp and sweaty under me.

I reluctantly pulled out and looked down. I watched as my cum leaked slowly out of her. I pushed it back inside and teased her with a finger. She moaned weakly. I didn't want my cum to escape. I saw an image of her in my head. She had a round stomach with my baby inside. Like an animal, I wanted to breed her. I'd wait, but as soon as she was ready, I'd plant my seed and impregnate her. I'd save that revelation for later. I had no idea I had that instinct until her. No other woman ever made me want or think that. This told me she was my mate, without a doubt.

I leaned down and kissed her gently before I lay beside her and took her in my arms. "You are so fucking amazing, wonderful, and incredible. I can't think of enough words. I love you, my She-Wolf."

She snuggled into my chest. "I feel the exact same, and I love you too." She yawned and closed her eyes. She'd so easily admitted she loved me for the first time. I was so thrilled. Nothing would ruin this. I wouldn't let it. I'd let her rest and then see if she was up for another round.

❦❦❦

We didn't get up until late the next morning. I was right. We did go another round. I could've gone again, but she was exhausted and I didn't want her so sore she couldn't walk. It had been a while since she'd had sex, and she told me shyly I was much bigger than she'd experienced before. It made me want to beat my chest even though I hated to know any man had her before me. I'd for sure make her forget they ever existed by drowning her in pleasure and making her feel like a queen.

We grabbed coffee and a Danish but didn't eat because we knew we'd be eating at the Highwaymen's clubhouse. They were having a cookout in December. Go figure. The weather was supposed to be in the mid-fifties, so it shouldn't be too terrible. I made sure she had on a sweatshirt just in case it got too cold for her. I hadn't presented her with a property cut yet, but I did get something for her to show she belonged to the

Punishers. On the back of the sweatshirt was our logo and club name. She'd lit up when she saw it. I made sure she was warm before we headed out.

I followed the directions to their place. It took us outside of town. I think a lot of clubs had their clubhouses outside city limits if they could. It made for less hassle from the cops. If your neighbors were further away, you had fewer complaints of noise or people sticking their noses into things you didn't want them to see. When we drove up, I saw they had their place fenced in, which was smart. I saw a large, one-story sprawling building on the right. On the left was another building, which appeared to be a garage. Past it a couple of houses. Bikes were lined up outside the large building. It had to be the clubhouse.

There was a guy at the gate. He came out to speak to me. I rolled down my window. According to his cut, he was a prospect. I nodded. "Hey, prospect, I'm Spawn. I'm with the Iron Punishers. Your president is expecting us."

He studied me and then glanced at Kimera. I saw him perk up and eye her with sexual interest. I couldn't blame him, but I wouldn't let it go either. I put him on notice. "I'd keep your eyes off my old lady if you know what's good for you," I said with menace.

He moved back and held up his hands. "No disrespect, man. Your old lady is a looker, and a man can't help but look, but I swear that's all I'll do. Let me get the gate. You can park anywhere. Find a spot in front of the building with all the bikes. Welcome," he said before scurrying to open the gate. I gave him a chin lift as I drove in.

"Aidan, no killing or maiming anyone. He didn't touch me," she reminded me.

"I know he didn't, and that's why he's still breathing. I'll always call out anyone who ogles you, babe."

"Can I do the same if women ogle you?"

"You can do whatever you want to them," I said with a smirk.

"You might regret that you said that."

I laughed as I found a spot and parked. I backed in. It was a habit no matter what I drove. It was in case I needed to make a quick getaway. I made her wait for me to come around to open her door. As I held her hand in my left, I reminded her. "Stick close to me. Don't go anywhere alone. I don't think we have anything to worry about, but just be alert. Tinker texted, and they came straight here instead of meeting us at the hotel. They came to feel them out in advance. If they'd gotten a bad vibe off them, we wouldn't be here." I told her. I hadn't mentioned it before we left the hotel. I think she forgot they were coming since she'd been so nervous when she got up and got ready.

I felt her relax a tad when she asked, "Who all came?"

"Tinker, Sandman, Gravel, and Crusher."

"Good," was her only response.

Walking inside, we were hit with the noise of

several voices, the smell of alcohol, and faint music. Thankfully, it didn't smell like pussy or smoke, although it most likely would later tonight. I planned to be gone before it happened. We barely got in the door before our names were yelled loudly, and Crusher and my other brothers came barreling over to us. They slapped me on the back and then hugged Kimera gingerly. They knew she was still leery sometimes to be touched. She seemed to handle it fine. When they stepped back, I saw three men behind them, and most of the others in the room were staring at us.

Crusher turned to them, and my brothers parted down the middle. "Spawn, let me introduce you to some of our hosts. This is Stallion. He's the president of the Highwaymen. On his right is his VP Stone, and on his left is Abyss. He's their enforcer. Guys, this is my brother Spawn and his old lady, Kimera."

They greeted us and shook my hand. When it came to Kimera, they smiled and welcomed her but kept their hands to themselves. I didn't know if it was because she was mine or if they did it due to knowing what she'd suffered. It made me like them better.

"Welcome, we're so damn glad we could get you here. Abyss tells me Maniac is a good guy, and so is your club. Everything I've heard says the same and that we have similar outlooks on life and people," Stallion said. I'd studied them as we were introduced. Stallion appeared to be in his mid to late forties. The other two were around my age. They stood straight and confident. I liked what I saw so far.

"Thank you for the invitation and for the offer of

help. We're hoping to complete our visit soon and get out of your hair."

"There's time for us to chat about that later. Let me introduce you to the gang and my old lady. She's probably over there chomping at the bit to talk to your woman. We only have the two old ladies here and, of course, a few kids," Stallion offered.

It didn't take long to meet the others. This club wasn't as large as ours, but I found they had three prospects. We were in the process of bringing in more at home. We only had poor Rhaines, and he was coming toward the end of his time.

Stallion's old lady was Mara. She was a few years younger than him, I think. Wrench and Diviner, two other members, were their sons. They appeared to be in their mid-twenties, so Stallion and Mara had been young when they had them. Whiskey, their treasurer, was in his mid-thirties. His old lady was Phoebe, and they had a seven-year-old son, Caleb, and a five-year-old daughter, Callie. The rest were Piston, their secretary, and Griller, their road captain, along with Tats and Boulder. In total, they had ten members.

Kimera stuck close, but she did great with everyone, and I was glad to see her talking. We sat down at a table with Stallion, Whiskey, their old ladies, and Abyss after all the introductions were made. Others rotated in and out at our table. As time went on, more chairs were pulled up. Those not at the table were either playing pool or darts. I was surprised to see they had a pinball machine in their common area. That was an idea for home.

After about an hour, we ended up migrating outside behind the clubhouse. They had barbecues and picnic tables out there. I saw they had two of the prospects manning the grill. Besides the picnic tables, there were a couple of fire pits.

We spent another hour just socializing before the food they were preparing was done. About a half hour before it was, their old ladies excused themselves to go get the other food they had in the clubhouse. I knew Kimera would want to help. She hated not being useful, and she'd think it rude not to assist them in some way. It was how she was, so I whispered in her ear to go. I made eye contact with Gravel. He knew what I wanted. He got up and followed her inside.

Stallion noticed. Nothing got by him. "I see you don't like her out of your sight. Are you unsure of us? I promise we'd never hurt her."

"No offense, but I don't trust anyone with her other than my brothers at this point. It's nothing against you, but after what she's been through in the past and not long ago, she's wary of men. I don't want her scared or uncomfortable. If I can't be with her, then one of my brothers will be. I don't mean any disrespect.

"Good. I don't blame you for doing it. I'd do the same for any woman. Maniac told Abyss why you're here and about the fucker from her past. He didn't mention anything about a recent incident, though. Mind if I ask what that was?" he asked gruffly.

This shifted the conversation from relaxed to tense. My remaining brothers stiffened, and his men got quiet and gathered close. It was as if an invisible signal went out to tell them to pay attention.

"One of our old ladies had a big issue with people beating her and leaving her with amnesia. We found her dumped body and rescued her. They thought they'd killed her. She's with our brother Lash. Anyway, I discovered who did it and why. They came looking for her. When they did, Kimera, who colored her hair to look like Troian, was taken by the four of them." I paused. Just recalling what she almost suffered made me want to punch something.

"Shit, don't tell me they raped her," Stallion muttered darkly.

"No, but one was seconds from it when we got there. It triggered some very unwelcome memories, as you can imagine. She's slowly relaxing around men, but I don't want to chance her becoming upset or scared. She's tough, but even the toughest person can break. Having this shit with the guy who raped her when she was a teenager come up only has made it worse. She's having nightmares. I want to end him so she never has to worry about him again."

"How did he come back into her life? You're in Virginia, and he's here," Stone asked.

"Kimera was raised in foster care since she was ten. The last home she was in was where this bastard was. He was the family's natural son. Anyway, another girl ended up there with her, too. She was younger, and Kimera thought she had protected her from his attention, but she was wrong. That woman was the one to track down my woman and tell her the cocksucker was back in town and had mentioned her name."

"Kimera protected her?" Whiskey asked with a questioning look.

"He forced her to have sex with him repeatedly for several months when she was almost sixteen. He threatened that if she didn't, he'd get it from the other one, a thirteen-year-old girl. Kimera had no idea the fucker was raping her too and using the threat of hurting Kimera on the other girl to make her submit and keep her mouth shut. Finally, Kimera told the parents, and those shitheads didn't believe her and sent her back to a group foster care. Their worthless piece of shit son went back to college to probably do it again and again. We're gonna stop this once and for all. No girl or woman will need to be scared of him again," I snarled.

The dark mutterings that broke out around me told me they were of the same mind. Stallion clapped his hand down on my left shoulder and squeezed. "Don't you worry. We'll gladly help in any way we can to rid the earth of this scum. It'll be our pleasure. We have a place we can take him to, where no one will hear his screams and another spot to get rid of his carcass afterward. You just say when." There was an unholy gleam in his eye. I grinned back just as evilly as all our brothers chuckled. Yeah, they were kindred souls. The conversation didn't go further because we saw the women coming back to join us.

We enjoyed the good food they had made. There was plenty of it and a big variety. The stories we shared had all of us laughing. Eventually, Kimera moved over to sit with Phoebe and Mara so they could chat about whatever. She was still where I could keep an eye on her, but she was smiling, so I figured she was at ease.

The hours flew by. I didn't keep track of them, to be honest, since we were having such a great time. It felt like having a get-together back home or at one of our friends' clubs. When it got dark, the fire pits were lit to provide warmth. I saw one of the prospects bring out blankets for the three women. The kids were tucked inside at Whiskey's house in their beds. His cousin had come to watch them so he and his old lady could party.

It was because they were such a great bunch and we were enjoying our time that I didn't pay attention to time. I groaned softly when I saw women coming around the clubhouse. It was obvious by their appearances they were either hang arounds or bunnies. Despite the cold, they were scantily dressed, and their faces were made up with way too much makeup.

I briefly wondered how the hell I'd ever been attracted to women like them. I guess the lure of easy pussy blinded a man. It took finding and falling for a quality woman to show you what you've been missing. I was even more grateful for Kimera when I saw them. I glanced over to see if she'd noticed them or not.

I knew she was aware of these kinds of women. We had them back home, but as far as I knew, she hadn't been exposed to them. All three old ladies were staring at them. Mara and Phoebe looked resigned and a bit disgusted. Kimera was studying them with a faintly curious expression. The other two watched but didn't get up. Kimera glanced at me. I smiled and winked at her so she'd know everything was cool. She smiled back and then said something to the two women.

"I see the entertainment is here," Sandman said with a smirk.

"Yeah, just watch the red-head. She's out to get a patched man, and I don't think she cares who. She's a decent lay but can get clingy," Wrench told him.

"She won't be getting more than that outta me," Sandman muttered.

In the firelight, I swear I could see the gleam of excitement when the women spotted there was new meat here. Jesus Christ, I hoped they would stay away from me. I had no idea how Kimera would react if any of them came onto me. A small part of me wondered if she'd challenge them, and the thought was hot, but I'd rather not find out. What if she was upset by them and blamed me for their behavior? I had no idea how much the ladies back home told her about these types of women in the biker world. I didn't want to be rude and bail suddenly, but I planned to give us another half hour, and then I'd get us out of there.

As I continued to talk to a few of the Highwaymen, I watched out of the corner of my eye what the new arrivals were doing. There were six in total. Two quickly went for some of Stallion's men, but a few approached Tinker, Crusher, and Sandman. I knew Sandman wouldn't mind. I didn't see Gravel. I was rather surprised when Tinker shook off the woman and sent her on her way. He scowled at her in irritation. Hmm, what was up with that? Lately, I noticed he'd been avoiding the women back home, too. Did he have a woman we didn't know about? If so, I wondered who she was.

I was distracted from my thoughts and keeping track of them as well as making sure Kimera was alright by Piston. He was showing me the bike he was restoring. He had pictures on his phone. It was a sweet ride already, even though he wasn't done. I was asking him about specs and telling him about the Warriors' custom work when two bunnies slithered up. One put her hand on Tats' chest. The other gave me what I guess was her sexy smile and reached out to touch me.

I opened my mouth to tell her hands off, but I never got the words out. Suddenly, Kimera was between us. She had her back to me. Her stance was stiff. When she spoke, I knew she wasn't thrilled.

"Sweetheart, I'll save you the trouble. He's taken. Now, I don't know if his brothers are interested, but they're single, so have a ball. Just leave this one alone. Spread the word." Her tone was firm, but she wasn't hateful. I was hopeful the bunny would heed her and turn her attention elsewhere. I was wrong.

I couldn't see Kimera's face, but I could see the bunny's. She got a pissed-off look and sneered at my woman. Shit, I had to stop this. I opened my mouth to tell the unknown woman to get lost, but the bunny, or whatever she was, beat me to the punch.

"I don't see a ring on either of your fingers, and you're not wearing a property cut. That means he's fair game. And even if he did have an old lady, it doesn't mean he wouldn't sample a better woman." She smirked. Her insulting remark pissed me off. She was nowhere near the quality of Kimera.

"Jazzy, stop it," Abyss growled.

"Oh, come on, Abyss. Are you jealous?" She fluttered her fake lashes at him and jutted out her hip, putting a hand on it. She was skin and bones.

"If you touch him, it's your ass," Kimera told her firmly.

I wrapped my arms around Kimera and pulled her back to rest against me. "She's right. I'm taken. Whether she has my ring or property cut on doesn't matter. She's my old lady. Her cut is at home being made."

Instead of Jazzy walking off gracefully, she snorted and scanned Kimera with a wrinkled nose. "Please, what does she have that I don't? I can rock your world. I know she can't."

Boulder snorted. "Jazzy, are you blind? She's a thousand times better than you. She's beyond gorgeous, sexy, and smart. I have no doubt she keeps Spawn happy in and out of the bedroom. All you do is give some temporary relief to whoever snaps his fingers. Sorry, but you're not now or ever gonna be old lady material."

Harsh, maybe, but it was true of most bunnies and hang arounds. Fury filled Jazzy's face. "Fuck you, Boulder! See if I ever let you fuck me again."

He laughed at her. "Honey, that's a promise I'll gladly take. There are plenty of other pussies out there, and you're not the best lay in the world."

She gasped in outrage. Now that the focus was off me, I was finding this entertaining. I heard Kimera giggle softly at Boulder's comments. Jazzy whipped her head back to glare at her. She'd heard her.

"What're you laughing at, bitch?"

"A dumbass, apparently. You keep it up, and no one here will fuck you again. I'd move on if I were you. Don't demean yourself like this. Have some self-respect. Men like that."

"Don't talk to me like that, cunt," Jazzy hissed at her.

"You're out of here," Stallion growled at the same time Kimera stepped out of my arms and got in her face.

"Call me a name again and see what happens. I promise you, you won't like it."

Jazzy stood a good five inches taller than Kimera. She had long, claw-like fake nails. She let out a strangled scream as she quickly shoved my woman. Oh, hell no. I reached out to bring Kimera out of range of her and get between them, but my She-Wolf was too quick for me. The punch thrown by her was a solid one to Jazzy's face. Jazzy screamed in pain and grasped her mouth. All the men around us erupted in laughter. I heard them calling out encouragement to Kimera.

"That's it. Show her."

"Beat that ass."

"Damn, that's hot as fuck."

Jazzy was sobbing, and blood trickled out from underneath her hand. Kimera sighed. "I warned you. Let me see. I'm a nurse."

"Don't touch me!" Jazzy shrieked before she turned and ran off.

Kimera faced Stallion. "I'm sorry if I offended you. It wasn't intentional, but I won't let another woman touch Spawn or myself."

He gave her a huge grin. "Sweetness, that was the best thing I've seen in forever. You didn't offend me a bit. Nice punch. Where'd you learn to punch like that? Spawn?"

"No, after I turned eighteen, I made sure to learn how to fight to defend myself and how to use a gun. I have a guard dog, too, but he stayed back home this time."

"I hate you had to punch her, She-Wolf, but I thank you for defending my honor," I teased her as I took her in my arms. She smiled at me and rolled her eyes.

"She-Wolf? I like it. Here's to She-Wolf. May she always defend her man and kick ass!" Stallion shouted. Everyone cheered and raised their drinks in a toast, except the remaining bunnies. It wasn't the way I saw our night ending there, but it would do. I think it was time to head to the hotel.

Kimera: Chapter 19

I hated to admit it, but going up against Jazzy and punching her had an odd effect on me. It made me crazy to have Spawn. It was all I could do to say our goodbyes to the Highwaymen and endure the drive home. He held my hand the whole drive back. Tinker, Crusher, Gravel, and Sandman decided to stay longer. They were adults. They could do whatever they wanted. Stallion was nice enough to offer them rooms at their clubhouse rather than staying at our hotel. We'd been offered the same, but we kindly declined.

As soon as we got behind the locked door of our room, I began to strip. Spawn watched with a hungry look on his face. He took off his cut and hung it over a chair. As he took off his boots, he spoke to me. "Are you eager to go to sleep, baby?"

I shook my head. "No, I'm dying to have my man get naked then fuck me. I need you, Aidan. God, I'm burning up inside," I whimpered as I tossed my bra on top of my sweatshirt and top on the floor. My shoes were off, too. Both hands shook as I undid my pants. My panties were wet from imagining what he would do to me. Last night was incredible. Even if my pussy was slightly sore still, I wanted him to take me again and again.

He let out one of those growls that made me melt last night. The feral look was returning, too. "On the bed, on your hands and knees. Spread your legs."

I didn't waste time removing the rest of my clothes. He was tearing his off almost as fast. I trembled as I got on the bed and assumed the position he wanted. I had my ass toward him. I felt vulnerable with my back, ass, and pussy exposed like that. I knew he wouldn't hurt me, but it was still slightly nerve-racking.

I jumped when he got on the bed behind me. His hands slid over my ass cheeks. "Relax, my love. I'll never hurt you. God, the sight of you like this has me about to burst. I want to taste your skin all over, kiss you, eat your pussy, and fuck you all at the same time. Since I can't, what should I do first? Hmm?" he asked in a sexy, gruff voice.

I moaned and glanced at him over my shoulder. "You can do anything you want. Eat me, lick me, taste me, or fuck me. I don't care. I want and love it all."

He grunted. "Lay down and spread your arms and legs for me. Close your eyes and let me pleasure you."

I did as he asked. Not being able to see him made my other sense heightened. I wondered what he'd do. My excitement increased.

"Another thing you should know about me is besides being primal. I seem to be wanting to be a pleasure Dom with you. That's new."

"What's a p-pleasure Dom?" I stuttered as his hands touched my feet, and he began to lightly caress then massage them.

"It's a dominant who likes control of his partner and uses anything he can to bring his partner as much pleasure as you can stand. That can be as simple as what I'm doing right now, to depriving your senses or using toys and other things to get you to lose control. The more you come and the more pleasure I can give you, the more I get."

"Making me feel good makes you feel good?"

"It makes me so fucking hard that I want to come over and over. Let me pleasure you, baby. I want you to scream loud, hard, and repeatedly as I make you come apart for me. Show me I'm the only one who can give you that," he groaned.

"Yes," I whispered. I jumped when I felt his lips on the soles of my feet. I had no idea what I'd agreed to. I lost track of time as he worked his way up my body. He would randomly whisper the things he looked forward to using when we got home to make it even better for me. I didn't know how it was possible without killing me.

He constantly switched between simple touches to using his nails, lips, and teeth. He rubbed his slight stubble on my skin, too. He caressed, kissed, licked, and bit me all over. I couldn't keep my cries inside as I got hotter and hotter. I felt like I was leaking a puddle underneath me. When he got to my pussy, he licked and sucked it, paying attention to my clit. I came quickly. I was barely back down from an intense orgasm when he left me. "Don't look," he ordered.

It was hard not to as he moved around. I heard a drawer, I think, open and close, and then there was a snapping sound. The mattress dipped, so I knew he was back. I jumped when I felt something cold touch my asshole. I moaned for sure this time. God, was he doing what I thought? A finger pressed against my asshole. I tensed up. I couldn't help it.

"Babe, can I? I think you'll like this once we get you past the first part. It burns, but then it can be so pleasurable. I can make you come even harder fucking this ass as I eat your pussy. Hell, I could make you come from just fucking your ass."

"Really? Women enjoy it? I know they show it in porn movies, but I thought that was just for show. Do you like that? Do you want to only use your finger?"

"Yes, some women do enjoy it, but not all. From what I've seen of you, I believe you will. It's not just in porn, and I do like it. If I'm being totally honest, I'd like to not only use my finger, but if you enjoy it, I'd want to try to progress you to taking dildoes and butt plugs. The ultimate would be if you'd trust me to use my cock to make you mindless." his voice got lower and gruffer as he explained.

Could I do it? Would I like it? Did this make me kinky because the thought was frightening and exhilarating at the same time? Of course, I now knew my man was kinky. If I was his woman, it made sense I would be too. He didn't press forward or say anything. He was letting me decide. I think it was his patience that made my decision for me.

"Show me. I want to see if you can make me come."

"Thank you, baby. I want you to try to relax as much as you can and push out as I press in. That'll help. If it becomes too much, tell me to either slow down or stop. If you detest it, we won't continue or do it again."

"I trust you, Aidan. I'm ready."

He groaned softly, then his finger pressed gently against my asshole harder. It reluctantly opened to let him slip the tip inside. I pressed out like he said, but it stung and hurt, although not terribly. I moaned.

"Okay?"

"Yes," I said. I wasn't about to chicken out this fast. I wanted to give it a true chance. Although if it was all like this, I didn't see myself wanting to do it again.

He barely eased his finger back, then pushed deeper. I hissed at the burn but didn't tell him to stop. "Fuck, you have no idea how hot it is to see your ass taking my finger, Hotcake. It's so damn tight, just like your pussy. Another deep breath and push," he ordered.

I did it automatically, and his finger went deeper. I don't know if I was getting used to the burning or if it was becoming less, but it didn't seem to be as bad. He began to thrust it slowly in and out. I jumped when his teeth nipped my ass cheek, and his finger pushed in further. Two fingers slid through my cream and then invaded my pussy. Lord, I felt full with his fingers in both holes. He ramped up the speed of his thrusts. I moaned and pressed back unintentionally. Lord, it was starting to feel really good. I tried to move my hips.

"That's it. Get up on your knees so you can ride my fingers. Fuck yourself on them. Ride 'em," he panted.

I awkwardly got up and tentatively pushed back on his fingers. The sensations it created made me moan. Forgetting to keep my eyes closed, I opened them and looked over my shoulder. His gaze was smoldering as he met mine. He licked his lips. "Harder," he muttered.

I let go, and within seconds, I was thrusting back hard again and again. I could feel the tingling and tightening low in my back and belly. I was getting close. I saw him fisting his cock with his other hand hard and fast. He was so hard and dripping precum. The head was dark red. I moaned and came thinking of his cock replacing his fingers in both my holes. I screamed and shook as I orgasmed. It was a hard and long release again.

By the time I was done coming, I was weak. I was about to sink to my belly again, but he had other ideas. Abruptly, his fingers were gone, then he was over the top of me, thrusting inside. I cried out as his much larger cock opened my pussy up. A hand reached up to grab my hair and pull it. The other went to my hip to help him jerk me back on his cock.

"Christ, you feel so fucking good. Ride my cock, baby. Come on it and make me come," he snarled.

I became mindless again as I pounded back as he hammered forward. It wasn't more than a few minutes before I came for him, and I screamed until I was hoarse. Wetness gushed down my legs. He was grunting, growling, and making snarling sounds. I was leaning with my head on the bed as I shivered by the end. Suddenly, he pulled out, and I felt warmth cover my lower back. I peeked to find him jerking his cock and shooting his cum all over my back. Damn, I was kinky because I found it sensual. I moaned, and I swear I had a mini orgasm.

When he stopped coming, he took some of his cum and pressed it up inside of me. The rest he rubbed into my skin. He even licked his fingers clean. I knew at that moment I'd never get enough of him, this, or be able to live without him. He moved up and rolled me so he could take my mouth. I eagerly gave it to him. Christ, I loved this man and the things he did to me.

"I love you, Kimera. No one can ever fit me like you do. When this is over, promise you'll let me fully claim you. I can't be without you. Move in with me."

"I love you too. What do you mean by claiming me completely? I thought you did already. You call me your old lady. As for living with you, what about my house? Toro?"

"I mean, you'll accept a property cut and my ring and agree to marry me ASAP. You can keep the house or sell it. It's up to you. As for Toro, he loves the compound."

"Yes, he does, but he'd have to live in the house with us. He's family to me."

"Babe, I love your dog. Hell yeah, he'll be in the house with us. Who else will help me guard our children and you? You didn't answer me. What about the cut and ring?"

His remark about kids made me picture myself pregnant again. It didn't scare me like it would've before. As for having his name on me and his ring, I had definite thoughts on that too. I know he mentioned it, and so had I, but I guess I hadn't considered it with us, truly. I waited almost a minute before I answered him. I smirked as I did. "Well, I guess if you insist, the answer is yes to both. You'll have to make sure to give me lots of orgasms so I don't change my mind," I teased him.

I squealed as he tackled me. I giggled and tried to get away as he wrestled me into submission. When I was trapped, he kissed me. It soon led to us moving on to round two. I'd be much sorer by morning, but I didn't care.

❦❦❦

I should've known our bubble of happiness would burst. I don't know what I was expecting, but it wasn't what happened. In some ways, it was one of my worst nightmare situations. Spawn had gone out with his brothers to do some recon, as they called it. They were taking a gamble that they might see Paden. I thought it was a waste of time, but if it gave them something to do, then who was I to ruin it? They were bored, and Spawn was frustrated.

His usual tricks weren't giving him results. For a man who lived by his computer, it was as if a best friend had betrayed him. Paden was staying well hidden. No one had sighted him, nor had he left any kind of digital trail Spawn could follow. I was beginning to worry we'd have to leave and go home, leaving this unresolved.

Neither of us could stay here forever. I was anxious to go back and start our life together.

It was while Spawn was out I decided to leave the hotel. I found something I'd been trying to find for Brent since before Christmas. He was such a cute little guy, and I wanted to give him this gift the next time we saw them. Other than the Punishers' kids for a few weeks and at Christmas, I hadn't been able to spoil any. I'd bought him and Brie gifts for the holiday, but this was one I'd been looking for, and it had been sold out. I got an alert saying a store in town had just gotten some in.

Lucky for me, I had the car. Spawn went in the SUV his brothers had rented. I hoped Claudia and Sonny didn't kill me. Brent's love of motorcycles was obvious even before he met Spawn. It was this love that made me look for this item in the first place. It was one of those toy motorized motorcycles for toddlers. It was similar to the motorized cars you saw all the time. I planned to get him a helmet and other safety equipment to go with it. I didn't think it would be worse than the scooter I saw him trying to ride in the driveway. He was a daredevil.

The store was across town. I called and asked them to hold one for me, and they said they could for an hour, so I got myself out the door and over there. One of the guys who worked there loaded it in the car for me. I was excited as I drove back to the hotel. As I sat at a light in town, out of nowhere, I realized I was only a mile or two from the neighborhood where I'd lived with the Gallaghers. I don't know why it popped into my head or why I put on my blinker to turn, but the next thing I knew, I was driving down their street.

It had changed since I lived here. The houses were showing their age and weren't as cared for as they used to be. The lawns were messy, and it had a sad air of neglect. It was a middle-class neighborhood back then. I wasn't sure what it was now. Seeing their house made my gut clench, and I felt sick to my stomach. I slowed to a crawl as I stared at it. Although they no longer lived there, I wanted to pound on the door and confront them. I was so shaken by the thought of it that I stopped, parked across the street, and put my head down on the steering wheel. I needed a minute. I sucked in deep breaths. I should've never come here, or at least not without Spawn.

Hoping he wasn't busy and knowing he'd be pissed, I called him. I had to hear his voice. Nightmares were crowding in on me. I was on the brink of a panic attack. He answered me quickly. "Hey, Hotcake, do you miss me already?" he said in a teasing tone.

"Spawn, I..." I couldn't get the words out.

"Babe, what's wrong? Are you alright?" he asked urgently.

I drew in a shaky breath before finding my voice. "I'm not hurt, but I did something stupid. I don't think I can drive back to the hotel." I cringed having to admit that. Boy, that made me sound weak.

"Where are you?"

"I'm outside the old Gallaghers' house. I never expected seeing it to affect me like this. I'm shaking, and

I feel sick to my stomach. Oh God," I sighed in defeat. The bastard wasn't even here, and he was messing with me.

"Sonofabitch! Hold on." I heard him talking muffled to one of the guys. He must've put his hand over the microphone. He was back in moments and continued. "We're coming. I know the address. What in the world made you go over there? If you needed to see it, why didn't you wait for me to take you?" I could hear how upset he was.

"I'm sorry, it wasn't on purpose. I had to go get something at a store. On the way back, I was at a light, and it dawned on me how close I was to the house. The next thing I knew, I was driving down the damn street. It was as if I was on autopilot or something. Who lets a house shake them up like this? I'm acting like a dingy drama queen," I huffed. Disgust at myself was evident.

"You're not dingy or a drama queen," I heard Crusher growl in the background.

"You have me on speaker?!" I practically shouted. My face began to burn.

"I do, and we're family. It's not like we're having phone sex," Spawn said in that sexy voice of his. This made my body shake but for a whole different reason. It was lust.

"Don't let us stop you having it," Sandman hollered.

"Why? Do you need pointers? Is your game that bad with the ladies?" Tinker joked.

Their banter put a smile on my face, and I chuckled. It helped to get my mind off where I was.

"Hey, I'll have you know the ladies love me, and I have no need in that department. I could give the rest of you lessons," Sandman shot back. Their laughter made me laugh hard.

"Wow, lessons, really? I can't imagine you're better than Spawn. He's a sex god," I blurted out.

"Jesus Christ, you've got that poor woman fooled. Sweetheart, I know I can put him to shame," Tinker informed me. I could tell he was trying not to laugh.

"I don't know about that old man. Can you still get it up?" Gravel asked.

"Fuck you, I'm not old, I'm seasoned. You haven't hit thirty yet. You're lucky you know where to stick it," Tinker informed him.

"He told me he puts it in their ears. His cock is that small," Crusher barked out as he chuckled. I lost it. They argued and teased back and forth. I was so diverted I forgot all about the house. I was startled when they pulled up behind me about ten minutes or so later. I hung up and waited for Spawn to get to the car.

He didn't waste time getting out and over to me. I unlocked the door so he could get in the front passenger seat. As soon as he was in, he leaned over, grabbed me, then tugged me toward him. He laid one of his brain-melting kisses on me. He didn't rush. When I came up for air, I was dizzy and ready to go back to the hotel and get out of our clothes.

"I'm here. Let's switch spots, and I'll drive. Come on," he said as he moved his hand to the door handle.

Before he could open it, I saw movement out of the corner of my eye. I glanced over, and all air rushed out of me. I cried out, "No!"

He followed my gaze, and when he saw what I did, he swore as he took his phone out of his cut. "You've got to be fucking joking," he snapped.

While he made his call, I sat there frozen as my rapist took his time going to the mailbox and then ambled back to the front door as if he didn't have a care in the world. I didn't listen to what Spawn was saying. My thoughts were scattered. I didn't come back to myself until Spawn grabbed my hand. That's when I realized I'd reached into my purse and was trying to pull out my handgun. In Louisiana, you had to have a permit to carry, but they accepted it from some states, and Virginia was one of them.

"Babe, look at me," he ordered. I looked at him.

"We can't kill him right here as much as I'd love that. We're gonna head to the Highwaymen's Club and tell them what we found. I promise he's not about to get away. Gravel is taking this car, and he'll keep an eye on him to be sure he doesn't go anywhere. I need you to drive down the street a bit so we can change out without attracting his attention. Can you do that?" he asked.

I numbly nodded. He watched me with concern as I started it and put the car in gear. Thank goodness

I didn't have far to go. I stopped when he told me to. In no time, I was out of my car and into the SUV with the others while Gravel took mine. We pulled away, leaving him behind to watch Paden. I sank into my mind, and unwanted memories came to mind. I couldn't get them to stop.

The image of him coming into my room the night he told me what he wanted and what he'd do if I didn't submit was crystal clear. As were all the other ones. The nights he'd come to visit me and hold his hand over my mouth so I couldn't make noise anyone could hear. I'd cry the whole time, and he'd get angry, but I couldn't help it. After he was done and left, I would run to the bathroom and puke, then take a shower and scrub myself almost raw.

I would lie in bed every night dreading it. I never knew when he'd come, so I barely slept. My foster parents were wondering why my grades were slipping since I had always been an honor student until then. I wanted to tell them so badly, but I was scared and didn't know what to say. I couldn't just blurt it out.

Finally, after several months, I knew I couldn't keep it a secret any longer. Paden was gone for the weekend with some friends. I knew I wouldn't have to worry about him. The first night he was away, I went to the living room. I was so nervous. My whole body was shaking, and I was trying not to throw up. The Gallaghers were watching television.

"Beck, Dorothy, can I talk to you?" They'd insisted I call them by their first names.

"Sure, honey. Let me turn off the TV," Dorothy said. She shut it off. The silence was deafening. She gave me a tiny smile. She'd been so sweet to me. We'd cook and bake together, and she did all those things you expect a good mom to do. I really loved being here, except for Paden. I had a little sister, and I'd always wanted one of those.

"I need to tell you something bad, but I don't know how to tell you. That's why my grades have been slipping."

"Kimera, you know you can tell us anything. We've been worried. You're not yourself, and then the grades on top of it. You're always so studious. We know you want to be a nurse when you grow up. That takes good grades. Whatever it is, just spit it out," Beck said kindly.

"He's right. Tell us. Is it a boy?" Dorothy asked.

I looked back and forth between them. They both wore expressions of concern. Taking a deep breath to quell my nerves, I decided to do what they said. There was no way to say it to make it sound better.

"It does involve a guy. It started about four months ago. He threatened me into having sex with him. Since then, whenever he wants it, I've had to give it to him. I don't want to, but I'm scared of him and what he'll do," I had tears running down my face by the time I got that much out.

Dorothy's look of horror was offset by Beck's look of anger. He came up off the couch. "Who? Who the hell would dare to do that? I want his name. I swear it'll stop, and he'll wish he'd never met you," he snapped.

My heart jumped for joy. They would help me, thank God. Shakily, I answered him, "I'm sorry to tell you this, but it's Paden. He said if I didn't let him, he'd do it to Claudia. I couldn't let him do that."

They both froze for several seconds. When they finally could talk, what came out of their mouths wasn't what I expected. The first was Dorothy. "How dare you accuse our son of such a vile thing! You ungrateful girl, we've been nothing but good to you, and you do this!" she shrieked.

I flinched. "I'm not lying," I protested.

"What do you hope to accomplish by accusing our son of this? He's a good boy and would never touch someone underage, let alone someone in our house. We've taken in others before you, and none of them have ever dared to say such things about him," Beck yelled.

"I don't know why they didn't. Maybe it was just me, but he's been raping me! I wouldn't lie about something that terrible," I cried back. Thank God Claudia was staying at a friend's house tonight. I didn't want her to know this. Her sleepover was another reason I picked tonight to tell them.

"Shut up! I don't want to hear another lie out of your mouth. Get out of our sight. If you dare to tell anyone that disgusting lie, you'll regret it. We should've never taken you in, you ungrateful little bitch," Beck yelled louder. His fists were clenched. I was afraid he was gonna hit me. I backed away from him. Dorothy was crying. I took off running for my room.

That was the beginning of the end for me. They refused to look or speak to me after that night. They acted like I didn't exist. Paden didn't come to my room when he got back. I had no idea if they told him what I said or not, but I was happy not to have any visits. A week later, my social worker came to the house unexpectedly and told me I was moving. I was forced to pack only my clothes and schoolbooks. As she walked me to her car, the Gallaghers watched from the window. They didn't even say goodbye.

It was after that I began to distrust people. Making friends became almost impossible. I finished out my time in a group home, which was fine with me. I kept to myself and focused on my studies so I could go to college when I got out of high school. By some miracle, I was given grants and scholarships. It was the only way I could do it since I had to work full-time just to live. I had a shitty studio apartment in the worst neighborhood. It was a wonder I hadn't been killed or raped there.

"Babe, we're here," Spawn said softly. His voice was what dragged me back to the present, and I looked up to see we were pulling into the Highwaymen's compound, I guess you'd call it. It's what the Punishers called their enclosed area around the clubhouse.

Spawn: Chapter 20

My need to jump out of the car and take Paden Gallagher as soon as I spotted him warred with common sense. I knew we couldn't risk taking him in broad daylight, but it was almost impossible not to do it. Only the threat of getting caught and being separated from Kimera, along with not wanting to drag four of my brothers down with me, stopped me.

The drive to the Highwaymen's compound was silent. I think we were all lost in our thoughts—I know Kimera was. I held onto her hand as she stared out the window. I wanted to talk to her, but I didn't want an audience. It was as we were entering their compound that I saw tears in her eyes.

"Babe, we're here," I said.

She jerked, and when her gaze met mine, I saw the pain there. I took off my seatbelt and slid over to wrap her up in my arms. She leaned her head on my chest. "Babe, it's gonna be alright, I promise you. He's not getting away. Gravel will stick to him like glue. Once we talk to Stallion and his guys and get our plan finalized, we'll go tonight. It's almost over," I whispered to her. I could see Crusher watching us with concern in the rearview mirror.

"I know you will. It's just seeing the house and

him. It brought back all the things that happened. His parents were so upset and mean to me when they found out. They called me a liar and a bitch, and within a week, they had my social worker come and pick me up. I had no idea they were doing it until she showed up and told me to pack. I thought they cared for me, but it was a lie."

Her sobs broke my heart. She'd suffered enough. I hadn't said anything to her about my other side project but maybe it was time I did. I raised her head so I could see her beautiful face. I wiped the tears away. We were now parked outside the clubhouse.

"They're just as guilty as he is in this. They hid it. Don't tell me there weren't signs or even niggling doubt somewhere in the back of their minds about him. They let him probably continue to do it to other girls. They're not getting off scot-free."

Her eyes widened as she sat straighter. "What does that mean?"

"They've been living quite a nice life since you left. They moved to another place, into a bigger and fancier house. They have luxury cars and take really nice, expensive vacations. I think they should know what it feels like not to be able to do all those things. To live how you did, especially when you had to support yourself and go to school."

"You're planning to take their money, aren't you?" she asked. I tried to tell if the idea bothered her. By the look on her face, it didn't. She was almost smiling, and her tears had stopped.

I smiled at her and nodded. "Damn right, I am. You and I can figure out who should get it."

Without missing a beat, she answered. "It should be something that benefits foster kids. I can do some research and see what's out there. It might be vindictive of me to like this idea, but I don't care. They refused to even consider I was telling the truth. I know he's their son, but they still should've at least checked into what I told them. What about his money? Does he have any?"

I grinned. "Not as much as his parents, but yes, he does well for himself. That's why I think it's weird he didn't take any out of his accounts, but his parents did, and there's no trail to show what they used it for, which makes me think it was given to him so he could stay off the radar. I'm not sure why. He doesn't know we're after him. He's up to something else."

"Hey, I hate to interrupt, but Stallion is staring at us. I think he wants to know why we're here without calling first," Tinker said.

I glanced over to see Stallion staring out the clubhouse door. "Okay, let's go. Babe, I'm not sure if Phoebe or Mara are around. We'll talk to Stallion and then probably at some point have church. I don't think they'll allow you in. Will you be okay by yourself in the common area?"

As I asked, Crusher and the others piled out. Crusher opened her door. She got out with me on her ass. She nodded. "Yeah, I'll be fine. You go do what you have to. I want this done so we can start the new year clean and get on with our lives." She took my hand. I placed a quick kiss on her lips, then headed over to greet Stallion. He had a worried look on his face.

"Sorry for dropping in like this, Stallion. I should've called, but we were taken aback by what we saw. We automatically headed here. We've found Gallagher, and Gravel is watching him. I'd like to see if we can make our move tonight." I informed him as I shook his hand.

A smile spread across his face. "That's the best news I've heard in a while. Come on in. Kimera, honey, you look like you could use a drink. What would you like?" he asked as he waved the prospect behind the bar out of the way when we got inside. Stallion stood there waiting for her order. It was a weekday, so the others were probably all at work. We'd have to wait until they got off, which was a bummer, but it couldn't be helped.

"I'll have a shot of whiskey. Would you happen to have any Jameson? If not, Jack Daniels works too."

I was surprised. I'd never seen her drink. I guess seeing that bastard had rattled her big time, not that I could blame her for being upset.

"The lady asketh, the lady getteth Jameson," he said with a wink and a smile. It made her laugh softly. He reached under the bar and brought out a bottle. He raised his eyebrows. "What about the rest of you? Is the lady drinking alone, or will you share her poison? I plan to."

"Hell yeah," Crusher muttered. Sandman, Tinker, and I all nodded yes, too. Shot glasses were set up, and he poured. In his case, it was a to the brim kinda shot pour. Those were the best. We all took one, but no one drank. Stallion held his up.

"A toast to making a disgusting, raping bastard pay for his crimes and to a future free of him. Let's show him what he gets when he messes with one of your old ladies. *Sláinte*."

I knew that was the Irish way of saying "health." We all repeated it, then drank. I thought Kimera might take a few tries to get hers down, but she surprised me by shooting it. She grimaced a tiny bit, but there was no choking. My brothers teased her.

"Will you look at that? Kimera is a bigger badass than I thought. She drank that like a pro. You've been keeping your talents hidden from us," Crusher teased her with a wink.

"She sure has. She's a secret party animal, I bet," Sandman added as he gently elbowed her.

"She'll have to be a drinker to put up with Spawn," Tinker added.

"Hey, I'm not that fucking bad," I objected.

She burst out laughing. "You're all insane, you know that, right? Just because I can take a shot doesn't make me a party animal, and I haven't been hiding it. As for needing alcohol to put up with Spawn, I don't see that happening. It's true. I rarely drink. I like to keep my wits about me, but I trust you guys to look out for me, so I relaxed."

"We'll always watch out and protect you, Kimera. You never have to worry about that not happening,"

Tinker told her soberly. The other two nodded. I rubbed her back. She knew I had her back.

"I know, and it means the world to me. So, what's next?"

Stallion answered that one. "Next, I get my guys' asses back here, and we sit down and get this party started. Kimera, Mara should be home by now. I'll see if she can come by and keep you company while we plan. Phoebe will be here later with the kids if she knows you're here. They don't get out of school until three, and she's working today."

"Don't go to any trouble. I can hang out here and read. I know you guys have stuff to figure out. They don't have to come to keep me entertained."

"It's no trouble. They've been talking about how much they enjoyed the other night. They told my guys to get off their asses and find themselves women like you so they have more company. It's been fun to watch them all try to run when it happens. The dumbasses don't know what they're missing. A good woman can make a man. I'm not ashamed to say it. I want my boys to find a woman like their mom and you. They have time, but she's ready for the grandbabies. If you know of any, send them our way," Stallion told her with a wink.

She giggled. "I don't, but if I do find any, I'll send them. That is if they want to come here. If not, I'll send them to Spawn's single brothers. The Punishers still have several single ones." She glanced at Crusher, Sandman, and Tinker.

"Oh hell no, don't get any ideas, woman!"

Sandman squawked.

"I wouldn't say no if she were the right kind," Crusher said, surprising me.

"I'm not looking, but thanks," Tinker said quietly. He had a frown on his face. His answer took me back. I knew for a fact he'd talked before about finding someone. What changed? When this was over, I'd have to get him alone and see if he'd tell me.

"I accept. Now, have a seat. If you want more to drink, he'll get it. If you're hungry, help yourself to whatever is in the kitchen. I'll be back. Just gotta go make some calls and send out the bat signal," Stallion said right before he headed toward a hall.

From our tour the other day, I knew he had an office down there. I think most presidents kept one in the clubhouse, whether they had a house nearby or not. We moved over to one of the tables. The prospect, I think his name was Zach, came over to us as soon as we sat down.

"I'm Zach, by the way. Just let me know what I can get you. I think there's some leftover chili in the kitchen, and if they haven't eaten it all, there's some cake Mara made. I can get you some if you're hungry."

"Thanks, Zach, I appreciate it. I'm not hungry. I can use a beer. Babe, what about you? Have you eaten?" I asked Kimera.

"I'm not hungry, but I'd take a drink, only not more alcohol, not yet. Can I have a soda? Anything other than Pepsi, please," was her answer. The others quickly gave him their orders. It seemed none of us was hungry at the moment. Nodding his head, Zach hurried off to get them.

"I wonder how long he has left to prospect and if they'll patch him?" Sandman mused.

"Ask him when he gets back. From the little I saw the other day, and now, he seems a good sort. Hopefully, he's been a good prospect," I said.

"What do you guys look for when they prospect, which determines if you vote them in or not?" she asked curiously.

We launched into what our club looked for. She listened intently. We were interrupted by Zach returning. As he passed them out, I asked him. "So, how long have you been prospecting, and how long will they make you do it around here? Our club usually does it a year, although sometimes it goes longer. Unless they're crap, then we cut them loose early."

"I've been here nine months. I was told they make you stay at least a year. Like you said, if you're not cutting it, they let you go early. I'm hoping since I lasted this long, it's a good sign."

"As long as you keep up whatever you're doing and don't fuck up big time, you should. You look a bit older. Mind if I ask what you were doing before you decided this life was for you?" I asked next. I was always interested in what brought men to our lifestyle. The reasons were plenty.

"I'd always seen them around town when I was

growing up, and they fascinated me. However, when I turned eighteen, my dad said I had to go to either school or the military. I chose the Army. I spent eight years with them, and then I had enough. When I got out, I decided I was going to see if they'd take me. I lucked out, and they did. Griller offered to be my sponsor. He said he knew my dad, which I didn't know. He's gone now."

"Hey, I was in the Army too. I learned a lot, but I had to finally get out, too," Crusher told him. They exchanged fist bumps. Before we could ask him more questions, Stallion came back. Like a good prospect, Zach faded away. He went back to the bar. Stallion sat down with us.

"I see Zach has been taking care of you. Good. Listen, the guys are wrapping shit up, and they'll get back as soon as they can. When they all get here, we'll have church. Mara is coming, Kimera. She should be here in the next half hour. She was in town running an errand, but it's done. Whiskey said Phoebe would head over after she got the kids from school so you wouldn't be alone. I think that's all until later."

"Thank you. I appreciate it, and I'm looking forward to talking to them again," she told him.

"I have a question for ya. Have you put any more women in their place since that night?" he asked with a twinkle in his eye.

She laughed hard as she shook her head. "Not in the last couple of days, but the day isn't over. I'm thinking of putting a bag over him that covers him from head to toe."

This set off my brothers and made Stallion grin like a maniac. "Baby, there's no bag for me unless you do the same. I have to put up with men lusting after you all the time."

"No, you don't! Men don't do that with me."

"Sure we do. I mean, hell, if Spawn hadn't called dibs first, I would've seen if you and I could've made a go at it," Crusher chimed in.

I knew several of my brothers would've been happy to go after her. She seemed shocked. She truly didn't know how attractive she was. I wasn't worried, though. Once a woman was claimed, none would poach.

"Really? You think not. I bet we could go home and ask the guys, and you'll see. Crusher isn't the only one. However, since I was the lucky one and got to you first, he and the rest know you're off-limits. If I were stupid enough to let you go, which I'm not, there would be a line forming. Although I'd have to kill them," I said with a snarl.

"You know we would never do that. I don't want to die or have my whole existence wiped out. Sorry, Kimera. You're gorgeous but not worth that," Sandman said.

"I don't blame you. It's sweet of you guys to say it, but I still think you're nuts. I'm nothing special."

"Yes, you are," I told her.

Just as I said it, the door opened, and Stone came in. This began the next hour. As more and more of the guys joined us, we told them what happened. They gathered around and had a drink. We talked about several things but nothing in depth about our plans for Gallagher. Mara showed up, too, and took Kimera off to talk. By the time we were ready to go to church, Phoebe and the kids arrived, and they were talking at a corner table. I went over to tell her we were going in. She nodded, and I gave her a kiss.

"Don't worry, we'll take care of her. I'm gonna take her to our house. If we're not here when you get done, have Stallion bring you to the house," Mara said.

"Thanks, I will. Have fun."

"I plan to," was Kimera's comeback.

Walking into their church, I looked around. The door had been pointed out on our tour, but we hadn't gone inside. It was set up like most MC churches, I think. A big table with lots of chairs. On the wall behind Stallion's spot at one end of the table hung a huge flag with their club's emblem and name on it. There were pictures of current and what I assumed were past members on the walls in frames. I felt right at home. My brothers and I waited until we were shown where to sit. Sitting down, we all looked at Stallion. The room got quiet.

"Now that we're all here, and thanks for getting here before the end of the day, let's talk. We all know what happened to Kimera, Spawn's woman. We've offered him whatever help he needs to take care of the issue. I said in my text we have an update. Spawn, tell them what happened earlier today."

I didn't delay in telling them what she did and how we saw Gallagher by accident. They all muttered excitedly when they heard it. I finished by telling them Gravel was watching him. His last message simply said he was still at the house.

"Yeah, let's get this bastard," Tats uttered as he rubbed his hands together.

"How do you want to do this, Spawn?" Stone asked.

"Assuming he stays in the house, then we'll have to wait until he's asleep and go in. There are houses all around him, so we'll need to do it on the down low and with as few as possible. My brothers and I can do it. It's getting him to a place where no one will hear his screams or disturb our time with him. You said you had a place. How far away is it?"

"It's about an hour away, and it's in the middle of nowhere. There are no neighbors for miles to stumble across us. If you're sure you don't need our help to nab him and transport him, we'll head out there while you take care of him. We've taken the liberty of getting it ready for our entertainment a while back. Since you flew, we knew you couldn't bring toys of your own," Stallion said with a smirk on his face. The others all chuckled darkly.

"What about Kimera? Is she going to stay here?" Tinker asked me.

I gave Stallion a chin lift. "Is that okay with you? I'd rather she not stay alone at the hotel. She'll stew on it enough as it is."

"We'll be glad to have her. She can stay with Mara. It'll be late, so why not have her stay the night? You're more than welcome to stay with her, too, although I don't know if you'll be done working until well into the morning. Mara will love the company."

"Thanks, I appreciate it more than you know. I'll tell her. We'll have to go back and grab her things, but we have to go to the hotel anyway."

After that, it was just talk about what we would take and how we'd get into his house. Getting in would require me to do some work to see if there was a security system registered with one of the local security companies and, if so, figure out how to bypass it. That would require me to have my laptop. We took a short break so I could get things started. Sandman volunteered to run back to get my laptop at the hotel. I had him take Kimera with him to get her things after I explained the plan. She wasn't thrilled to be left without me tonight, but she understood the need and agreed to do it.

I sent them off while we continued to talk. Crusher or Tinker would fill him in while I worked. At some point, we'd have to tell Gravel what we planned. I didn't want to pull him off Gallagher and risk him getting away. I wanted to know what the hell he was doing in that house. His family sold it. The title transfer I found was for a family named Kilpatrick. As far as I had found, they had no connection to the Gallaghers. I hated mysteries.

After Sandman came back, I set up in an empty room in the clubhouse to do my work. Before I got started, I checked on Kimera. She was doing fine with the ladies and assured me she was okay. They were busy at the clubhouse cooking for everyone.

I worked as fast as I could. Since we were on a deadline, I reached out to Outlaw in Hunters Creek to see if he could help me check some of the security companies. He said sure, then the next thing I knew, I had all the rest of them helping. I hadn't wanted to bother them, but this was what I loved about being part of an extended MC family. They were always willing to help. Even Diviner came to give me a hand. That was when I learned he was the Highwaymen's hacker slash computer guru or whatever you wanted to call it. His club name made sense now.

He joked his brother was the mechanically inclined one while he was the opposite, but he could do some work on his own bike, he told me. We sat there tapping away and muttering back and forth. While I drank coffee, he was drinking energy drinks. More power to him. I couldn't stand the taste of them.

We took a short break to eat dinner, and then we were back at it. I hated to leave Kimera alone for so long, but I had to do this. Gravel kept reporting hourly. So far, Gallagher had gone out to grab dinner and then came back home. He ate alone. As nightfall came, Gravel took a chance and snuck through the dark to recon his house. He said he was inside watching television and drinking beer. He promised to text when all the lights went out in the house. That was our cue to head over to take him in an hour. Surely he'd be asleep an hour after turning out the damn lights.

In the end, none of us could find a security company that was monitoring his address. This was good news. It meant we didn't need to worry about tripping it. I planned to cut the electricity to his neighborhood, and the phone lines would be jammed. I could do it remotely and then turn it back on when we were done. The days of having to do it manually were over. Everything was going digital. In some ways, it was good, but in others I worried. As much as I loved the digital world, it scared me, too.

We were set. I got to spend about an hour with Kimera, and then we were back at it. This time, it was making sure we had all the equipment we needed. When we left to go to get him, Stallion and his guys would be off to the location that they found for us. He'd shown us the spot on a map. I'd scoped it out using Google Maps and other tricks I had. He was right. It was out in the middle of nowhere. They'd be waiting for us there. His prospects were staying behind to keep a watch over their compound, the ladies and the kids. They didn't expect trouble, but it was a precaution we all took.

It was midnight, and we were sitting around the common room. Some were playing pool. Sandman was trying his hand at the pinball machine. A couple was playing darts, and the rest were talking. My phone chimed. I glanced at it as my heart sped up. It was Gravel.

Gravel: Lights just went out.

Me: Good. Stay there. Will join you shortly.

Gravel: Got it.

When I looked up, everyone was staring at me. "It's almost time. He turned out the lights. My guys and I will roll out in fifteen minutes," I informed them.

"We'll leave when you do. Take your time. If something comes up and you can't grab him, let us know, and we'll find another way," Stallion offered. I gave him a nod.

I turned to Kimera. She'd joined me not long ago, but she had been quiet. I saw her fidgeting, so I laid my hand on hers. "Babe, there's nothing to worry about. We do this all the time. Just think, by morning, it'll be over."

"I know, but I still worry. I wish I could go."

I jerked in surprise. This was the first time she'd said that. "You never said anything about wanting to go. Why the sudden desire?"

"I've been thinking. Troian told me no details, but she was there when you took out her cousins, and she said she needed it. It made it real for her. She asked if I'd want to do it. I told her I didn't know until the time came. Well, it's time, and the more I think about it, the more I don't know if I can face not giving him a piece of my mind. Will I be able to relax and know in my soul he's gone if I don't see him die? Not that I think you'll lie to me. It's just a case of seeing is believing, you know. God, I'm sorry. I shouldn't be telling you this now. Forget it. Go do what you need to do. I'll be here when you get done."

The others had gathered as she talked and heard the gist of what she said. The Highwaymen were exchanging worried looks. I could understand. They had shot down the idea of Sonny coming along, which I knew would happen, and I didn't blame them. He was an outsider. At least we were part of their MC world. My brothers had more contemplative looks on their faces.

"Kimera, honey, you know I'll give you just about anything in the world if it's within my power, but I'm not sure this is one of those things. What if you can't forget what we do to him? Or it makes you scared of me or my brothers? I can't risk losing you over him. I know Troian seems to have done fine with it, but her doing it doesn't mean you need to."

"Do you think she's stronger than me?" was her immediate response.

"No, I don't. You're very strong, or you wouldn't have made a life for yourself after what he did. You didn't turn to drugs or alcohol. You didn't hurt yourself or even kill yourself. You came here to help find him without backup."

"Spawn, I know it's more between you two, but if you're worried about what we think, I have no problem if she wants to come. If she ends up not wanting to watch it or only part of it, then one of us will bring her back. I think she deserves the chance to face her tormentor," Sandman said out of the blue. Crusher and Tinker nodded their heads, yes.

"It's not just us we have to worry about," I reminded them. The Highwaymen would be there, and although it was unlikely they'd get a chance to touch him, they might not want a woman seeing it. Even knowing about it, they could see it as a risk.

"I don't need to go. Forget it," she said.

"I don't have a problem if she wants to go. Do you have your old ladies participate in stuff like this?" Stallion asked, raising his brow.

"A few and other clubs we know have had it happen. Sometimes, just to tell the people off, a few have gotten their hands a bit dirty and others very dirty. It's not expected," I explained.

"Hell, if I had an old lady and she wanted to get her licks in and she could handle it, I'd have to think about it," Abyss mused.

Others murmured. Not seeing another way around it, I laid it out: "It would have to be a unanimous vote, babe. I don't like it, but I can understand why you want to do it."

To my surprise, when each Highwayman was looked at by Stallion, every one of them said yes. I was sure some would vote against it. I glanced at my brothers. All three said yes. That left Gravel. I called him.

"What's up, Spawn?" he asked as he answered. He was talking softly.

"Kimera wants to come. I told her it has to be unanimously yes from all of us and Stallion's guys. I need your vote."

He was quiet for about a minute, then he answered me. "I don't want her to see him, but I know it helped Troian to be there. If anyone deserves to see this, it's her. Hell yeah, bring her."

"I'll tell them. See you soon."

I hung up and faced them. "It's unanimous. Let's get you ready. There are a few things you'll need, and I'll go over the rules on the way," I told her. She nodded. God, I hoped I wasn't making a mistake.

Spawn: Chapter 21

On the way to extract Gallagher, I covered the rules. She'd stay in the car with Gravel. He would remain as our lookout. She was dressed in dark jeans, boots, and a plain black hoodie she had borrowed from Mara. Her hair was up under a black skull cap. I didn't want anyone to be able to identify her if we were seen. I didn't smear her face with tactical paint like ours were. She made me laugh when she whispered to me how sexy it was. I ended up kissing her and smearing some on her anyway.

As I went over the rules, one of the big ones was that I had the final say on whether she had to leave. It could be in case she was too upset by what she saw or if there was a risk to her. If, by some rare chance, we were found, I would do everything I could to get her out of there. I tasked Crusher with that job. I trusted all my brothers, but he had the most tactical experience. He could do it when none of the rest of us could. He promised me he'd get her away.

In the end, we left her in the care of Gravel to be a second lookout as we crept down the street to the dark house. The neighborhood was so quiet. There weren't any dogs barking, which was weird to me. Not that I wasn't grateful, but it seemed odd this whole set of houses didn't have a single outdoor dog.

Before we went in, I'd shut down the electricity to the house. We had to get in and out before someone in this section reported it to the electric company, and they figured out what happened and turned it back on. However, based on what I did, it might take them a while to fix it. The cell service was easier to handle. I was carrying a signal jammer. It would affect anything electronic we had, but we weren't relying on anything like that for this anyway.

Picking the lock to get in the backdoor was a joke. When we got inside, I shined my flashlight on the inside of the door. There was a deadbolt on it, but he hadn't engaged it. Good for us, bad for him. One of the things Kimera had done for us was draw out a detailed layout of the house. She was able to show us where the bedrooms were. Knowing him, she figured he'd be in the master, but just in case, she also pointed out which had been his room.

We split up into teams of two so we could check both at the same time. It was better than chancing him, possibly hearing something, and coming to investigate. Tinker went with me to the master bedroom, while Crusher and Sandman went to his old bedroom. I listened at the door to be sure I couldn't hear anything. I heard faint snoring. I signaled to Tinker. He hurried to get the other two. We agreed if we somehow determined before entering which room he was in, we'd fetch the others.

I had no doubt I could subdue him myself, but better safe than sorry. I felt, rather than heard, the three of them come up behind me. I held up three fingers.

When I dropped the last one, I turned the knob and opened the door. It was pitch black, but it wasn't an issue for us. We had night vision. We all packed them this time. I bet the TSA people were wondering what the hell when they saw them and our guns, but we followed the rules for declaring and flying with the weapons, so there wasn't much they could say.

There was a big lump on the left side of the bed. I eased up beside it. I could see his head. The desire to start beating the hell out of him was almost more than I could resist, but I fought for control. There'd be enough time for that soon enough. To ensure he would give us no trouble and to decrease even more the chance he might alert someone, Stallion had suggested we use a fast-acting tranquilizer on him. If Lash were here, he could've given us one, but he wasn't, so we figured we'd have to make do. Apparently, the Highwaymen had someone who could get that kind of thing for them, and he or she came through. Tinker had it out and was ready to hit him with it on my signal, but first, I wanted him to know what hit him.

I reached down and sealed my hand over his mouth. His eyes flew open. Even in the odd greenish light of the goggles, you could see his fear. It made me smile. You couldn't even see our outlines in the room. He must have blackout shades or something. He tried to struggle to get loose. "Don't move, or I'll slit your throat," I hissed. No, I wouldn't. That would let him get off too easily, but he didn't know it. He froze. He was breathing hard.

"Your day of reckoning has come. Time to meet the Devil. Night night."

That was the signal Tinker was waiting for. He hit him in the neck. It was easy to get it straight into him there. It took a minute to feel him relax underneath my hand. I cautiously lifted it. Nothing. Working quickly, we got him tied up, gagged, and out of the bed. Crusher was the biggest, and he offered to carry him in a fireman's carry. We didn't waste time getting back out of the house. We made sure to lock the door behind us. We'd worn gloves and had our hair covered. Nothing would be left behind for anyone to know what happened to him. He'd become one of those missing person mysteries you hear about.

We took a different route to get back to the vehicles. There was no way I'd make Kimera ride in the same one as him. He was going in the SUV with my brothers, and she and I would be in the car we rented. Before returning them, we'd wipe them down with bleach. Since we didn't spill any blood, it should take care of any possible DNA he left behind. When we got to them, Sandman opened the back door, and Crusher dumped him inside.

I saw Kimera staring out of the car. Gravel got out and came over. Wordlessly, they got in, and I went to join her. I shut the door and started it. I pulled out behind them. She gave me an anxious look. "Did you have any trouble with him?"

"Nope. Not a bit. He was in the master. It went like clockwork. Are you alright? Do you still want to do this? It's not too late for me to drop you off to stay with Mara."

"Aidan, I'm not backing out no matter what you say. I have to be there. I need to get this rage I feel vented. Don't worry about me."

"Baby, I'll always worry about you and try to protect you from anything that scares or hurts you. Okay, let's go get this done so we can go home." I squeezed her hand, then raised it so I could kiss it. She smiled at me.

We took our time and weaved our way through the streets to get to the one we needed and would follow out to the meet site. We rode in silence. I let her be alone with her thoughts. Stallion was right. It took almost an hour to get there. If it weren't for the GPS on my phone, I wouldn't have found it. I'd wipe it from my phone's history and whoever's phone used it in the SUV. Erasing things is possible if you know how to do it.

When we got there, I saw three vehicles. Stallion and his men decided it would be less conspicuous to be in regular cars rather than on their bikes. I agreed. They were gathered in a semicircle in front of the entrance. A lantern was shining out front. Standing there were Stallion, Stone, Whiskey, and Piston. The others must be inside. We parked next to their rides.

As we got to them with Crusher carrying Gallagher again, I noticed Kimera didn't even glance over at him. She was holding herself stiffly. I prayed she wouldn't regret this. Stallion grinned. "I see you brought the sacrifice."

"I aim to please. Let's get this show on the road," I said.

"Follow me," he said. As he led, we fell in behind him. His three brought up the rear. The walk inside was twisted and long. I was about to ask when we were getting there when we came around a turn and into a large open area. I looked around. I'd never been in one of these before, and I wasn't too thrilled about it, but they had assured us it was safe despite not being used for years.

We were inside of an abandoned aluminum mine which had played out years ago. It was cold and damp down there. I eyed the dirt ceiling. The thought of being trapped down here made me uneasy.

"Don't worry, it's safe. We've used it before, and it's fine. You probably didn't see the steel gates over the entrance. They're closed and triple padlocked when we're not here. We're good," Abyss told us. Deciding to trust him, I perused the rest of it. There was an old wooden chair in the middle. It looked like the old-fashioned ones that they used to do electrical shock treatments on people in the old days. It was sturdy, for sure. On the arms and legs were metal shackles, which were part of the chair. Off to the side were wooden crates. On top of them were a variety of tools laid out.

"He should be coming around soon. The shot was calibrated to last about an hour and a half, two max. Milady, why don't you sit and rest?" Boulder suggested to Kimera as he waved his hand toward a crate without anything on it.

"Thank you," she told him as she went to sit.

Not wanting to leave her alone long, I only did a

quick check of the toys they'd brought us. They'd do the trick. As much as I might want to prolong his misery, I wouldn't. The risk was higher here than at home, and I wanted to get this over with. We'd have to tell Claudia and Sonny he was no longer a threat without saying more. They could draw their own conclusions. Then we'd be back on our way home. If we couldn't book flights, we planned to rent the SUV longer and drive back. Today was New Year's Eve. The Highwaymen were planning a party, and they'd invited us. I'd have to see how Kimera felt afterward.

I stood, rubbing her back, as we waited. The murmur of low conversations kept flowing around us. I was about to go slap him to wake his ass up when he twitched then I heard a faint moaning sound. I gave her a kiss and then walked over to stand in front of him. I wanted to be the first person he saw when he woke up.

He moved more, then lifted his head. He blinked like an owl at the lights. They had it well-lit in here. His eyes widened when he saw me. He glanced around and saw the others. The only one he didn't see was Kimera. She was behind me. I wanted it that way. She and I had talked about this. His gag had been removed when they chained him to the chair.

"W-who are you?" he croaked.

No one said anything. He tried again. "I don't know you. You made a mistake. I'm not whomever you're after. I'm not the owner of the house. He's working out of state for three months. I'm just house-sitting for him." Well, this explained why he was back in his old house. We all stood there with our arms crossed, staring menacingly at him. Sweat dotted his forehead despite the chill.

He swung his head side to side before he tried again. "Listen, you don't want to hurt me. If you do, my family will make sure you're hunted down and put in prison. Let me go, and I'll forget I ever saw you. I don't know what the owner did to you, but it's between you and him. I don't want any trouble." That was what broke my silence.

"You don't want trouble? Why not? You sure like causing it. Along with causing pain and suffering, don't you, Paden Gallagher?"

He jumped when he heard I knew his name. More fear entered his face. "Please, I have no idea what you're talking about. Whoever told you I hurt someone or caused suffering lied."

I turned my head and nodded. Kimera stood up and came up behind me, then walked around me. As she came to a standstill in front of us, I put my hands on her shoulders. He stared at her, trying to puzzle out where he knew her from. I could read his face.

"Hello, Paden. Don't tell me that you forgot me. Or is it because you've hurt so many girls that you can't remember them all?" she asked, her voice strong as she said it.

"I don't know—," he started to say, but she cut him off.

"Yes, you do. You told Claudia you wanted to see me, so here I am," she said sweetly.

I saw when it registered who she was. Not only did panic take over, but he began to shake. "Kimera?" he whispered.

"Yes, Kimera. Have you hurt so many girls and women that you can't remember what we look like anymore? I know I've changed a bit, but not that much. Maybe it's the red hair. I dyed it to help a friend catch her tormentors so they could be made to pay for their crimes. I'd like to introduce you to these men." She pointed to Stallion and his men first.

"This is the Savage Highwaymen MC. I know you've heard of them. These five are the Iron Punishers MC. They're not local, but they made the trip especially to help me take care of you. And this big hulking man behind me is Spawn. I'll let him explain how he got his name. He's my old man. He's been chomping at the bit to meet you." I swear her tone had gotten sweeter.

I saw him turn green when he heard all that. He was shaking his head. "Kimera, please. I don't know why you're doing this, but we can sort out whatever the misunderstanding is. Tell me how I supposedly hurt you. I did see Claudia, but all I said was that I wondered if she had ever heard from you or not. I was hoping you were doing okay."

She lurched closer to him. "Liar," she hissed.

"I'm not lying. Guys, I don't know what she's told you, but I haven't hurt her or anyone else," he said in a pleading tone. The urge to punch him in the face was growing.

"So it wasn't you who raped me repeatedly when I was fifteen and told me if I didn't submit and keep my mouth shut, you'd do it to Claudia. The same Claudia I now know you were raping at the same time. Your parents didn't believe me when I told them. They sent me away rather than face the truth that their precious son is a pedophile. How many girls have you raped, Paden?" Her voice was rougher now.

"I didn't rape you, Claudia, or anyone else! She's crazy. The reason my parents sent her away was she was a troublemaker and a compulsive liar. They tried to teach her manners and not to lie, but she wouldn't listen. They had no choice but to send her back."

She let out a scream and lunged at him. He screamed, and when I tugged her back, I saw why. She'd gotten her hands on a knife, and it was buried in his thigh. She'd sunk it deep, too.

"You lying fucking bastard! I wasn't lying then or now. You raped both of us. You were a man, and we were kids. We didn't want it. You deserve to suffer and die for what you put us through, and that's exactly your fate. I hope you burn in the fires of hell for the rest of eternity. While you do, know I'll be living a happy life full of love and family. Oh, and don't worry, your parents aren't getting off either. Spawn has something planned for them."

She turned and buried her face into my chest. I held her tightly as I glared at him. He was shaking like a leaf. I leaned down to whisper in her ear. "Do you want to do anything else to him? Or do you want to watch?

You can leave too if you prefer."

She looked up and shook her head. "I'm not leaving. For now, I'll watch. If I change my mind, I'll let you know. Is that alright?"

"It's perfect." I gave her a deep kiss and then took her back to her crate. When I faced him again, I let my inner demon show. He'd been growing louder and louder since she told me what this fucker had done to her. He wanted blood in the worst way, and I was about to let him out to play. He craved this man's pain and blood worse than he did the Gusevs. He was about to learn why I was called Spawn, and so were the Highwaymen and Kimera.

"No, you can't! If you kill me, someone will figure it out, and you'll fry for it!" he yelled frantically.

I walked up to him. I hadn't even started on him yet, and he appeared ready to pass out. I showed my teeth as I yanked the knife out of his thigh. He screamed in pain. The blood came out faster, but I noticed it wasn't arterial. She knew where to stab him.

I thought back to what we'd done to the Gusevs. First came the beating. I'd gladly do it. I had brass knuckles, but I didn't start with those. I wanted to feel his flesh giving under my blows. I was strong, and I could pound on him for a while before my hands needed rest or help. I landed the first one on his jaw. His head snapped to the side. I did it on the opposite side. From there, I landed blows wherever I thought they would cause the most pain and either break bones or cause internal injuries. As I worked him over, I talked.

"The men Kimera mentioned, those bastards only kidnapped and tried to rape her. I helped to take them apart. You raped her over and over. Imagine what I'm gonna do to you. You'll wish for death and to meet the Devil long before I'm done. Tell him I said hello. He knows me. I've sent more than a few fuckers like you to him."

He pleaded, but nothing he could say would save him. I beat him until he was unconscious. As we waited for him to come around. I checked on her. She was pale but refused to leave. Tired of the delay, I went back to him and slapped his ass awake. He moaned weakly. Next, I took the wooden baseball bat someone had been nice enough to include in the unusual arsenal. I took a couple of practice swings. It sang through the air.

"Honey, can I try that?" she asked softly from behind me.

"Sure, baby, if you want. Here ya go," I handed it to her. She got close to him and studied him as if trying to decide where to hit.

"Please, Kim, don't do this," he begged.

"How many times did I beg you not to rape me, and you didn't listen? Dozens of times. Sorry, I don't understand," she said right before she let loose. She slammed the bat into both shins, his thighs, and both arms. When she was done, he was a blubbering mess. She handed the bat back and retook her seat.

For good measure, I landed a blow across his shoulder and his ribs on both sides. There were audible cracking sounds on the ribs. Hopefully, I didn't puncture his lungs. If I did, he'd die too quickly.

With the Gusevs, we'd broken all ten of their fingers. I had a better idea for him. As I hunted for something to use, Crusher came over. "Brother, do you need us to work on him so you can take a break?"

"I can't, Crusher. My rage right now is too high to do it. I know I'm spoiling your fun, and I'm sorry."

"You don't have to tell us sorry. We understand. Just know we're here if you want to. Stallion and his guys knew there was no way they'd get any licks in, but they seem to be enjoying the show. I think he misses you. You'd better get back to him before he gets lonely," he said with a smirk and chuckle. I grinned at him.

I found what I needed. As I passed Crusher, I changed my mind. I leaned in and softly told him what I wanted him to have at the ready. He lit up, and so did Gravel, Tinker, and Sandman.

I held up my tool. Gallagher's look of horror grew. "No, no," He screamed as I walked behind him and yanked the first finger away from the others.

It took some hand strength to do it, but I had it. His agonizing scream thrilled me as his pinky finger fell to the floor. I moved on to the next one. Crusher was next to me by then, and he quickly cauterized the wound with a small blow torch so Gallagher wouldn't bleed out. The smell of burned flesh made me almost gag. I saw Abyss hand Kimera a piece of cloth to put over her nose.

After a couple of fingers, Crusher traded off with Tinker. As I snipped, my brothers took turns cauterizing. He passed out long before we were done. I wish Lash were here with his whips. I'd have him show me some of his moves. Gallagher was in pretty bad shape. I thought of what else I could do. There wasn't a lot. The way he was breathing made me think I had damaged his lungs. I wiped the sweat from my brow, streaking the tactical paint on my sleeve.

I studied him. There wasn't much I could do before the final two acts. They were gruesome, and I hoped Kimera would leave before then. If not, she may never look at me the same again, but the demon insisted it had to be done, and I wasn't fighting him this time. I went over to her. "Babe, it's gonna get really ugly. Will you go outside so you don't have to see this?"

"Spawn, you can't do anything to that monster that'll make me think badly of you or chase me away. Do it, and then let's go home. I'm tired, and I want to see Toro and the rest of our family."

"Okay, baby, I love you."

"I love you too," she gave me a kiss after she said it.

Choosing not to prolong it, I chose one more thing. I picked an item on the crates. Abyss nodded. I guess I knew who brought it. He handed me a pair of gloves. "Have you used this before?"

"No."

"You don't want to get any on you. If you'll allow

me, I'll do it for you. What do you want it to be used on?"

I leaned in and told him. His grin was outright wicked. He laughed as he walked over to him. I grabbed the knife. When I got to Gallagher, I slapped him awake again. As he surfaced, I took the knife and cut away the crotch of his pajama bottoms. He whimpered as I did. His flaccid cock reminded me of the last time I saw another man's cock. He wasn't impressive, either.

"No, don't cut it off," he cried.

"I'm not," I told him.

He looked startled, and I continued, "He's got something special for you. Abyss, show him."

"My pleasure," he said before he lifted the container and poured some of the contents over Paden's cock. Instantly, I saw it start to eat away the flesh. His screams were deafening as the hydrochloric acid ate away at his cock.

"Jesus, I knew it," one of the Highwaymen muttered. I guess they were used to Abyss using this stuff.

"What else do you want to do to him? It won't take long for it to eat into something important. If you want to do more, get it done," Abyss advised.

"I do, but what about the acid? I don't want it on me. I should've had you do this last."

"What do you want to do?"

I whispered to him. He threw back his head and roared. "Oh fuck yeah. You're a diabolical fucker.

No wonder they call you Spawn. Hold on, I got this." he walked back to the crate and came back with a container. He soaked Gallagher in it. As he did, he explained to those of us who had no idea what it was. "This is a neutralizer for the acid. Let it soak in for a minute or two, and then Spawn has the finale. It's a great one."

We waited. When Abyss nodded, I turned to Crusher and Tinker. "Get him up and take his pants off. Turn him around and bend him over the chair."

They didn't question why. They jumped to it. As they did, I gave her a raised eyebrow look. She shook her head. It didn't take them long to get him up. I grabbed the item I needed. I don't think anyone had brought it to be used as a tool, but it would do nicely. As I approached him and the others saw what I had, they flinched, and I heard the remarks. Gallagher was trying to see over his shoulder, but Gravel was holding his head while Crusher, Tinker, and Sandman held his arms and back.

"Oh fuck, is he?"

"Shit, I think he is."

"I don't know if I can watch."

"Jesus Christ, that's gonna hurt like a motherfucker."

I snapped on a pair of gloves from my pocket. With those in place, I got close, and I spoke to him. "This is for all the times you raped Kimera and Claudia and God knows who else."

Without further delay, I spread his ass cheeks

which made him squeal like a pig. He tried to clench his cheeks together, but he was no match for me. With them spread wide, I shoved the glass soda bottle up his ass hard and definitely without lube. His scream was animalistic, but I didn't stop. I sodomized him with it until he was bleeding and passed the fuck out. I left it inside him and hesitantly turned to see what my woman was doing. Would she run from me?

She had her hands over her mouth, Her eyes were huge, and she was pale. Fuck, I went too far. I stayed away from her. I didn't want to scare her even more. Taking off the gloves, I balled them up and shoved them in my pocket. I walked out of the inner chamber. The guys were calling my name, but I kept going.

Outside, I crouched down and hung my head. I let the demon have free rein, and the bastard had lost me my Kimera. Why didn't I hold back? Why did I have that side to me? Hot tears ran down my face. Without her, what was there to go on for? I was so lost in my misery I didn't know anyone had left the mine until a hand touched my shoulder.

Then I heard her voice. "Aidan, why did you leave?"

"You know why. I went too far, and now you're disgusted with me. My demon got loose. How can you even bear to touch me? I fucking lost you over a piece of shit."

"You don't disgust me, and I have no problem touching you. You haven't lost me. Yes, it was gruesome, but he deserved it. If I believe that, then I must have a demon inside of me, too. I think it makes us a perfect couple. Don't you?"

It took several seconds for what she said to sink in. When it did, I stood and turned. She was smiling at me, and her face was full of love. I picked her up and kissed her. Everything was gonna be alright. As long as I had her, the world was good. We kissed until we heard more voices coming closer. It was time to finish up the last part and then get our asses back to Bristol. I had a woman to put a property cut and ring on.

Kimera: Epilogue- Three Months Later

Since our return from Louisiana, so much has happened. Thankfully, it was all good. The day after Paden was dispatched, Spawn and I went to see Sonny and Claudia. We didn't give them details or outright say he was dead, but they knew he was gone. She was as relieved as I was. The Highwaymen took care of disposing of Paden. While his death was cringe-worthy, I meant what I told Spawn. He deserved it.

When we returned, he didn't waste time presenting me with my property cut. The thrill it gave me to have it and see *Property of Spawn* shocked me. I breathed a sigh of relief when I saw my club name he chose. I was worried it would say Hotcake, but instead, he put *She-Wolf*. I loved it. Hotcake was my special name, like Studcake was his. Then, to make it even better, he presented me with an engagement ring a week later.

If he had his way, we would've been married the following week, but I told him we couldn't get married before Troian and Lash. Thankfully, they got married at the beginning of February. I was able to convince him to let everyone have a small breather. Our wedding was set for May sixteenth. Theirs was wonderful, and I got the opportunity to meet most of the people from the other clubs I had heard so much about. It had been a huge event, and it seemed ours would be too. I found that bikers loved any chance to party.

Spawn and his hacker posse, as I called them, worked quickly and not only drained Paden's money away but also his parents. The last I heard, they were living in a one-bedroom apartment in a crappy neighborhood. Their money, investments, and everything else had gone bad, and they had no clue why or how. The small part of me that might have felt bad for them didn't in the end. Why? Because the posse discovered Paden had done what he did to us to three of the five girls before me. They were the recipients of a secret benefactor who gave them money. It wouldn't make up for what he did, but it was something. The rest went to a couple of foster care programs.

Another thing Spawn did, which was all for me, was he tracked down my parents and told me what the deal was with them. At first, I wasn't sure I wanted to know, but the more I thought about it, the more I needed to know. It seemed they had both been flighty people who didn't work, always were on public assistance but wasted their money on drugs and alcohol. They even were known to sell drugs to pay for their vices. Having a child cramped their style. After they gave me to Granny, they left Lake Charles for another part of Louisiana. They died from overdoses a few years later and only a couple of months apart. What a sad ending.

Even though I made it back in time to keep my

job, I didn't stay long. Not long after my return, Alisse told me Dr. Simpson was hiring more staff. Her partner was starting in the new year. My interview went well, and I think she liked me too because of my association with Alisse and Chey. I was offered a job the next day, which I happily took. I loved working with everyone there, especially Cheyenne and Alisse. It wasn't as hectic as surgical recovery could be, but I enjoyed it. It left me more time to spend with Spawn, my new Punisher family, and Toro. Speaking of Toro, he was loving life. He was free to run and explore every day and had so many more adoring fans. He never lacked attention.

Right after we returned, the club brought on not one or two but three new prospects. Their names were Dekian, Trigg, and Knox. I wasn't sure yet if they'd make the cut, but so far, they seemed to be doing okay. The club wanted to make sure Rhaines had time to teach them the ropes before he was patched in. Of course, they didn't tell him that. They were terrible to him and kept hinting that the new prospects were needed since he was to be kicked out. The poor man almost killed himself trying to show them he was Punisher material. In the end, they patched him in, thank God. They decided to play off his name when they gave him his road name. His name was now Hail. I liked it, and he seemed to as well.

As I watched the guys, especially Hail, run the prospects ragged tonight, I had to laugh. I was so glad to become an old lady. We didn't have to go through a year-long audition. I didn't know if I could've stood it. Movement caught my eye. Turning further to the right, I saw Spawn coming toward me. He had an intense, passionate expression on his face. My body lit up instantly. I knew that look. He was about to take me home and make love to me. I wondered what new things he might introduce to me next. The man was nothing if not creative, and my pleasure was always guaranteed.

He scooped me up and growled. "She-Wolf, what would you say to a chase at the house? You get naked, and let me try to catch you."

I moaned, "Yes." It was one of my favorite games. I loved being the prey to his predator. He loved to tease me and say it was only fair I submit since I was paying off my debt. It seemed repeated sexual submission was his idea of me paying for losing the childbirth bet. He had promised to give me sex, which would make me lose my voice and weak, and he made it happen often. It was a debt I wanted to keep on paying for the rest of my life. I adored this man and the happiness he brought me. There was nothing I wanted more than to be Spawn's She-Wolf.

The End Until Tinker's Witch
Book 6 of the Iron Punishers MC

Made in the USA
Las Vegas, NV
14 May 2024

89937040R00203